SLAVES
OF THE
MASTERY

WILLIAM NICHOLSON

EGMONT

EGMONT

We bring stories to life

First published in Great Britain 2001
This edition published 2011
by Egmont UK Limited
The Yellow Building, 1 Nicholas Road
London, W11 4AN

Text copyright © 2001 William Nicholson

The moral rights of the author have been asserted

ISBN 978 1 4052 3970 7

www.egmont.co.uk
www.williamnicholson.co.uk

A CIP catalogue record for this title is available from the British Library

Typeset by Avon Dataset Ltd, Bidford on Avon, Warwickshire
Printed and bound in Great Britain by the CPI Group

38254/18

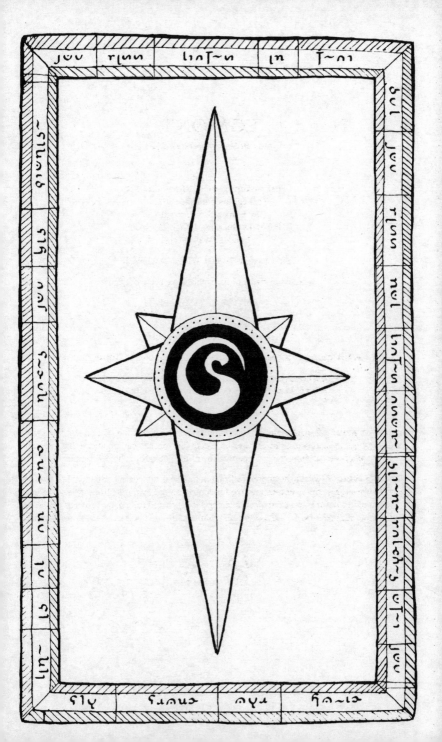

Contents

Prologue: Sirene

On a clear day the island can be seen from the mainland, the long ridge of its tree-ringed hill breaking the horizon to the south. Fishing fleets sometimes pass its rocky shores, and the fishermen stare at the stark outline of the great ruin that tops the hill, but they don't stop. The island has nothing for them. Little grows on its bare sides, only tufts of dusty grass, and the circle of ancient olive trees round the roofless hall. Also there are stories about the island, of wizards who can summon storms, of talking animals, of men who fly. Such matters are best left alone.

The island is called Sirene. Long ago a band of travellers settled here, and built the high stone walls on the top of the hill, and planted the olive trees for shade. The building has no floor, other than the grass and rock that was there before. It has no roof. Its tall windows have no glass, its wide doorways no doors. But it's not a ruin: this is how the people who built it meant it to be. No timbers to rot, no tiles to slip and fall. No glass to break, and no doors to close. Just a long light space swept by sun and wind and rain, a house that is not a house, a place to meet and sing and then to leave again.

Now after many years the sound of footsteps is heard again on Sirene. A woman is following the long rising path from the shore. No boat lies moored in the cove, and yet she is here. She wears a plain faded woollen robe, and is barefoot. Her grey hair is cut short. Her face is weathered, lined, brown. How old is she? Impossible to say. She has the face of a grandmother, but the clear eyes and agile body of a young woman. She barely pauses for breath as she makes her way up the hillside.

There is a freshwater spring where the hill levels off, and here she stops and drinks. Then she goes on, and passes between the twisted trunks of the olive trees, touching their jagged bark lightly with one hand. She steps through the doorless doorway into the roofless hall, and stands there, gazing, remembering. She remembers how this hall was once full of people, and how they sang together, and how she was filled by the song and wanted it never to end. But there is a time for singing and a time for waiting. Now it is all to begin again.

She walks slowly down the centre of the hall, looking out through the high windows on either side at the ocean beyond. A lizard, unaccustomed to human intruders, rattles away into a crack in the stonework. A cloud sails across the sun, and its shadow slides over her.

She is the first. The others will join her, soon now. The time of cruelty has come.

1

Sunset over Aramanth

Marius Semeon Ortiz crested the brow of the low hill at a gallop, and drew his panting horse to a halt. There below him lay the broad coastal plain, and the ocean: and not so far away, no more than an hour's march, his goal, his prize, his gateway to glory, the city of Aramanth. Ortiz stood up in the saddle, and holding himself steady, breathing rapid breaths, fixed his keen young eyes on the distant city. The walls were long gone, as his scouts had reported. There were no signs of any defences. Aramanth lay before him in the fading evening light as fat and as helpless as a mother hen.

His line captains clattered up beside him, and they too smiled to see the end of their long journey. The food wagons were almost empty, and for the last three days the men had been marching on short rations. Now Aramanth would feed them. The wagons would sit low on their axles when the lines turned for home.

Ortiz twisted round in the saddle, and saw with silent approval the orderly approach of the raiding force. Close on a thousand men, three hundred and twenty of them mounted chasseurs, were making their way up the rising land. Behind them rolled the horse-drawn wagons which carried the tents, the cages, the rations for the men and

1

the provisions for the horses: sixty wagons, and twice that number of teams to haul them, for horses could not be asked to bear great weights for long without resting. Young as he was, Ortiz was a commander who left nothing to risk. No lame horse would slow his lines on the long march.

He raised one hand. The silent signal flashed from squad to squad, and men and horses shuddered gratefully to a stop. Today was their nineteenth day on the march. They were tired, far from home, and uncertain of success. It was his will alone that had sustained them: his certainty that this, the longest raid in the history of the Mastery so far, would yield its greatest prize. For years now travellers had told tales of the prosperous and peaceful city on the plains. It was young Ortiz who had sent out scouts to confirm the reports. Aramanth was rich, and it was undefended. 'How rich?' he had asked. The scouts had made their best guess. 'Ten thousand. At the very least.' Ten thousand! No commander had ever delivered so much, nor half so much, to the Mastery. Just twenty-one years of age, and he now held within his grasp such glory, such honour, that the greatest prize of all would surely follow. One day soon the Master would make his choice of successor, his adopted son; and Marius Semeon Ortiz dared to dream that it would be he who knelt and said, 'Master! Father!'

But first the wealth of Aramanth must be harvested, and brought safely home. He turned back to look once again at the distant city, where dusk was gathering and the lights were beginning to be lit. Let them sleep in peace for one more night, he thought to himself. At first light I will give the command, and my men will do their duty. Aramanth will burn, and ten thousand men, women and children will become slaves of the Mastery.

* * *

Kestrel Hath stood with the rest of her family towards the back of the crowd of guests. Her young sister Pinto, seven years old and jumpy as a sparrow, twisted and fidgeted beside her. The betrothal ceremony was taking place in the centre of the city's arena, where the old wind singer stood. The base of the structure had been dressed with candles for the occasion. The light breeze kept blowing the candles out, and the bride's mother, Mrs Greeth, who hated anything to be out of place, kept creeping forward to relight them. The wind caused the wind singer to hum and coo, in its sweet everlasting way. Kestrel was not interested in betrothals, and so she listened instead to the voice of the wind singer, and as always, she was soothed.

Pia Greeth, the bride, was fifteen years old, the same age as Kestrel herself. Pia looked lovely by candlelight. The boy she was marrying, Tanner Amos, seemed overwhelmed by the ceremony. Why is Pia marrying him, Kestrel thought? How can she know she'll love him for ever? He looked so uncertain; so timid, and so young. But he too was just fifteen, the age when young people became marriageable; and this was the start of the marriage season.

Kestrel frowned and shook her head, and turned her eyes away from the young couple by the wind singer. At once she met the eyes of Pia's older brother Farlo, and realised he had been staring at her. This irritated her. He had taken to following her around in the last few weeks, and looking at her in a hopeless yearning way, as if he wanted to speak to her, but was waiting for her to speak first. Why must she speak to him? She had nothing particular to say. Why must everybody suddenly start pairing up? She had liked Farlo well enough until he had begun gazing at her in that goggly fashion.

So she looked away again, and there was her twin brother Bowman gazing into the distance. She felt into his mind, and realised his attention too was not on the ceremony. He was sensing something else: something that troubled him.

What is it, Bo?

I don't know.

Now the young couple were saying the vow of betrothal.

'Today begins my walk with you.' The boy spoke in a shy hesitant voice. The vow came from the old days, when the Manth people had been a nomadic tribe, forever travelling over the barren land. Many of the guests moved their lips with the familiar words, unaware that they were doing so.

'Where you go, I go. Where you stay, I stay.'

Now Bowman was moving quietly away. Kestrel saw Pinto follow him with her eyes, desperate to go too. She saw her speak low to their mother, who nodded, knowing her youngest child simply couldn't stand still and stay silent for long. Then Pinto too slipped away.

'When you sleep, I will sleep. When you rise, I will rise.'

Kestrel did not follow Bowman. More and more these days, he chose to be alone. She didn't understand it, and it hurt her, but it was what he wanted, and she loved him too much to complain.

She listened to the ending of the vows.

'I will pass my days within the sound of your voice, and my nights within the reach of your hand, and none shall come between us. This I vow.'

The boy then held out his hand, and the girl took it.

Kestrel saw her mother feel for her father's hand and squeeze it, and knew she was remembering the time of her own betrothal. A sudden sadness came over Kestrel, a new and unfamiliar feeling. She dug the nail of one forefinger into the palm of her hand until it hurt, to stop the tears that were rising in her throat. Why should I be sad, she asked herself? Because ma and pa love each other? Because I never want to be married? But it wasn't that. It was something else.

Now the guests were crowding round to congratulate the young couple. Mrs Greeth was blowing out the candles and putting them away in a box, to be used again later. Kestrel's mother and father were making their way up the nine stone tiers of the arena, hurrying a little, because there was a city meeting that evening, and the ceremony had gone on longer than expected. Bowman and Pinto were gone.

That was when Kestrel found the right name for the feeling of sadness that had come over her. It wasn't loneliness. While her twin brother lived, she could never be lonely. It was a glimpse of something more terrible: a premonition of loss. One day she would lose him, and she didn't know how she could go on living after that.

We go together.

The words, an echo from the past, meant to her that when the time came to die, as one day it must, they would die together. But this new feeling told her otherwise. One would die, and one would live on.

Let me be the one who dies first.

At once she was ashamed of herself. The one who died first would be the lucky one. Why should she wish the misery of survival on her beloved brother? She was stronger than him. She must bear it.

This was the feeling that made her want to cry: not loneliness, not yet, but the certainty that the day was coming when she would be alone.

Mumpo Inch sat on the tumble of stones that had once been part of the city walls, and gazed out towards the dark ocean. If he looked long enough he could make out the crests of the bigger waves, rolling in under the moonless sky. He let out a long sad sigh. Another day gone, and he had still not spoken the words he had so carefully prepared and memorised. It was now eleven weeks and two days since he had passed his fifteenth birthday, and four weeks and four days since Kestrel Hath had done the same. Mumpo adored Kestrel more than life itself, and had done for five long years. He couldn't bear to think she might marry anyone but him. And yet, if he were to ask her, he knew she would say no. He was sure of it. They were too young. He felt it himself. Neither of them was ready to be married. But what if someone else asked her first? And what if she said yes?

He heard sounds behind him, and turning, saw Pinto hopping over the stones. Pinto was small for her age, skinny and lithe and sharp as a blade of grass. Because she was so much younger, Mumpo always felt easy with her. She never criticised him, or smiled at the things he said, as others did. She only ever got cross when he called her Pinpin, which had been her baby name. She was not a baby any more, she would tell him fiercely, staring at him with those bright hurt eyes that seemed always to be about to cry, but never did.

'I knew you'd be here.' She dropped to her knees behind him, and twined her arms round his neck.

'I come here to be alone,' said Mumpo.

'You can be alone with me.'

It was perfectly true: she was no intrusion. He reached one arm behind him and pinched her bony leg.

'What have you done with Kess?'

'Oh, I've killed her,' said Pinto, wriggling happily. 'I got fed up with you always asking me about her, so I killed her.'

'Where did you leave her body?'

'At the Greeths' betrothal.'

Mumpo rose to his feet, dropping the girl to the ground with a gentle shake. He was tall and well-built, like his father, but unlike his father in his prime, he had no air of authority about him. He was too easy-going to impose his will on anyone; too simple, some said. As for Pinto, she thought he was the dearest person in the entire wide world.

'There's something I have to ask Kess,' he said, more to convince himself than to inform the girl.

'I shouldn't bother,' said Pinto. 'She'll say no.'

Mumpo blushed a deep red.

'You don't know what I'm talking about.'

'Yes, I do. You want her to marry you. Well, she won't. I asked her, and she said no.'

'You never did!'

As it happens, Pinto had not asked her big sister this vast and frightening question. She had wanted to many times, but she had not dared. However, she was quite sure that if she were to ask it, the answer would be as she declared.

'You're an evil interfering rat-girl. I shall never talk to you again.'

He was angry and ashamed. Pinto repented at once.

'I didn't ask her, Mumpo. I just made that up.'

'Do you swear?'

'I swear. But she will say no.'

'How do you know that?'

Pinto wanted to say, I know because you belong to me. Instead she said,

'She doesn't want to marry anyone.'

'She will,' said Mumpo gloomily. 'They all do in the end.'

It was quite dark now, so they held hands as they made their way back over the uneven piles of rubble. Pinto felt how his strong dry hand held hers, so light and yet so sure, and twice she pretended to stumble just to feel his fingers close tight round hers, and his muscular arm hold her from falling. In reality she was as nimble as a goat, and could find her way by starlight or by no light; but she was playing a secret game that they were betrothed, and in her head she was saying to him the familiar words of the betrothal, 'I will pass my days within the sound of your voice, and my nights within the reach of your hand.'

They passed the abandoned buildings of the old Grey District, now used only by gangs of unruly children for their secret games, and entered the lamp-lit streets of Maroon District. The old names were still used, though few of the houses retained their old colour. After the changes, the citizens of Aramanth had been seized with a rage for house painting, and all over the city a rainbow of bright colours had sprung up, on doors and window frames, walls and even roofs. But five years of sun and wind and rain had worn away the hastily applied paint, and the old municipal colours were beginning to show through once more.

They found the main plaza full of people and noise. It turned out the meeting had ended almost as soon as it had begun, following a dispute about procedure. Everyone was streaming out of the city hall and making their way home, arguing eagerly. Mumpo never attended the city meetings. All that happened, it seemed to him, was that everyone talked at the same time as everyone else, and nobody listened, and so they all went out at the end with the same opinions they'd come in with.

His searching eyes soon located Kestrel at the centre of a group of young people, all talking with passionate conviction. Mumpo came to a stop at the fringe of the group, and wouldn't join them, even though Pinto pulled at his hand.

'They're just going on about nothing,' Pinto said. 'Like they always do.'

Mumpo wasn't listening. He was watching Kestrel. In common with many of the younger set, she cropped her hair short and ragged, and wore faded black robes in reaction against the multi-coloured look favoured by the older people. Her face was odd and bony and wide-mouthed, not beautiful in the usual way: but there was about her a restless intensity that drew and held the attention. To Mumpo, she was entirely beautiful. More than beautiful: she was so alive that sometimes he felt her to be life itself, or the source of life. When those eager black eyes met his, he felt the jolt of her vitality, and everything around him seemed brighter and more sharp-edged.

'Why weren't you at the meeting, Mumpo?'

With a start, he realised she was talking to him.

'Oh, that sort of thing's not for me.'

'Why not? You live here, don't you?'

9

'Yes,' he said.

'Then don't you care about the city that's your home?'

Mumpo said the first thing that came into his head, as he usually did.

'It doesn't feel like my home.'

Kestrel stared at him, and said nothing for a long moment. Then she turned back to the others, made some abrupt goodnights, and walked away.

Mumpo and Pinto followed more slowly. Mumpo's rooms, where he lived with his father, were close by the Hath family's quarters, in the heart of the city.

'I always say the wrong thing,' he told Pinto sadly. 'And I never know why.'

Bowman had not been at the meeting. He had walked the streets of the city, trying to locate the source of the danger he had felt at the betrothal. It was as elusive as a smell. Sometimes he thought he had it, then he lost it again. He turned his face to the wind and sniffed the air, hoping this would guide him. But it wasn't a smell, or a sound: it was a feeling. Bowman could feel the presence of fear a mile off, and could sense the joy that bursts out as laughter before the smile was even begun. But feelings were hard to trace. They came as often from inside himself as from the outside world.

Now it was gone again. Maybe he was making it all up. Maybe it was hunger. He decided to go home.

When the rest of the family returned, they found him standing on their little balcony looking out at the night. The stove was almost out. Hanno Hath bent down to coax it back into life.

'You've let the fire go out, Bo.'

'Have I?'

He sounded surprised, so Hanno Hath said no more about it. People said Bowman was a dreamer, or more unkindly, that he went about half-asleep, but his father understood him. Bowman was as awake as any of them; more so, perhaps. But he was attending to different things.

'That was a waste of time as usual,' said Kestrel, coming into the room. 'The only person who said anything worth hearing was Mumpo, and he's the biggest fool of all.'

'He's not a fool!' protested Pinto, entering after her.

'Oh yes, we all know Mumpo's your pet.'

Pinto flew at Kestrel, fists tight-clenched and flailing, hot tears springing up in her eyes. Kestrel struck back at once, hitting her on the nose. Pinto fell sobbing to the floor.

'Kestrel!' said her father sharply.

'She started it!'

Ira Hath picked Pinto up and soothed her. Pinto's nose was bleeding. When Pinto discovered this, she was secretly elated, and stopped crying.

'Blood!' she said. 'Kess made me bleed!'

'It's not much, darling,' said her mother.

'But she made me bleed!' Pinto was triumphant. The one who draws blood is always in the wrong. 'Tell her off!'

'You made yourself bleed,' said Kestrel. 'You hit my hand with your nose.'

'Oh!' said Pinto. 'Oh! You lying witch!'

'All right, that's enough.' Hanno Hath's mild voice had the effect of calming everyone down, as always. 'So Mumpo said something interesting, did he, Kess?'

'I was going to tell you, only Pinpin –'

'*Don't call me Pinpin!*'

'Am I allowed to speak?'

'I don't care. Say what you like.'

Actually Pinto was interested, because it was about Mumpo.

'He said Aramanth doesn't feel like his home.'

'Oh, that poor boy.'

'Yes, but it made me think. It doesn't feel like my home, either.'

Hanno Hath threw a glance towards his wife.

'So where is your home, my Kess?'

'I don't know.'

'Well, you may be right. All the old books say this was only ever meant to be a way station on the journey to the homeland.'

'The homeland!' His wife snorted crossly. 'What is this homeland? Where is it? I'll tell you where it is. It's somewhere else. That's where it is. Wherever you live in the real world you find troubles and discontents, so you make up a somewhere else that's better. That's all your precious homeland is. So we might as well make the most of where we are now.'

'You may be right, my dear.'

'But ma,' said Kestrel, 'don't you feel it too? We don't fit in here.'

'Oh well, as to that, I'm just one of those odd-shaped people who doesn't fit in anywhere.'

'We're an odd-shaped family,' said Pinto. The notion pleased her.

'There is a homeland,' Kestrel persisted. 'Don't your books tell you where it is, pa?'

'No, darling. If they did, I'd have gone there long ago.'

'Why?'

'Oh, I'm an old dreamer.'

'Well, I'm going to go.'

'Wait until you're married,' said her mother. 'You'll find things will look different then.'

'I don't want to be married.'

Ira Hath looked up and met her husband's eyes. He gave a small shrug, and his eyes turned towards Bowman.

'We'd never make you marry against your will,' her mother began gently. 'But darling –'

'I know I'll end up lonely when I'm old,' said Kestrel, to show she didn't have to be told. 'But I don't care.'

'Kess'll never be lonely,' said Pinto enviously. 'She's got Bo.'

Their mother shook her head and said no more. Hanno Hath went out on to the balcony to stand beside Bowman. He didn't speak, because he was feeling for the right words with which to begin. But Bowman knew well enough what he was thinking.

'I really am trying, pa.'

'I know you are.'

'It's not easy.'

Hanno Hath sighed. He hated asking this of his son. But Ira was right, now that the twins were growing up they must learn to be a little more apart.

'Do you still share thoughts?'

'Not as much as we used to. But yes.'

'She has to make a life of her own, Bo. So do you.'

'Yes, pa.'

Bowman wanted to say to his father, we're not like everyone else, we're not to have a life like other people, we're marked out for something quite different. But since he didn't know what, or even why he felt it, he said nothing.

'I'm not asking you to stop loving each other. Just to have other friends as well.'

'Yes, pa.'

Hanno put one arm lightly round his son's shoulders. Bowman let it rest there for a moment. Then he said,

'I think I'll go out.'

As he headed for the door, Kestrel looked up and met his eyes.

Shall I come with you?

Better not.

Kestrel knew as well as he did that their parents wanted them to spend more time apart. But she also knew there was something else.

Tell me what it is.

I will. Later.

Then he was gone: down the steep stairs, and out into the night street. He had no destination, he needed only to be away from other people, away from his family. He would have walked away from himself if he had known how. He was sure now that the sense of danger that hadn't left him all day was coming from the fear buried deep inside himself. He needed a place of stillness to understand it better, and to know why it had awoken after all these years. So he headed south, towards the ocean.

Once past the city boundary the streetlights gave out, and he made his way by starlight. It was a cool autumn night, and he shivered a little as he walked. His eyes adjusted to the darkness, and soon he could make out the shoreline far ahead, and the line of low hills that formed the horizon to the east. When at last he stopped, it was not because he had reached anywhere in particular, but because he judged he was far enough from the bustle of the city. Here, alone in the night, he stood still and closed his eyes. He felt for the sensation of fear, and found it at once, shockingly close. It was powerful, and cruel. He spoke to the memory of power within him.

I don't want you. I never wanted you.

But it wasn't true. He had wanted the power once. All those years ago, in that time that ever since had felt like a dream, he had wanted it. He had let himself be filled by that intoxicating spirit. And now the Morah was in him, and he would never be free.

He walked a little way eastward, up the rising land, feeling the fear all around him. He came to a stop, seeing only the black line of the hilltops, and the grey blur of the sea. He turned, and there lay Aramanth, twin-kling softly in the night. There lay everyone he loved, everyone who loved him, in all the world. How could he tell them he was a source of danger to them? A traitor who carried the living spirit of the Morah into their safest home? How could he tell his sister, his half-self, that she must not come too close, lest the Morah possess her too?

The evil is in me. I must carry it alone.

It was so strong, so all-pervading: it filled the night air round him like a dark cloud. Suddenly he felt he could no longer breathe. He turned and walked fast back towards the city, unaware that had he continued for a few minutes more up the hill, he would have seen the army of the Mastery encamped on the farther side, burning no fires or lamps, their horses' harness muffled, waiting soundlessly for dawn.

2

Terror at dawn

That night, Ira Hath had a dream that was so intense it woke her before her usual time. She sat up in bed, and found that she was sobbing. She was unable to stop herself. She tried to smother the sobs with the hem of the blanket, but this produced a snuffling noise that was even worse, so she got out of bed to get herself a drink of water. Once up she found she couldn't stand properly, and she had to sit down again rather suddenly on the bed. That woke Hanno. He saw the streaks of tears on her cheeks and became alarmed. So she told him her dream.

She had been walking along a snow-covered road, together with all the rest of the family and many others besides, and the road led to a pass between steep hills. On either side of the road, the slopes rose high up, white and smooth, while the road itself climbed to a summit, and then fell away on the far side. They were going west, it seemed, because directly ahead, in the great V formed by the hills on either side, the sun was setting. Though all round her the winter air was cold, she felt a warmth on her face that seemed to come from the sunset ahead.

She walked in the lead, in front of everyone else. So she was the first to reach the summit of the road, and stand within the V looking over the brow. As she reached this point, a flurry of flakes of new snow began to fall around her, and ahead the setting sun turned the western sky a deep red. Through the falling snow, by the light of the sunset sky, she found herself looking down on a broad plain, where two rivers flowed into an unknown sea.

Then in her dream, as she gazed down at the land framed by the V of hills, with the snow falling and the warmth on her cheeks and the wide red horizon beyond, she felt a sudden rush of happiness that was so intense it brought tears to her eyes. Faint with joy, she turned to Hanno and her children, and saw from their faces, knew in an instant, that they could not follow where she was going. She had found the greatest happiness she had ever known, and in the same moment knew she must lose everyone she had ever loved. In her dream she had wept for her joy and her loss, and sobbing, she had awoken.

Hanno dried her tears and held her in his arms, and told her it was only a dream. Slowly the shock of it passed, and Ira became her old self again, and said that it was all his fault for indulging in foolish talk about the homeland.

'Why did you fall over?' he asked her.

'I didn't fall over. I sat down.'

'Why?'

'I felt wobbly.'

He didn't say anything more, but she knew what he was thinking. Her distant ancestor Ira Manth had been a seer, the first prophet of the Manth people. *Every time I touch the future*, he had written, *I grow weaker. My gift is my disease. I shall die of prophecy.*

17

'It was only a dream, Hanno. Nothing more.'

'I expect so, my dear.'

'You're not to go putting ideas into the children's heads. They're full of enough muddle as it is.'

'I won't say anything.'

Ira stood up once more, stronger this time, and went to the window. She drew the curtains, and saw outside the first light of the new day spreading over the eastern horizon.

'Nearly morning.'

Hanno Hath joined her at the window, putting his arms around her.

'I do love you so much,' he said softly.

She turned her head and kissed his cheek. They stood like this, very quiet, for a long moment.

Then Hanno said, 'Do you hear it?'

'What?'

'The wind singer.'

She listened.

'No.'

The wind singer had stopped singing.

Marius Semeon Ortiz sat in the saddle on the brow of the hill, his chasseurs lined up behind him. A breeze from the ocean carried the hiss of waves and the tang of salt on the dawn air. Ortiz was watching the city below, where his raiding parties were already at work. Halfway down the hill on his left flank crouched the attack squads, waiting on his command. He sensed the nervousness of the ranks of horses behind him, straining at the bit. His own mount shifted her weight, flared her nostrils, and let out a soft whinny.

'Easy,' he said. 'Easy.'

A flaming arrow arched up from the city high into the silent sky: the signal that the warehouses were breached.

'Provisioners!' said Ortiz. 'Firing squads!' He had no need to speak loudly. His men were alert to his slightest word.

The provision wagons rolled down the hill on padded wheels, accompanied by their bands of silent raiders. They moved fast, knowing they had very little time to do their vital work. Ahead of them, loping at speed, ran the firing squads, each man carrying on his back a bundle of oil-soaked kindling. Ortiz raised one hand, and the remainder of his force of foot-soldiers rose up and ran in a long curving path to the seaward side of the city. After them, more slowly, rolled the empty cages known as monkey wagons.

There came a shout from the city. A watchman had encountered the provisioners. Now others began to wake, and lights were flickering on. But already a greater light was burning, in one of the abandoned apartment blocks of Grey District, and the breeze was fanning the flames. Another sprang up, and a third: a line of fires, along the northern and windward side of the city.

Ortiz felt his horse shudder beneath him. She had smelt the sting of smoke, and knew her moment was near. There were shouts and screams coming from the city now, and the rattle of running feet. Ortiz could picture the scene, which he had witnessed so many times before: the people, waking to find their streets ablaze, pouring out of their houses, half-dressed, confused, frightened.

Slowly, he drew his sword. Behind him, the lines of his chasseurs followed suit, and he heard the shivering hiss of three hundred blades leaving their scabbards. He released the bit, and his horse took a step forward. Behind him, the chasseurs swayed and moved. He spurred his horse to a trot, and then to a canter. Behind him, the drumbeat of following hooves. His eyes fixed on the burning city ahead, he held the chasseurs at a canter, covering the stony ground. This was the moment on which all depended. If the blow fell with speed, surprise, and terror, then a force of a thousand men could overwhelm a city, and take captive ten times their own number. It was the horror of that first attack that would turn free men into slaves.

He glanced to his left as he rode, and saw that his foot-soldiers were in place. Behind him, the first rays of the rising sun were reaching over the black line of hills. This is it, he thought, the moment of no turning back, the all or nothing: and rising in the saddle, he was swept by a sensation of pure joy. Eyes bright, lips parted in a smile, he raised his sword as he rode, spurred his mount into the gallop, and cried,

'Charge!'

The wind singer was burning fiercely. Hanno Hath trained the nozzle of a fire hose on the flames, while Bowman and Kestrel, one at each end of the handle, pumped with all their might. Already the tiered arena was alive with running figures. The cry of 'Fire!' spread through the city. Ira Hath and Pinto were racing down the streets, banging on doors to wake the sleeping people. From all sides families in nightclothes came streaming into the arena. Kestrel wept as she pumped, saying, 'No! No! No!' with each downward stroke. Bowman didn't turn to look at the smoking wind singer for fear he too would cry.

Hanno's fire hose succeeded at last in dousing the flames, leaving the tower half-destroyed, charred and hissing.

'Keep pumping!' he cried, turning the hose on a burning building. But Kestrel had already left the pump and was swinging herself up onto the smoking ruin.

'Be careful, Kess –'

Her father's voice was cut short by a terrible screaming. A great rush of men, women and children burst into the arena. With a thunder of galloping hooves, the chasseurs of the Mastery crashed through the pillared arcade, swords flashing, and the people of Aramanth ran before them. Those that fell or turned back were cut down by the long swords, so that as the lines of horsemen advanced, their horses rode over the bodies of the wounded and the dead. Behind the chasseurs came foot-soldiers with short spears, with which they stabbed the bodies lying bleeding on the ground. Terrified, the people of the city fled before this savage killing machine, across the arena, down burning streets, out of the city, towards the ocean shore.

Kestrel clung to the burnt-out wind singer, and in her black clothing she wasn't noticed by the invaders. The scorched wood hurt her arms and legs, but she dared not move; and unmoving, she watched the slaughter. She saw her father and brother forced back with the rest. She heard the piteous cries of the wounded, and the brisk blows of the spearmen. She watched the leader of the invaders ride by on his horse, saw him clearly in the light of the rising sun, his handsome young face framed in a cascade of tawny hair, his eyes cruel as a hawk hunting vermin. She stared as long as she could, printing the image deep in her memory.

I won't forget you, my enemy.

As the last soldier passed out of sight, an unearthly silence fell. Kestrel reached up for the slot in the wind singer that held its silver voice. The metal throat was almost too hot to touch, but she made her fingers feel into the slot, and quickly, before she knew she was burned, she snatched out the voice. It fell to the flagstones below. She followed it, dropping swiftly down the tower, feeling the skin tear on the fingertips of her right hand. She found the voice on the ground, already cool enough to handle, and with her left hand slipped it into her pocket.

All round her now she heard the sound of flames, and felt the heat in the air. The great circular arena was built of stone, and there was little there to burn. But beyond the ring of pillars there rose a wall of fire. There was nowhere for her to go.

Outside the city, the fleeing people now found themselves penned in a broad space between the fire and the ocean. Here the foot-soldiers of the Mastery were waiting for them. The soldiers made no move to attack. They stood in menacing clusters, swords drawn, while the thousands of helpless townspeople milled about, dazed and frightened, looking for members of their families, crying and sobbing, unable to take in what had happened. There was no leadership, no organisation. The blow had fallen too suddenly.

Marius Semeon Ortiz rode up and saw the stunned looks all around him, and was satisfied. His provisioning parties were withdrawing from the torched city, their wagons full. It was time to calm the prisoners, and teach them obedience.

'You will not be harmed! Do as you are ordered, and you will not be harmed!'

Mounted officers rode through the crowd repeating the cry.

'Remain where you are! You will not be harmed!'

Ortiz now ordered the monkey wagons to be brought forward. Teams of horses hauled the high-wheeled cages into the heart of the crowd, where the horses were unharnessed and led away. Ortiz looked round for a suitable victim among the conquered people, to demonstrate why the cage had acquired its name.

Hanno Hath had succeeded in reuniting all his family except Kestrel. The way back into the city was barred by armed men, but even had they been able to slip past the cordon, the fire was raging too fiercely. They could only hope that somehow Kestrel had found a means to escape the inferno. Meanwhile, here and now, too many people were wounded. The first priority was to survive, and to help others to survive.

A mounted officer clattered past, crying, 'Do as you are ordered, and you will not be harmed!'

'Are you all right? Pinto, you're bleeding.'

'I'm all right, pa,' said Pinto, her voice trembling. 'It's not my blood.'

'Did anyone see what happened to Kess?'

Ira Hath looked at Bowman. He had his eyes shut, his mind reaching out for his twin.

Kess! Can you feel me?

He shook his head.

'Would you know if she was –?'

'Yes. I think so.'

Pinto caught sight of Mumpo, with his father Maslo Inch.

'There's Mumpo! He's all right!'

Marius Semeon Ortiz, high on his handsome charger,

was looking in the same direction, his eyes drawn by the tall man in the white robes. Maslo Inch, once the all-powerful Chief Examiner of Aramanth, had no pride any more. Ever since the changes, he had grown increasingly confused, and in recent years he had come to depend entirely on his only son. All that was left of his former glory was the white robe, the old sign of the highest rating, and his dignified bearing. His heart was broken, his mind bewildered, but his body, through force of long habit, walked tall. It was this that singled him out.

Ortiz pointed, and his men pushed through the crowd and seized Maslo Inch by either arm. Mumpo tried to stop them, but they brushed him aside, and a mounted officer shook his sword at him. His father, only half-understanding what was happening, smiled for him as he was led off.

'Let them be, son. What does it matter?'

Mumpo followed, as did many others, including Hanno Hath. They saw Maslo Inch pushed into the high cage, and the barred door locked after him.

Mumpo turned to Hanno Hath in distress.

'What will they do to him?'

Hanno shook his head, afraid to speak.

'My orders will be obeyed!' Ortiz cried out, his horse wheeling round and round. 'Without question! Without delay! The first sign of disobedience –' he pointed to the cage, 'and this man will die!'

Ortiz looked round and heard the rushing murmur of voices. His words were being repeated all across the great crowd of prisoners. This was good: fear made them attentive. They must learn that he did not make empty threats. As the Master himself had taught, a single act of brutality could control an entire city, so long as it was carried out without hesitation, and without mercy. Ortiz had his victim. Now all he needed was a pretext.

Mumpo knew nothing of this. All he knew was that the father he had come to love had fallen into an unexplained danger. The horseman with the sword had frightened him, but he had now ridden away, and Mumpo was angry. He possessed the courage of the uncalculating soul: wishing to save his father, he thought nothing of the risks he might himself face. So marching forward to the cage, he rattled its blackened bars and shouted,

'Let him go!'

Ortiz swung round on his horse. He pointed his sword at Mumpo.

'Stand back!'

'He's my father,' said Mumpo, saying not what was needed, but what he felt. 'Let him go!'

Maslo Inch reached his hand through the bars and stroked Mumpo's cheek.

'My son,' he said proudly.

Ortiz saw with grim satisfaction that his order had been disobeyed.

'You were warned. Now the price will be paid.'

He gave a sign, and one of his men stepped forward with a burning torch. Beneath the cage there was an iron tray, in which lay a deep bed of firewood topped by oil-soaked kindling. Above the kindling, the floor of the cage was an open iron grid. As the kindling caught fire, and the smoke began to rise, the people nearest to the cage realised with horror that Maslo Inch had no way of escaping the flames. He was about to be burned alive.

'You will be silent!' commanded Ortiz. 'For each person

25

who speaks, I will take one more from among you, and they will die in the same way.'

A terrible silence fell over the people of Aramanth. How could they think of disobeying? Even the bravest of them, even those willing to risk death, dared not bring about the death of others. So they made no noise at all, as the fire spread in the deep tray beneath the cage, and the poor lost man inside tried to climb the bars to escape the heat.

Ortiz watched, as he had watched before. It was unpleasant, but it was necessary. All new slaves must witness a death in the cage before entering the provinces controlled by the Mastery. It was the Master's order.

Maslo Inch didn't make much of a monkey for the watching soldiers. After his first desperate efforts, he fell limp, and his white robes caught fire. He then folded noiselessly to the cage floor, without so much as a scream, which was unusual. But the sound of the burning was sufficient. Ortiz could see from the drawn white faces of his prisoners that the lesson was well learned.

There came a low cry, and a thud. The young man who had disobeyed him had fallen to the ground. The people around dared not stoop to help him, and so he lay there, apparently in a faint. Ortiz decided to overlook the incident. It was time to prepare for the long march home.

'People of Aramanth,' he called to the shocked and silent crowd. 'Your city is destroyed. Your freedom is at an end. You are now slaves of the Mastery.'

Bowman stood utterly still, his eyes fixed on the burning

city, searching with all his senses for Kestrel. He heard the flames and smelt the smoke. Here and there he found pockets of buried pain among the ashes, which burst like bubbles against the touch of his mind, releasing the last cries of those who lay there, dead but still warm. So much sadness rose from the smoking ruins, so much hurt and loss. He flinched as he felt it, but made himself search on. Then a soldier pulled roughly at his sleeve, and turning, no longer searching, he caught a fugitive touch of her, no more than a flash of a figure seen through scorched pillars, through heat-distorted air: but he knew her. She was there. She was alive. It was enough.

Already the soldiers were forming the new slaves into lines. He let himself be pulled and commanded. He didn't care. She was alive, and the future now had a shape. In parting him from his sister, his half-self, his enemy had drawn taut the cord that linked them, shivering taut, like the bowstring on an archer's bow. They would find each other again. The drawn string would be loosed. Then the hunter would become the hunted, and the arrow would fly.

3

The wind is rising

K estrel remained by the burnt-out wind singer all that day, while the fire raged through the city. As night fell and the air grew cold, the flames began to die down at last, and slowly, fearfully, she climbed the nine tiers of the arena to see if anyone else was left alive.

Aramanth was gone. In its place, by the orange glow of the burning houses, she saw ruined streets littered with bodies over which carrion birds screeched. She called out as she went, at first low and afraid; but hearing nothing, she called louder and louder. No one answered.

The statue of Creoth, the first Emperor of Aramanth, still stood, the white stone now blackened by smoke. The fountain no longer flowed, but there was water in its basin. She cleared the ash floating on the water's surface and drank deep. The water tasted bitter, but she forced herself to drink until she could drink no more.

She made her way back to the building in which her family had lived, and found it roofless and still burning. The stairs had caved in. There was no way she could reach their apartment, even if she had dared to brave the fire. Looking up, she made out the space that had once been her room, now a skeleton of black beams against the night sky.

Her foot stumbled against a dark mound in the street. It was the dead body of a woman. The face was pressed to the ground, but Kestrel recognised that plump back. It was Mrs Blesh, their one-time neighbour when they had lived in Orange District, before the changes. Her hand, outreached in the dirt where she had fallen, still clutched a merit medal that had been awarded to her son Rufy, for a prize poem he had written. Kestrel remembered that medal well. Mrs Blesh had carried it with her everywhere, and shown it to everyone. She remembered the poem, too. It was called 'Waiting to Smile', and was about being afraid to smile until someone else smiled first. Kestrel remembered how astonished she had been that dull studious Rufy Blesh had had such feelings at all, let alone put them in a poem. His mother hadn't understood the poem, but she had been ridiculously proud about the medal, to her son's embarrassment.

Gently Kestrel detached the medal from the dead fingers, and slipped it into her pocket, alongside the silver voice.

Where is Rufy Blesh now? Where is everybody?

Bo! Where are you?

No answer.

Suddenly she felt faint, and knew she was going to fall. She closed her eyes, and a greater darkness swallowed her up.

When she woke, it was light. She stood up, and shook her stiff aching limbs. She made herself walk down the smouldering street. She followed the trail of devastation across the city, and out onto the plain. As she walked, her strength slowly returned. She could feel the cold ocean breeze on her face. She began to be

29

aware that she was hungry. And she began to ask questions.

Why has this been done to us?

She turned and looked once more at the burned shell of her world, and knew that nothing would ever bring it back again. Now that it was gone, she found she had loved her city more than she had known. In its clumsy fashion it had tried to make them a home.

Who has done this to us?

In a flash, she recalled an arrogant young face, a tumble of tawny hair.

Who are you? Why do you hate us?

The attack had been so violent, so personal, that she felt as if her own insides had been ripped out, and she had been made hollow. Whoever had done this had meant to destroy them all – perhaps had destroyed them all. She hadn't seen a single other living creature since she had left the arena. She could be the only one of the Manth people left alive in the world. This unknown enemy had meant to destroy her too.

Why?

Suddenly her fierce will caught like a slumbering fire. All her being rose up to defy the unknown enemy.

I will not let you destroy me!

She looked south at the great grey heaving ocean. She looked back towards the last of Aramanth. Then she looked east, and knew that this was the way they had gone, the people-killers, the city-burners. The stiff grasses of the coastland were trampled in a broad swathe, and not far away there lay the huddled shapes of dead bodies.

She had only to follow the march. Her family may be dead. Her people may be dead. But her enemy would be alive. For this reason alone she had survived the death of her city. For this reason alone she would not die.

I am the avenger.

This single simple idea filled her up, it was food and drink. Half-intoxicated with passion and exhaustion, she reached both hands high into the air above her head and spoke aloud, shouted aloud, to her unknown enemy who neither knew nor heard, and to herself who would never forget.

'I will follow you! I will find you! I will destroy you! This I vow!'

For all of that first long day on the march, the people of Aramanth could see behind them the smoking ruins of their home. At first, as if drawn to look on their lost happiness against their will, they turned many times, and wept at the sight. But as the dying city became smaller in the distance, and their tears were all used up, they turned to look no more.

Bowman marched with his family, striding steadily onwards, seeing nothing. With all the power he possessed, he was reaching out, listening, feeling again for the familiar vibrations of his sister's mind. But now he could hear nothing.

Marius Semeon Ortiz came riding slowly down the line. Bowman, seeing him approach, woke from his half-sleep, and tuned his acute senses towards him. This was the man who had taken everything from him, including Kestrel. This man was his enemy. More steadily, more surely, he looked on the tawny-haired man on the horse, and reached out his mind towards him, in order that he might know him.

Ortiz saw the young slave staring up at him. For a moment, their eyes met. Then he rode on, paying him no more attention. Most of the slaves looked at him as he rode by. No doubt they hated him, but they said nothing. They had learned that his punishment was instant and harsh. So it was only a few moments later that he realised the young man had been looking at him in a way he had not known before. Ortiz rode on down the line, puzzling over the sensation. It hadn't been the look of a captive, or a slave, but of an equal. Somehow, in that short moment in which their eyes had met, the young man had seen inside him. What had he seen? Ortiz was not much given to introspection. He was a man of ambition, a man of action. But now he was intrigued.

He turned his horse round, and rode back to find Bowman.

'You,' he said, tapping him on the shoulder with his sheathed sword. 'What's your name?'

'Bowman Hath.'

Ortiz walked his horse alongside the marching slaves, keeping to their pace.

'Why do you look at me like that?'

Bowman didn't answer. Instead, he turned and looked once more into Ortiz's eyes.

This time, because Ortiz had sought the contact, Bowman entered far more deeply into his mind. Ortiz started as if he'd been stung. He jerked his eyes away, and spurred his horse into a trot.

How dare he! he thought to himself as he rode off to the front of the line. He didn't put the thought clearly into words, because he found it too unsettling, but what he had felt, inexplicably, tantalisingly, was that the slave called Bowman Hath had understood him.

The slaves were not chained or roped. They marched in

whatever order they chose. The pace was punishing for the little children and for the old people, so the stronger young men took it in turns to carry those who couldn't keep up. This was more than an act of kindness: those that were left behind on the march were killed by sweepers, mounted soldiers who followed the tail of the long line.

Mumpo carried the heaviest burden of all, for the longest time. He stumped steadily along, with his former foster-mother Mrs Chirish on his back. She was not too young or too old to keep up, she was too fat.

'I don't like to be a burden,' she said each time he heaved her up onto his back.

Mumpo never complained, and never seemed to grow weary, but he didn't smile any more. He didn't speak unless he was spoken to, and then answered as if from somewhere far away. He couldn't forgive himself for having caused his father's death.

'But Mumpo, you didn't.' Pinto tried many times to make him understand. 'They did it. Not you.'

'They did it because of me.'

'It wasn't your fault, Mumpo.'

'He needed me, and now he's dead.'

Pinto pleaded with him, stroked him, tried to make him feel all right again, but nothing she said made any difference. What she knew but didn't say was that his heart had been doubly broken. He had lost Kestrel, too.

Their only hope was that Bowman insisted Kestrel wasn't dead.

'She'll find us,' he said. And every night, as they curled up on the stony ground to sleep, Pinto would watch Bowman, his eyes open, sitting very still, listening for her faraway voice.

* * *

Ira Hath soon developed blisters on her feet, and was in constant pain as she marched. Under her breath she cursed the soldiers who drove them along, muttering a steady stream of the old oaths.

'Pocksicking udderbugs! Hogging pongos!'

Her exclamations meant nothing at all to the soldiers, which kept her safe from punishment, but denied her any satisfaction. At last, in a torment of frustration and foot-ache, she found a way to vent her hatred on her captors without putting herself at risk. She lashed them with praise.

'You giant! You immensity! You have thighs like young oaks! They creak in the wind.'

'What did she say?'

'The beauty of your countenance dazzles the unwary! Small buzzing creatures are drawn to the light in your eyes.'

'Don't bother with her. She's a mad woman.'

'The substances you expel from your nose are a precious ointment for the buttocks of the blessed!'

By the second day, the mood of the prisoners on the march began to change. The food was basic but adequate, the pace of the march tiring but bearable. There had been no stragglers and no attempts at escape for some time. This strange and fearful new life was starting to become familiar, and new friendships began to spring up.

'Look here, young man,' said a voice behind Mumpo. 'Why don't I take a turn carrying the good lady? You need a rest.'

Mumpo looked round to see that this offer came from no less a person than the former Emperor of Aramanth.

Creoth the Sixth was a big bearded man with a friendly manner that even the rigours of the march could not affect.

'No thank you, sir. I can manage.'

'Nonsense! Beard of my ancestors! I have as strong a back as you.'

Mumpo found that Creoth would not be denied, so he lowered Mrs Chirish to the ground.

'Do you mind, auntie?'

'I hate to be a burden,' she said. 'Really, I would walk, only my legs go too slow.'

'Come along, good lady. Up you get.'

Mumpo could not deny that he was glad of the rest. From this time on, he and Creoth took turns in carrying Mrs Chirish, and so became friends. Mumpo found the one-time ruler of Aramanth to be an astonishingly good-tempered companion. He was always grateful for his meagre rations, and at night he blessed the ground he slept on.

'I should have thought you would have found it harder than any of us,' said Mumpo. 'Being an Emperor.'

'Oh, that's all done with,' said Creoth. 'I'm just the same as you now.'

It turned out that this was what he had wanted for a long time. After the changes in Aramanth he had told his people that he no longer saw any need for an Emperor, and wished to lead the life of an ordinary citizen. However, it soon became clear that he possessed no skills of any kind whatsoever, and was quite unable to make a living. So he went back to being Emperor for ceremonial purposes only, and for the past five years had been much in demand for neighbourhood parades, and graduation days at district high schools. He never asked to be paid for these duties, but since they always involved a large meal, he lived well enough from ceremony to ceremony. After a while he had taken to carrying a basket with him, which he filled with leftovers, and so was able to eat even when not acting in his official capacity.

Now a slave among slaves, he was required only to do as he was told, eat what he was given, and keep marching.

'I find it all so much simpler,' he told Mumpo.

In this way, Creoth naturally became part of the group that ate and slept with the Hath family. His good temper made him welcome; though they were a little taken aback to find that it extended to the guards.

'Well, why not? I expect they have their troubles too.'

'They're murderers,' said Pinto. 'I hate them.'

'So do I,' said Mumpo. 'I'm going to kill them.'

The words sounded strange coming from friendly easygoing Mumpo. But over these last days, he had been slowly finding his way to a resolution. His grief and guilt over the death of his father was giving way to a simple powerful desire. He would make his father's murderers suffer as he had suffered.

'Are you any good at that sort of thing?' asked Creoth. 'Killing, and so forth?'

'I don't know,' said Mumpo. 'I've never tried.'

'You have to know what you're doing.' Creoth made some cuts and thrusts in the air with an imaginary sword. 'I was taught when I was young, but I've forgotten it all now.'

'Mumpo would be good at it,' said Pinto. 'He's terrifically strong. He could kill anybody.'

Hanno Hath overheard this.

'Mumpo won't do anything so foolish,' he said. 'We don't want any more people burned in the monkey cages.'

Mumpo looked down and said nothing. Pinto went pink.

'Does that mean none of us can do anything ever?'

'It means none of us can do anything until all of us can do everything,' said her father.

On the third night of the march, Ira Hath dreamed again. This time she woke screaming. Hanno took her in his arms and soothed her as best as he could.

'Hurry!' she was sobbing. 'Faster! Faster! The wind is rising!'

As she came out of the dream, she calmed down again, but for a while she was too weak to speak. Then she said, drawing slow careful breaths, 'Tell me it's just a bad dream.'

'It certainly was a bad dream.'

'I dreamed that we were on our way home, and the wind was rising – such a wind! A wind that destroys everything! I knew that if only we could get home before the wind caught us, we'd be safe, but we weren't going fast enough. You, Hanno, and the children, and all the others, you were walking so slowly – I shouted at you to hurry, hurry! But you wouldn't! Why wouldn't you listen?'

'It's all right. It was only a dream.'

She looked into her husband's gentle face, wanting him to reassure her, but instead she saw there a deep concern.

'I'm not a real prophetess, Hanno. I'm truly not.'

'I expect you're right.'

But as soon as he had a chance, Hanno spoke to

37

Bowman about Ira's dream, and the thoughts that were beginning to form in his mind.

'Perhaps this is the beginning of our journey after all,' he said. 'We may have less time than we think.'

'But we're prisoners. And we don't know where to go.'

'Ira knows. She has the gift. I've known it for a long time.' He took his son's hand in his and kissed it. 'You've known it too, I think.'

'Yes.'

'We must watch, and listen, and learn. Wherever we're being taken, the walls that imprison us will have doors, and the locks will have keys. We will escape.'

Suddenly orders could be heard, calling the lines of marchers to a halt.

'Why are we stopping?'

It was the middle of the afternoon, and the sun was still high in the sky. On each of the three preceding days they had been given no rest until darkness fell. Hanno looked round to make sure the rest of his family were near and safe. On all sides he saw people sinking gratefully to the ground, rubbing their aching feet. Soon there came the clinking sounds of the cook-pots. It seemed they were to have an early supper.

Hanno assembled his particular group. Apart from his wife and children, they included Mumpo and Mrs Chirish, the tailor Miko Mimilith and his family, Creoth, and Scooch the pastry-cook. It so happened that the rations being passed round for their supper that afternoon included pastries looted from Scooch's bakery in Aramanth. Little Scooch shook his head sadly over them.

'When they're fresh out of the oven, they float into your mouth,' he said. 'But this –' he held up the five-day old pastry, 'this would stun a small pig.'

'Not bad,' said Creoth, eating eagerly. 'Not bad at all. Another for you, Mrs Chirish?'

'I don't like to be a burden,' said Mrs Chirish, taking two.

Bowman suddenly stiffened, and raised his head. He had felt a distant wave of pain. A moment later there came a sharp cry from the front of the column. They all heard it. Bowman closed his eyes, and let his acute senses piece together the nature of the pain.

'Skin,' he said. 'Burning.'

Now they saw them: a group of soldiers some way off, hauling a small wheeled iron drum, doing something to the slaves that made them scream.

Bowman rose and walked up the line to see for himself. He didn't want to see, but knew he must. This is how it was for him now. He felt compelled to know everything about their captors, and their captivity, to prepare himself for the time when he and Kestrel were together again, and together they struck back.

A woman was screaming. Bowman could see her struggling and shrieking. He saw the soldiers club her about the head until she was silent. Then the men round the iron drum pressed something to her arm, and there was a hiss of smoke, and the smell of burning meat.

He watched as a new set of metal stamps were clamped into the branding-iron, and the iron was thrust into the red-hot coals burning in the drum. He saw how the soldiers seized the next slave's arm, and how the heated brand was pressed to the back of the shaking wrist. He felt the pain of the branding as if it were his own.

'You! Get back to your place!'

The soldier gave him a push to send him on his way. He returned to the group round his father.

'It's quick,' he said. 'But it's going to hurt.'

'I don't care,' said Pinto.

Bowman saw how she trembled at the approach of the branding team. For all her angry pride, Pinto was only seven years old. He wanted to hold her in his arms when the moment came, but knew she would be too proud to let him. So to conceal his object, he said to his father,

'Let's have a wish-huddle, pa.'

Hanno Hath understood. He opened his arms.

'Come, Pinto. Wish-huddle.'

Pinto came into his embrace. Bowman joined them. Pinto called to Mumpo.

'Come on, Mumpo. You can wish too.'

Ira Hath was watching the branding team with angry eyes. 'How brave they are,' she said bitterly. 'Such manly figures.'

'Hush,' said her husband. 'Come.'

Mumpo joined the huddle gladly, pressing his head against theirs, feeling the hug of their arms around him. Pinto wished first, as the youngest.

'I wish for it not to hurt too much.'

Then Bowman wished.

'I wish Kestrel would come back to us.'

Pinto said quickly. 'I wish that too.'

Before anyone else could wish, the branding team reached them, with their rattling tray and smoking drum. A man with a list took down Hanno's name, and gave him a number. Hanno held out his arm, and because he hadn't made a wish, he now said softly,

'I wish Kestrel to be safe.'

The red-hot iron seared his skin. He twitched, but he made no sound. His wife then held out her arm in her turn, saying, 'My wish is for you too, Kestrel.'

Mumpo said simply, 'For you, Kestrel.' He never moved when the iron burned him. He didn't even blink.

Bowman said nothing. But in his head he spoke to her as he was branded.

Love you, Kess.

Then Pinto held out her thin arm, unable to stop it shaking.

'Oh Kess –' she said. The iron pressed to her young skin, and the pain plunged deep into her, making her sob aloud. But she only sobbed once.

That night as Bowman sat awake listening for Kestrel, he could still feel the pain of his burned wrist. He had not resisted the branding, or made any complaint, but deep inside he was angry. More than the burning of his home city, this burning of the skin of children made him hate the Mastery. In his anger and his powerlessness, he did as he had done long ago, and reached out into the unknown.

You who have watched over me before, whoever you are, help me now.

Then he thought, in the silent chill of the night, I want more than help. I want power. I want the power to destroy these people who seek to destroy me.

You who watch over me, give me the power to destroy.

First Interval:

The butterfly

On the island called Sirene three people stand between the high arched windows beneath the racing clouds, and sing together a wordless song. On either side of the woman who was the first to return stand a young man and an old man. All three are bare-headed and barefoot; all three wear plain woollen robes that reach to the ankles, and are held around the waist with a knotted cord. The song they sing sounds like the rustling of stream water, or the whisper of wind in the trees, but there is a melody here, a pattern of notes that follow after each other in tranquil cycles. It's the song of foreknowing. As they sing, their minds become clear and receptive, and they begin to sense what is to come.

They see the cruelty spreading over the land. They see cities burning, and people on the march. They see young women weeping and old women lying down to die. They feel the hatred in young men's hearts, and know the killing will go on until the time of consummation.

They hear a boy calling to them, crying out for help. They see a girl walking alone, feeling between the fingers of her hand a silver instrument made in the shape of a long-tailed S. They feel her anger, her weakness, her danger.

The singing comes to an end. The young man is filled with a desire to act, to strengthen the weak, to bring an end to the cruelty. The old man feels his desire.

'They must find their own way,' he says. 'We are to do nothing.'

The woman doesn't speak. But later that day she takes herself off alone to the end of the island, where she can watch the distant coast of the mainland. Here she settles herself down and without closing her eyes enters a kind of sleep, in which she slips from quietness into a deeper quietness.

In a little while a butterfly comes jigging and dancing through the air. It settles briefly on a nearby olive tree, and closes its wings. The butterfly's wings are a brilliant iridescent blue, the blue of lapis lazuli, the blue of a kingfisher's breast. They shimmer in the autumn sunlight, in the gleaming light reflected from the great ocean.

Then the wings flicker into motion once more, and the butterfly dances beneath the crooked olive branches, and settles on the woman's cheek, on the high weathered cheekbone beneath her left eye. Here it remains for some little time, while the woman speaks to it in a way that the butterfly understands. Then the brilliant blue wings tremble again, and the butterfly is gone.

4

The Delight of a Million Eyes

Kestrel lay on her stomach on the ground, with her legs and arms spread wide, and one cheek pressed to the earth. With her eyes closed, and all her attention on the feel of the land against her body, she poured out her energy in radiating waves.

Bowman. Where are you?

If he was within reach of her silent call, he would answer. But even if there was no answer, and there was none, by lying very still she could hear, as if in an echo of her cry, that he had passed this way. Not a sound: not the print of a foot on the earth: just a distant familiar feeling that was fading fast, but not yet gone. At home she had always known on entering an empty room if her brother had been there. His presence lingered, the shape he had made in the air, like the disarrangement of cushions in an armchair where someone has been sitting. His gentleness lingered. That quiet gaze in his troubled eyes, that knew everything she felt without the need for words, his loving gaze lingered.

Oh Bowman, where are you?

This faint touch of his passing was enough to drive her

onwards. He was alive, and he had come this way. She rose to her feet, and set off once more.

She followed the trail of the slave march eastward, rising at dawn, walking steadily all morning, resting at noon, and walking until sundown. She slept on the earth where she stopped, and waking, set off again without hesitation. She lived off the refuse of the march, eating the stalks discarded from vegetables, and the bones thrown out of the stewpots. The land was low and undulating, and clothed in a dry spiky grass which scratched at her ankles. At the high point of each rise she looked ahead, hoping to catch sight of the great march, but every time she saw nothing but the next long rolling hill, and the hazy autumn sky.

From time to time she passed dead bodies, most commonly of old people, people she had once known. She made herself look at them, made herself see the wounds of the spears that had killed them, because the sight fuelled the anger and hatred that drove her on. But after a while she avoided the sad bundles. She was growing weaker, and was fighting the temptation to lie down herself, and slip into a sleep from which she would never wake.

Then the day came when there were no more leavings from the march. After ten days, the provisions were evidently running low, and everything that could be eaten was being eaten. On the eleventh day, Kestrel found nothing at all. There was no shortage of water, each shallow valley had its stream, and for a while, by filling her belly full of water, she could forget her hunger. But when the hunger returned, the pain was worse.

On the twelfth day she began to feel dizzy. When she

stopped to rest at noon, her legs gave way beneath her, as if only the rhythm of walking step by step had kept her upright. She folded to the ground, and lay huddled on one side, and knew no more.

Some hours later she was woken by the flickering of a bright light. The sun was low in the sky, and was dazzling her eyelids. Then came blackness. Then the brilliant light once more. She became aware of sounds: the rumble of carriage wheels, the clatter of horses' hooves. She forced herself up onto one elbow, and opened her eyes.

There before her, quite close, moving slowly in a long line of coaches, wagons, and men on horseback, was an exquisite high-wheeled carriage, painted orange and green, ornamented with gold. In the carriage sat a young woman, looking out. Kestrel stared at her, not knowing whether she was dreaming or awake. The young woman stared back. Then she started to scream.

'She's looking at me! She's looking at me!'

The immense column of carriages came to a halt. Tall men seized Kestrel and lifted her into the air. She was carried before a man in a gold cloak, who said things to her she didn't understand. Then she lost consciousness again.

Kestrel half-woke to the sound of voices. One, the voice of a cross-sounding man, was saying in an impatient sort of way, as if it should be obvious to everybody,

'Put her to death, put her to death.'

The other was the voice of a haughty young woman.

'Nonsense, Barzan. She must be made to understand what she's done, then she must have her eyes put out.

Everyone knows that.'

'But radiance, we can't wait until she wakes up. We're late already.'

'Who said we were to wait? You can put her in my carriage, and Lunki will watch over her.'

'In your carriage, radiance?' The one called Barzan sounded very surprised.

'Why not? She's seen me already. And she's only a girl, you know.'

Kestrel hadn't opened her eyes, so the unknown people who were arguing over her still believed her to be unconscious. She now felt herself lifted up by several hands and carried up steps and into a darker place, which she supposed must be the young woman's carriage. Here she was laid down on a soft bed, and shortly felt the rumbling motion of the carriage wheels rolling over the rough ground. The shock of all that had happened to her, and the softness of the bed, and the jogging motion of the carriage, combined to send her back into a deep sleep.

When she woke for the second time, she opened her eyes for a brief moment, and saw in the half-light of the curtained carriage two ladies, one fat and one thin. The thin one was about her own age, and astonishingly beautiful. Kestrel closed her eyes again, and lay there listening to their conversation, hoping to find out what they meant to do with her.

She heard one of them return to her bedside and sit down to gaze at her. It was the young one, the beautiful one, with the haughty voice. After a while she said, in an approving tone,

'She's not at all fat.'

'The poor thing's starved,' said the fat woman.

'She won't like having her eyes put out, will she?'

There came no answer to this. The young woman evidently took this silence as a criticism.

'She shouldn't have looked at me, darling. You know that very well.'

'Yes, sweetie. But my baby should have been wearing her veil.'

'She still looked at me. So it's too late now.'

'I wonder what she thought.'

'So do I, rather.'

There was a silence. Then the young woman went on,

'You know, Lunki, apart from you and mama and papa, no one's seen my face since I was seven years old.'

'Quite right too. My baby mustn't show her face, not until she's married.'

'Yes, I know.' She sounded unenthusiastic.

Kestrel felt her come closer. She felt her curious fingers touch her cropped hair.

'Wake her up, darling. Poke her.'

'It'll take more than poking, sweetie. That one needs food.'

'Feed her, then. At once. Now.'

'But she's asleep.'

'Push it into her,' said the imperious young woman.

Kestrel heard the one called Lunki, evidently a servant, rattling about in a cupboard. She began to think she had better open her eyes before some strange substance was forced into her mouth. But then she heard the young woman clap her hands and say,

'Honey! How clever you are, Lunki!'

Kestrel smelled the honey on the spoon. Then she felt the cool trickle on her lips. Still pretending she was half-asleep, she poked out the tip of her tongue and licked

the sticky sweetness. It tasted of wild clover in summer
meadows.

'She ate it! Give her more!'

Honey drip by honey drip, Kestrel felt her strength
returning. After a while, she judged the time was right to
admit that she was awake. She fluttered her eyelids and
opened them, and looked up at the two ladies who were
leaning over her.

'She's awake! Look, Lunki, she's awake!'

The beautiful young woman clapped her hands once
more.

'Can she speak? Make her say something.'

Kestrel decided she had better speak.

'Thank you,' she said quietly.

'Oh, you darling! Can I keep her?'

'What about –?' The fat servant touched her eyes.

'Oh!' The young woman was shocked. 'I can't possibly
let them put out her eyes. That would be too horrible.'

Kestrel heard everything, and said nothing. She had
decided to say as little as possible until she learned who
these people were.

'She can be my servant. My servants are allowed to
look at me. That is, you are, you know, Lunki.'

She turned to Kestrel and spoke as if to a small child.

'Would you like to be my servant? Or would you rather
have your eyes put out with red-hot skewers?'

Kestrel said nothing.

'She's thinking about it. I don't mind.'

The young woman's sharp eyes suddenly caught sight
of the silver S that was hanging on a string round
Kestrel's neck. She reached one hand and touched it,
turning it this way and that to study it.

'I like this,' she said. 'I want it. Give it to me.'

'No,' said Kestrel.

'No?' Astonished, the young woman turned to Lunki. 'She said no. But I want it. She must give it to me.' And to Kestrel, 'You have to give me what I want.'

'No,' said Kestrel again, and took the silver voice away from her elegant white hand.

The young woman stared at her.

'How dare you!'

She slapped Kestrel's face. Without thinking twice, Kestrel slapped her back, as hard as she could. The young woman burst into tears. The servant saw this aghast.

'Baby!' she exclaimed. 'Oh, my poor baby!'

'You've been kind to me,' said Kestrel, 'and you're very beautiful, but if you hit me again I'll kill you.'

The young woman gasped for breath.

'Oh! You'll be so punished! Oh! You'll cry! I'll make you cry! Oh, you creature!'

She took Kestrel's hand in her own violently trembling hand and pulled it and twisted it, as a confused rush of words came tumbling out.

'Why aren't you afraid of me? Did I hurt you? I'm sorry if I hurt you, but you're not to – you're not to –' She raised Kestrel's hand to her lips and kissed it. 'Why are you so unkind to me? Do you really think I'm beautiful? How would you kill me? Why aren't you afraid?'

Gently, Kestrel drew back her hand. The young woman became calmer. Her huge amber eyes gazed at Kestrel, and her sweet soft lips trembled.

'Please tell me. Am I really beautiful?'

'I've never seen anyone so beautiful in all my life.'

'Oh, I'm so glad.'

She was entirely sincere. It seemed that it was somehow necessary for her to be beautiful. Kestrel picked this up at once. Whatever other faults this imperious young woman had, she was not vain.

Somehow the slaps had been forgotten, on both sides.

'Who are you?' asked Kestrel.

'Who am I? Don't you know?'

'No.'

'I'm the Johdila Sirharasi of Gang, the Pearl of Perfection, the Radiance of the East, and the Delight of a Million Eyes.'

'Oh.' There seemed nothing else to say.

'I'm on my way to be married.'

'Who to?'

'I don't exactly know.'

'So how do you know you want to marry him?'

'I have to marry him, whether I want to or not.'

'I wouldn't.'

'Wouldn't you?'

Kestrel could see that no one had ever talked to her like this in all her life. On her face was a look of astonishment, as if a curtain was being swept aside, to reveal a vista on a new and exciting world.

Lunki saw this too, and was alarmed.

'Baby, take care, won't you? We don't know anything about her.'

'Then she can tell us.' To Kestrel, 'Tell us.'

'Tell you what?'

'Who you are. What you're doing.'

'My name is Kestrel Hath. I'm looking for my family.'

'Why? Where are they?'

'If I knew, I wouldn't have to look.'

Again, Kestrel saw the shock of surprise on her face.

She thought to herself, she's a princess, she always gets what she wants, no one's ever answered her back before.

'You're really not afraid of me?' the Johdila asked.

'No,' said Kestrel. 'Why would you want to hurt me?'

'I don't. I did to start with. But not any more.'

'So we can be friends.'

Kestrel meant nothing very much by this, but the word made a great impact on the young princess.

'Friends? I've never had a friend.'

She studied Kestrel with close attention, wanting to understand her.

'Why do you wear such ugly clothes?'

'So no one will look at me.'

The Johdila puzzled over that. Then,

'I've decided to keep you,' she announced.

'You can't keep me. I'm not a pet.'

'But I want to.'

'Then you must ask me.'

'Ask you? But what if you say no?'

'Then you don't get what you want.'

'But that's – that's –' She clearly wanted to say, that's not right, but something in Kestrel's face made her hesitate. 'But that will make me sad.'

'Not for long.'

'Can I keep you? Please?'

Kestrel couldn't help smiling. She felt so much better, now she'd eaten. And the Johdila did look so comical, with her pretty face all puckered up and ready to cry.

'Maybe I'll stay just until I'm well again,' she said. 'If you'd like me to.'

The Johdila looked in wonder at Kestrel's smile.

'What do you want me to give you?'

'Nothing.'

'Then why are you smiling at me?'

'You're funny. You make me smile.'

The Johdila considered this gravely.

'Is that how friends smile? For no reason?'

'Yes.'

So the Johdila smiled back.

'Oh!' exclaimed Kestrel, caught unawares by the radiance of her smile. 'How lovely you are!'

5

Looking, listening, learning

Ozoh the Wise took the sacred chicken from its basket, and carefully dusted its feet with powdered chalk. Nearby, his royal master the Johanna of Gang, the Lord of a Million Souls and the father of the Johdila Sirharasi, stepped down from his royal carriage, lowered his enormous body into a camp-chair, and emitted a long loud groan.

'Be quiet, Foofy. You'll disturb the chicken.' This from his wife, the Johdi of Gang, Mother of the Nations. Though known affectionately to her people as 'Little Mother', she was as large as her husband, her girth made even more imposing by the stiff heavily-ornamented tent-like garments she wore.

The Johanna groaned because he was hungry. He slept poorly while travelling, and when not sleeping, he thought about food. At home if he woke in the night, which he never did, he could call for any food he wanted. On this journey, if he woke in the night, which he did every night, he must go hungry. His wife had introduced a strict rule that no breakfast was to be served at court until the day's signs had been read. After all, as she had pointed out, if the reading called for a day of fasting, and they had already eaten, who knew what the consequences might be?

The royal augur held the sacred chicken over the sign mat, which he had unrolled on a level patch of ground. The chicken was white and fat and fluffy, with sticky-out feathers all round its mad pink eyes. Ozoh was thin and bald and bare, at least from the waist up, so that everyone could see the intricate blue-green patterns that twined all over his body, the proof of his claim that one of his grandmothers had been a snake. Below the waist he wore the traditional baggy pantaloons of Gang, so no one knew whether the markings extended over his bottom; but many wondered.

'Oh! Ha!' he muttered, and lowered the chicken carefully onto the mat. The whole watching court went still, tensed to see what the chicken would do. Two men watched with particular attention. Barzan, the gloomy stooping Grand Vizier, standing behind the Johanna on his right side, kept his eyes on the movements of the chicken. The other man, a tall handsome soldier, watched the royal augur. His name was Zohon, and he was the Commander of the Johjan Guards.

The chicken looked back at them for a moment. Then, moving its head in abrupt jerks, it strutted off the mat towards its dish of corn.

'Aaah!' went the court.

A short line of white footmarks had been left on the mat by the departing chicken. The augur looked at them closely.

'Excellent.'

Everyone relaxed. That meant there would be breakfast.

'As your mightiness can see, the signs enter through Fang and exit through Yanoo.'

'They look clear enough to me,' said the Johanna.

'Indeed so. Nothing untoward will happen today.'

'That's all right, then.'

The Johanna started to rise.

'So long,' added the augur, 'as all members of the royal party do their duty with a glad heart.'

'Ah,' said the Johanna. He looked towards his wife.

'What if they don't?' asked the Johdi, thinking at once of her daughter, the Johdila Sirharasi, still asleep in her carriage. Sisi was not known for doing her duty, with a glad heart or otherwise.

'If they don't,' said the augur gravely, 'there will be consequences.'

'Oh dear,' fretted the Johdi. 'I was afraid of that.'

Happily, Ozoh the Wise understood her well.

'The Johdila, of course, has no duties,' he said. 'Not in the strict sense of the word. Being as yet unmarried.'

'Oh! Ah. Not in the strict sense of the word,' said the Johdi, greatly relieved.

'And in the matter of signs, as your gloriousness appreciates, only the very strictest sense of the word applies.'

'That's all right, then,' said the Johanna again. 'Bring on the hot buttered pancakes.'

The Johdila Sirharasi did not breakfast in the dining tent with the rest of the court. Her breakfast was carried to her own private sleeping carriage, by two servants wearing blindfolds. They were afraid of dropping the heavily-laden trays, and so they proceeded very slowly from the kitchen wagon to the Johdila's carriage. By the time they arrived, the melted butter on the pancakes had formed a hard yellow crust. This happened morning after morning, but no one thought to improve the arrangements, because the Johdila never complained. She never complained because she never ate her breakfast. It was eaten later, and in secret, by her maid Lunki. The rule at court was that the servants did not eat until their masters had eaten, and since the Johdila sometimes went for days without eating, Lunki had learned to take the opportunities that fate placed in her path.

The two servants stumbled their way into the outer room of the Johdila's carriage, where Kestrel now had a bunk bed alongside Lunki. They handed over their trays, and stumbled out again. They made no attempt to peek through the blindfolds. Any man who looked on the unveiled face of the Johdila would have his eyes burned out with red-hot skewers.

'Breakfast, sweetie,' cooed Lunki through the dividing curtain.

'Boil me a glass of water, darling.'

Kestrel did not participate in the Johdila's morning ritual. Instead, she slipped out of the carriage after the departing kitchen servants, and finding a secluded space between the stationary carriages, she lay down and spread herself out face to the ground. It was harder here among the stamp of grazing horses and the rattle of passing soldiers, but she lay still, reaching into the ground, until she began to touch the memories of the road. Yes, the dust recalled him. He had passed this way. Her brother, her sister, her parents, the Manth people, had passed this way.

She heard footsteps. The footsteps stopped. Someone was standing near her, watching her.

She got up off the ground. There, staring at her, frankly curious, was a very tall, very good-looking soldier. He wore a beautifully-cut uniform of dark purple cloth trimmed with gold braid, closely moulded to his slim waist and his muscular chest. In one hand he carried a slender-shafted hammer, made of silver, which he flicked idly back and forth so that it struck the palm of his other hand.

'So you're the one who saw the Johdila unveiled,' he said.

'Yes,' said Kestrel.

'Is she beautiful?'

'Yes,' said Kestrel.

'You realise that according to the law you should have your eyes burned out?'

'It's a stupid law.'

The soldier raised his dark eyebrows and smiled.

'Well, maybe it is,' he said. 'Fortunately, she seems to have taken a liking to you.'

Kestrel said nothing to this. She decided she had better return to the carriage. But the handsome soldier reached out his silver hammer to detain her. She noticed then that the end of its shaft was fashioned into a fine sharp blade.

'Do you know who I am?'

'No.'

'I am Zohon, Commander of the Johjan Guards. After the Johanna himself, I'm the most powerful man in all the Sovereignty of Gang.'

He looked round, to make sure that no one was near enough to overhear him, and he lowered his voice.

'If you help me, I'll help you.'

'Help you do what?'

'The Johdila is being taken to a country known as the Mastery. She's to marry the son of its ruler.' Zohon's lips curled into a sneer. 'A fine gentleman who goes in for robbing and burning and taking slaves. His son will make a fine sort of husband for the daughter of the Johanna of Gang, don't you think?'

'They take slaves?'

'The wealth of the Mastery is built on slaves.'

Kestrel saw again the horsemen bursting into the arena of Aramanth, and the screaming people running before their swords. She shivered.

'How can the Johdila be given to such people?'

'How indeed?' Zohon saw the horror on her face, and he approved. 'The marriage must be stopped.'

There came a bustle all up and down the caravan. The carriages were about to start moving again. A servant passed nearby, carrying the sacred chicken in its cage. Zohon saw the royal augur following behind, and knew that Ozoh had seen him.

'We'll talk later,' he hissed to Kestrel. And turning aside, he sauntered nonchalantly away towards his men.

When Kestrel rejoined the Johdila's carriage, she found Sisi out of bed and seated at her mirror-table. This table had six mirrors so placed that she could see herself from every angle. Lunki stood behind her, and together they were repairing the ravages of the night.

'Where have you been?' asked Sisi, spotting Kestrel in one of the mirrors.

'Just walking,' Kestrel replied.

'Walking? In the open air? Your skin will dry out.'

This turned her attention back to her own lustrous creamy skin.

'It seems so unfair,' she complained, 'that I should have to lay my head on a pillow when I sleep. I can't help turning over in the night, and I know for a certain fact that it makes wrinkles. Look, darling! That line wasn't there yesterday.'

'We can pat it out, sweetie. Lunki will pat it away for her baby.'

Lunki was as deeply engaged in the Johdila's appearance as the Johdila herself. It was understood between them that Sisi was beautiful for both of them. In a wider sense, Sisi was beautiful for all the Sovereignty of Gang, as was indicated by her titles, the Pearl of Perfection, Radiance of the East, and the Delight of a Million Eyes.

'My neck has grown fatter. I'm sure of it.'

'No, sweetie. It's only the way the shadows fall.' Lunki massaged soft oils into her mistress's skin. 'Now why doesn't my baby drink the smallest glass of milk?'

'Don't bully me, darling. I feel as if today will be a fat day.'

The Johdila was so slender and lissom of form that Kestrel found it hard to believe she was the daughter of her parents. Sisi assured her that her mother had been as slender as she was, before her marriage.

'It's marriage that makes you fat. That, and having babies. I don't think I shall have any babies. Lunki can have them for me. Would you do that for me, Lunki darling? Do say you will.'

'No need to worry about that for now, my precious. There's the marrying to be done with first.'

'Yes, I know.'

'What sort of man is it you're marrying?' Kestrel asked, wondering how much the Johdila knew.

'Oh, someone or other.' Sisi's mind was running along a different track. 'What is it married women actually do, Lunki?'

'Do, sweetie? How do you mean?'

'They must do something that makes them fat.'

'Ah, well, my pet, it's not so much what they do, as what they don't do. You see what a lot of trouble it takes to keep you beautiful. Well, once you're married, you won't need to be beautiful any more, will you?'

'I suppose not.'

'So naturally you'll stop taking trouble. Then before you know it, you're as fat as a badger.'

'What's it like being fat, Lunki?'

'Oh, it's not so bad, once you get used to it. You don't feel the cold so much. And you'd be surprised how much extra time it gives you in the day.'

When the elaborate morning toilet was done, and Sisi's long hair was braided and coiled, both she and Lunki took one last look at their joint creation, sighed with admiration, and lowered the veil. All this time the carriage, in common with the rest of the caravan, had been in steady motion. But now the Johdila was dressed, Lunki pulled on the bell-rope, and the long line of carriages heaved and rattled to a halt once more. It was time for Sisi's dancing lesson.

The dancing tent was erected by the roadside, and the dancing master, Lazarim, approached the Johdila's carriage and tapped respectfully on the door. The Johdila then emerged, swathed from top to toe in layers of blue and silver silk, so fine that they floated about her mysterious form like smoke. Kestrel went with her, in her role as servant and unofficial friend. Lazarim escorted them to the dancing tent, which though windowless was open to the noonday sky. And there, to the music of a blind-folded piper and drummer, he taught the Johdila the dance called the tantaraza.

Kestrel could see at once that Sisi was not a natural dancer. The tantaraza was a difficult dance. It required concentrated attention to memorise the intricate sequences of steps; and then conscientious practice, to turn the mechanical copying of the step-sequences into the fluid rhythms of the dance. Sisi had never been required to give concentrated attention to anything in her life; and as for practice, if she found she couldn't do something the first time, she became bored and gave up.

Lazarim longed with a fierce and terrible longing to smack her bottom. He longed to pinch her until she screamed, or wept, or made any sound at all, other than that languid monotonous whine.

'Do I ha-ave to? I feel so-o tired this morning. Be a darling pixie, and don't bore me too-oo much.'

'But you must learn the dance, radiance. It is your father's wish that you marry, and to be married, you must dance.'

'Yes, I know, darling. Don't bully me. But I don't have to dance much, surely? Just the once is enough, isn't it?'

'Just the once is enough, my lady, but that once must be perfect. The lords and ladies of the Mastery must say, nowhere in the world is there beauty and grace to match the Johdila of Gang.'

'But that would be true, darling Lazarim, whether I danced or not.'

'If it is your wish not to dance, my lady, I say no more. But if you wish to dance, you must dance well.'

'Oh, well. I suppose we could go over a few steps. But you're not to muddle me.'

While Kestrel sat quietly and watched with growing interest, Lazarim took the Johdila through the opening sequence again: the sidesteps, the salute, the three spins away, the arrest, the heel-toe drumbeat of the re-join, the clasp, and the swirl. The tantaraza was a sublime dance, the dance of dances, to Lazarim it was art and passion, love and religion, life and death. This tiny but exquisite man was a true master of its mysteries, and with all his being he longed to be released from the torture of teaching, and to fly away into the ecstasy of the dance. Instead, here he was, hobbling through the steps like a cripple.

'No, radiance, no! The spins are fast, very fast, like a spinning top, remember? Then the arrest is sudden! Like this! See how my skirts fly away without me?'

'Your skirts, Lazarim?' She tinkled a little laugh. 'You mustn't make me smile, pixie. Every smile leaves a line.'

'Once more, please.'

When the dancing lesson was over, Kestrel accompanied Sisi to lunch with her father and mother in the royal carriage.

'You are lucky not to have to dance, Kess.'

'I thought it looked like fun.'

'Fun? Why do you say that? It's difficult, and annoying, and not fun at all.'

The royal carriage was guarded by Johjan Guards. On this occasion, as they approached its canopied steps, Kestrel saw that Zohon, their commander, was standing with his men. He looked round, and for a brief moment his eyes met hers. He gave her a look that said, we understand each other. Then his gaze rested for a moment on the veiled Johdila. Then he said something to one of his men, clapped him on the shoulder with a loud and careless laugh, and turned and sauntered away. That over-loud laugh, that over-carefree swagger, told Kestrel much. A man so intent on showing his lack of interest must be very interested indeed.

They entered the royal carriage. Lunch was already on the table, and the Johanna was eager to begin. No attention was paid to Kestrel. The Johanna and his wife disapproved of her, both because they thought she looked odd, and because they felt it was unbecoming for a princess to have a friend. They had made their views known to their daughter. Sisi had replied sharply,

'Kestrel is my friend, and she goes where I go.'

As a compromise, when in the royal carriage Kestrel did not eat at the main table, but at a little table of her own. This suited her very well, because she found that quite quickly everyone forgot about her, and talked as if she wasn't there.

'How is my precious one today?' said the Johanna, removing his daughter's veil and looking proudly on her face.

'Oh, papa,' sighed Sisi. 'I wish we were home.'

The Johanna sighed too. He hated travel in all its forms. He too wanted to be back in his own city of Obagang, in his palace, with his dogs and his horses, sleeping at night in his familiar-smelling big old bed.

'It must be done, precious one.'

In a melancholy frame of mind, he settled down to eat his pie.

'I don't understand why you have to do anything, papa, unless you want to.'

'Eat up, Sisi,' said her mother. 'You're looking a little peaky.'

'It's my duty to my people,' the Johanna began; and then stopped, to take another mouthful. Also, it wasn't easy to explain. The faraway land called the Mastery was just one among many satellite nations that orbited the great sun of Gang; but somehow, like an ageing giant, mighty Gang had grown weaker as the Mastery had grown stronger, and its ruler, the Master, was now annexing land that had long owed allegiance to Gang.

There came a knock at the outer door. The Johanna frowned, and signed to his daughter to replace her veil.

'Enter!'

The Grand Vizier entered, and bowed. Grand Vizier Barzan was the only one of his subjects who would dare to intrude on a meal. His intrusions were frequent, always urgent, always accompanied by warnings of catastrophe, and always delivered in low respectful tones, as if from beyond the tomb.

'Our hopes are scattered to the winds, mightiness,' he intoned. 'The caravan master reports that he has completed his calculations. At our present rate of progress, we will arrive a full month late.'

'A month late! We can't arrive a month late. It will be taken as an insult. Whose fault is it? Someone must be punished.'

'Naturally, mightiness. I will see to it myself. In the

meantime, in view of the problem, might we consider not stopping the caravan for the dancing lesson before lunch, or for lunch itself, or for the rest after lunch, or for dinner?'

'You're right, Barzan. We must press on.'

'We must stop for my rest,' objected the Johdi. 'I can't rest in a moving carriage.'

'No, my dear. Of course not.'

'And you know if you eat while travelling, your stomach gets upset.'

'No, no, we must stop for meals. The dancing lesson, then. We must not stop for the dancing lesson.'

'The Johdila is to dance in a moving carriage, greatness?'

'Ah.'

'The dancing lessons must continue, sire. This marriage is all that stands between us and war. And if there is war –'

'Yes, yes,' said the Johanna, getting flustered. 'So what are we to do?'

The Grand Vizier sighed.

'The escort, mightiness –'

'I won't have you send my guard away, Barzan. You're only saying it to spite Zohon, you know. I won't arrive in a foreign city with a few house-servants. I won't shame my ancestors.'

'But mightiness, three thousand men, all heavily armed, most of them marching on foot – no wonder we travel too slowly.'

'The Johanna of Gang is always escorted by his Johjan Guards. It's traditional. No, Barzan, that's not the answer. We are travelling too slowly. Seek out who is responsible. Punish them. That is the answer.'

'As you wish, sire.'

The Grand Vizier bowed gloomily, and withdrew.

'I do wish Barzan and Zohon would stop this squabbling,' complained the Johanna. 'They're as jealous of each other as a pair of schoolgirls.'

'Papa,' said Sisi, lifting her veil, 'why will my marriage stop there being war?'

'I've told you, precious one. Once you marry, your husband becomes our son and heir. His father can't make war on us if his own son and heir is our son and heir.'

'But doesn't that mean he gets everything he wants without the trouble of a war?'

The Johanna gazed at his daughter for a long thoughtful moment.

'These are matters of state, Sisi. You wouldn't understand.'

Kestrel, listening to these exchanges unnoticed at her little table, gained more information to add to her growing store. Out of such overheard fragments, out of observations and guesses, she was beginning to make a plan. At the heart of her plan was the Commander of the Johjan Guards.

6

The Hammer of Gang

Sisi and her parents always rested after lunch. Kestrel took this opportunity to walk down the entire length of the caravan. For a while she counted the carriages and wagons she passed, but there were too many, and after the fortieth vehicle she gave up counting. Apart from the grand gilded carriages of the royal court, there were plain carriages for officials, and plainer ones still for upper servants. There were carriages with chimneys for the cooks, and carriages with arrow slits for the soldiers. There were the quartermaster's wagons, and feed wagons for the horses, and tent wagons, and bed-roll wagons, and more and more, to carry the necessaries of this great moving town. Near the rear of the line she came upon the tethered horses of the Johjan Guards, and beyond the horses, in the shade of a line of trees, the mess tables where the men were to eat. On the far side of the trees the entire force, almost three thousand men, were formed up in long regular lines, doing their daily exercises.

Kestrel came to a stop, concealed from their view by the quietly-grazing horses, and watched. It was an impressive sight. The men were naked but for their tight black under-britches. They were all tall, powerfully-built,

68

and bronzed by the sun. They all wore their hair drawn back tight over the head, and knotted in a small roll on the back of the neck. They moved together, in perfect time, the long ranks of men dropping to the ground and springing into the air, dropping and springing up, seemingly without effort, but for the glisten of sweat on their shapely torsos.

At their head, facing them, as naked as his men, but even taller and more magnificently-muscled, stood Zohon, their youthful leader. He issued no commands. He moved, and like a reflection in a thousand mirrors, his men moved with him. He was still, and they were still. Kestrel, watching, knew that so perfectly-disciplined a force of fighting men were more than equal to the raiding parties of the Mastery.

As the sequence of exercises came to an end, she was about to show herself, to speak to Zohon, when she saw Barzan approaching from the farther side. To the fury of the Grand Vizier, the sentries insisted on searching him for concealed weapons.

'Really, Commander,' he objected. 'If I wanted to assassinate you, I could do it without coming anywhere near your guards.'

Zohon stood magnificently still, his great chest rising and falling, his eyes fixed on Barzan with total concentration.

'Show me how.'

'Well – for example, with a bow and arrow.'

'And where would you stand, to take aim?'

Barzan looked round. He hadn't intended to go into so much detail.

'Well – there, between the carriages.'

Zohon smiled, and clapped his hands. From all round,

from behind the carriages, from the branches of the trees, from concealment in the long grass, appeared hidden guards. Fortunately for Kestrel, they all looked to their commander; and so she remained unnoticed.

'You would be dead, my friend,' said Zohon, 'before you could set an arrow to your bow.'

Barzan drew a long breath, to control a rising wave of irritation.

'Exactly who, Commander, do you expect to attack you, here, in your own country, surrounded by your own men?'

'That is the difference between you and me, my friend. You do not believe there will be an attack until it happens. Then you believe it. But then you are dead. I believe the attack will come before it comes. I believe it before there is any threat of an attack. I believe it most of all when there is no reason whatsoever for an attack. That is why I am still alive.'

'Yes, but so am I.'

'Ah, my friend. Be very careful.' He smiled, and gestured to his batman to come forward with the water bucket. Taking it from him in one hand, he emptied it over his own head, splashing the Grand Vizier in the process. His batman then handed him a rough towel, and he rubbed himself down.

Barzan brushed water droplets off his gold robe with impatience.

'I understand you wished to speak to me, Commander. I'm extremely busy.'

'Too busy to ensure the safety of the Johanna? I think not.'

'The Johanna is perfectly safe.'

'Now, yes. But then?'

'When? What are you talking about?'

'This city,' said Zohon with maddening calm, 'this famous Mastery's famous High Domain. I am told it has only the one entrance.'

'What of it?'

'What else has only one entrance?'

'I have no idea.'

'A trap!' said Zohon. 'Once we are lured into this city with only one entrance, they have only to close the gates, and we are trapped!'

The Grand Vizier passed a hand across his brow.

'Why should anyone want to trap us?'

'To force the Johanna to hand over all his power.'

'Commander, the Johanna is giving his only daughter in marriage to the only son of the ruler of this city you fear to enter. What possible reason could that ruler have for using force to gain what is being freely given?'

'To the true ruler,' said Zohon, drawing on the jacket of his magnificent uniform, 'the use of force is an end in itself. I insist that if the royal party enters this city that has no exit, the Johjan Guards accompany the Johanna at full strength.'

'At full strength! Three thousand armed men at a wedding! Impossible!'

Dressed now, glorious in his gold-encrusted purple tunic, Zohon held out his hand and his batman gave him his silver hammer. The Grand Vizier eyed it with open disgust.

'I will not insult our host with such an offensive suggestion,' he said.

Zohon swung his hammer back and forth.

'I consider it my duty to alert the Johanna to the danger.'

71

'By all means do so, Commander. I for my part mean to alert the Johanna to the danger of allowing a large force of halfwitted louts to trample over our host's exquisitely beautiful city.'

He turned and strode away. Zohon watched him go with a smile.

'We shall see, my friend,' he murmured to himself. 'We shall see.'

Kestrel now stepped out from the concealment of the horses and let the sentries discover her.

'You! Halt! Stay where you are!'

She did as she was told. Zohon, hearing the sentry's cry, turned and saw her. He beckoned to the sentry, indicating that he was to bring her to him.

'Dismiss the men,' he instructed his officers.

The lines of men, who had been standing rigid and motionless all this time, now broke up, and crowded round the mess tables, eager for their belated lunch. Zohon stood gazing into the distance, speaking to Kestrel without looking at her.

'What do you want?'

'You said you would help me,' replied Kestrel.

'Why do you want my help?'

'I'm alone. I have no one to protect me.'

Zohon nodded, still without looking at her.

'Do as I ask,' he said, 'and you will come under the protection of the Hammer of Gang!'

He struck a nearby tree-trunk with his silver hammer.

'I don't speak of this –' he held out the hammer, 'but of myself. I am known as the Hammer of Gang. Under my protection, no one will dare to harm you.'

'Thank you,' said Kestrel.

'But if I am to help you, you must help me.'

He turned and fixed her with his stern eyes.

'I believe this marriage to be a mistake. Worse, a disaster. Why is the Johdila to be married to a man she has never met? Who is this man? Some undersized pygmy with a fat belly and black teeth? Some ancient wreck with no hair and a squint? He could be. We know nothing about him. Is the loveliest, the sweetest, the most perfect creature in all the world to be sold to this monster because her father hasn't the guts to stand up to a petty dictator?'

The Commander was almost shouting. Aware that he was making too much noise, he calmed himself down, and went on in a fierce whisper,

'She should marry one of her own kind. She should marry a strong and healthy young man who is respected by her people, and who is powerful enough to protect her. Doesn't she deserve this, and more? Is she not the most beautiful young woman in all the world?'

This question seemed to require an answer.

'She is very lovely,' said Kestrel.

'Ah!' Zohon sighed, and a faraway look came into his face. 'I know it in my heart! I've never seen her face, but her loveliness – how can I explain? – her loveliness calls out to me.'

As he spoke of the Johdila's loveliness he thought also of his own handsome looks. The two images were linked in his mind.

'At home,' he said, 'there's a secluded woodland pool, where I go to swim. After I've swum, I stand by the bank and let the water run off my body, and wait for the surface of the pool to be still. Then I look down, and see my reflection.'

He fell silent, contemplating the memory of his own manly form. Then he turned to Kestrel.

'How do I look to you? Short? Tall? Plain? Handsome? Be honest.'

'Tall,' said Kestrel. 'Handsome.'

'I'm not asking for compliments, you understand. I want facts. Simple undeniable facts. I believe I am considered a fine figure of a man. I'm twenty-nine years of age. I'm Commander of the Johjan Guards. These are facts. Would you not say, when you consider these facts, that I am a suitable consort for the Johdila?'

'Oh, yes.'

'Has she said as much to you?'

'No.'

'But she might. Were you to ask her. Were you to lead the talk round to the subject of marriage, and husbands, and how it might have been better managed, and who might be a better choice, and young men of her acquaintance. You follow me?'

'Yes,' said Kestrel. 'You want to know if she'd rather marry you.'

'Hush!' Zohon was a little shocked to hear it put so plainly. 'Some things are better understood in silence. These are dangerous matters.'

'But it's too late, surely.'

'We shall see about that.' He walked moodily up and down, swinging his hammer. 'First, I need to know her heart. That is where you must help me.'

'What am I to do?' Kestrel knew very well, but it suited her to have Zohon think he was the one with the plan.

'Speak to her. Find out if she fears this marriage. Speak of me. Then come to me and tell me what she says.'

Horns sounded from the lead end of the caravan. Soon now the carriages would be moving off.

'Go now. Keep my secret. If you betray me –' he raised his hammer, and reversing it, lopped off a cluster of leaves from a low-hanging branch, 'I will show no mercy.'

As the leaves fluttered to the ground, Zohon's ever-alert eyes caught a movement on the far side of the trees. It was Ozoh, the royal augur, hurrying to his carriage, his gaze firmly fixed on the ground.

'And don't trust the snake man,' he added.

Ozoh the Wise was worried. He made it his business to notice what went on around him, even the little unimportant things, and he had noticed that the Johdila's new servant had some unexplained dealings with Zohon.

He decided he had better share his suspicions with Barzan. The Grand Vizier, his friend and patron, had promised him an estate in the hills by the southern lakes, with its own vineyard, once the royal marriage was successfully concluded.

'I've just seen the Commander –'

'That scheming squirt of squirrel droppings!'

'He seems to be making friends with the Johdila's new servant.'

'I should have started a war somewhere, to get him out of the way.'

'I wondered if you'd noticed.'

'Of course I've noticed,' said Barzan, not wanting to appear unobservant. 'What of it?'

'I just wondered what they might have to talk about.'

'Ozoh,' sighed the Grand Vizier, 'Zohon is a virile

young man. This servant is in her way an attractive young woman. Need I go on?'

'Ah. So you think it's that.'

'It usually is.'

'So you think there's nothing to worry about?'

'Quite the contrary. If Zohon has his eye on the girl, so much the better. He's far too keen on playing with his toy soldiers. There's nothing like a woman to take a man's mind off soldiering.'

Ozoh the Wise returned thoughtfully to his own carriage. The sacred chicken clucked at him from its cage. Ozoh opened the cage door and took the chicken onto his lap, and sat stroking its white feathers as he pondered the situation.

'What am I to do, my dove?' he murmured. 'What am I to do, my silky one?'

The chicken scratched at his baggy pantaloons and cooed contentedly.

The immense caravan rolled across the land in a north-easterly direction, through the subject kingdoms and on into the border territories. From the first outriders of the Johjan Guards to the last baggage wagons, the column took over an hour to pass by. The peasants and traders in the path of the royal progress took care to prostrate themselves on the ground as the caravan went by, and press their faces to the dust. Many closed their eyes and went to sleep, as the thousands of marching boots and hundreds of rumbling wheels ground slowly past. It was safer to go to sleep than to risk a peek at the magnificent carriages, in case the fabled Johdila was looking out of a carriage window. The simple peasant folk believed that one glance from her radiant eyes was a preview of paradise, but they also believed that one glance would cause their own eyes to catch fire and melt. Wise in their fashion, they chose to sleep in the dust, and let paradise go by.

7

Into the Mastery

Marius Semeon Ortiz and his long lines of captives reached the borders of the Mastery on the twenty-fifth day, just as he had planned. There was no wall surrounding this country of slaves: only a pair of stubby stone markers, on either side of the road. The true indicator that they had passed into a new realm lay in the countryside around them. Hanno Hath and his family saw it with astonishment: on one side of the stone markers, a bare windswept land, where only the hardiest of plants, gorse and heather and thorn, clung to the stony ground; on the other side, tilled fields, many still tawny with the stubble of a late harvest, divided by hedges, and criss-crossed by deep-ditched watercourses. Here and there, groups of farm workers could be seen driving teams of plough horses, or digging potatoes. They paused in their work as the march went by, and gaped in their turn in surprise. Ortiz, his body aching from the long days in the saddle, noted this with satisfaction. No one had ever brought back so many slaves, in such fine condition, in a single raid.

He beckoned one of his chasseurs to his side.

'Ride on,' he said. 'Present my compliments to the Master. Tell him I bring him the Manth people to kneel at his feet.'

His captives looked around them as they marched, their weary spirits rising with the news that the end was in sight. The more they saw of this new country, the more they marvelled. The road down which they passed was now paved in smooth cut stone. Where it met a ditch or stream, a new well-built stone bridge carried it onward without interruption. On either side they saw farm buildings with steep roofs that hung almost to the ground: large handsome houses made of timber and clay, with well-swept sandy yards, set among pastures stocked with plump cattle. Smoke rose from tall chimneys. Children's voices could be heard chanting their lessons from a many-windowed schoolhouse. A jaunting wagon passed them on the road, carrying a crowd of young people sitting back to back, who were shouting out and laughing as they went. There were no prisons to be seen, no bars, no chains, no guards. Wherever the slaves were kept, it was not here.

Bowman strode along steadily beside his father, on the outer edge of the column of slaves. To his right marched a stout round-faced soldier, one of the lower ranks, for whom the long trek from Aramanth had been almost as arduous as for the captives. His name was Joll, and he was a Loomus, from the coastal region of Loom. The Loomus were mostly fishermen, a slow-moving slow-thinking race, not much given to talking. Bowman had made friends with Joll in the last few days, and he now turned to him with a question.

'All these people. Where are they going?'

The further up the road they marched, the more it became apparent that others were heading in the same direction. From fields and paths they came, in an ever-growing stream, to make their way up the rising land towards the band of trees on the near horizon.

'To the manaxa,' replied Joll. And pointing with his chin towards the mounted figure of Ortiz ahead, he added, 'He's clever, that one. He's bringing in his prizes on the day of the manaxa.'

'What's the manaxa?'

'The manaxa? Well now, it's like nothing in the world excepting itself. How would you speak of the manaxa, Tell?'

Tell was another Loomus guard, marching immediately in front of Joll.

'The manaxa?' said Tell. 'I would speak of it as a kind of dancing.'

'And a kind of killing,' said Joll.

'It's not every day you get a killing,' said Tell. 'You don't want to raise the lad's hopes.'

'True enough, true enough. As often as not the loser takes the jump.'

'You get a killing,' Tell explained to Bowman, 'when the fighters are evenly matched, and neither one will give up. That's quite something, I don't mind telling you. That really oils your britches.'

'Are they forced to fight each other?' asked Bowman.

'Forced? Why would they be forced? It's an honour to be a manac. An honour and a glory. Am I right, Joll?'

'You are, Tell. An honour and a glory. And then there's the doing of it, you know. The manaxa is what I'd call very dangerous, but very beautiful. Am I right, Tell?'

'You are, Joll. Dangerously beautiful. That's it, in two words.'

They had now reached the trees, and for a little while they marched in tree-shadow. The long days of walking had worn down the Manth people, and there was little spirit of resistance left in them. Even Ira Hath had become quiet. Her blisters had passed from raw wounds to calluses, and as her feet had hardened, the pain had faded. Ortiz had been careful not to force the march for too many hours at a time, and with careful rationing the food supplies had lasted. All in all, he had judged it well. The slaves were in need of good food and rest, but they were not broken. Knowing that they would not reach the marshalling yards until later that evening, he ordered the last of the supplies to be distributed as soon as he gave the command for the march to stop.

The Hath family stayed close together, as they had done all through the march. Ira Hath and Pinto followed immediately behind Hanno and Bowman. Mumpo, whose turn it was to carry Mrs Chirish, lagged some way back. As they passed through the trees there was little to see, so each of them turned to whatever thoughts were uppermost in their minds. Hanno was worrying about whether they would be split up on their arrival. Ira was remembering the kitchen of their old house in Orange District where Pinto had been a baby, and how Bowman had rolled her back and forth on the floor and made her laugh. Bowman was missing Kestrel. And Pinto, slogging determinedly along on her much shorter legs, was day-dreaming about a heroic act in which she rescued them all from their enemies. She was not clear about the exact way she would do it, and so had moved on, in her imagining, to the part where everyone cheered, and said how wonderful it was that they owed their freedom to a child of seven.

So all of them were caught entirely by surprise when they marched out of the trees and saw the view before them. The Mastery lay in a wide shallow valley that bordered an immense lake: and everything about it was beautiful.

The road wound down through green fields, past farms and villages and great estates, to the shores of the lake. A causeway reached out from the shore, carried on timber piles for half a mile or more to an island, where there rose a walled palace, or city, that seemed to be built out of light and colour alone. There were buildings, they jostled close one against the next, but their thousand roofs seemed to float, each one sustained by a weightless shimmering umbrella. The late afternoon sun was falling aslant into the city, and the domed roofs, seeming to drink it, were gorged with light, and flushed rose-pink, emerald-green, blood-red.

All round the city ran walls of creamy stone, walls that rose up directly from the waters of the lake, and went on rising for thirty feet or more. Yet even this massive edifice was so constructed that it seemed light: the upper stonework, becoming thinner as it rose, was pierced with intricately-patterned holes, so that from this distance the great walls seemed no more substantial than a curtain of amber lace.

Marius Semeon Ortiz saw the wonder on the faces of the slaves, and felt again, as he always did on returning to the Mastery, a renewal of awe and gratitude to the Master.

'That is the High Domain,' he said. 'The most beautiful city built by man.'

As the slaves marched on, Hanno looked for the prisons or fenced compounds where they were to be kept, but all he could see were farms and villages, and the glowing city on the lake. And everywhere he looked, he saw people wending their way along paths, in cheerful bands, converging on a great gathering now visible below them. Here a large arena had been cut out of the hillside: a great earthwork that could only have been dug by thousands of slaves. But where were the slaves now? Not these people streaming onto the grass-topped terraces, so excited, so happy, and so free.

Mumpo plodded on with the rest, the weight of Mrs Chirish on his back forcing him to lean forward and keep his head down. Mrs Chirish, knowing he couldn't see far ahead, supplied him with a running commentary on the scene as it unfolded before her.

'Oh, my! I never did see anything so – You'd never believe such a – Oh, the colours! It puts me in mind of a jar of boiled sweets, only you don't get the pretty ones any more – Oh, you'll be glad of this, my Mumpy, they're setting down – Sweets like jewels, they were, you could see right through them – Yes, I do believe we're to be let to rest, and about time – There's some sort of a what do you call it, where people watch people – Not much further now, and the grass is soft, I should say – Baskets coming out, that'll be bread – So many people, they've all come to watch, though what they're going to watch I couldn't begin to say – Yes, they're setting us down, and not before time.'

Mumpo came at last to a stop, and lowered Mrs Chirish carefully to the ground. The slaves were being allowed to rest on the open land just above the arena. Mrs Chirish patted Mumpo gratefully on the arm.

'You're good to your old auntie, Mumpy.'

Mumpo was staring at the crowded grass terraces. Tired though he was, he felt a shiver go through him as he sensed the crowd's excitement. All round him he heard voices speaking of the manaxa, and although he had never heard of it before, he soon understood that this arena was to be the setting for some form of combat.

The terraces descended to a sandy floor, where there stood a flat-topped mound, also covered with sand. This mound was some twenty yards across, its steep sides rising to the height of a man. Evidently it was on this simple stage that the manaxa was to take place. Beyond the flat-topped mound could be seen the shadowy entrance to a tunnel, cut into the banked terraces. This tunnel emerged a little further down the hill, nearer the lake. On the terrace directly above the tunnel's mouth stood a crimson and gold pavilion, inside which a servant could be seen arranging chairs.

A cheer now went up from the crowds packed onto the terraces. Mumpo looked up, and following their pointing arms, he saw that the gates in the walls of the palace-city had opened, and a procession of men on horseback was crossing the causeway.

Ta-tara! Ta-tara! Hunting horns sounded across the water, heralding the leaders of the column, the lords of the Mastery, riding two by two. Their richly-coloured cloaks streamed behind them as they came jogging all in time with each other, hammering over the timber causeway. After them came another double line of horsemen, who seemed from this distance to be naked. Finally came a cluster of officials, guards, and servants surrounding a figure in a crimson cloak.

Bowman stood watching, the piece of bread he held in his hand frozen in midair. The riders were coming closer all the time; and as they came, Bowman felt a mounting fear. This was something more than soldiers, with their stabbing spears and slashing swords. This was a power that reached into hearts and minds. The power radiated from the man in the crimson cloak.

He was big, taller and broader than those around him, and beneath his billowing cloak glinted a breastplate of golden armour. On his head he wore a golden helmet, from the sides and back of which a curtain of gold chain fell over his neck and shoulders. Framed in this flying golden mane, glowing in the rays of the sun, he came riding high and hard on his great black horse, heralded by horns.

'The Master!' cried voices on all sides. 'The Master!'

Marius Semeon Ortiz, watching as intently as any of his captives, felt the familiar rush of heat that always came when the Master was close. Instinctively he found himself speaking the oath of service, the beautiful words that always brought him strength and tranquillity.

'Master, all that I do, I do for you.'

The mounted procession now passed into the far end of the tunnel, and shortly all were lost to view. Then the lords were streaming into the red and gold pavilion on foot, and the naked men came stalking out of the tunnel mouth onto the floor of the arena. One by one they circled the mound, arms raised, and received the applause of the crowd. They were powerful-looking men, with scarred bodies and wary eyes. Not entirely naked: now that they were close, they could be seen to be wearing tightly-bound loincloths. Their hair was long, but coiled and held in a net on the back of the neck. These were the manacs, the men who would dance and fight: the most deadly fighting men in the world.

Mumpo watched the manacs with rapt concentration. The shiver he had felt at the first sight of the arena had grown into a trembling that shook his diaphragm and chest. He watched the way the manacs held themselves, and the way they moved, and the way they acknowledged the cheers of the crowd, and without realising he was doing it he too spread his arms, and bowed his head very slightly to this side and that.

When the manacs had each completed their circuit of the mound, they lined up facing the pavilion. The lords moved back, to either side. The cheering from the terraces stopped, and a strange silence fell. Then, as if at some unheard command, the manacs went down on their knees. The lords in the pavilion went down on their knees. So did Marius Semeon Ortiz, and all the spectators in the arena, and all the soldiers guarding the slaves. In a long rippling motion, the great crowd buckled and knelt in silence.

The Master then appeared alone from the back of the pavilion, and walked slowly to the rail at the front. He could now be seen to be an immensely large man, with a great belly and a barrel of a chest and a huge head. He had removed his helmet, to reveal a shaggy mane of long white hair, and a short thick white beard, that framed a nut-brown face. He stood still and looked on his people and smiled, his eyes twinkling as they roamed over the terraces. Every one over whom that benign look passed felt sure the Master had seen him and known him and sent him a special wordless sign of approval.

He raised one gold-gloved hand, and with a long sigh of movement, the lords on either side of him, and the manacs in the arena, and the great crowd, all rose to their feet once more. The manacs filed away down the tunnel. A seat was drawn forward for the Master. And he sat.

Bowman had never taken his eyes off the Master. While those around him saw his comfortably fat stomach and his amiable smile, Bowman felt the power within him. It was not the power of the Morah he had felt all those years ago. It had none of the intoxicating thrill that had filled him then, or the sense of invincibility. But it was a very great power nonetheless, and in its quieter way it now gripped the many thousands gathered to watch the manaxa.

The horns sounded again.

Ta-tara! Ta-tara! Out from the tunnel at a run came two of the manacs. To wild cheers from the crowd, they sprang up the slope to the flat surface of the mound.

They were now armed. Each man had steel casings strapped to his lower legs, from ankle to knee. At the top of the steel guards, over each knee, there projected a short blade. Similarly their lower arms were covered, from elbow to hand, the steel casings ending in short blades over the fists. On their heads they wore close-fitting helmets, from the brow of which protruded a fifth short blade. Apart from these armoured sections, their bodies were naked and exposed.

They presented themselves to the cheering crowd, moving from side to side, raising their arms to receive the applause of their supporters. One was bigger than the other, and from the pattern of scars all over his torso and thighs, had survived many bouts already. The other seemed to be slighter and younger, and the cheers for him were less enthusiastic.

Mumpo, who had moved forward to join the Hath family group, felt Pinto come up and put her arms round his waist.

'What will they do to each other, Mumpo?'

'They'll fight,' he replied.

'Will they kill each other?'

'One lives, one dies,' said Mumpo, hardly aware what he was saying. He was entranced by the manacs.

As he watched, the opponents retreated to opposite sides of the mound, and stood there with their heads bowed, suddenly still. The crowd fell silent. Mumpo had an odd feeling all over his body: he felt as if he knew how the fighters would move. It would begin slowly, like cats stretching and prowling.

And so it was. The Master gave the sign. Limb by limb, the manacs reached towards each other, separated by a wide space, and they danced. There was no other word for it. Rising, swooping down, curving their hands through the air, arching their legs, curling and twisting, they advanced towards each other as if connected by invisible threads. Both men were very strong, and it was beautiful to see the way they could move so slowly and with such control. But what gave the keen edge of antici-pation to the beauty of the dance was the knowledge that soon now those flashing limbs would draw blood.

Pinto turned her eyes away, not wanting to see the hurting. Her father felt how his heart pounded with excitement, and was ashamed to be so affected. Bowman looked from the Master to the fighters, and understood at once that the spirit of the manaxa was the spirit of the Master: it was he who had willed this terrible elegance. Beauty and blood, dancing and death, were joining hands before their eyes in a few moments of perfect concentration.

The younger manac struck first, sending a fist-blade slicing towards his opponent's throat. The big man swayed backwards, and almost in the same movement, turning his weight onto his right foot, lifted his left knee and struck. The knee-blade gouged into the young man's flank, and bright blood streamed out.

The crowd called out their hero's name. 'Dimon! Dimon!'

Suddenly the dancers were spinning at speed. The

young manac was fast, very fast. Wounded though he was, he had curled away and round and back, so rapidly that his fist-blade flashed under Dimon's guard, and skimmed his thigh. Second blood to the newcomer. Now Dimon seemed to explode. With a flurry of flying limbs he drove his young opponent back and back, to the very edge of the mound, knees slamming out, fists striking, parrying with his arm-guards, bounding into the air, forcing the newcomer to defend and defend, until with one last driving blow he sent him tumbling off the mound.

A great cheer broke out. Dimon raised his arm high in victory. The defeated manac climbed back onto his feet, and stood still, panting. Dimon lowered his arm. The loser then looked up, and the crowd rained down jeers and boos. Followed by mocking insults, he walked slowly out and into the tunnel.

Pinto was horrified.

'He did his best. Why do they jeer at him?'

'He lost,' said a guard standing nearby.

Mumpo's entire body was vibrating. He felt as if he was burning inside.

'I could do that,' he said.

'What, lose?' said the guard, laughing. 'Oh, yes, we could all do that.'

Mumpo said no more, but that wasn't what he meant. He meant he could dance that deadly dance, and win. His body told him so. His body had understood.

Another bout now proceeded, between two new manacs, and this too ended with one of them driven off the mound. Mumpo realised as he watched that there were a limited number of moves, and that the skill lay in the way they were combined and countered. Because both fighters knew once a move was begun how it would unfold, much of the art of the combat lay in creating patterns of expectation and then breaking them. The best fighters could change course even in the middle of a high-speed sequence. The most glorious moves, the ones most admired by the crowd, involved the highest risk.

The third bout brought on the manac who was clearly the favourite of the crowd.

'Here he comes,' said the guard to Pinto. 'That's Arno. Now you'll see what the manaxa's all about.'

The one he called Arno was very big and very heavy. It seemed unlikely that such a mass of flesh could escape the blades of his lither opponent. But once the fight began, it was clear that Arno was a master. Turning on the tips of the toes of one foot, bowing low and curling high, he became weightless, his moves so fast and graceful that they seemed to require no effort. Almost with unconcern, he flicked at his opponent's body, striping his skin with thin bloody lines. He himself had many scars on his great barrel chest, but this time his opponent was given no chance to add to them. Disdainfully, as it seemed to the spectators, he drove his opponent to the edge of the mound, and there flicked him, almost gently, with one fist-blade: his signal to the loser that he should now jump. Assuming that he would do so, Arno permitted his concentration to slip for one brief moment. The loser, seizing his chance, dropped and jabbed, driving his knee-blade deep into Arno's thigh.

Pinto cried out loud. Arno bellowed with wounded pride. His left fist flew. His right armoured forearm parried. His left forearm swept aside a return strike. His head went down and in. With a crunching sound, his head-blade drove deep into his opponent's chest. For a moment, the two fighters were still, locked in a strange embrace. Then Arno pulled back. Dark blood came bubbling out of the wound. The stricken manac sank to his knees. Then he fell forward onto the ground, and his heart-blood spread in a deep red stain over the sand.

Arno stood still, his own blood flowing unnoticed down his thigh. Then, slowly, he raised his right arm, to claim his victory and do homage to the Master. The cheer that greeted him shook the arena, as thousands of voices bayed for the joy of a kill.

'He should have taken the jump,' said the guard, shaking his head, as arena servants carried the dead man away.

'It's horrible,' said Pinto trembling, looking round at the shouting stamping crowd.

'Yes,' said Mumpo. 'But it's beautiful.'

There were no more kills that afternoon. As the manaxa came to an end, the shocked and excited captives were congratulated by their guards.

'First day in the Mastery, and you see a manaxa *and* a kill! Someone's watching over you.'

Ira Hath spoke low to her husband.

'What sort of people are they? To make a show out of killing?'

'People like us,' said Hanno sadly. 'People like us.'

Marius Semeon Ortiz now gave the command, and the soldiers moved down the lines ordering the slaves onto their feet. After their hour's rest on the soft grass, it was a weary business returning to the march.

'How much longer, pa?' asked Pinto.

'I don't know, my darling. Shall I carry you?'

'No, I'm all right.'

Pinto had never once asked to be carried. In the early days of the march she had come very close. When her legs were so tired that the muscles shook even when she stood still, she had said to herself, soon now I'll ask to be carried. But just knowing she could ask had been enough, and she had struggled on by herself. Now she knew she would never ask.

The lines of slaves were marched down the sloping road, and into a cutting between high banks, and through a tunnel. They heard the sound of the great crowd, and saw evening light on sand ahead: and so discovered they were to be marched into the arena itself.

The spectators had remained on the terraces, because the Master had not yet left the pavilion. Marius Semeon Ortiz rode into the sandy arena floor at the head of his column, and spurred his horse up onto the mound. Here he faced the Master, still as a statue, as the Manth people marched through the arena, flowing round him on the mound in two streams.

As they passed, the great crowd of spectators applauded. The lines went on and on, and the crowd applauded more and more. The Master looked on, his broad benign face beaming as if all these weary strangers had come to do him homage of their own accord. Bowman, following behind his father, looked up at the red pavilion just before passing into the tunnel, and for the briefest of moments he met the Master's eyes. The bearded fatherly face was smiling, but the eyes were not. In this half-second, Bowman caught the flash of an implacable will, and a chilling indifference to the human traffic on whom he smiled. The impression made on him formed rapidly into a single realisation: *this man has no need of love*. Then the arched tunnel exit cut him off, and he was following his father into the underground service chambers of the arena.

As they passed through this shadowy stone-vaulted space, they saw the manacs who had fought earlier, now lying on benches to have their wounds dressed and their muscles massaged. Mumpo trailed more slowly than the rest, his eyes lingering on those scarred gleaming bodies with longing. They also passed the corpse of the dead manac, lying covered on a bench. Then they came out into the open once more, and followed the long column down the slope to a series of marshalling yards.

Ortiz stayed motionless on his horse until the last of the slaves had left the arena. Then he bowed low to the Master, and raising his head, looking up into the face he knew and loved, called out in a loud clear voice:

'Master! All that I have done, I have done for you!'

The Master slowly inclined his head.

'You have done well,' he said, in his deep soft voice. 'You have pleased me.'

Ortiz flushed with pleasure. It was more, far more, than he had dared hope for. A nod, a smile perhaps, would have been enough. But the Master had actually said, in public, that he was pleased! Surely soon now he would send for him and speak the word he so longed to hear: the word that would make him his son.

His heart glad, his tiredness long forgotten, Ortiz spurred his horse off the mound and out of the arena.

The new slaves were already being quartered in the series of inter-connecting courtyards built for the purpose. Here beneath the open-fronted barns that walled each courtyard they were drinking mugs of hot thick soup, and washing themselves in the long troughs, and lining up for the latrines. Tonight they would sleep on the ground for the last time. Tomorrow they would be allocated their rooms, and put to work.

The Hath family lay down in their clothes with the rest. Hanno and Ira slept side by side, their hands clasped, as was their habit. Pinto curled up against her mother's other side, Bowman beside his father. Too weary even for a wish-huddle, they felt each other's closeness, shut their eyes, and were soon asleep.

All but Bowman. He lay with his eyes closed, and saw again the Master's smiling bearded face, and felt the power of his limitless will.

Come quickly, Kess. I can't do this without you.

He was missing his sister more intensely than he wanted his family to know. It was at night, when the distractions of the day fell away, that the pain returned at its keenest. He had never been parted from her for more than a few hours from the day they had been born. He was so accustomed to the wild tumble of her thoughts and the violence of her desires, that this silence in which he now lived was almost unbearable. Without Kestrel, he was half-alive: less than half, since she had always been the more vital part of his being. He pined for her keen and restless spirit.

Where are you, Kess? Come back to me, I can't live without you.

He poured his longing out into the silent night, reaching as far as his strength allowed. But wherever she was, she was farther away yet, and there came no answering voice.

Second Interval:

The hermit

The great yew tree stands alone, near the top of a ridge of land that shelters it from the prevailing north-west winds. It has stood here longer than anyone knows, certainly for hundreds of years, guarding a small spring of clear water that, it's said, never runs dry. Dogface chose the old yew for its solitary position, and for the fresh water supply. He eats very little, but he drinks a lot. The tree has other virtues: it's evergreen, and so provides shelter in winter and shade in summer; its principal branches fork above the main trunk in such a way that he has been able to build a small but secure house here; and the view to the south is spectacular.

Dogface is a tree hermit, and therefore in theory he has no possessions. There's the snug thatched tree-house, which he occupies but doesn't own. There's a water jug on a long cord, which he uses but doesn't own. And there's a long thin sinuous grey cat called Mist, who keeps him company, but he doesn't own. Here at least there's no doubt of any kind. Nobody owns Mist.

This morning, the morning that everything changes, begins no differently to any other. When Dogface wakes with the dawn, Mist is there as usual, sitting on the sill of the glassless window, watching him with a look of mild disapproval.

'I do sometimes ask myself,' says Dogface as he sits up and stretches, and shrugs off his nightgown, 'why you trouble to stay with me. You seem to get so little pleasure from my company.'

'I don't stay with you,' replies Mist. 'I'm here. You're in my vicinity.'

'So you say, Mist, so you say.' Dogface makes his way to the hole in the tree-house floor through which he relieves himself. A narrow line of brown yew leaves below testify to the daily cascade, as does the circle of brown grass on the ground. 'And yet you must like me, I tell myself, or you would choose some other vicinity.'

'Like you?' says Mist. 'Why would I like you?'

'I don't say there's any reason to like me.'

Dogface is not a vain man. He knows he's strikingly ugly, with his long dog-like features and his bad eye. He knows he smells, not because he can smell himself, but because he hasn't washed since he settled in the tree, which is now three years, eight months and eleven days ago. Furthermore he knows he has nothing the cat wants, for the simple reason that he has nothing. But the cat still chooses to stay.

'I've come to the conclusion,' he says, unreeling the jug on its long cord, 'that your kindness to me, which I haven't in any way earned, must come from your own affectionate nature.'

'My own affectionate nature?' Mist watches the hermit lower the jug all the way down into the little pool at the foot of the tree. 'You know perfectly well I'm incapable of affection.'

'So you say, Mist, so you say.'

Dogface draws up the cord hand over hand, and swings the heavy dripping jug back into the tree-house. He holds it towards the cat. Mist jumps down from the sill, and takes three or four laps at its brimming top. When he's done, Dogface drinks, long and steadily, and then splashes the remainder over his face. Refreshed, he draws a deep breath, and settles down to sing the morning song.

Had there been a passer-by, and there are none, for there's no road or track within sight, he would have heard nothing of the discussion between the hermit and the cat. It has taken place, but not aloud. Dogface has lived alone for so long now that he has forgotten there's a kind of speech that makes vibrations in the air. As for Mist, cats can't talk. But in every other way than sound, they have ordinary conversations, much like anyone else; and had Dogface stopped to think about this, he would have realised that this is his special value to the cat. The more thoughtful species of animals greatly appreciate conversations with humans, but very few humans know how to do it. Mist finds Dogface ridiculous, and his chosen way of life incomprehensible, but at least he replies when spoken to. From Mist's point of view, there's no way of telling which humans have this knack. All you can do is address them and see if they hear you. It's typical, Mist thinks, of the generally bungled nature of existence, that the only human he's found who talks back is a one-eyed hermit who lives in a tree.

The conversation between man and cat has been silent. Dogface's song is not. Here is another bond that keeps Mist in the hermit's company. He has grown to like his songs. The morning song in particular has a sweet waking stretch to it, as the wordless melody hums and buzzes around the tree-house, calling up life and vigour and the new day itself. Dogface has dozens of songs. There's an eating song and a sleeping song, songs for rainy weather and songs for sunshine, songs for cramp and songs for indigestion and songs for loneliness. Mist has come to know them all.

As the morning song heads towards its end, the cat slips out of the tree-house and stalks along one of the yew tree's spreading branches. Here he chooses a spot and lies down, still and silent, and waits for breakfast.

Dogface finishes his song, stands up, stretches so high he pushes on the underside of the thatched roof with the palms of both hands, and then shakes out his day robe. It's the simplest garment imaginable: a tunic of coarse undyed wool, with long baggy sleeves, and a hem that comes down almost to the ground. Dogface never washes it, but every morning he shakes it violently out of his window, and so, he hopes, prevents the dirt from settling.

This shaking of his shift acts as a signal to the birds that live in the tree. At once they all rise up from their various perching places, skitter around in the air, and flutter down to land on the branches round the hermit's door. Dogface pulls the robe over his head, jerks it straight, and steps out onto the broad branch he calls his front porch. Here, forty feet above the ground, he sits down on a convenient seat-like protuberance, long worn smooth by his bottom, and all the birds come and sit on him.

The birds love Dogface: the small birds most of all, the tits and robins and finches. A pair of woodpeckers live in the tree, and never fail to greet him, occupying always the same place on his left shoulder. The starlings come in a rowdy gang, but they never sit still for long. The blackbirds like to stand on his head, and the sparrows hop about all over his thighs and knees.

'Good morning, birds,' says Dogface, lifting one gnarled finger to smooth the feathers on a chaffinch's breast. 'The days are getting shorter. The swifts will be with us by and by.'

The birds chirrup back at him, and cock their heads to one side when he speaks, and chirrup again. Birds' brains are too small to manage conversation, but they hear the hermit well enough, and find everything he says interesting. They're proud that he's come to their tree. The morning gathering gives them something to think about all day, and lends variety to their life. Dogface senses this, and tries to say at least one new thing every morning, like a calendar that prints a wise thought at the top of each page. But first, he receives his gifts.

He holds out his hands, and the birds fill the air with their beating wings as they deliver their tributes. Over the time he's been among them they've learned what he likes, and no longer offer him worms or beetles. Now each morning his hands are filled with berries and grains and seeds, and nuts carefully pecked out of their shells. Dogface waits until one hand is full, sorts through the offerings to put aside some for his winter store, and puts the rest into his mouth. He chews the grains and the fruits all together, his hand back out again for more. This is his only meal of the day, and it's entirely supplied by his friends the birds. In winter they don't feed him, because they can barely feed themselves, and he hibernates, half-starved, till spring. Fortunately there's a song for hunger that takes away most of the pain.

When the last of the birds' gifts is received and eaten, they all fly down to land on him once more, covering him completely, and listen for his morning thought.

'My mother,' says Dogface, 'always told me I was a beautiful baby. She made me a little blue bonnet.'

The birds find nothing comical in what Dogface has told them. They don't know he's ugly. They don't know what a bonnet is, either. That makes it all the more interesting.

Mist hears it all from a branch above, but makes no comment, because he's occupied in hypnotising a sparrow. The unfortunate bird has caught Mist's eye, and hasn't been able to look away. Now Mist creeps up on it, and it sits frozen on its twig, and utters not so much as a squeak when he pounces.

Dogface hears the pounce, and sees Mist bounding away with the bird in his mouth, and shakes his head. When the cat reappears a few minutes later, he makes a gentle complaint.

'It really is too bad, Mist. I've asked you before not to eat my friends.'

'They're not *my* friends,' says Mist, settling down on the hermit's lap to digest his breakfast.

'Couldn't you eat mice or something, as a favour to me?'

'Why would I want to do a favour to you?'

'Now, really, Mist, this is all a pose. You know very well I'm your friend.'

'Friendship is nothing more than habit and convenience,' says the cat.

'Listen to you! Purring on my lap!'

'The human body is a source of warmth.'

'The human body, indeed! You mean my body. You mean me.'

'Yes, you are the nearest available person.'

'So what will you do when I die and my body turns cold?'

'I shall manage.'

Dogface shakes his head again, and strokes the cat's back with firm steady strokes, the way he likes it. When they first knew each other, the hermit wasn't good at stroking, but Mist set him right. Now being stroked by him is a positive pleasure. He strokes in the right direction, and maintains a regular rhythm, with just the right amount of pressure.

'Are you proposing to die any day soon?' asks Mist.

'When the times comes,' Dogface replies.

'Oh, I see. Just the usual run of things.' The cat loses interest. 'Don't stop stroking.'

Dogface says nothing more, not wanting to distress his friend, but in using the phrase 'when the times comes' he's not referring to the usual run of things. Dogface the tree hermit is one of the Singer people, and like all Singer people, he is waiting for the call. In recent weeks he has felt tremors from far off, shifts and shivers in the pressure of the air, that make him more alert than usual. It's coming soon, he's sure of it.

While the cat dozes on his lap, the hermit does his morning forgetting exercises. He starts at the bottom, by feeling his bare feet, how they dangle in the cool air. Then, moving up his ankles, he forgets his feet: pushes the thought of them out of his mind, and they're gone. He feels his shins and calves, tickled by the hem of his robe, and then forgets them in their turn. His thighs and buttocks, pressed from below by the branch of the tree and from above by the sleeping cat; his stomach, slowly digesting berries and nuts; his lungs, drawing in sweet air; his slow-beating heart; his arms, one moving, one still; all in turn felt, known, and discarded. Finally his face, the stroke of the breeze, the hiss of the leaves, the brightness in his good eye, and the very mind that knows these things, all slip away and are forgotten, and he is entirely quiet.

The bright blue butterfly comes dancing round the spreading branches of the yew tree, and settles on the windowsill of the hermit's house. Here it remains for some moments, its wings glinting in the sunlight. Then it flutters back up into the air, circles the hermit's sleeping head, and comes lightly to rest on his left ear.

Dogface wakes with a jerk, nearly toppling off the tree. The cat springs off his lap and stands with his back arched, hissing.

'What?' says the hermit, looking round. 'Who is it?'

Then he feels the tickle on his left ear. He bends his head and becomes silent, as if he's listening to something. Then he nods.

Mist sees this with concern. Something unusual is happening. The cat dislikes change; particularly change without explanation or warning. He sees the blue butterfly fly away from the hermit, away over the treeless plains. He sees the clouds streaming by overhead, massing on the far horizon. He sees birds circling, cawing, a flock of rooks. Nothing out of the ordinary in that. But the hermit is stirring, long before his accustomed time.

Dogface stands up, and returns to his tree-house. He bundles up his night robe, his jug, and its cord. Mist watches him with irritated surprise.

'What are you doing?'

'I have to go,' says the hermit.

'Go? Go where?'

'I have a message to deliver.'

He emerges once more onto the branch that is his front porch, and calls to the birds.

'Birds! I have to leave you!'

Word spreads rapidly among the birds, and they all come flying down to settle on the branches round him.

'I'm going now,' he says to them. 'Thank you for your kindness to me. I will repay you in my own way.'

Then he steps off the branch, and floats slowly to the ground. This doesn't surprise the birds, who can all fly, but it astounds the cat. Mist gapes as the hermit's feet land gently on the ground below. Hastily he claws his way down the rough bark of the yew's trunk to follow him. The birds too follow.

'How did you do that? Humans can't fly.'

'Some humans can,' says Dogface, attempting clumsily to walk for the first time in almost four years.

'All right,' says Mist, running beside him, 'I admit it. Now I'm interested.'

The birds follow overhead in a long stream, calling to each other and to the hermit. Some are saying goodbye, others are asking questions, but they still can't talk in a way that he can understand. Dogface, being a Singer, could make contact if he really tried, but all he would hear, after long effort, would be, 'What's a blue bonnet?'

As it is, his mind is on other things. He's excited. If the time has come to deliver the message, then that other time, the time for which he trained, for which he's been waiting for so long, must be approaching at last. How far off now? It can only be a matter of weeks. It will take him several days to find the child of the prophet; and then many days more before he can meet up with the others. He half-regrets having chosen to be a tree hermit. His legs haven't been exercised enough in the tree, and now, already, they're aching. He realises he'll never complete the journey in time on foot. Under normal circumstances no Singer uses his powers for personal convenience, but Dogface judges this to be a special case.

'Mist,' he says to the cat loping beside him, 'are you coming with me?'

'What does it look like?' says the cat.

'Then you'd better jump up on my shoulders. I'm going to be going too fast for you.'

'I may not be staying with you long.'

'All you have to do is say the word, and I'll stop for you to get off.'

On this understanding, Mist climbs up and settles himself on the hermit's right shoulder.

'Hold on tight.'

Dogface focuses his mind carefully, and starts to hum a song the cat hasn't heard before. Shortly, he rises a few inches into the air, tilts forward at an angle, and begins to glide over the ground. At first he moves slowly. Then he picks up speed, without gaining height. Soon he's scooting along as fast as the clouds that stream by over-head.

Mist has all his claws out, gripping tight to the

hermit's robe, but once he's become accustomed to the speed of their travel, and finds his point of equilibrium, he becomes very excited.

'Now this is something!' he cries. 'This I like!'

He leans his furry face forward, and feels the speed-wind ruffle his whiskers, and imagines how it would be if he could fly. He pictures the fieldmice rooting in the grass, unaware that he's gliding above them. He sees himself floating through the air in absolute silence, unheard, unseen. He sees himself drop, in the perfect inescapable pounce.

'You must teach me how to do this,' he says. 'This I have to learn.'

'It would take too long,' says the hermit. 'We have too far to go. And it wouldn't get you what you want in the end.'

He doesn't want to share his secret, the cat reflects, not really surprised. But I shall find it out. And then, ah, then, an end to the arrogance of birds! Let them flap their silly wings and fly away from me. I'll rise up and spring, and up! Up! I'll scoop them from the very clouds!

Mist has found his dream. He will go wherever he must go, he will do whatever he must do, but one day he will be a flying cat.

8

Kestrel learns to dance

Kestrel's travel-stained black clothes were taken away and burned. She now wore the uniform of the Johdila's servants, a plain pale green robe with a white head covering. Beneath, on a thin cord hung round her neck, the voice of the wind singer lay close to her skin.

'Now you look just like Lunki,' said Sisi. 'Only thinner.'

Most of the day they spent in the Johdila's carriage, as it jolted its way over the land. But whenever the Johdila went out, Kestrel went with her. By now the other members of the court had become used to her, and took her for just one more of the Johdila's servants.

'You mustn't mind, darling. They don't understand about friends. It would only confuse them.'

'I don't mind.'

When not required by the Johdila, she would sit and gaze out of the carriage window.

'Why do you look out of the window all the time?' Sisi asked her. It wasn't that she objected: she simply wanted to know. Everything Kestrel did fascinated her.

'Because my people came this way.'

Every day Kestrel saw the signs. They were following the same road as the march.

'Oh!' said Sisi, surprised. 'Do you still care about your people?'

'Yes.'

'Even though you've got me now?'

'Yes.'

'But you don't care about them more than me, do you? I'm terribly nice to you. Lunki says I spoil you.'

'Yes, I care about them more than you. Just as you care about your father and mother more than you care about me.'

Sisi thought about that. She did love her father and mother, she supposed, quite a lot really, only they weren't at all interesting, and if they were to be taken away, as Kestrel's father and mother had been taken away, she wasn't sure she'd miss them so very terribly.

'But your people are gone, darling,' she pointed out. 'And I'm not. So really and truly, I think I'm more important now.'

Kestrel turned her great dark eyes on her, and Sisi felt the thrill she always felt at her friend's strength and mystery. It was as if however long she looked she could never see to the bottom of her.

'I have a brother,' said Kestrel, 'a twin brother, who's as close to me as I am to myself. He knows what I'm feeling without me having to say it. If he died, I would die. But he's alive. Every day, I come closer to him. Soon we'll be together again, as we have been from the day we were born.'

Tears came into Sisi's eyes as she heard this.

'I wish I had a twin brother,' she said.

'No, you don't. It's not good to be so close to another person.'

'Why not?'

'It makes you not need other people.'

'What's wrong with that?'

'Oh, Sisi,' said Kestrel. 'However are you going to cope with being married?'

Sisi shrugged. It was a subject she preferred not to think about.

'They'll tell me what to do, and I'll do it. That's how it is when you're a princess.'

Kestrel looked away out of the window once more, saying as casually as she could,

'Wouldn't you rather marry one of your own people?'

'One of my own people?' The question surprised Sisi. 'Who?'

'I don't know. There must be some young man who's caught your eye.'

'No. There isn't. Who would there be?'

'Well –' Kestrel didn't want Sisi to see through her motives, and cast round in her mind for some plausible candidates. It wasn't easy. 'Ozoh the augur?' she said at last.

'Ozoh? He's half-snake!'

'Barzan?'

'Old, dull, and married.'

'Zohon?'

'He's always smiling when there's nothing to smile about. And anyway, he only loves himself.'

Kestrel was impressed. She hadn't realised Sisi was so sensible.

'And there's another thing, darling,' Sisi went on. 'All my people are inferior to me, because I'm a princess, and my husband has to be superior to me, so he'll have to come from somewhere else.'

'He doesn't have to be superior to you.'

'Would you marry an inferior husband? Don't be silly, darling. It wouldn't work at all.'

'He could be superior in some ways, and you could be superior in others.'

Sisi thought about that.

'Yes, that would work. I think I'd quite like that. Only there still isn't anybody, is there? So I might as well marry this man my parents have chosen for me.'

'Well,' said Kestrel, feeling she'd done all she could, 'I'm just glad I'm not a princess.'

After a short silence, Sisi said in a quiet voice,

'It isn't at all what people think. Nobody ever tells you anything. You never go anywhere. You never meet anybody. You're supposed to be better than everyone else but really you're a sort of doll in a doll's house.'

Kestrel was touched.

'You could always stop being a princess.'

'What else am I good for? I've never been taught to do anything for myself. All I know is how to be beautiful.'

'Oh, Sisi.'

'Don't tell anyone I talk like this. They wouldn't understand. The doll princess is supposed to be radiant, and happy, and –'

She gave Kestrel the oddest smile, and turned her head away.

While they had been talking, the long column of carriages had rumbled to a halt. It was time for the Johdila's dancing lesson. Soon they heard the dancing master's tap on the door, and Sisi groaned and lowered her veil.

Kestrel went with her to the roofless tent. The little dancing master was in a state of nervous excitement.

'Ten days, radiance! They say we will arrive in ten days!'

'Yes, pixie, I know. This horrible journey just goes on and on. Still, it will end, you know. In the end.'

'You misunderstand me, my lady. Only ten more days, and you have not mastered the dance. It will be a disaster. I will be blamed. I will be punished.'

'Yes, I suppose you will. After all, you are my dancing master.'

'But radiance,' pleaded Lazarim miserably. 'You don't try. How am I to teach you the steps if you won't try?'

'It is a very difficult dance. It is, isn't it, Kess?'

'Yes,' said Kestrel. 'It's difficult, but it's beautiful.'

Lazarim threw Kestrel a look of gratitude.

'There, radiance! Difficult, but beautiful! If my lady were to try harder, and practise the steps, the difficulties would fall away, and the beauty would remain.'

'Well,' said Sisi, unconvinced, 'I'll try a little. But you're not to bore me.'

She adopted the opening position, left foot forward, right hand raised, and Lazarim took his place beside her. The piper and the drummer began to play, and Lazarim stepped lightly to his left. Sisi, stepping to her right, collided with him.

'No, my lady, no! The left foot goes back and to the side, like so.'

'Oh, yes. I remember now.'

They started again. This time they managed the side-steps, the salute, and the spins, but Sisi could not master the arrest. Instead she went on spinning until she came slowly to a natural stop.

'No, radiance. One moment you are spinning, the next moment you are still. Listen to the beat. There!'

He demonstrated, flying round on one toe, and stopping, frozen in mid-turn, apparently effortlessly, as if his body had no weight.

'You see how I bend my body, my lady? As you turn, the curve of your body counterbalances the spinning motion, so that all you have to do is make your back straight, at just the right moment, and –'

He did it again. Kestrel, watching, was fascinated. She longed to try for herself.

'It's easy for you, pixie,' said Sisi petulantly. 'You've got a bendy body. I don't think my body bends that way.'

Kestrel could resist no more.

'Maybe I could show you,' she said.

'Could you, darling?' Sisi sounded surprised, but not at all offended.

Lazarim was only too pleased to release his reluctant pupil.

'It might help if you were to watch the steps a few times, my lady.'

'Oh, good. I'm much better at watching. Kess, you're a darling sweetie.'

So Lazarim took Kestrel's hand, and Kestrel adopted the opening position for the tantaraza. She had watched the dancing master for several days running, and without having tried a single step for herself, she knew by heart every move he had demonstrated with so many repetitions. She held Lazarim's hand lightly in her own, and all her body tingled. She had not told the Johdila, but as she had watched, she had caught the spirit of the tantaraza, and once that has happened, you long more than anything to dance.

'Now,' said Lazarim, 'we begin with three steps to the left, and three to the right.'

'I think I know,' said Kestrel. 'But I may lose you towards the end.'

She poised her body on her toes, and Lazarim felt it from the touch of her hand: she was a dancer. A surge of joy swept through him. He forgot that the Johdila was his pupil, and this girl no more than a servant. He wanted to dance.

Controlling his excitement, disciplining his breathing, he too rose onto his toes, and clicked his tongue at the musicians. The drumbeat began, then the sweet melody of the pipe. He moved, and she moved with him. And back, and she was there, lithe and sure. The salute, not perfect, but charming. And she was spinning, round, round, round, and there! Her arms snapping, her hips curling like the crack of a whip! She held his eyes, still as a statue, eyes bright with the electricity of the dance, and click-click-clack! Click-click-clack! In she came, a pin-sharp sequence of steps for the re-join, and they were away. From that moment, Lazarim forgot his day's task, and the Johdila, and all the Sovereignty of Gang. He surrendered himself to the dance.

Kestrel flew like a bird in his arms. At first her mind was tracking the steps she had watched so many times, but now it was as if there were no more steps, only movement, that came as naturally to her lithe young body as breathing. She responded without question to the dancing master's touch, unaware that they had moved beyond the strict form of the tantaraza into the rare and highly-prized stage known as free flight. The musicians played as if entranced, their blindfolded eyes following the dancers' every move, their rising rhythm urging the dance simultaneously towards formal perfection and to complete freedom. Sisi watched in astonishment, and was filled with a loving admiration for her extraordinary friend.

As for Kestrel, she felt like a bird that has lived all its life in a cage, and now for the first time spreads its wings and rides the boundless wind. She trusted her partner completely, and so released herself into the dance without fear. Her heart was pounding, her cheeks were flushed, and yet within herself she felt cool and sure. Nothing in the world existed but the dance. Let it go on for ever!

Lazarim knew better than Kestrel that one part of the perfection of the tantaraza, the dance of dances, was that it came to a climax. He changed his step, and the musicians heard it, and the drummer began to beat the final rhythm, that is called the arise. This Lazarim had never practised with the Johdila, and so Kestrel had had no opportunity to study the steps. She felt at once the change of pace, and did her best to follow the dancing master, but inevitably they lost the beat. He took her by both hands, and spun her gracefully to a stop, and made her a bow.

She was panting and laughing, full of vitality, and beautiful in a way that Sisi had not noticed before.

'Sorry,' she said. 'I don't know that part.'

Lazarim took her hand and kissed it in silence. His eyes thanked her with unreserved passion. Sisi clapped her slender hands together, not too hard.

'Darling, how beautiful you are!'

She was genuinely pleased. It was as if Kestrel had suddenly become a comrade in arms. They could be beautiful together.

Lazarim turned to her.

'That, my lady, is the tantaraza.'

'Yes, pixie, I saw. Wasn't Kess fine?'

'Do you think you could learn to do it, my lady?'

'Oh, no! Do you think I could?'

Lazarim sighed. No, he didn't think she could, not in a thousand years. And yet, somehow, she must.

'If your radiance's servant here can learn the steps . . .'

'Don't be silly, pixie! Kestrel's different. You must be able to see that.'

'What then are we to do?'

Sisi understood the dilemma, but all she could think was that matters had been arranged very unfairly. She was the one who must be married, and to marry, she must dance; and dancing, she now saw, was not something that came naturally to her. Kestrel, on the other hand, danced as if she was born to it, but was not the one who was to be married.

'If only Kess could do the dancing for me,' she said, 'I believe I could manage the rest.'

'No doubt,' said Lazarim. 'But your future husband is expecting to marry one bride, not two.'

'You yourself said one dance was enough.'

'So it is, radiance.'

'Well, how would he know?'

'Know what, radiance?'

'I must be veiled, pixie. You know that. Why couldn't Kestrel wear my robes and veils, and dance for me? Nobody would know it wasn't me.'

Kestrel heard this in silence: her mind at once racing, to calculate where her own advantage lay.

Lazarim was shaking his head.

'Your father would never permit it.'

'I don't see why we should tell him.'

The dancing master stared at her. She was right: who else would ever know? The plan really might work. It was madly dangerous, of course. But it could work.

Sisi too was all at once seized by her idea. She turned eagerly to Kestrel.

'Would you do it for me, Kess darling? Do say you would! You know I can't do the stupid dance, however much I practise, and if I don't dance I can't marry, and if I don't marry everything will go horribly wrong, and there'll be wars and things, and my father will be so cross!'

Kestrel looked at her, and then at the dance master. Would her plan be helped if she put on the Johdila's wedding dress, and danced in her place? Not in any obvious way that she could see at present. On the other hand, if she agreed, she would be part of a dangerous secret, and secrets were always a source of power.

'Please, darling. You'd look so beautiful in my wedding dress.'

Sisi was gazing at her anxiously. Kestrel realised she hadn't given an answer.

'What about them?' Her eyes indicated the two musicians.

'What about them?'

'They might tell.'

The Johdila turned to the musicians.

'If you tell anything you've heard here, I'll have your tongues pulled out, and rabbits' heads pushed into your mouths, and your lips sewn up.'

The musicians hung their heads, too terrified to speak.

'And your eyes will be burned out with red-hot skewers,' added the Johdila, for the sake of tradition.

'They'll say nothing, radiance,' said Lazarim.

'So there you are. Nobody will ever know but us three.'

It seemed to Sisi that the whole intractable problem, that had hung over them since the start of their journey, was now solved. She felt proud of herself.

'Do friends tell friends they've done something clever, if they have?'

'Yes,' said Kestrel.

'I have, haven't I? It is a clever idea, isn't it?'

'Yes. It's a clever idea.'

Kestrel looked at Lazarim, and in both their eyes was the unspoken question: can we make it work? For Lazarim, it was a godsend, a delivery from what had seemed certain disaster. For Kestrel, it was just another chance, placed in her way by fate. And of course, it would mean she would have to dance.

'If I'm to dance,' she said, 'I'd better learn to do it properly.'

9

The shadow of the monkey wagon

The Manth people were woken to their first full day in the Mastery by the creak and rattle of food wagons. Their breakfast was mugs of dark sharp-tasting tea, and lard cakes. The tea was wonderfully stimulating, and the lard cakes rich, moist, and filling. Their strength returned.

Bowman and Mumpo walked the perimeter of the marshalling yards, looking for weak points in the walls that penned them in. There were many. They found loose planks that could be forced aside, and places where the timber stockade could be scaled. Soldiers were on duty on the far side, but not in any great number, nor were they paying much attention. The big gates, barred on the outside, looked as if they could be forced open, given enough determination.

'We can get out of here,' said Mumpo.

'They'd come after us,' said Bowman. 'They have mounted soldiers.'

A different voice spoke from behind them.

'We could hide.'

They turned to find Rufy Blesh following them, listening to them. He had a wild look in his eyes.

'You're thinking what I'm thinking, aren't you?' he said. 'There's not so many of them. We could make a run for the trees.'

'All of us? The children and the old people too?'

Rufy looked away. 'Not all. But some is better than none.'

'No,' said Bowman. 'We must go together.'

He was surprised to hear the authority in his own voice, but he knew he was right. The Manth people must stay together.

'Then we'll never go.' Rufy's voice was harsh. 'Don't you see what's happened? Our people have been whipped like dogs. They're frightened now. They'll do as they're told. They'll choose to be slaves. You watch.'

'Not me,' said Mumpo. 'I shall fight.'

'Come with me, then, Mumpo!' Rufy cried. 'You're like me, you've no family left. We can slip out in the night, and hide in the forest.'

'And what then?' said Bowman.

'What then? Freedom!'

'It's not enough.'

Pinto came running up to them.

'You're to come,' she said. 'There's a meeting.'

'Of course,' said Rufy Blesh bitterly. 'The Manth solution to everything. Call a meeting.'

Hanno and Ira Hath attended the meeting along with everyone else. The meeting had been called by Dr Greeth, one of the few high officials of old Aramanth who had survived the changes with dignity.

'Jessel Greeth is a sound practical man,' said Hanno to his wife, 'but I don't think he understands what's happening to us, or why.'

'Better to be a slave and live,' said Ira Hath, 'than to be free and die.'

Hanno Hath turned to her in astonishment.

'What did you say?'

'I'm not sure,' said Ira, going a little pink. 'Did I say something?'

'Yes.' Hanno looked at her thoughtfully for a moment. 'It doesn't matter.'

Dr Greeth stood on a food wagon to address the gathering.

'My friends,' he said, 'it's time for us to face the truth of our situation. Our beloved home is destroyed. There is no going back. We are prisoners, slaves, exiles in an alien land. What are we to do? Are we to fight for our freedom, when we have no weapons? Are we to attempt escape, when we have nowhere to go?'

'Cowards!' cried out Rufy Blesh from the back. 'Do you want to live and die as slaves?'

Dr Greeth frowned. Hanno Hath realised he knew what he was going to say.

'Better to be a slave and live,' he said, 'than to be free and die.'

Hanno looked at his wife. Ira Hath blinked and shook her head.

'Coward, coward, coward!' cried Rufy Blesh.

'Maybe I am a coward,' said Dr Greeth evenly. 'Maybe you're a braver man than me. But look around you. Look at our people. Do you ask them all to choose death? For what?'

'For the honour of the Manth people!'

'You ask them to choose honour over life?'

'Over a life of slavery, yes!'

There were some scattered murmurs of approval.

'Let's not do anything in haste,' said Jessel Greeth. 'Winter is coming. We don't yet know what our life here will be like. If it proves unbearable, we may all come to agree with our fiery young friend. That will then be the time to fight and die. For now, I propose that we wait and see. We have everything to gain, and nothing to lose, by waiting for the spring.'

There was a silence. Then Miko Mimilith the tailor called out:

'What does Hanno Hath say?'

Hanno Hath had never been more than a librarian, but he was widely respected; and his wife, some said, had the true gift.

'I must tell you,' said Hanno in his quiet voice, 'I believe we have less time than we think. Somewhere, not here, our homeland is waiting for us. I believe we must find it before it's too late.'

His words caused uproar.

'Too late for what? What is to happen? Where is this homeland? How do you know?'

Jessel Greeth put the question in its most un-answerable form.

'You propose that we leave here, though we may die in the attempt, to seek a homeland, though you don't know where, to escape some fate, though you don't know what?'

'Yes,' said Hanno.

'I take it this revelation comes from your wife, our good prophetess?' Jessel Greeth didn't mean to make fun of Ira Hath, but there was a smile in his voice as he spoke.

'Yes,' said Hanno.

'What exactly does she say?'

Hanno hesitated, and met his son's eyes. Bowman was looking at him steadily. 'Tell them, pa,' he said.

'She says, the wind is rising.'

At that, Jessel Greeth actually did laugh.

'The wind is rising?'

Ira Hath jumped up, goaded beyond endurance.

'I am not your good prophetess!' she cried. 'I'm not any kind of prophetess! You can all do as you please. Nobody needs to listen to a word I say.'

At this point, the gates to the marshalling yards swung open, and in came a troop of soldiers, escorting teams of clerks with ledgers under their arms. The meeting broke up. Ira Hath, wanting to hit somebody, hit her husband. She drove him backwards with a series of sharp pushes to his shoulders and chest.

'Don't do that! Never do that again!'

Hanno Hath didn't resist. He waited till she stopped hitting him, and then said,

'You know it's true.'

'I don't!'

'You knew the exact words he'd say. You heard him speak them before he spoke them.'

'I was guessing.'

'No, you weren't.'

'What's the use, Hanno? They won't listen. Why tell them?'

'Because it's true.'

She said nothing, but her eyes looked frightened.

'It is, isn't it? Something terrible is going to happen.'

Slowly, she nodded her head.

The clerks were moving among the captives, allocating them work according to their skills. One of them, ledger in hand, now stopped by Hanno Hath.

'Slave number,' he said.

'What?'

'On your wrist.'

Hanno pulled up his sleeve and the clerk noted the number branded there.

'Skill,' he said.

'Skill?'

'What can you do?'

'I'm a librarian.'

'Librarian? That's books, isn't it? You can work in the depository. They've got books there. You!'

'Me?' said Ira Hath.

'Number. Skill.'

Ira met her husband's eyes as she replied,

'Prophetess.'

'What's that?' said the clerk in surprise.

'It's someone who says things you don't want to hear.'

'What use is that?'

'Very little.'

'Can you do anything else?'

'I can stare,' said Ira, her nose beginning to twitch. 'I can wave one hand slowly from side to side –'

'She can sew,' said Hanno hastily, seeing that matters were about to get out of hand. 'She's good with a needle.'

'Sewing,' said the clerk, writing in his ledger. 'Basic repair work. Laundry.'

He moved on.

'I won't,' said Ira.

'Just for now,' said Hanno. 'Please.'

Scooch, who had made the best pastries in Aramanth, was assigned to work in one of the big bakeries. Miko Mimilith was sent to cut cloth at a dressmaker's. Creoth, the former Emperor, was not so easy to place. He told the clerks that he had no skill of any kind.

'What, nothing at all?'

'Nothing at all.'

'Don't you find that time passes rather slowly?'

'Yes,' said Creoth. 'I do.'

'Well, you look healthy enough. You'd better work on the farms.'

Mumpo told the clerk he wanted to be a manac. Pinto heard this with horror.

'No, Mumpo! You can't! You'll be killed!'

But Mumpo proved stubborn.

'I can do it. I know I can.'

'We've never had a new slave ask to be a manac before,' said the clerk. 'You know they only take the very best fighters?'

'They'll take me.'

The clerks consulted with each other.

'Well, I suppose there's no harm in sending him for an assessment.'

Bowman asked to be a night-watchman. His reason was simple. In the night, when everyone else was asleep, he could listen for Kestrel.

'Night-watchman,' wrote the clerk in his ledger.

Once the lists were completed, the slaves were led out to start their new jobs. As they left the marshalling yards, armed soldiers moved among them and picked out individuals from the groups of families and friends. Pinto was chosen from the Hath family group, and led off to one side.

'Where are you taking her?' said Ira Hath.

The soldiers didn't reply, but the answer came soon enough. On either side of the paved road stood long lines of monkey wagons, with their cage doors open, some already half full. Up to twenty people were herded into each cage. The space beneath the floor grids was stacked with bundles of firewood. Pinto shook violently as she was put in the cage. Hanno called out to her before he was led off.

'Nothing's going to happen to you, my darling. See you at the end of the day.'

No explanations were given, no warnings. They had all seen the function of the iron cages. Bowman and Mumpo became very thoughtful. Now they knew that the walls that penned them in were unbreachable, unclimbable after all, even if they were invisible. Any attempt at escape, any disobedience at all, and their loved ones would be burned alive. They were to live from now on in the shadow of the monkey wagon.

Hanno felt his wife's anger seething within her.

'Please, my dear,' he begged her, 'control yourself. Think of Pinto.'

And so they parted, each to their place of work.

Mumpo stood before the chief trainer of the manaxa school, waiting for him to speak. Lars Janus Hackel sat at his desk and stared at him, letting his eyes roam over Mumpo's body.

'Ha!' he grunted, unimpressed.

He got up and felt Mumpo with his huge hands. Once, in the days of his arena career, he had been a great mass of muscle. Now he was a great mass of fat. The scars that cross-hatched every visible part of his body had puckered and turned mauve, so that he looked like an uncooked sausage forced into a net.

'You're soft,' he said. There was nothing about the boy, with his moon face and dangling limbs, that showed he had the makings of a manac. Hackel was not interested in romantic dreamers who got themselves chopped to pieces in their first bout. The manaxa was an art, not an execution. He turned aside, dismissing the boy.

'Go away.'

'I can do it,' said Mumpo.

'Go away.'

'My body knows what to do.'

'Go away.' Hackel turned back. 'What did you say?'

'My body knows what to do.'

Hackel stared at him. Long ago he had had just this feeling himself, and had spoken in just these words. For nine years he had been the undefeated champion. Was it possible this gawky lad had the true grace?

He lowered himself back into his chair, grunting with the effort, and pondered.

'All right,' he said at last. 'I'll take a look at you.'

Hackel was a reasonable man. There was no call to kill the boy for having a foolish dream. He summoned one of his more recent recruits, a good solid fighter called Benz.

'Put on your training guards. I want to try out a new lad.'

Mumpo was stripped and fitted with leg and arm guards, but unlike the ones worn in the arena, in the place of blades on the knees and fists and helmet they had stubby metal knobs. He was led into a training ring, where a raised timber floor took the place of the sandy mound. His sparring partner gave him a friendly pat on one arm and said,

'Don't worry. I won't hurt you.'

'You won't touch me,' replied Mumpo.

Mumpo's confidence surprised the trainer. The boy was either very good or very stupid.

For Mumpo himself, limbering up for the bout, it was

all simple. He sensed he could fight well in the style of the manaxa, but more than this, he was burning to fight. Within him, driving him on, was an engine of fury that Hackel dimly perceived, though not its object. Mumpo meant to learn to be a manac, and then to turn his killing power on his masters.

The trainer settled down on a ringside bench, and signalled to Benz that he could begin. Benz came out dancing, according to the custom of the manaxa. Mumpo followed him with his eyes and his limbs, dancing the same moves. Hackel grunted with approval. The boy moved nicely. Benz then curled in close, for a classic knee-fist-knee strike, but Mumpo seemed to know what was coming. He blocked each punch with clean fast moves, and all at once he was behind Benz, grazing his back with one arching fist. Hackel chuckled. A simple spin-and-lift, but nicely done.

Benz realised he would have to try harder. Turning on Mumpo, he executed the attack called the pump hammer, a high-stepping flurry of blows that is meant to overwhelm the opposition's defences. Mumpo knew instinctively how to respond: he leaned back, then drove forward with a single fist hit to the head. The blow landed short, but threw Benz off balance. Mumpo closed in with a series of punishing knee and fist strikes to the body, that battered his opponent to the floor.

'Stop! Stop! Stop!'

Hackel was astonished by Mumpo's ferocity.

'No need to kill him!'

Mumpo backed off, still jigging from foot to foot, so powered up with aggression that his fists went on striking the air before him. His opponent staggered to his feet, giddy and aching from the blows he had received. Hackel went to him and checked his face and chest.

'Go and lie down.'

Benz limped away. The trainer turned to Mumpo.

'Well,' he said slowly. 'What was that about?'

'I want to fight.'

'So I see.'

Hackel didn't tell the boy how impressed he was. It didn't do to let them get too high an opinion of themselves.

'Will you teach me?' said Mumpo.

Hackel put his head on one side, pretending it was a difficult decision.

'You punch like a baby,' he said. 'And you haven't the first idea of how to build an attack. But I'll make a manac of you yet.'

Pinto's day passed slowly in the monkey wagon. The first terrors soon wore off, as she saw how the others in the lines of cages complained more of the boredom than the danger. One group two cages down sang songs for a while, until their neighbours complained. Mostly the prisoners either gossiped or dozed. Titbits of news were passed from cage to cage and eagerly discussed, while the guards yawned and speculated on what would be for lunch. Pinto stayed very quiet, afraid that if she attracted attention in any way they would all be burned. To occupy herself, she thought about Mumpo, and how when she was fifteen and old enough to be married, he would be twenty-three, and much more grown-up, but not really different at all.

Hanno Hath appeared briefly, just before lunch-time, to see how she was managing. She held his hands through the bars, and smiled for him so he wouldn't worry about her.

'It's not hard at all,' she told him. 'It's just boring.'

'It'll be over soon, my darling,' he said. 'Nothing at all bad will happen to you.'

'I wonder what they do when it rains.'

'You get wet, I suppose.'

'I mean, they wouldn't be able to light their fires.'

Her father gazed at her with pride.

'You're the bravest girl in the world,' he said.

Hanno Hath himself had been assigned to a huge warehouse, which was crammed with every kind of object imaginable. Part junk-store, part treasure-trove, here were heaped the spoils of numberless raids, including the most recent attack on Aramanth. The wagons carrying the plunder had not been unloaded yet, and he found books from his own library, tipped loose between the piles of furniture, as packing material.

The warehouse manager gazed wearily on the wagons from Aramanth.

'Why do they bring back all this rubbish? Slaves I don't mind, they can move themselves about. But who's going to move all this? Yours truly, that's who.'

'What would you like me to do?' asked Hanno.

'Let's see.' He studied Hanno's docket. 'So you're a librarian. You'd better do books.'

'What am I to do with them?'

'Move them about. Make a pile. That's what we do here. Chairs go with chairs. Pictures go with pictures. Books go with books. You'll pick it up.'

'What happens to the piles?'

'What happens to anything? They decay and die.' He

swept one arm round the great crowded space in which they stood. 'Think of this depository as the world. What do we all do here? We move about a bit, and then we die.'

Hanno found that he was to be left alone. For a while he stacked books as he had been told. When he realised the manager was not returning to inspect his progress, he set about retrieving the more valuable books plundered from his own library.

The books had been pulled in haste from the shelves, and thrown higgledy-piggledy into the raiding wagons, and many had fallen open, and been crushed. Hanno couldn't bear to see a book with its spine cracked and its pages crumpled. He took each one and gently set it right, smoothing out the thick creamy pages until their edges were aligned once more. In doing this, he glanced over the texts here and there, and so, inevitably, began to read.

He was so deeply immersed in one of the early Manth chronicles that he never heard the approaching footsteps.

'What do you think you're doing?'

The question was barked at him in a huge and terrible voice. The owner of the voice, however, was a very small man wearing a hat with a very broad brim.

Hanno jumped to his feet.

'Just a short rest –'

'Give, give!'

The little man held out an imperious hand. Hanno gave him the book, cursing himself, terrified that Pinto would come to harm because of his lack of vigilance. The warehouse manager came bustling up.

'Professor Fortz! I had no idea!'

'Of course you had no idea. You're a witless buffoon. When did you last have an idea?' To Hanno he said accusingly, 'This book is written in old Manth. Nobody can read old Manth.'

'I can,' said Hanno.

'Is that so?' The little professor looked at him with interest. He swung round to the warehouse manager. 'You don't need him, do you? You do nothing whatsoever here, so it doesn't take two to do it.'

'Well, Professor, I do find –'

'Don't. Just do as you're told, there's a good fellow.' He turned back to examine Hanno. 'I take it you're a Manth yourself.'

'Yes, I am.'

'Interesting people. Interesting history. All over now, of course. Aramanth burned, was it?'

'Yes,' said Hanno.

'Don't glare at me, my good sir. I didn't burn it. Well, we won't waste your talents here. The Mastery knows how to use people. Good day to you.'

He turned and made his way out, moving at considerable speed for one with such short legs. The warehouse manager hurried after him.

'Professor! What am I to do with him?'

'Nothing,' came the booming reply. 'I'll send for him in due course. Just go on doing nothing, my good fellow, as per usual.'

At the end of the day, the monkey cages were unlocked and the people inside let out. A new batch of slaves was lined up to take their place, complete with rugs to keep them warm through the night. Hanno and Ira Hath were there to see Pinto released, and Bowman too. All up and down the roadway people were hugging and kissing, as their loved ones were given safely back to them; while others looked on with quieter sadness, as their loved ones climbed up into the cages, and saw the iron gates locked after them.

Pinto let her mother hold her tight in her arms and kiss her, but she didn't cry. The long hours in the cage had had their effect.

'These are wicked people,' was all she would say.

'They are, my darling, they are.'

It was the turn of Mrs Chirish to spend the night in the cage. Mumpo was there to help her in.

'I'll come for you in the morning, auntie.'

'You're a good boy, Mumpy.'

'All you have to do is lie down and sleep.'

'I don't like to be any trouble,' said Mrs Chirish looking round, 'only I am on the large side, and there doesn't seem to be enough room.'

'Yes, there is, auntie. You squeeze yourself up against the bars here.'

'Oh, yes. That's all right, then. Good night, Mumpy. Friends in dreams.'

'Good night, auntie.'

As they walked back up the road, Pinto asked Mumpo what Mrs Chirish had meant when she said 'Friends in dreams'.

'When I was young I was always sad, because I had no friends. So every night when auntie tucked me up she said, never mind, you'll make friends in your dreams.'

'Oh, Mumpo. Did you?'

'Sometimes.'

'But you've got us now, haven't you?'

'Oh yes, I'm all right now.' Then he remembered. 'Except for Kess.'

'We'll find her,' said Bowman. 'Or she'll find us.'

Back at the marshalling yards they found the clerks with their ledgers, and learned that they had been allocated new living quarters. They were to sleep from now on in specially-built two-storey slave barracks, dispersed all over the countryside on the fringes of villages. The Hath family were led off, together with many others, to Slave Barracks Seventeen, a mile or so down the hillside, nearer to the lake.

The long building was partitioned into many smaller rooms, each reached by an open passage at the front. They were plain rooms, with no curtains on the windows or rugs on the floor, but they offered privacy of a kind, and best of all, beds. The beds were wooden frames strung with rope, the mattresses coarse bags stuffed with straw, but to the weary slaves this was luxury. The beds stood close together, eight to a room. At the foot of each was a slave number. For a while there was a great to-ing and fro-ing as people searched for their places, checking their wrist numbers as they went. The Hath family had all been placed together, along with Mumpo, Scooch, Creoth, and the absent Mrs Chirish. Bowman, who was to work through the night, ate an early supper and went to lie down on his bed. There was still an hour to go before dark.

Creoth appeared later than the rest, as dusk was falling, glowing with happiness. He joined the others for supper in the big communal kitchen on the ground floor, and told all who would listen, in between mouthfuls of soup, about his day on the farm.

'Cows!' he exclaimed. 'Excellent fellows! Beard of my ancestors, what a day!'

It turned out he had learned how to milk a cow.

'It's a knack, you see. You don't squeeze, or pull.

Oh, no! You close your fingers one after the other, like this.'

He wiggled his fingers to demonstrate. Everyone laughed, and he laughed with them.

'You can laugh,' he cried, 'but you should try it! Not as easy as I make it look.'

Creoth was not the only one who had enjoyed his first day of slave labour. Miko Mimilith was full of the wonders of the materials he had found at the dress-maker's.

'I've never seen such finely woven silk. Like air, I promise you. No, finer than air. Like thought!'

Dr Batch, a teacher in Aramanth, had been assigned to a class in one of the schools set up for the slave children.

'I must confess I've been given all that I need. And as for discipline – well, no problems there, believe me. I will say this for our masters, they have created a climate of respect for authority, and I can't altogether disapprove.'

Mumpo revealed that he had been accepted into the manaxa school. Pinto was horrified.

'You can't! You mustn't! They'll kill you. I don't want you to die.'

'I won't die.'

She followed him when he went outside to stretch his legs.

'You'll be stabbed to death. You mustn't do it. We need you.'

She clung to his arm as she pleaded with him. 'Say you won't.'

'I want to do it,' he replied. 'So I'm doing it.'

'Plee-ease, Mumpo.'

'Leave me alone.'

'I won't let you go till you promise me you won't do it.'

'Leave me alone!'

He tried to shake her off, but she clung tight. The dim sense that Pinto was right only made him crosser.

'Get off me, you skinny little rat!'

He gave a vigorous jerk of his arm, and Pinto was thrown to the ground. She bruised her shoulder in falling, and started to cry. The sight of her crouched on the ground crying made Mumpo more angry still.

'Why are you always hanging round me?' He shouted at her, to make the hurt be her own fault. 'I don't want you. Leave me alone.'

Pinto crept away. Later her mother found her curled up in a corner, her eyes red from crying, but she wouldn't say why.

Jessel Greeth, who was quartered in a different building, called on Hanno Hath before nightfall. He was well aware that most of the Manth people had found their first day more bearable than they had expected.

'What do you say now, Hanno? Still calling for rebellion?'

'It's not going to be easy,' said Hanno.

'Indeed not. Not easy, and maybe, not wise.'

'I think we should put aside a little food each day. Anything that can be stored. That way we'll be able to feed ourselves on the journey.'

'The journey, eh? You've got to get away first. How do you do that?'

'I don't know.'

'Well, before you go stirring everyone up, just listen to this. I've been given a job in the Department of Supply. I helped organise the meal you had this evening. They must have seen that I have a natural talent for management. Anyway, my boss, the fellow who oversees the supplies for the whole sector, is a slave! He showed me his brand number!'

Hanno looked back on Greeth's beaming face without understanding.

'Don't you see? They promote slaves! There are slaves in positions of authority! We could do well here.'

'But Jessel,' said Hanno, wrinkling his brows. 'These are the people who murdered our families and burned our home.'

'Well, yes, yes, there's that, I realise that, of course. But what's the point of looking back, eh? Here we are, so let's look forward.'

'The point is, whatever's good about this country is built on force and cruelty. It's poisoned at the heart.'

Greeth looked uncomfortable for a moment. Then he shrugged, and said,

'Nothing's perfect. We live in the real world. Our duty is to make the best of it. And ask yourself, what is the alternative? A journey to nowhere?'

So saying, satisfied that he had won the argument, he went over to shake Dr Batch's hand, and share experiences of their first day.

Hanno Hath confided his worries to his wife.

'I don't know how to make them listen to me.'

'They hear you,' she said. 'The time will come soon enough when they'll believe you.'

'How soon?'

'Before winter comes.'

10

A visitor in the night

When night fell, Bowman's work began. With a lantern in one hand and a staff in the other, he was sent out into the pastures by the lake shore to watch over a herd of cows and their calves. His job was to scare away any wolves that might come sniffing round the herd, looking to steal a calf.

A hut had been provided for the cowherd, a small windowless shelter against rain or cold, and here Bowman took up his post. He sat on the earth floor, with the door open before him to pasture and lake, and watched the cows moving placidly past, tearing softly at the grass. As the sounds of voices in nearby villages faded into quietness, he turned his mind to Kestrel, and listened for her in the night. Once or twice he thought he felt her, but so faintly and so far off that he couldn't be sure. The moon rose in the sky, a half-moon, its light shining faintly down on the palace on the lake. One by one the lights in the beautiful buildings were going out.

He had no way of measuring the passing of time, and so time itself seemed to come to a stop. The stars turned, and the moon crossed the sky, but these were cycles that were outside time; or so Bowman felt. The night grew cold. He had been given a long sheepskin cape, which he drew ever closer about him. The cows settled down to sleep. A wind sprang up, and ruffled the waters of the lake. The palace across the water was in darkness now. All was quiet.

Then he heard a sound: the soft swish of grass, and a low tuneful humming. Someone was approaching. He took hold of his staff, and stepped out of the hut, wondering what sort of person could be out at this time of night. The humming sounded more clearly now. Out of the darkness, slowly entering the reach of the lantern-light, there came an ugly one-eyed man.

He was evidently making for the hut. He held his arms folded across his chest, the hands inside the loose sleeves of his robe. The robe was a plain garment of undyed wool, not nearly thick enough for warmth on this chill night. His feet were bare. Bowman wondered as he approached who he was and what he could want. Perhaps a poor man hoping to share the shelter of the hut. Perhaps one of the lone witless creatures to be met with on remote roads, who live and die like animals. Except the tune he was humming was no random noise: it made a pattern of sound that, once you caught it, was quite pleasant. Behind him, no more than a shadow in the lantern's light, loped a grey cat.

The stranger reached him at last. He stopped humming, and looked at Bowman without speaking, and Bowman looked at him. He had a melancholy face, and one of his eyes was a milky colour, and didn't move. He examined Bowman closely with the other eye, as if to satisfy himself about something.

'Are you the child of the prophet?' he said.

'Am I –?' Bowman was greatly surprised. 'Which prophet?'

'Is there more than one?'

He shuffled his way into the hut, and sat down on the floor. Then looking up at Bowman, he patted the ground beside him.

'Sit.'

Bowman sat.

The stranger began to hum again. It seemed to be a deliberate humming, that it would be rude to interrupt, so Bowman sat quietly and waited for him to stop. After some time, he brought his wordless song to an end, and stretching out his fingers, worked them together.

'Ah, that's better,' he said. 'I get pain in my hands, especially on a damp night. But I'm all right now.'

'Is that why you were humming?'

'Yes. That was the song for relieving pain in the extremities. Really I should accept the pain, and put it to use. After all, pain is just another form of energy. But we all fall short of perfection.'

He looked out over the lake towards the dark city.

'That would be the High Domain.'

'Yes.'

'Have you been there? Have you seen it?'

'No.'

'They say it's quite something. Beauty. Learning. The human spirit in flower.'

Bowman stared at the city-palace with anger.

'All I know is they kill people and they make slaves.'

'Yes, well, that too.'

The grey cat suddenly appeared, jumping out of the darkness onto the stranger's lap. Bowman stared.

'You have a cat?'

'I wouldn't say I *have* a cat. He travels with me.'

Mist looked up at Bowman with dislike. To Dogface, he said in their silent form of communication,

'Who is this halfwit?'

'He's someone we need. I have to make sure he knows what to do.'

'What?' said Bowman. Dogface had spoken aloud.

'Sorry. I was talking to the cat.'

'You were talking to a cat?'

Mist slowly turned his head away. He wanted nothing more to do with this dull youth.

'Leave him to the cows,' he said. 'He seems to have their level of intellect.'

Dogface noticed the cows for the first time.

'So they've put you to watch the cows?'

'Yes.'

'And are the cows grateful?'

'Are they grateful? I've no idea.'

'Ask them.'

'I can't talk to cows.'

'Of course you can. You just haven't tried.'

'Spare me!' said Mist. 'Do we really have to sit here getting colder by the minute, listening to cows?'

'It's as good a beginning as any,' said the hermit.

Bowman supposed this was addressed to him.

'Beginning of what?' he said.

The hermit fixed his good eye on the nearest cow, and spoke to it.

'Wake up, my friend,' he said. 'Forgive me for disturbing you. The young man here would like a word.'

To Bowman's astonishment the cow lumbered to its legs and came over to them. The big head swung down, close to where he sat, and he felt the cow's moist breath on his face.

139

'I believe you already know what to do,' the hermit prompted.

Bowman had no idea at all how to begin, so he just looked into one of the cow's big unblinking eyes, and let himself go quiet and empty inside, as he did when listening for Kestrel. After a few moments, the cow trembled violently, and Bowman sensed a confused buzz of sound. The cow was frightened.

It's all right, he told the cow, not so much in words as in feelings. *I won't hurt you.*

Slowly he felt the cow grow calm, and the vibrating noises faded to a single slow pulse of sound: *oomfa – oomfa – oomfa.* The cow's big wet nose pushed very close to him, and he felt the suck of air as she snuffled at his face.

Then he found it. It was like that moment when you're in a room full of people all talking at once, their voices mingling into a meaningless jumble of sound, and suddenly you catch a voice speaking your own name. From then on, you hear that voice alone, and understand it, and all the other voices slip into the background. Only, the cow didn't exactly have a voice. She had a flow of observations. She had concerns.

Monster night stillness juice of grass don't-trust always near calf smell of my own one no sudden moves monster sleep my own one pale monster in moonlight shivering . . .

'I'm your friend,' said Bowman aloud, so the hermit could hear too.

Friends move slow monsters jump . . .

It was the strangest thing. The cow wasn't talking, but he received the answer, feeling by feeling, with perfect clarity. He had always assumed cows were stupid. He now understood that they just worked more slowly than people.

He raised one hand to touch the cow, but deliberately made the hand move very slowly through the air.

'I – can – be – slow,' he said, also speaking slowly.

The cow contemplated him gravely.

Miserable monster no peace no rest sudden moves hurt stillness monster grieving . . .

Astonishing! The cow thought he was the one with the problems.

'Do you pity me, cow?'

Sad monster rush rush and odd stick creature jerky jerky go about and about ha ha ha . . .

Now the cow was laughing at him! In her slow and wordless way, she found him amusing.

'Laugh at me if you want,' said Bowman, a little offended. 'But you're still afraid of me too.'

Ah monster hurt monster hurt all jerky jerky funny monster terror monster death monster and at the end ha ha ha . . .

Bowman understood.

'We monsters bring so much fear, what can you do but laugh at us?'

The cow gazed at him a little longer, with what seemed to Bowman to be a deep compassion, an acknowledgement that he had understood how she felt. Then she swung slowly away, and plodded off in search of her calf.

'There you are,' said the hermit.

'It's so strange. I feel quite different about cows now.'

'Wonderful,' said Mist. 'Can we go now?'

'I'm not done yet,' said Dogface.

Bowman was looking at the cat.

'Does it work with all animals?'

'Of course. And with plants. And even rocks, though

141

you have to work very hard with rocks.'

'How do you know these things?'

'How does anyone know anything? I've been taught.'

'Who are you?'

'You mean you want to know my name? Names are greatly overrated. We can all manage perfectly well without them.'

He shivered as he spoke.

'Why, you're cold!'

Bowman pulled off his sheepskin cape and drew it over the hermit's shoulders.

'You should wear warmer clothes.'

'I have to say I agree. But where I come from, it's very much frowned on. If you're cold, they say, sing the song against cold. Or accept the cold, and put it to use. Still, you're very kind. And you were most sensitive with that cow. I can see you'll do a decent enough job when it comes to it.'

'When it comes to what?'

'What you asked for.'

'I don't understand. What have I asked for?'

Dogface rubbed at his bad eye with one hand and cast his mind back.

'The power to destroy, I think they said. Not what I'd call a noble request. Nor a sensible one, really, given that you have the power already. More power than me, at any rate.'

The cat heard this in surprise.

'This boy has more power than you?'

'Oh, yes,' said Dogface. 'He was born to it.'

Bowman too was amazed, though for a very different reason. Could this truly be the answer to his cry in the night? And if so, who was this strange one-eyed man?

'So he could fly, could he?' said Mist.

'He could do anything he wanted,' replied the hermit. But after a moment's reflection, he added, speaking now to the bewildered Bowman, 'I'm not saying your power will be enough, when the time comes. But you can always ask for help.'

'When what time comes?'

'The time to destroy.' Dogface raised one arm towards the dark city on the lake. 'You want to destroy all this, I take it?'

'I – I – don't really know.'

'Oh, yes. I believe so.' He spoke in the vague manner of one who recalls something he's been told. 'You've been sent to destroy and to rule.'

'To destroy and to rule? There's been some kind of mistake. No one sent me. I'm a slave. I was driven here against my will.'

'Against your will, perhaps. Not against theirs.'

'Whose?'

'Sirene.'

Bowman stared at the hermit, once again reduced to silence. This time it was because of a name he had never in his life heard before, but which at once seemed familiar.

'So you see, there's no mistake. It's like with the cows. You have the power, but you haven't tried to use it yet. It's just a matter of practice, and wanting it enough.'

'Just a matter of practice, eh?' said Mist. 'Just a matter of wanting it enough?'

Dogface nudged the cat off his lap, got up, and pulled the heavy sheepskin cape off his shoulders.

'Thank you for your warmth. Now I must be on my way.'

He started up his humming once more.

'But I don't know what to do! You haven't told me. You haven't explained –'

The hermit stopped humming, and his good eye fixed Bowman with a severe look.

'You really must get out of this habit of expecting other people to do everything for you. It's not good, you know. You don't learn anything that way. Think of the cows, and try and do it for yourself.'

He reached out and took Bowman's staff from him, and let it fall to the ground. Then he looked down at it and was silent for a moment. Suddenly the staff jiggled where it lay, lifted itself up, and pushed itself back into Bowman's still open hand.

'See? Not at all hard, really. Now I must be on my way. Not much time left.'

With that, Dogface departed, shuffling over the grass in his bare feet with surprising speed. The grey cat ran by his side.

'You say that boy has more power than you?'

'Yes, poor lad. He's a true child of the prophet.'

Bowman pulled the sheepskin cape close round himself once more, and stared after him. Even well wrapped, he found he was trembling.

Sirene . . .

Why should the unknown name be so familiar? Why did it make him shiver? And could he really do what the one-eyed man had done?

He let his staff fall to the ground once more. He looked down on it. Feeling both foolish and excited, he tried to concentrate on the staff, saying to it with his mind, *Move!*

Nothing happened.

He stared at the staff for a long time, urging it in every way he could think of to rise up, but it simply lay there in the light of his lantern, showing no inclination to obey him.

After a while, he sat down on his haunches and glared at the staff, sensing that it could move if it wanted to, but was being stubborn. Just a matter of practice, the stranger had said. But how was one to practise when nothing happened?

Bowman didn't notice the grey cat return, and sit silently outside the pool of lantern-light watching him. All his attention was on his unmoving staff.

Just a matter of wanting it enough.

He settled down onto the earth, sitting cocooned in the thick cape, as he had been when the hermit had first appeared. He realised his thoughts were all in a racing tumble, from everything his visitor had said. So for a little while he looked up at the sky, and followed the half-moon as it sailed over the world, forever moving, and yet never seeming to get anywhere. Then in a calmer frame of mind, he returned his attention to his staff. He thought of how it had been with the cow. Perhaps this stick had feelings too, in its own way.

More respectfully, he reached out his mind towards the staff, and – what? Talked to it? That was ridiculous. Nobody talks to a stick. Instead, he attended to it. He felt gently all around it with his eyes, and through his eyes with his inner senses. He found nothing unusual. It was, well, stick-like. It was quite a young stick, he found. There was still sap beneath its hide of bark. The core of the wood had a pleasing density, in which there was no brittleness. The wood was in its prime. Round its smoothed top end he felt the impress of many hands, and he felt the stick's pride that those hands had clasped it tight, had leaned on it with great weight, and it had supported them. It hadn't bowed, or snapped. This staff was reliable, and it knew it.

He nudged it lightly, to see the underside, and it moved. Not much, just a half-roll, as he had intended. Only, his hands had remained buried deep in the warmth of the cape. He had moved it with his mind.

He fought back the impulse of surprise, determined to maintain the quiet contact he had made. He nudged at it again, and again it shifted a little. It was rather like blowing on a leaf: all he had to do was push with his mind, and the stick felt the force.

He held the smooth end of the staff with his mind, and gently levered it up. It rose, its other end still on the grass. He lifted it almost upright, and started to pull it towards him. But he wasn't quite strong enough, or practised enough, and it fell clattering back to the ground.

The cat saw, and was impressed. The boy did have power. That was all he needed to know.

He stood up, and stalked majestically into the light.

'Hallo,' said Bowman. 'You've come back.'

'Are you telling me?' said Mist. The boy heard nothing, of course. The cat sat down and stared at him. 'If you've got so much power, how about learning to talk?'

'Where's your master?'

'Oh, spare me!'

Bowman looked out into the darkness. There was no sign of the one-eyed stranger. The night was passing, and he had much to think over. He returned to the doorway of the hut and sat down there with his legs crossed, his staff and his lantern by his side. Mist climbed onto his lap and curled up there and started to purr. Bowman stroked him.

'I think you like me,' he said.

'Please,' said Mist wearily. 'You give me what I want, and I give you what you want. Let's just leave it at that.'

That same night, Ira Hath dreamed again, the dream in which snow fell over a red sky, and the coastal plain with the two rivers lay before her, between the steep hills. She cried out loud in her sleep, 'Wait for me! Don't go without me!' This woke her up, as well as her husband. She lay in his arms and they whispered together about the dream.

'I hate it,' she said. 'It's not fair. I wish it would go away.'

'No, my darling. It's not fair.'

'I don't want to be a prophetess. It's too tiring.'

'The land you see in your dream. Is it a good land?'

'Yes.'

'Is it our land?'

'Yes.'

'Can you lead us there?'

'Yes.' She hugged him close and kissed his familiar face. 'I'll never leave you. They can't make me.'

Hanno kissed her in return, and said nothing.

Bowman came back to the slave quarters at daybreak, and the cat followed him at a distance. At the first opportunity, Bowman took his father aside, and told him about the visitor in the night.

'Sirene!' exclaimed his father. 'That was the ancient home of the Singer people!'

'I think he may have been one of them.'

'I didn't know they still existed.'

'What are they, pa?'

'I know a little. If only I had my books!'

'They built the wind singer, didn't they?'

'Yes. They were a people who had no homes, no possessions, no family. They wore plain robes, and went barefoot, living off the kindness of strangers. They had no weapons, no armour, nothing, and yet they alone had the power to resist the Morah.'

'What kind of power?'

'I don't know. It was all written down once. But so much has been lost.'

He fell silent, deep in his own thoughts.

Bowman did not tell his father about the power he had discovered within himself. He was still unsure about it, and shy of exposing it to the scrutiny of others. For similar reasons, he did not say that the stranger had told him, *You have come to destroy and to rule.* He only half understood it himself. What he did understand, and did tell his father, was that he now believed he was part of some greater plan.

'I think I'm here for a reason, pa. I think there's something I'm to do.'

'We're all here for a reason, Bo. We must watch, and wait for our moment.'

As the others departed for their day's work, Bowman went to his bed, in the many-bedded room. Mist followed him silently, almost unnoticed, and lay down under the bed. Here, as Bowman slipped into sleep, when he was least expecting it, he caught the tremor he had strained for night after night: the sound too distant to hear, the movement too distant to see, the passing of a shadow in the dark –

Kess!

So faint that even thinking the thought made too much noise. Now it was gone again. But it had been his sister, he was sure of it.

She was coming.

11

Preparations for marriage

Kestrel was lying in her narrow cot bed in the Johdila's carriage when she felt that brief tremor of contact. She made herself as still as she could in the lumbering creaking vehicle, but it did not come again. When finally she relaxed her intense concentration, she found that Sisi was speaking to her from her nearby bed, just a few feet away in the shadows of the curtained carriage.

'Why don't you answer, Kess? Are you angry with me?'

'No, no. I was thinking about my brother.'

'Oh, your brother. You're always thinking about him.'

'You'd like him too, if you knew him.'

'I don't expect I would,' said Sisi sulkily. 'I don't really like anybody, except Lunki, who doesn't count. And you.'

But as she said this, a new thought came to her.

'Is your brother like you?'

'I don't know that he's like me. It's more as if he's half of me.'

'Is he the same height as you?'

'A little taller.'

'And what else?'

'What do you want to know?'

'Well, what colour is his hair?'

'He's dark, like me. And a pale face. He's quiet. He often looks sad. He can feel what other people are feeling, just by looking at them.'

'Does he have someone he wants to marry?'

'No, I don't think so. He's quite a lonely person.'

'Like me,' said Sisi.

She lay in her deep downy bed, and as she was rocked by the steady motion of the carriage, she let her new thought blossom within her. Kestrel was her only friend, the only one outside her family she had ever loved. Bowman was just like Kestrel, only he was a man. Why should she not love him?

'I think I shall marry your brother,' she announced shortly.

Kestrel laughed aloud.

'Don't you think you should ask him first?'

'Why? He's bound to want to marry me. Because I'm so beautiful.'

'Oh, Sisi. You're so – so –'

'So what?'

'So uncomplicated. I don't know how else to say it.'

'Do you mean I'm stupid?'

'No, not stupid. Only, there's so much you don't understand.'

'Mama told me men want to marry women who are beautiful. She said it doesn't matter if you're stupid, so long as you're beautiful.'

'Bowman's not like most other men.'

'You mean he doesn't want a beautiful wife?'

'I don't think so.'

'Then what's the point of being beautiful?' She gave a little scream, out of anger at all the wasted effort. Kestrel said nothing, so she screamed again.

'Stop it!' said Kestrel. 'You're not to scream over such nonsense. Screaming's for when you're hurt.'

'All right, Kess. Don't be cross with me, or I'll – no I won't.'

'And anyway, you can't marry my brother. You're going to marry this other person. Whoever he is.'

'No, I'm not.'

'You said you have to.'

'You said you wouldn't if you were me.'

'I'm not you.'

'Oh, Kess, how I wish you were! Then I could be you. You are going to dance for me, you know. You've already started being me, just a little. And think how much you'd like being so beautiful.'

'I shouldn't,' said Kestrel.

'Why not?'

'Because I'd rather be me.'

'But what if you were you and beautiful?'

'I couldn't be,' said Kestrel. 'If I was very beautiful, I'd stop being me. Or at least, people would see my beauty and wouldn't see me.'

'What an odd idea. That's not how it is at all.'

They fell silent. The Johdila had been told how beautiful she was so often she found it difficult to imagine herself apart from her beauty. But one day soon a man would see her unveiled. What would he think? She wanted him to see her beauty, but she wanted him to see her, too.

'Oh, Kess, darling,' she sighed. 'How hard it all is.'

Later that day, the Johdila was summoned to her father's carriage, where she was to be instructed by her mother on the ceremony of marriage. This gave Kestrel the opportunity she needed to speak with the Commander of the Johjan Guards.

She found Zohon drilling his men. He was standing on a set of steps he had had made for the purpose, which raised him high enough to oversee the entire formation, watching as his officers issued the drill commands in a series of staccato barks.

'Wheel! Merge! Cross under!'

Kestrel waited to one side, and also watched. The long lines of men in their deep purple uniforms created intricate patterns that flowed in and out of each other, as if, ceasing to be individuals, they had become one vast pulsing organism. Zohon had forged his men into a superb fighting machine, and Kestrel rejoiced to see it. Already as her plan matured in her mind she thought of the Johjan Guards as her army, the force that would set her people free.

Zohon saw her at last. Impatient to learn her news, he signed to his officers to bring the elaborate drill to an end.

'Turn! Face! Salute!'

The troops saluted their commander.

'Dismiss!'

Zohon strolled over to his campaign tent, paying no attention to Kestrel. She let a few moments pass, and then followed.

As soon as they were alone together, Zohon fixed her with his burning eyes.

'Well? Have you spoken to her?'

'Yes,' said Kestrel.

'And?'

Kestrel lowered her voice. 'The Johdila is very afraid.'

'Afraid! Go on.'

'She's afraid of this country called the Mastery. She's

afraid of disobeying her father. She's afraid of failing her people.'

'Of course she is. They ask too much of her.'

'She believes she must do her duty, even though . . .'

'Even though her heart isn't in this marriage?' Zohon was eager to learn his instincts were right.

'It isn't,' said Kestrel.

'And me? You spoke to her of me?'

'I was very careful. I slipped your name into the conversation.'

'And what did she say?'

'Nothing. Her eyes looked down. She was silent.'

'She looked down. She was silent.' Zohon strode up and down the tented space, pondering this information. 'She looked down. She was silent. What does it mean? I'll tell you what it means. She dared not look, or speak. And why not? Because of the strength of her feelings! Yes, count on it, she did not trust herself even to speak my name!'

Excited by this conclusion, he turned back to Kestrel to instruct her on the next phase of his plan.

'You're to say to the Johdila that you've spoken to me. You're to say that I will save her from this marriage. But I must know her heart. You understand?'

'Yes,' said Kestrel.

'Let her send me a message, through you. Then I will know what to do.'

'Very well.'

'Now go! I have matters to attend to. Fortune favours the bold!'

Meanwhile the Johdi was rehearsing her daughter in the wedding ceremony. It was many years since she had performed the five steps herself, but she remembered every moment vividly.

'My mother cried all through my wedding day. I shall cry, I know it. Now, the most important thing to remember is to keep the steps small. Like this.'

The Johdi shuffled forward, one small step.

'Remember, every time you step forward, he steps forward. You don't want to bump into him. I've known weddings where they never had room for the fifth step. And you know what that means.'

'No, mama. What does it mean?'

'One of you will die ten years before the other. Each step stands for ten years together. So let's practise. I'll be the man.'

They stood facing each other at opposite ends of the main saloon of the royal carriage.

'Hands clasped. Look down.' Sisi did as she was told. 'He moves, then you move. There. Now you.'

Sisi stepped forward.

'Pause. There'll be music. Don't look up until after the third step.'

'Why am I not to look up?'

'In the early years, a good wife is ruled by her husband.'

'But you're not ruled by papa.'

'Only in the early years, darling. Now I step. And off you go again.'

Sisi stepped forward.

'Before you were married, mama, did you want to be married to papa?'

'Of course I did, darling. He was the son of the Johanna of Gang. The old Johanna, that is.'

'But did you love him?'

'Now the third step. How could I possibly love him, dear? You can't love a man if you've never so much as said good morning to him.'

'What if you hadn't liked him?'

'Fourth step. Keep it small.'

Sisi stepped forward.

'Now look up. Keep your head up from now on.'

Sisi looked up at her mother. She was close now.

'I chose to like him. As you will do. Fifth step.'

The Johdi stepped forward, and Sisi followed. Now they were close enough to touch. Her mother parted her plump hands and declared,

'With these five steps, I stand before you as your husband. Do you receive me as my wife?'

'And all I say is, yes?'

'You say yes, my darling. And you're a wife.'

Sisi felt a great sadness come over her. Not wanting her mother to see, she put her arms round her and buried her face in the Johdi's ample bosom.

'There, my sweet one. There, there.'

'Mama,' said Sisi after a moment. 'Have you been happy, married to papa?'

The Johdi sighed.

'I know no other life,' she said. 'He's a good man. Who's to say it would have been any better with anyone else?'

When Sisi was alone with Kestrel in their carriage that night, in the soft secret time between going to bed and falling asleep, she listened for Lunki's soft regular snores, and then spoke to her friend.

'Kess, darling. Are you awake?'

'Yes.'

'I was wondering. Have you ever wanted to run away from everyone and everything, and be a quite different person?'

'Yes,' said Kestrel. 'Often and often.'

'But you didn't ever do it?'

'I ran away once. But I didn't become a different person.'

'Did you go home again?'

'Yes.'

'Did everything go on just the same as before?'

'No. Everything was different after that.'

'Was that good or bad?'

'I'm not sure.' Kestrel thought about it, wanting to answer truthfully. 'I think maybe it was bad. I've never felt I really belong anywhere, ever since.'

'Maybe you don't belong anywhere. Maybe some people don't.'

Kestrel touched the silver voice that hung round her neck, night and day.

'Maybe not.'

There followed a silence, in which Kestrel thought how her mother had wanted her to marry, and how Sisi was going to be married, and for the first time she felt Sisi was someone like her.

'Kess,' said Sisi out of the dark. 'I don't want this wedding. But I don't know how to stop it.'

Kestrel had a short struggle with herself. She was beginning to be ashamed of the way she was using Sisi in her plan. But she had no choice. She must trick Sisi into playing her part, or her family and her people would never be free.

'Maybe you should talk to your parents.'

'They'll just tell me I have to be married. Mama will

say it'll be the same whoever I marry, and I won't want to in the beginning, but after a while I'll get used to it.'

'Well,' said Kestrel, to quiet her conscience, 'you're not married until the wedding, and that's days and days away. Maybe something will happen to change everything.'

'Maybe.' Sisi's voice sounded small and sad. 'But I don't expect it will.'

Kestrel steeled herself to carry out the next step in her plan. She reached an arm out to where Sisi lay.

'We'll still go on being friends, won't we?'

'Oh yes! Always!'

'We could have a secret sign, if you like.'

'A secret sign for what?'

'Just to tell each other we're friends.'

'Oh, yes. I'd like that. What shall it be?'

'When we're in public together,' said Kestrel, 'and I can't speak to you because you're a princess and I'm a servant, I shall press the palms of my hands together, and then clasp my fingers, like two people hugging. That'll tell you I'm thinking of how we're friends.'

'Oh, Kess! How lovely! And what's my sign?'

'You do the same for me.'

There was a silence. Then Sisi spoke happily out of the dark.

'I'm doing it now. Are you doing it?'

'Yes.'

'I do love you, Kess. I've never had a secret friend sign before.'

'Nor have I.'

'Then I'm your first secret friend, and you're mine.'

Warmed by this thought, Sisi settled down at last to sleep.

* * *

The next morning Ozoh the Wise awoke to find his chicken gone. The cage door was open, and the chicken nowhere to be seen. He searched the carriage in mounting panic.

'Where are you, silky? Cluck-cluck-cluck! Where are you, my dove?'

The chicken was gone. It couldn't let itself out of its cage. Someone, therefore, had stolen it.

Ozoh sat on his chair by the empty cage and tears crept down his painted cheeks. He loved his chicken. He knew it was ridiculous to love a chicken, but the fowl had been a friend to him, and he was lonely on the journey.

Then he dried his tears and did some serious thinking. The time for his morning sign reading was rapidly approaching. It would not do much for his reputation if he admitted he had lost his sacred chicken, and had no idea what had become of it. So he made a short discreet visit to the provisions wagons.

That morning, the Johdila chose to attend the sign reading. With each passing day, she was becoming more interested in predictions of the future. Kestrel accompanied her, remaining discreetly in the background.

Ozoh the Wise arrived, with his escort of guards. He carried his sign mat, and he was followed by his servant. But Kestrel, along with the rest of the assembled court, saw that his servant did not carry his caged bird.

The royal augur proceeded to unroll the sign mat on the ground, and squat down before it, and study it, all in profound silence, as if nothing was amiss. The Johanna looked from side to side, and at last said to his wife in a loud whisper,

'I can't see the chicken.'

'Silence!' hissed the royal augur.

'Be quiet, Foofy,' said the Johdi.

Ozoh began to groan. He swayed back and forth, his eyes closed, crooning.

'He's never done that before,' said the Johanna.

The Johdi looked on in alarm. Something terrible was going to happen, she was sure. Kestrel looked at the Grand Vizier, who was watching with furrowed brows, trying to work out what the augur was up to. She then looked at Zohon. He had no expression of any kind on his smooth handsome face. Kestrel knew at once that this change was somehow his doing.

'Haroo! Haroo!' crooned Ozoh. Suddenly he bounded into the air, fell back down prostrate onto the sign mat, and bounced back into his squatting position.

There on the mat, spinning round and round, was an egg.

The entire court gasped. Even Zohon was surprised.

'To see the future,' Ozoh intoned, 'I must reach into the past! The sacred chicken has returned to the egg!'

'Oh, Foofy!' cried the Johdi in terror. 'We shall all have to grow backwards!'

'The egg,' said the royal augur, 'is the sign of new life, the sign of joyful beginnings.'

'Joyful? Are you sure? That poor chicken.'

'See how it comes to rest, Little Mother.'

The Johdi calmed down. She liked being called Little Mother. The egg had now stopped spinning.

'The narrow end favours Haroo. This is the dawn of a new age of love. A blessed sign for the coming marriage!'

He bowed towards the Johdila.

'So everything's all right, is it?' said the Johanna.

'Better than all right, mightiness. The sacred egg

shows the way. Your magnificence has only to look for himself.'

'Well, I do see it, that's true.'

'You see love. You see peace. You see soldiers returning home to their rejoicing families, and putting away their swords, and turning with glad hearts to honest toil.'

Kestrel saw Zohon frown and look away.

'I see breakfast,' said the Johanna; and laughing heartily at his own joke, got up out of his folding chair and waddled off to his carriage.

Kestrel was following the Johdila back to their own carriage when Barzan approached, and asked the Johdila for permission to speak to her servant. The Johdila was surprised.

'You want to speak to Kess? What about?'

'A personal matter, radiance.'

Sisi took Kestrel aside.

'You don't want to talk to him, do you, darling? He'll probably put out your eyes with red-hot skewers. He's been wanting to do it ever since I found you.'

'I'm sure he only wants to ask me about you.'

'What about me? What will you tell him?'

'What would you like me to tell him?'

This was a new way of seeing the matter. Sisi reflected.

'You could tell him I don't like this whoever I'm to marry, and I won't marry him.'

'He'll say you can't not like him if you don't know who he is.'

'Oh. Do you think I can't?'

'Maybe I should try to find out who he is.'

'Yes, that's a good idea. How clever you are. Find out who he is, and then say I don't like him.'

The Johdila returned to her carriage, and the Grand Vizier spoke with Kestrel.

'No doubt you heard the augury,' he said, smiling in what he meant to be a fatherly way. 'The dawn of a new age of love.'

'Yes,' said Kestrel.

'Love is in the air. The sacred egg has pointed the way.' He lowered his voice. 'Perhaps the egg also points towards you.'

'Me?'

'I believe you have an admirer.'

'Who?' Kestrel was genuinely surprised.

'The handsome and eligible Commander of the Johjan Guards, no less! The man for whom the hearts of the maidens of Gang go pitter-pat!'

Kestrel began to understand.

'You're very kind,' she said, 'but the Commander has given me no reason to suppose that he favours me.'

'He's spoken to you, hasn't he?'

'Yes.'

'Well, there you are! Why would a man like that speak to a girl like you if he didn't mean to marry you? No, no, depend upon it, he's courting you.'

'I see,' said Kestrel.

'I admit I can't imagine why – that's to say, you're a bright-eyed little thing, and if he likes you, why not? He has rank, he has wealth, he has – some would call him handsome, and so he is, in an obvious sort of way. Personally I believe looks of that sort age rapidly, and I'm sure he'll run to fat – however –' recovering himself, 'you'll not find a man to match him in all Gang. A fine figure of a man. A noble fellow. One of the best.'

Looking round, he saw that Zohon himself was watching them from a distance.

'You see! He can't take his eyes off you. A sweet smile, a soft touch, and he's yours.'

He nodded twice, satisfied that he had planted the necessary seeds of love, and went on his way.

Zohon waited until the Grand Vizier was out of sight, and then approached Kestrel himself. He did not want to be seen talking to her, so he passed close by without seeming to pay her any attention. But as he passed he said loudly enough for her to hear,

'Meet me in my carriage.'

Kestrel waited a few minutes, and then did as she was told. In Zohon's carriage, she was surprised to find the royal augur, Ozoh the Wise, but no sign of Zohon himself.

They looked at each other with mutual suspicion.

'What are you doing here?' asked Ozoh.

'I was told to come,' said Kestrel.

'So was I.'

They said nothing more for a few moments. Ozoh was looking at the silver voice hanging round Kestrel's neck.

'That pendant. It's unusual. Where did you get it?'

'From home,' said Kestrel.

'I'd like to buy it from you. I'd pay you well.'

'It's not for sale.'

Before Ozoh could speak again, there came a chuckling cooing sound, from somewhere very near at hand. Ozoh jumped up.

'My chicken!'

He spun round, his baggy pantaloons billowing.

'Where are you, my silky one?'

The sound was coming from the bedroom half of the carriage, which was reached through an open door in the dividing partition. As Kestrel watched, Ozoh passed through the door, and approached the curtained bed beyond. The cooing had now become an alarmed cackling.

'I'm coming, my dove! I'm coming!'

Ozoh pulled back the curtains, and froze, staring. On the bed lay Zohon, fully dressed, holding the chicken by its legs, upside down.

He smiled at the augur, and swung himself into a sitting position. Reaching out his free hand, he took his silver hammer from the table by the bed.

'Did your signs foretell this?' he said.

With one rapid sweep of the bladed hammer, he sliced off the chicken's head. Ozoh gave a terrible croaking sob. Zohon held out the headless corpse, blood streaming, and Ozoh took it, and pressed it to his bare painted chest.

Zohon rose to his full height.

'From now on,' he said, 'you work for me.'

He looked through the open doorway at Kestrel, and smiled for her in the way he had smiled for the augur. He scuffed the toe of one boot sharply over the floor. The chicken's head came skittering over the planks to rest at Kestrel's feet.

Kestrel heard Ozoh sobbing quietly, as he stroked the little bundle of white feathers he held in his arms.

'Oh, my dove,' he was saying. 'Oh, my silky one.'

Zohon turned to stare at the augur.

'I expect to hear signs favouring my ambitions from now on,' he said. 'You will speak of the need for a strong leader. You will speak of the treachery of strangers. You will say that the purest love is found at home. Am I making myself clear?'

'Yes,' said Ozoh, bowing his head.

'You may go.'

Ozoh shuffled out of the carriage, with the remains of his chicken still clutched in his arms, its blood smeared over his turquoise-painted stomach.

Zohon turned his merciless gaze on Kestrel.

'I make a good friend,' he said, 'but a dangerous enemy.'

Kestrel knew he had meant her to see him kill Ozoh's chicken, to frighten her. He had succeeded. She had always thought him stupid, but now she thought him cruel as well as stupid. The combination frightened her very much.

'Why were you talking to Barzan?' he demanded.

'He was talking to me. I never went to him.'

'Why was Barzan talking to you?'

He swung his silver hammer back and forth, never taking his eyes off her.

'Because of you. He thinks you're showing an interest in me. He wants me to encourage you.'

'He thinks –!'

Suddenly he burst out into a peal of rich full laughter.

'He thinks I'm interested in you! Wonderful! What a fool the man is! Well, why not? Let him think it. Tell him I'm courting you. Tell him the great Zohon is lovesick for the Johdila's servant girl.'

He rocked with laughter at the thought.

'Well, well, well! I wasn't expecting that.' He calmed down, and became serious once more. 'What of the Johdila? Do you have a message for me?'

'Not quite a message,' said Kestrel.

She felt her cheeks begin to flush. She had prepared for this moment, but that was before she had seen Zohon's cruelty. She was glad to deceive him, but she feared for Sisi. Zohon interpreted her awkwardness differently.

'You mustn't be shy,' he said. 'Just tell me what she says.'

'The Johdila is afraid to speak,' said Kestrel. 'But to let you know her heart, she will give you . . .'

Again she hesitated. Then, with her eyes lowered, she went on,

'She will give you a secret sign.'

Zohon's eyes widened.

'A sign of her love! What is the sign?'

Kestrel slowly pressed the palms of her hands together, and slowly interclasped the fingers.

'The sign of eternal love.'

Zohon looked on Kestrel's clasped hands as if mesmerised. He drew a long sigh.

'The sign of eternal love,' he murmured. 'When will she show me this sign?'

'When she can. You must be patient. She is very frightened.'

'I understand. Tell the Johdila – tell Sisi – no harm will ever come to her. Tell her she is under the protection of the Hammer of Gang.'

He raised his silver hammer as he spoke. On its blade Kestrel saw the lingering stain of the chicken's blood.

12

Reward and punishment

Marius Semeon Ortiz climbed the wide stairs to the upper levels of the High Domain, forcing himself to maintain a dignified pace, though his heart was racing. From above he heard the sound of an orchestra playing, led by a virtuoso violin. A good sign: the Master only played when he was in a contented mood. Surely, thought Ortiz, the moment has come. The Master can't delay much longer. The wedding party was said to be only days away, and the Master had yet to name his son and heir.

Here in the great light-filled spaces beneath the jewelled domes, where no objects, no items of furniture, no curtains, no lamps, were permitted to interrupt the glowing emptiness, the huge figure of the Master was striding up and down, violin to his shoulder, bow sawing on the strings, leading his private orchestra and chorus. The musicians stood, their eyes on the Master, accompanying him from memory. The chorus waited in silence, their eyes also following the Master, all swivelling at once as he swept past them and back again. Over to one side stood two patient figures, one with a large book in his hands, the other with a bucket and mop. The man with the book was Meeron Graff, Keeper of the Master's

Household. The other was Spalian, the Master's personal servant.

The sweet chords of the strings gave way to sonorous brass, as the Master, lifting his bow, turned to greet his visitor. Striding down the cavernous space, eyes half-closed, bearded face uplifted, his bow now striking the air, the Master commanded great climbing flourishes of trumpets, and piled on mountain ranges of drumbeats, before returning to his own instrument, and with a breathtaking display of vaulting notes, drew the composition to a close in a mighty final chord.

Ortiz stood still and marvelled. The Master was bare-headed, his shaggy mane of white hair falling about his shoulders, his great grey eyes alight with the passion of the music. How often Ortiz had gazed on that noble face! In that generous brow he saw wisdom, in that great jutting nose he saw power of will, in those broad and ruddy cheeks he saw kindness. How old was the Master? No one knew. Perhaps sixty, perhaps more. He was as vigorous as ever, as strong in his appetites, and as loving. It was said that the Master had only to look into your eyes to know the secrets of your heart. But Ortiz had no secrets from him. He had been brought to the Mastery as a tiny child, after the death of his father. The Master was the only father he had ever known. Everything he did was done to win his approval and his love.

Now the last vibrations of the music died away, and the musicians lowered their instruments. The Master let his violin fall from his shoulder, and beckoned. Ortiz stepped forward, and prostrated himself on the floor before him.

'Up, boy! Up!'

Ortiz rose.

'You've done well.'

'To please you, Master.'

The Master nodded. 'Walk with me.'

He turned and strode over the echoing floor. This was how the Master was always to be found, pacing the upper levels, violin in hand, his eyes on the far mountains or the lake or the boundless sky. He hated crowds and silence, walls and stillness: so he was always in motion, always surrounded by great space. It was as if his outsize figure could not be contained in any ordinary room.

'Your new slaves are being well looked after?'

'Yes, Master.'

'Reward and punishment.'

'Yes, Master.'

'The Manth were a fine people once. A people of great gifts. And now . . . You should study history. It humbles us all.'

'Yes, Master.'

'After the cruelty, the kindness. At present they hate me. In time they will love me.'

'All your people love you, Master.'

'Of course they do. It's a natural human instinct, to love those in power. It needs very little encouragement.'

He was looking out of the wide windows at the city beyond. Two pigeons fluttered down to alight on a parapet outside. They were both silver-grey, but one had a white breast. The Master studied them with interest.

'You see the two birds out there? The white breast will fly away first. My dinner on it!'

He moved closer to the window and waved the bow of his violin. The pigeons took to the air, the white-breasted one in the lead. The Master boomed out a great laugh.

'There! I shall eat tonight after all!'

Ortiz said nothing. There were many things the Master did and said that he didn't understand. It was safer to make no comment.

'I lose as often as I win, you know? Not so long ago I lost five wagers in a row. Didn't eat for two days.'

He laughed again, and looked at Ortiz.

'Why do you think I do that?'

'To train your will, Master?'

'Not bad, not bad. I do it to keep myself in check. I have absolute power. No one can command me. Therefore I must command myself. I make my little wagers, and if I lose, I pay. How old are you?'

The personal question shot out without warning.

'Twenty-one, Master.'

'Do you think of marrying?'

Ortiz controlled the excitement that came surging up within him.

'Yes, Master. When the time is right.'

'The time? Not the person?'

'And the person, Master.'

'There is a royal party approaching our borders. The ruler of our neighbour empire has asked that our two countries be joined in marriage. He offers his daughter. I am to offer my son. You know all this?'

'Yes, Master.'

'It seems I am in need of a son.'

Suddenly the Master came to a dead stop. He reached out his violin and his bow for Meeron Graff to take, and bellowed,

'Stand clear!'

Ortiz stepped back. The Master hitched up his robes,

opened his britches, and urinated in a long powerful stream over the smooth stone floor.

'Aaah!' he said with evident satisfaction. 'One of life's unfailing pleasures. The summons so imperious, the release so sweet! Spalian!'

His servant had not waited to be called. Hardly had the Master finished emptying his bladder when Spalian was before him with bucket and mop. The members of the orchestra and chorus looked aside, pretending they had seen nothing. Within moments, the puddle on the floor was gone, the stone flags buffed clean and dry, and the Master had taken back his violin.

'A perfectly disgusting habit, isn't it?' he said to Ortiz, as Spalian departed to empty his bucket. 'Like an animal. Why do I do it?'

'Another of your ways to keep yourself in check, Master?'

'Very good. So it is. No one dares criticise me, you see. I must criticise myself. But for what? Everything I do, I do for the best. So – I piss on the floor! Disgusting! Like an animal! I'm ashamed of myself! Do you see?'

He threw his violin to his shoulder, and as if in illustration of his self-disgust, played a sequence of angry notes, chasing each other up the scale.

'I think so, Master,' said Ortiz.

The violin was lowered again.

'So where were we? Marriage. You'd better go and take a look at her. See if she'll do for you.'

'Master! Is it your wish – am I to assume –?'

'Well? What?'

'You yourself just said, Master, that you're in need of a son.'

'So I am. Someone must marry the girl.'

'And you think that I –?'

Ortiz couldn't bring himself to speak the words. The Master stared at him, eyebrows raised, waiting for the rest. Then he burst out laughing again.

'Yes, yes, I'm thinking of you, boy. Of course I am. But don't get too excited. I may name you as my son. You may marry the girl. But that doesn't mean you'll be Master after me. It takes more to do what I do than marrying a princess.'

'I know that, Master.'

'You're not big enough for that job. Not yet.'

He smiled affectionately at Ortiz, and slapped his own enormous belly.

'I shall grow, Master.'

'Good answer. Well, one step at a time, eh? Go and look at the girl. See if you can stand her. Then we'll decide.'

'Yes, Master.'

'Off you go, then! Brush up your tantaraza, eh?'

'Yes, Master!'

'And look after those Manth slaves. They'll serve us well.'

The Manth people, in their various places of work all over the Mastery, soon found that their skills were noticed, and put to good use. Scooch remained as a lowly dough-mixer for just one day. He was now established in his own pastry bakery, with three trainee assistants under him. Miko Mimilith the tailor worked up some garments that attracted attention, and now he was busy making a dress for a fine lady from the High Domain. He described his design to the others in the barracks.

'Just a simple sheath, but with a high neck, and a

train. There's a loop of material sewn to the train that she slips over her wrist, so that the train moves with her as she walks.'

He demonstrated, swaying slightly from side to side, exaggerating the movement of his hips, so that everyone laughed.

'Swish, swish, swish,' he said, to show the moving of the train.

Creoth was given charge of a small herd of milk cows.

'I know every one of them,' he declared, 'and I've given them all names. Whiteface, Tawny, Dreamer, Hop. Cherub, Angel, Cloud. Clumper, Stumper, Star . . .'

Mumpo had left them, to live at the training school. He was to make his debut at the manaxa to celebrate the coming wedding. Pinto missed him badly: all the more so because she was now made to go to school every day, and she didn't like it. The other children were happy enough, because they had been given a new exercise book each, and a new pencil-case, with four pencils in it, and an eraser and a ruler. The pencils were all beautifully sharpened. Dr Batch told them they were to keep them sharp, and he would inspect them every day. 'Dull pencils for dull writing,' he said. 'We want sharp pencils for sharp thoughts.'

Pinto hated having to sharpen her pencils, without quite knowing why. Her companions put it down to her being a Hath, and having a peculiar mother. Once more, as in the old days of Aramanth, the Hath family seemed to be out of step with the rest. Alone among the slaves, they were not settling down to their new life, nor were they taking advantage of the new opportunities.

Hanno Hath went on stacking books at the depository. Ira Hath refused to be moved to a more demanding job than laundry seamstress. She didn't speak of it to anyone, but she felt she was growing weaker. When she prophesied now, it was in a quieter voice. However, few people listened to her any more. They knew she only ever said the same thing.

'O unhappy people!' they told each other, mimicking her prophetess voice behind her back. 'Seek the homeland. The wind is rising!'

They laughed, and flapped their arms up and down, pretending her wind was blowing them away.

'It doesn't matter whether they listen or not,' said Hanno. 'What matters is that you prophesy. Let your voice be heard. If all they do is laugh at us, well, we can bear that, I think.'

Bowman too remained at his humble post as nightwatchman. Here as the cows grazed and later slept, watched by the silent grey cat who always accompanied him, he listened for Kestrel's slow approach and practised his secret powers. Ever since the visit of the hermit, he had known that he was destined to destroy the great power that ruled all their lives. So every night, alone in the pasture, he worked away at his mind control exercises as steadily as an athlete in training to run a champion's race.

One night while he was engaged in this way, he heard a voice calling to him from the darkness.

'Bowman! Are you there?'

'Yes. I'm here.'

A slight figure appeared, loping over the night-damp grass. It was Rufy Blesh. He joined Bowman in the circle of lamplight. He looked at the cat, and the sleeping cows, and the distant dark lake.

'This is what you do all night? Just sit here?'

'Yes.'

'Is this what you're going to do for the rest of your life?'

'I hope not.'

'Well, it is. Unless you do something about it.'

Bowman could feel the restless anger in him. Rufy was not a safe person to confide in.

'We have to wait, Rufy.'

'Wait for what? Wait for how long? Until we're all old? Aren't you ashamed of every single day you live here?'

'There's nothing we can do. You know how they punish us. You know the price we'd pay.'

'Yes, I know.' He became excited. 'Don't you see? That's how they make us enslave ourselves. I've been thinking about it, and there's only one answer. We can only ever escape by paying that price. A few will suffer, but the rest will go free.'

'Can you do that?' asked Bowman. 'I can't.'

'Why not? If this was a war, some of our people would die. Well, it is a war. Some of our people have died already. If we never fight back, what did they die for?'

'I can't do it, Rufy.'

'Then you've surrendered. You're defeated. You've truly become a slave.'

'I don't think so –'

'Yes! You have! You're as bad as all the rest. You've given up!'

'Rufy, I know they killed your mother –'

'This isn't about my mother! This is about me! She's dead. I'm not dead. I have all my life ahead of me. So have you, Bowman. I thought that you at least would want to fight back.'

'I do. But this isn't the time.'

'This isn't the time. Wait. Be patient. That's all I ever hear. But nobody ever does anything, and nothing ever changes.'

He jumped up, and suddenly held out his hand for Bowman to shake.

'Goodbye, Bowman. You're the best of them.'

Bowman shook his hand.

'Don't do anything rash, Rufy,' he said. 'Remember you're not alone.'

'In the end, we're all alone in this world. That's what I've learned.'

With that he walked off into the darkness.

Bowman looked after him, his mind full of troubled thoughts.

'I should have said more,' he said aloud. 'But what else is there to say?'

The grey cat stared back at him with reproachful eyes. Bowman had become so used to the cat's presence that he often spoke to it aloud, although this was really no more than a form of speaking to himself. Mist found this one-sided conversation particularly galling.

Bowman returned to his exercises.

'Watch this, cat! Watch the staff!'

Now he could lift his staff the way the one-eyed man had done, and make it come into his hand.

'Believe me,' said Mist, 'when you've seen one flying stick, you've seen them all.'

'These are the powers of the Singer people, cat. I'm going to be a Singer one day.'

'One day? How about now?'

'You look at me so oddly, cat. I wonder what you're thinking.'

'So why don't you try to find out?'

'I wonder if you understand every word I say.'

'Oh, spare me!'

'Raise one paw.'

Mist thought about it. On the one hand, the request was demeaning. Raise a paw, indeed. He wasn't a kitten. On the other hand, he had to find some way to make this child of the prophet work harder at their communication problem.

Yawning, to show he felt no kittenish eagerness to please, he raised one paw.

Bowman stared.

'You do understand me!'

'Wonderful! Now let's work on you understanding me.'

'Turn round in a circle.'

'Oh, please. I'm not going to lie on my back and wave my legs in the air, so don't even ask.'

Mist turned round in a slow dignified circle. Bowman looked down at him in silence for a few moments. Then he sank gently onto his knees.

'Forgive me if I've not shown you proper respect,' he said. 'There are so many things I don't understand.'

This was an improvement. Mist was almost touched. The boy's not as stupid as he looks, he thought. He approached him, tail raised high, and rubbed his body against the boy's legs, as a gesture of goodwill.

'If you'll be kind enough to come close to me, and sit still,' said Bowman, 'I'd like to know you better.'

Mist did as he was asked. The boy was so polite he could hardly refuse.

Bowman lowered himself onto his elbows and rested his forehead against the cat's face. At first Mist found this made his whiskers tickle, and he moved his head away.

But Bowman waited patiently, and they found a position in which both were comfortable, where the cat's brow was pressed to Bowman's right temple. Here they remained in silence for some time.

Bowman worked hard. First he cleared out his own mind. Then he sat in silence, seeking nothing at all. Then, very gently, he started to reach into the cat's mind.

He felt the cat flinch at the first intrusion.

'I won't hurt you,' he said.

Mist found the experience quite unlike anything he had ever known before. The hermit had simply been able to hear him. This was something else. As the boy had said, he was seeking to know him.

'Too fast,' the boy was saying. 'Slow down.'

Mist tried to slow down the race of impulses within him. It wasn't easy. His senses were constantly feeding him impressions, sounds, smells, flickers of movement, that kept him forever on the alert. Everything that was other than him was either danger or prey. All the time, even in sleep, his body was coiled like a spring, ready to hunt or flee. Slow down, the boy said. Not easy.

He tried to let his mind drift. Suddenly he fell into a memory, a sensation of close warmth, of small shrill sounds, of great joy. Above him in his memory the sky was moving, a sky that smelled sweet and felt warm. He wriggled his body, as it was wriggling in his memory, wanting to feel all round him those other wriggling bodies – and there it was! The full moment returned! He was lying on dry leaves in a sandy burrow, among his brothers and sisters, and his mother was moving her long body over him, and he was reaching up to suck. Startled by the intensity of the happiness the memory brought him, Mist nuzzled his head against Bowman's and whimpered aloud. Bowman found the memory, or at least, the way the cat felt it.

'There,' he said softly. 'There, there.'

Oh, you boy! said Mist to himself. What are you doing to me? I've been alone too long.

'Alone too long,' said Bowman.

He had heard.

'You heard me?'

'Yes. I heard you.'

'Oh, you boy! The hermit was right!'

Eagerly, gratefully, he licked Bowman's cheek and brow, tasting the sharp salty tang of human skin.

'Well now, cat. I've found you at last.'

'You're a dear boy. You're a fine boy.'

Mist went back to licking, astonished to hear himself. Anyone would think he was expressing affection. Of course, it was nothing more than an overflow from the memory, an echo of the emotions of his kittenhood.

'Have you come to tell me what I'm to do?' said Bowman.

'Yes,' said Mist.

'Then tell me.'

'You're to teach me to fly.'

Mist felt the boy's head move away, and saw the dark eyes looking at him with a quizzical expression. Then Bowman started to laugh.

'But I don't know how to fly.'

'It's just a matter of practice,' said the cat. 'And wanting it enough.'

But before they could pursue the subject further, a bell began to ring from the nearby village, the urgent clamour of an alarm. Soon other bells were joining in, and lights were being lit. Bowman jumped up.

'Something's happened.'

There were troops of grim-faced soldiers moving everywhere, searching with lanterns, checking the people out on the roads. Bowman was stopped three times on his way back to his slave quarters, and each time his brand number was examined and checked. Late though it was, he found everyone in the barracks awake, and gathered in anxious clusters. He soon learned what had caused the alarm. One of the slaves was missing.

The officials of the Mastery ordered a room check. But the word was already out. Pinto whispered to Bowman as he joined them.

'It's Rufy Blesh. He's run away.'

Clerks with ledgers moved up and down the lines of shivering slaves, checking off their names and numbers. Then they checked the kin group of the missing slave, and from the night's lists they identified which of the monkey wagons contained his relatives. The Greeths were cousins to the Bleshes. Pia Greeth, the young woman who had been betrothed on the last night before Aramanth was burned, was even now incarcerated in Cage Number Eleven.

'But they can't, can they? They wouldn't!'

The soldiers moved away down the road, following the chief clerk and his team. Behind them trailed the Manth slaves. To their horror, they found the guards already stacking extra firewood in the under-tray of the cage where Pia Greeth was held. Nearby an iron brazier burned red in the darkness.

The Hath family followed with the rest; and the grey cat loped along at Bowman's feet.

There were twenty men and women in Cage Number Eleven. Within a very short time, all their husbands and wives, parents and children, had gathered, fearful of the punishment. No official threat or announcement had been made. The guards were surely acting without instructions. Tanner Amos, holding his young wife's hands through the bars, was certain it would all end in nothing.

'They're just doing it to frighten us,' he said. 'They can't burn you all. You've done nothing wrong. It would be too cruel.'

Pia Greeth's father, Dr Greeth, arrived panting, and started shouting at the guards.

'Who's in charge here? Who's in authority?'

The guards paid him no attention. Dr Greeth saw the chief clerk standing to one side, looking at his ledger.

'Are you in charge here?'

'I don't know that I'm in charge,' said the chief clerk. 'I'm just here to make sure everything's done right.'

'Then you will tell these fools to leave the firewood alone. The people in the cage are innocent. They've made no attempt to escape.'

'There's been an escape,' said the chief clerk. 'Now there's to be a punishment. That's how it's done right.'

'No! It's not right! Where's the sense in punishing people who haven't done anything wrong?'

'Where's the sense in punishing people who *have* done something wrong?' said the chief clerk. 'That's too late, isn't it? They've already done it. No, punish people before they've done anything wrong, and then they won't do it, will they? You nip it in the bud. That's what the Master orders, and the Master's always right.'

Dr Greeth realised to his horror that the nightmare was really going to happen. Tanner Amos started to bang his fists against the bars. The chief clerk saw this, and called out loud so everyone could hear him.

'Any trouble, and another wagon will be burned.'

There was no trouble after that.

Bowman stood in silence with the rest; but alone among them, he knew he was not powerless. Now if ever was the time to use his secret strength. He fixed his mind on the burning brand that the guard was even now carrying from the brazier towards the cage. He gripped it, as he had gripped his staff in the night pasture, and he pulled hard. It jerked clean out of the guard's hand, and fell to the ground.

'Clumsy oaf!' said the chief clerk.

The brand was still burning. Puzzled by what had happened, the guard stooped down to pick it up. Bowman held the brand with his mind, and pulled it away, over the ground. The movement through the long damp grass doused the flame. The guard stared in bewilderment.

'What's the matter with you?' said the chief clerk.

'I'm not sure,' said the guard.

'Idiot! You!' The chief clerk pointed to a second guard. 'You do it. And don't drop it!'

The second guard pulled a burning branch from the brazier, and carried it towards the monkey cage. Once again, Bowman reached out to grasp it. But this time the guard was holding the branch firmly in both hands, and when Bowman tugged, he didn't let go. The struggle between them was short but intense. Bowman found he was strong enough to stop the guard moving the burning branch closer to the cage, but not strong enough to pull it from his grasp. For a few tense moments they strove with each other, the guard leaning forward as if against a strong wind, and Bowman pulling him back.

'Come and help me here!' shouted the guard.

Two of his companions, willing but bewildered, came alongside him and pushed. Bowman knew then that he couldn't hold them. He just wasn't strong enough. As soon as this certainty entered his mind, his power collapsed. The guards, suddenly released, tumbled forward, falling to the ground. But the branch was still burning. Now Bowman could do nothing but look on, helpless and exhausted, as they lit the firewood.

It caught quickly. The flames spread. The people in the cage climbed the bars. They started to scream. The guards went round the cage, banging their sticks at the fingers clinging to the bars, to make the people inside fall down into the fire. The onlookers, unable to help, sobbed and turned away. Bowman too turned away at last, bitterly aware of the cost of his failure. Only Tanner Amos never took his eyes off his young wife. Jessel Greeth knelt on the ground and howled like an animal. The screams of the dying grew louder for a while, and then quieter. The bright orange fire raged, lighting up the crossroads and all the wagons along the four ways.

No one, not even Tanner Amos, watched the horror to the end. One by one they knelt before the fire, and bowed their heads, and blocked their ears so as not to hear the sounds of the burning. There they stayed until the fire burned low, and the agony of their loved ones was over.

Jessel Greeth then rose up on unsteady legs, and trembling all over his body, he tottered over to Hanno Hath, his face contorted in bitter rage.

'You killed them!' he shrieked. 'You and your sick dreams! You made the Blesh boy run away! You filled his head with your lies! And now – look!'

'Don't hate me, Jessel,' said Hanno. 'Hate the Master.'

'I hate you!' screamed Dr Greeth. 'I blame you! We don't want you, and we don't want your poisonous dreams, and we don't want your mad wife!'

'Shut up!' shouted Pinto. 'Shut up! Shut up! Shut up!'

'Oh, yes, you've still got a daughter,' sobbed Dr Greeth, frantic with pain. 'There she is, spitting at me. But where's my daughter?'

'I'm more sorry than I can say –'

'I don't want you to be sorry! I want you to be punished! I want you to suffer as I'm suffering now!'

Hanno Hath saw the faces of the others, all looking at him with the same reproach in their eyes. He knew then there was nothing he could say.

'Come, my dear,' he said to his wife. In silence, he led his family back to their rooms.

Bowman followed, lost in self-punishing thoughts. Then he felt Pinto's arm creep through his, and he realised she was crying. He put an arm round her and hugged her close, and felt the torrents of fear and anger within her.

'It won't go on like this forever. I promise you.'

'Oh, Bo, I can't bear it! I hate being a child! I want to be grown-up, and strong, so I can do something. I feel so useless.'

'You're not useless. Every one of us has something we can do.'

'What am I to do?'

'I don't know. But our time will come. We must watch out for it. We'll know it when our time comes. Then the strength will be given to us, and we won't just have to stand and watch.'

Once in their room, they sat together on their beds and held hands.

'How much longer?' said Hanno.

'Not long now,' said Ira.

'All this will be destroyed,' said Bowman.

'How can it be?' said Pinto. 'How can we fight them? How can we hurt them? How can we destroy anything?'

In answer, Bowman took her exercise book and her new pencil-case from the end of her bed, and opened it on his lap. He fixed his mind on one of the pencils, and picked it up. His mother and father and sister watched in silent amazement. With a steady motion, he lifted the pencil over the exercise book, and set it in motion, looping round and round.

'That's how the Mastery will be destroyed.'

He held up the exercise book to show her what he had made the pencil draw. It was the curled-over S of the Singer people.

'Sirene,' said Hanno softly.

Pinto looked up and saw from her parents' faces that they understood this, and believed it, and the fear in her began to subside.

'Oh, my darling,' said Ira, kissing her son. 'You have a greater gift than me.'

Pinto crept her arms round her brother, and crawled onto his lap, wanting to feel him close.

'When will it end?' she asked him. 'When will the hurting end?'

Bowman held her in his arms, and remembered how she had been when she was little, so round and happy, and how she had looked up at him with her sunny face and said, 'Love Bo'. He was filled with a desire to make her happy again, so he rocked her in his arms, and told her his own dearest hopes.

'One day,' he said, 'we'll get to the homeland, which is

our own country, and we'll not go wandering any more. We'll build a town for our people, by a river that leads to a sea. We'll work hard all day, and at the end of the day we'll sit round a big table and eat our own good food and tell stories about how it used to be. You'll grow up, and maybe have children of your own, and they'll hear the stories too, about how we used to live in a great city, and then how we were slaves, and then how we searched and searched for our homeland. But to your children they'll only be stories, because they'll be so safe and happy sitting round that big table they won't be able to believe such frightening things could really have happened. They'll sit on your lap like you're sitting on my lap now and they'll say, "Weren't you terribly afraid, mama?" And you'll say, "I expect I was, my darling, but it was all long ago now, and I've almost forgotten."'

Hanno and Ira listened to him, and saw how he stroked his little sister and calmed her wounded spirit, and they were prouder of the love in him than of all the powers of Sirene.

'Thank you, Bo,' whispered Pinto.

'Thank you, Bo,' said his father.

Mist the cat had seen and heard it all. He had watched the burning with as much horror as any of the onlookers, and now from his position under the bed he heard Bowman's gentle words, and he too was soothed.

This boy of mine is a fine boy, he thought. A good boy. He will do great things. I've chosen well.

13

The Lost Testament

Hanno Hath was at work in the depository the next day, when Professor Fortz came for him.

'You!' he boomed. 'Time to find out how good you are at deciphering old Manth script.'

Hanno followed the professor on foot towards the lake. The slaves they passed were subdued, and avoided meeting their eyes, as if they had done something shameful. Because the ones who had died in the night were innocent, every one of the Manth people who remained unharmed felt guilty.

Professor Fortz noticed the familiar signs.

'I gather there was a burning last night,' he said. 'I hardly need say that it shocks me. All acts of barbarity shock me. On the other hand, the Great Library, which is the glory of our academy, is entirely filled with priceless manuscripts seized in acts of war. So what is one to think?'

He seemed not to require an answer. He was much shorter than Hanno, and wore a very wide-brimmed hat, so that all Hanno saw of him was a black circle bouncing along by his side, like a large beetle.

'It's the kind of dilemma that used to trouble me,' the professor went on. 'But I've found that moral scruples fade over time. The treasures, however, remain. If anything, they grow ever more precious. Our collection of old Manth texts is second to none. The pity is no one can read a word of them.'

Hanno realised he was to be taken into the High Domain. He followed the little professor onto the long causeway, wondering very much what he would find within the towering walls ahead. Professor Fortz was still talking: and suddenly his words caught and held Hanno's attention.

'It was the Master himself who wanted the old Manth collection,' he was saying. 'He has great respect for one of your people, a tribal elder or prophet known as Ira Manth.'

'The Master has heard of Ira Manth?'

'Yes, certainly. But even the Master can't read the old texts.'

Hanno's mind began to spin. How would the Master have come to know of the first prophet of the Manth people? Why would he care? Preoccupied with these thoughts, Hanno followed the little professor through a door in the gate, and down a long cloister-like passage; and so found he had arrived at the Great Library without taking in anything of the High Domain.

'This,' said Professor Fortz, 'is our rare documents archive. We keep all the manuscripts in excellent condition, which is yet another benefit of war. Many of them were mouldering and unread in their original homes. And here's the old Manth section. Take a seat.'

Hanno Hath took a seat at the wide table, and stared at the carefully-wrapped bundles being opened before him. As he looked, he felt his heart begin to hammer with excitement. Never in all his life had he dared to hope he would find such treasure.

'There! Make any sense to you?' The professor tossed manuscript after manuscript onto the table. 'There's another!'

'This is extraordinary,' marvelled Hanno. 'You have some of my people's most precious documents here.'

'What's precious about them?' boomed Fortz.

'We lost so much, in the tribal wars long ago,' said Hanno. 'We thought they were destroyed.'

'Well, you thought wrong. Now you can stop thinking, and copy them out in a form I can read. No one can read that wretched Manth scribble.'

Hanno sorted through the papers, eager to begin.

'Do you want them transcribed in any particular order?'

'How can I, when I don't know what's in them? Do try to think before you speak. So few people do these days.'

'Maybe I should start by listing the documents for you.'

'Do as you think best. Just get on with it. Let me know if you find anything of any significance.'

He then left Hanno alone. Hanno said nothing, but he knew already that he had found something of very great significance indeed. He had recognised it as soon as Professor Fortz had tossed the manuscript so carelessly onto the table.

It was the Lost Testament.

Bowman slept during the day, while the others worked. He was just waking when the soldiers came for him. He was alone in the barracks, but for the grey cat.

They checked his wrist number.

'Bowman Hath?'

'Yes.'

'Put your boots on and come with us.'

'Where to?'

'You're wanted.' They would say no more.

The early autumn dusk was already gathering as he followed the soldiers down the road to the lake. Ahead, where the causeway joined the shore, a man stood waiting. As they came near, Bowman saw that it was Marius Semeon Ortiz.

The soldiers saluted. Ortiz studied Bowman carefully.

'Yes, he's the one.'

He dismissed the soldiers with a wave of one hand.

'Come with me.'

He set off over the causeway towards the High Domain. Bowman accompanied him in silence. On either side lay the placid waters of the lake, reflecting the lights of the city. Above, stars were beginning to show in the evening sky. All was at peace.

'I picked you out on the march,' said Ortiz.

Bowman remained silent. He was trying to sense Ortiz's mood, so that he could prepare himself for whatever was to be done with him.

'You're a quiet one,' said Ortiz. 'I like that.'

They walked on. Bowman found the causeway was longer than it appeared from the land side. The walls of the High Domain grew ever more immense as they approached them. Behind, he heard the soft pad of the grey cat, following in the shadows.

'I find I need a servant for a particular duty,' said Ortiz. 'The task is not a menial one. I have chosen you. Are you willing to serve me?'

'Do I have a choice?'

'No.'

Bowman said no more.

'You don't ask the nature of the particular duty.'

'You'll tell me, when I need to know,' said Bowman. 'I must do it, whether I want to or not.'

Ortiz glanced at him, and for a few moments they went on in silence, their footsteps sounding softly on the boardwalk.

'You hate me, of course.'

'Yes,' said Bowman.

'I burned your city. I drove you from your home. I enslaved you. Why would you not hate me?'

They were now close to the great gates in the city walls. In one corner of the left gate there was a small door, of a size to admit people entering singly and on foot. Ortiz now rapped on this door. He turned his handsome young face to Bowman and said,

'But I'm also your liberator. I'm the man who has set your people free. One day you'll understand this.'

The small door opened from the inside. Bowman said nothing, but secretly he was astounded by what Ortiz had just said. He had assumed this brutal young warlord was no more than a fighting machine in the service of a cruel state. Now here he was speaking aloud the belief that he shared with his mother and father, but which even they had not dared to put so plainly: the destruction of Aramanth, and this time of enslavement with all its cruelties, was somehow necessary. The Manth people had to leave, in order to arrive. But where?

Ortiz had gone through the low door into the city. Bowman followed. The door closed again before the cat could reach it.

* * *

The first and strongest impression was the sound of music. From all sides came the jaunty melodies of fiddles, and the sweet lament of pipes, and the carolling of voices in song. It was the time of evening when the people have done with their day's work, and have not yet settled down to sleep; when night has fallen, but every lamp is shining. The clustered buildings that crowded the alleys before him all glowed from within, the soft lamp-light making the many-coloured glass with which the walls and roofs were set shine like jewels. Through and behind and before these splashes of red and amber moved the people of the High Domain, paying their evening calls, meeting in groups to talk or to dance, making music and singing. A sweet confusion of sound filled the air.

Bowman looked round in a daze. Could such cheerful kindly people know that across the lake, on the night just gone, others had been burned alive? If they knew, surely they would rise up in horror and overthrow the Master who commanded it. Ortiz was ahead, beckoning Bowman to follow him up the broadest alleyway. They passed a small food market, where stalls displayed sweet cakes and wines, outside the entrance to a tea house. From within the tea house came eager laughing voices, raised in debate. A little further on, the windows of an upper room were thrown open, and inside a choir could be heard practising a set of harmonies. Bowman heard the conductor rapping on his music stand, and calling out, 'Keep in time, please, ladies! Once more!' They passed a little piazza surrounded by lime trees, where old men sat playing chess in the night air. Beneath the arches of a covered arcade a dancing master was leading a class in an intricate series of steps. 'You must concentrate, please! Give your mind to your feet! Think with your toes!'

The alleyway opened up suddenly into a wide space, on the far side of which stood, or floated, an immense exquisite building, roofed by four domes. Each dome rested a little way above the next, with a poised lightness that seemed impossible in so great a structure; each fashioned out of a delicate filigree of stonework, each glazed in a different colour, pale gold and orange, rising to red and violet, so that the many lights within its different levels caused it to shimmer like a sunset sky.

'Oh!' said Bowman. 'How beautiful!'

Ortiz watched him, nodding with approval.

'This is how men were meant to live,' he said.

He led Bowman through arches into the great hall. Here, in the centre of the pillared space, a fountain played.

'Look at the fountain,' said Ortiz.

The fountain represented a platform of rocks on which stood a cage, all carved from the same single block of translucent grey-white marble. The door of the cage stood open, and from beneath it, up through its marble bars and out of its open marble door, there burst a rising gush of water. At the point where the arching water fell back to earth there hung three birds, seemingly sustained in midair by its power alone. Their wings were spread in upward flight, to show that they had just, mere moments ago, sprung from the imprisoning cage. The birds were carved from the very same block of pale stone, but the ribs of stone which supported them were concealed by the flow of water. The spray that broke beneath their wings created the illusion that they were in motion, forever on the point of flying free.

'The man who made that,' said Ortiz, 'had worked all his life as a stonemason before he came here. All he had ever cut was square blocks for buildings. And all that time, this was locked up inside him, waiting to be released.'

'Is he a slave here?' asked Bowman.

'Of course.' He gestured around him, at the great glowing vaulted space. 'Everything here is the work of artists. This whole city is a work of art. There's nothing like it in all the world.'

Bowman was awed, and confused.

'What's it all for?' he said.

'For us who live here. The Master says men were made to live in beauty.'

'Except for the slaves.'

'The beauty exists for the slaves as well. You're a slave. You feel it.'

He set off across the hall, followed by Bowman. On the far side, a series of arcaded passages led to a smaller hall, where several people sat on tiered seats watching a training session. Sixteen fighters from the manaxa school were being drilled by their trainer, in a display that was designed both to hone their skills and entertain spectators. The half-naked manacs glistened in the lamplight as they executed their crouching turns and sudden high springs, working in matched pairs.

Ortiz and Bowman lingered a few moments to watch.

'There's to be a festival manaxa on the day of the wedding,' said Ortiz.

'Will they kill each other?'

'It's possible.'

Bowman found it hard to believe that these graceful movements could be the prelude to brutal death. But he had seen it for himself. When the manacs entered the arena, they danced to kill. It was all part of the riddle that was the Mastery: beauty and slavery, civilisation and terror, dancing and death.

Suddenly Bowman realised he knew one of the manacs.

'That's Mumpo!'

'Don't call to him. He won't hear you.'

Bowman knew Mumpo had gone away to be trained: but how was it possible that so quickly he had been so changed?

'But it's Mumpo!'

Mumpo, whom he had known since he was five years old, whose nose had dribbled, who had always been at the bottom of the class, who had followed his sister Kestrel like a pet dog, who had grown tall but still spoke with that same slow look of bafflement – how could he have turned into this sleek dangerous manac, who was scissoring the air with his limbs just below him?

Ortiz knew none of this. But he did know how the Mastery found and exploited the talents of its captives.

'Everyone changes when they come here,' he said. 'Even you will change.'

He moved on, and Bowman followed.

Now they were in a passage off which opened many smaller halls. From each came the tap-tap-tap of dancing feet, and the brisk commands of dancing instructors. Ortiz paused outside one set of doors.

'I'm to have a lesson now,' he said. 'The dance called the tantaraza.'

'A dancing lesson?' It was all so unlikely. This soldier,

this conqueror, this destroyer, evidently cared how well he danced.

'The Master has taught us that we come closest to perfection in dance.'

He entered the room. A slender lady was waiting inside, talking quietly to two musicians, a pipe player and a drummer. She rose at once, and made Ortiz a delicate curtsey.

'My dance teacher, Madame Saez,' Ortiz told Bowman. 'How old do you think she is?'

Bowman hardly knew how to answer without giving offence. The lady wore a tight-fitting slip and light skirt, that revealed clearly a lissom body in its prime; but the lines on her neck and face told a different story.

'Under or over forty?' prompted Ortiz. The dance teacher dimpled with pleasure.

'Perhaps around forty?' said Bowman.

'She's sixty-eight!' Both Ortiz and the lady enjoyed Bowman's surprise.

'And I've never danced better in my life,' added the lady. 'But come, we have work to do. Remove your outer garments.'

Ortiz stripped off his cape and his jacket, and prepared to dance. Bowman realised that he was to watch. Ortiz had still said nothing to him about why he had singled him out, or what he was to do.

Madame Saez adopted the opening posture of the dance.

'Play! Acha!'

The musicians played, and the dancers danced. Bowman knew nothing of the tantaraza, but he could see at once that Ortiz was an excellent dancer, and extremely well practised in the steps. They spun and parted before him, following the intricate patterns of steps, slowly increasing in speed and variation, until –

'No, no, no!' The teacher stamped her elegant shoe in irritation. 'How is it possible that you miss that turn? If you truly know the tantaraza, such mistakes are unthinkable! You speak words in the order that makes sense, don't you? So dance the steps in the order that makes sense. Acha!'

The musicians began again at the beginning, and the dance unfolded once more. Bowman watched, and allowed his feeling mind to enter the dance. Without knowing anything of the steps, he could tell where the problem lay: the teacher was dancing without premeditation, as if her body was a spring that was unwinding of its own volition. Ortiz was dancing by following a script in his mind. Inevitably he was falling behind his partner, following where he should lead, if only by a fraction.

'Stop! Stop!' The lady was not pleased. 'You do not improve. You must take more care.'

'No,' said Bowman. 'He must be careless.'

Madame Saez stared at him.

'Well!' she said. 'You are the dance teacher now? I have been instructing pupils for nearly fifty years. But no doubt you know better.'

Ortiz was amused. 'He may be right, you know.'

'Careless, indeed! You will be precise. Exact. Perfect. When you leave my class you may be as sloppy as you choose, but here – precision! Acha!'

They danced again. Ortiz danced better. He had understood Bowman, even if his teacher had not. Against his will, Bowman felt himself warming towards Ortiz. That hawk-like face, that head of tawny hair, presently so absorbed in the complex dance, was like the Mastery itself: cruel, but beautiful. And harder yet to understand, Bowman sensed that his young master believed himself to be doing, to the best of his ability, what was right and good. There seemed to be no guilt in him when he let his eyes meet Bowman's eyes. As he danced, he seemed almost innocent.

Bowman himself did not feel innocent. He didn't know yet what duty he was to perform for Ortiz, but he sensed it would lead him to his greater duty. Beautiful though this city was, it must be destroyed. Bowman was certain of it. And somehow, he was to be the destroyer.

Hanno Hath sat at the library table, holding the brittle cream-coloured pages in his trembling hands, reading and re-reading the line of text that ran across the top of the first page:

For the child who bears my name, and must complete my work.

For generations, Manth scholars had known of the existence of the Lost Testament, but no record had ever been made of its contents. All that was known was who had written it, for whom, and why.

The author was the first prophet of their people, Ira Manth. It was known that he had written it for his seven-year-old granddaughter, who was also called Ira Manth. His purpose had been to leave an account of all that the prophet had learned. Some even said that the prophet had foretold the future of his people in the Lost Testament.

And here it was, on the table before him: a few small

sheets covered with line after line of carefully-penned old Manth script. Beneath the opening line, the blocks of handwriting were divided at irregular intervals by lines drawn across the entire page. These blocks were numbered, using the old Manth hand-signs, which counted in fives. At the end of the document the author had sketched the looped-over S that was the symbol of the Singer people. Hanno was astonished to see it on so early a document.

He steadied his hands to hold the paper to the light, as he read the first page.

The time of the consummation has come. Now I and those who have travelled with me must sing the song to the end. Out of our stillness, out of our love, out of our song, will come the wind on fire.

In the first generation after the consummation, there will be a time of kindness. In the second generation, the mor will rise, and there will be a time of action. In the third generation, the mor will fill the people, and there will be a time of cruelty. Then the song must be sung again.

I charge you, my child, to carry my knowledge through the time of peace, which is also the time of forgetting. Let the unwritten song be passed on to the next generation. Let there be singers. Let them live in stillness, and know the flame. They will lose all and give all. In the sweet moment before the consummation, they will be tossed in the storm of bliss. This shall be their reward.

14

Ortiz falls in love

When the great caravan of Gang reached the borders of the Mastery, it came to a halt. Here the seventy-seven carriages, the royal court, its officials, its servants, and its enormous retinue of guards, pitched camp and settled down to make final preparations for the wedding. There was a great deal to do. The bride's wedding dress must be taken out of its travel trunk and assembled. The Johanna's regalia must be polished. The ceremony must be rehearsed. And in general, everybody began to bustle about and become anxious.

Kestrel knew that she was now close to her brother, because the feeling of him came to her strong and clear: but she didn't realise just how close she was, until all at once, she heard his voice. She was in the Johdila's carriage with Sisi and Lunki when there came a flurry of moving air, a tingle of warmth, and then, far off but recognisable, Bowman calling to her.

Kess! I'm coming!

She stood absolutely still, and forced all other thoughts out of her mind.

Kess! I can feel you! You're there!

Yes, she called back to him. *I'm here!*

At once she felt a wave of joy flow out from him to

embrace her. She couldn't see him or hear him, but she sensed that he was coming nearer all the time. Her own dear brother was coming!

Are ma and pa –

All well! came the joyful reply.

Are you slaves? Are they hurting you?

Not free, he answered her. *But not hurt.*

Tell them I love them.

She wanted to cry, and knew he could feel it.

Love you, Kess. We'll all be together again soon.

Shortly after this a messenger arrived from the Mastery, to announce that a party was on its way to welcome the travellers. With them rode the bridegroom, the Master's son, coming to view the bride.

The Johdila received the news with fury.

'Coming to view the bride!' she exclaimed. 'What does he think I am? A menu? He can't pick and choose, you know.'

'Don't forget,' pointed out Kestrel, 'you will be veiled.'

'Oh, yes.' The Johdila had forgotten this. 'He can view me till his eyes pop, but he won't see me.'

'But you'll see him.'

'I will! Serve him right!'

'What if you don't like him?'

'I'll run away. Will you run away with me, darling? We'll live in the trees like squirrels, and never marry anybody. Or do squirrels get married?'

'Let's wait and see what happens. After all, who knows? Something may happen to stop the marriage taking place.'

Kestrel could feel Bowman coming closer all the time. She realised he must be riding with the bridegroom's party. This coincidence, that her brother was accompanying the bridegroom while she accompanied the bride, first astonished her, and then gave her renewed confidence. It couldn't be chance. Somehow, it must have been arranged. Someone was watching over them. And soon now, very soon, they would be in each other's arms –

No! They mustn't give each other away.

Bo! You're not to show you know me.

Don't worry. I won't.

He understood. Of course he understood: he always had.

Zohon came striding by, followed by a stream of armed men. He was engaged in positioning soldiers in hiding places on either side of the road. Kestrel saw this, and was disturbed. She sought out the Grand Vizier.

'Should the Johdila be better protected, sir? If there's to be fighting.'

'Fighting? What fighting?' exclaimed Barzan. 'This is a wedding party.'

'It's just that, when I saw the soldiers hiding in the bushes –'

'Soldiers hiding in bushes!'

This had the desired effect. Barzan stormed up to Zohon, and demanded to know what he was doing.

'Defending the Johanna,' replied Zohon curtly. 'If they think they can creep up on me, they'll learn their lesson soon enough.'

'They're not creeping anywhere, you great baboon! They're coming to view the bride!'

'How do we know that?'

'Because a messenger was sent to tell us.'

'They'd hardly send a messenger to say, "We're coming to attack your camp and kidnap the Johdila", would they? Really, Barzan, I do sometimes wonder if you're up to the job.'

'Kidnap the Johdila? What for? We're giving her to them!'

'We might be. And we might not. We might be only pretending to give them the Johdila, in order to spring a trap and attack their country.'

'But we're not!'

'They can't be sure of that. So they may decide to strike first. But I will strike before them!'

'You'll strike first, before they strike first?'

'Exactly!'

'How will you know they were ever going to strike first, if they haven't yet struck?'

'That is my skill, Barzan. That is why the Johjan Guards have been undefeated for the last five years, since I took command.'

'No it isn't. You've been undefeated for the last five years because we haven't had a war in the last five years.'

'Precisely! I think my point is made.'

'I think you're barking mad.'

Barzan went to the Johanna to protest against the arrangement of the guards.

'Don't you see, greatness? It strikes the wrong note entirely. The note of suspicion, and veiled aggression.'

'I don't know about that,' said the Johanna. 'They're fine-looking fellows, you know.'

'They're soldiers, gloriousness. Soldiers fight wars. We do not want a war.'

'Oh, poo poo, Barzan,' said the Johanna.

At the request of the Johdi, Ozoh the Wise held a special sign reading before the arrival of the bridegroom and his party. The royal augur, badly frightened by his encounter with Zohon, was now struggling to please both sides. He spun the sacred egg with trembling fingers.

'Oh! Ah!' he murmured as the egg came to rest.

'Well?' said the Johdi, who was becoming more anxious every day.

'You see for yourself, fragility! The egg is in Spong!'

'In Spong! Foofy, the egg is in Spong!'

'Well, well, my dear. If it is, then it is, you know.'

'In Spong,' said Ozoh, 'the blessings of peace are sustained by the flower of manhood.' Ozoh was pleased with this phrase, 'the flower of manhood'. It seemed to him that it showed an inclination towards the Johjan Guards, which would satisfy Zohon, but in a peace-loving way, which would satisfy Barzan.

'So will everything be all right?' fretted the Johdi.

'Where there is shadow, there must be light,' said the augur. 'Though the sun sets, it rises again.'

'That's quite right, you know,' said the Johanna, impressed and cheered.

Zohon's lookouts now shouted that the visitors had been sighted.

'To your places!' cried Barzan. 'Everyone in position!'

The courtiers and officials formed up in two angled lines, reaching out from the royal carriages in the shape of welcoming arms. The horn players raised their horns to their lips and waited for the signal. Zohon strode up and down, swinging his hammer with suppressed violence. The Johdila and Kestrel pressed close to the gauze-covered window of the carriage, each as eager, though for different reasons, to see the bridegroom's party arrive.

Then the horns sounded on the highway, followed by the horns on the approach track, followed by the horns in the camp itself. Into view rode a handsome and brightly-coloured group of young men, wearing cloaks that billowed behind them, over elaborately-embroidered tunics, with plumed hats on their heads.

'Peacocks!' sneered Zohon to himself as he saw them. 'I'll set them squawking before I'm done!'

Kestrel, peeping through the carriage window, recognised Ortiz at once. He rode in the lead, bareheaded, his thick tawny hair rippling in the breeze. He sat tall in the saddle, conscious that hundreds of eyes were now upon him, and slowed his horse down to a walk. Behind him came his gentleman companions. Behind them his servants. Kestrel looked on him, and felt her whole body stiffen. The memory swept through her so vividly that she could almost smell the burning houses and hear the screams: she saw again that arrogant face turning towards her, not seeing her, the cruel eyes reflecting the red and dancing flames that were destroying her home. This was her enemy. This was the one she had sworn to destroy.

'He's not so bad-looking,' said Sisi. 'And he's not at all old.'

'He's a murderer!' said Kestrel.

'Is he?' Sisi was surprised. 'How do you know?'

Kestrel longed to tell Sisi, but she didn't trust her not to blurt it out to all the court. For now, her secret was her power. So she replied,

'Look at his face. Don't you think he looks cruel?'

'Not especially. What does cruel look like?'

Now Ortiz had dismounted, and all his party were swinging down off their horses. The Johanna and the Johdi descended from their carriage, and the Grand Vizier presented the bridegroom to his royal master. Kestrel could feel Bowman's nearness, but still she couldn't see him. Then the gentlemen round Ortiz moved forward, clearing a space, and there he was, standing quietly at the back, holding Ortiz's horse. He looked just the same; if anything, a little smaller, frailer-seeming beside the big handsome horse. She knew he felt her too, but couldn't yet see her. A glow of happiness came over her as she gazed at him.

I can see you.

Where? Where are you?

His head turned this way and that, hunting her.

In the green and gold carriage, with the bride. We'll be coming out soon.

Now his eyes were turned directly towards her. But he couldn't see through the gauze-curtained window.

The formal introductions were over. The time for the viewing of the bride had come. Footsteps approached the Johdila's carriage.

'Lower your veil, pet,' murmured Lunki.

The door was opened from the outside. The Grand Vizier proclaimed,

'The Johdila Sirharasi, Pearl of Perfection, Radiance of the East, and the Delight of a Million Eyes!'

Sisi stepped out of her carriage, followed by Lunki and Kestrel. As soon as she was out, Kestrel felt Bowman's eyes on her, but she avoided looking at him. Her eyes on the ground, she went meekly behind the Johdila, as a good servant should.

The Johanna took Sisi's hand as she came up to him,

and held it tight. Now that this imposing young bride-groom had come to view Sisi, the Johanna found himself not wanting to let his little girl go.

'Speak, mightiness,' whispered Barzan.

'Oh, very well,' sighed the Johanna. So he raised his royal head and addressed his son-in-law to be.

'I present my beloved daughter. May she find favour in your eyes.'

Ortiz looked at the Johdila. He had not been told she would be veiled. Of course, this marriage was more in the nature of an alliance than a love match, but even so he couldn't help feeling cheated that he wasn't to see her face.

'My lady,' he said, making her a low bow.

A silence followed.

'It is our custom,' said the Grand Vizier, in case there was any misunderstanding, 'for the bride not to speak to the groom until she is married.'

'Oh,' said Ortiz, feeling even more cheated.

'Her first word to you will be the word which makes her your wife.'

'Ah,' said Ortiz.

He looked round, a little at a loss, frowning to conceal the fact; and so caught sight of Kestrel. The Johdila's young servant, as he presumed her to be, was standing just behind the Johdila, with her eyes cast modestly down, and unveiled. As he looked on her, it seemed to him that he recognised this young woman's face. He searched his memory, wondering where he could have met her before, not guessing that what was striking him was her resemblance to her twin brother.

Suddenly her eyes lifted, and met his. He saw a flash of recognition burn there, just for a moment. Then she looked down again. Ortiz felt a shudder of surprise go through him.

At exactly the same time, Sisi had discovered, standing some way behind her husband to be, a slight young man with a pale face and big dark eyes. The young man was gazing steadily, not at her, but at Kestrel. As she looked at him, his eyes moved to rest on her. Because she was veiled, she was able to gaze directly into his eyes, and he couldn't tell that she was looking back. She found those dark eyes fascinating. There was so much quietness in them, and so much understanding. She realised then that most men's gaze was rough and bossy, as if their eyes were forever trying to force something onto her; whereas this gaze was gentle, receptive, kind.

Bowman, for his part, longed with all his being for one look from Kestrel. He understood that they must not give themselves away, and had made no attempt to reach out to her with his mind. But the temptation to catch her eye was too strong. He turned his gaze from the veiled princess back to his beloved sister, and just at that moment she looked up, and their eyes met. For a fraction of a second, they told each other through their eyes all there was to be said: all their love, all their deep gladness that they were both safe, all their gratitude that they were near each other again. Bowman longed with a terrible aching longing to run into her arms, to feel her touch, as he had done every day of his life, until the coming of the Mastery. But he never moved so much as a finger, and almost as soon as their eyes met, the look was broken again.

Not before Sisi had seen it all. The look in Bowman's eyes was unmistakable. He knew Kestrel! At once, gazing on him with this clue to help her, Sisi saw the resemblance. This must be Kestrel's brother! Secretly excited, she now studied him all over again. He was not as tall as she had hoped, nor did he look strong; but his face was so interesting. It kept changing. He didn't laugh the way Kestrel laughed, but then there was nothing here to laugh at. He seemed not to know what he was supposed to do. Sisi liked him for that, because she didn't know what she was supposed to do either.

She felt a pinch on her arm.

'Make your respects.' It was her mother, whispering. 'Return to your carriage.'

The Johdila did as she was told. Kestrel and Lunki followed behind. As soon as they were back in the carriage, Sisi sent Lunki out on an errand, and turned eagerly to her friend.

'I saw him! He's your brother! He is, he is, I know it!'

Kestrel's confusion gave her away.

'Please,' she said. 'You mustn't tell anyone.'

'Oh no, I won't, darling! It'll be our secret. But you have to let me meet him.'

'What for?'

'So I can marry him, of course! You have to meet people you're going to marry.'

'You're not marrying my brother, Sisi.'

'I am so. He's sweet.'

'You're marrying that – that –'

'That murderer, you called him.'

'Well, so he is.'

'I like your brother better.'

'You're to forget about my brother. No one's to know he's my brother.'

'Why? I don't understand. Why can't we just send for him to come and visit us? Don't you want to see him?'

Reluctantly, Kestrel realised she would have to explain, at least in part.

'He's a slave, Sisi. So are all my family. I'm looking for a way to help them escape.'

'Kess, how simply thrilling! What way?'

'I don't know yet.'

'I have an idea! I'll ask the Master to give them to me, as a wedding present.'

Kestrel was touched. She smiled, but shook her head.

'It's not just my family. It's my people.'

'How many is that?'

'Thousands and thousands.'

'Oh.' Sisi was dismayed. 'That's too many, Kess. You'll never find a way for thousands to escape.'

'Yes, I will. I want to, and I have to, and I will!'

Her fierce determination thrilled the Johdila.

'I expect you will, too, Kess,' she said. Then, with sudden dismay, 'But what will happen to me? I'll have to marry the murderer, won't I?'

'Who knows? No one ever knows what will happen until it happens.'

But Kestrel had no intention of waiting for some unknown fate to intervene. Now that she had seen Bowman, now that they could communicate, she was determined to carry out her plan to the end. All the necessary pieces were falling into place. She and Bowman, working together, could do anything. And as for Sisi – she preferred not to think about Sisi. The unfortunate fact was she was growing fond of her. She had thought at first that Sisi was stupid, but now she realised she was simply ignorant. If anyone was stupid, it was Zohon. She had laughed at him to start with, but now she knew that a vain and stupid man with a sharp knife is not funny at all. How could she deliver Sisi into the clutches of a man like that? But would she be any better off with the murderer Ortiz, to whom her family were selling her? So Kestrel resolved to pursue her plan whatever the consequences, and to trust to the inspiration of the moment to save Sisi.

Marius Semeon Ortiz rode back to the High Domain in a thoughtful silence. His mind was on the young woman who had attended the Johdila. She wasn't what anyone would call beautiful, but there was something about her that was hard to forget. What was it? A directness of manner, a boldness in her eyes, even a touch of wild-ness. And the mouth – he imagined that mouth smiling. He imagined the lips forming into a kiss. He imagined kissing – With a start, he forced himself to break off such a ridiculous train of thought. If his circumstances had been different, he might perhaps have sought to know the young stranger better. But his duty lay clear before him. He would marry the Johdila, and so bring the immense Sovereignty of Gang under the Master's control. The Master would be proud of him, and would make him his heir. In time, all the power and wealth of the Mastery would be his.

He gazed down the gentle sloping land towards the lake, and the city-palace that rose from its waters. In just a few short days now he would be married. His bride, the Johdila Sirharasi of Gang, would come to live with him in his beautiful rooms. Her servants would come with her. The fascinating young woman with the dark eyes would have a bed under his roof. He would pass her in the passages. Her eyes would look up and meet his. Her arm would brush against his arm. He would turn, to find she had also turned, and was looking at him. He would reach out a hand, draw her close, kiss her neck, her cheeks, her lips –

Boomba-boomba-boomba – The horses' hooves clattered over the timbers of the causeway. Ortiz blinked, roused from his daydream.

What's happened to me, he thought in alarm? I don't know this young woman's name. I've not spoken a word to her. I've looked at her once, for barely a second. It's ridiculous, impossible, and untrue, to suppose that I've fallen in love.

Fallen in love!

The words alone, spoken only in his head, made him tremble with delight. Fallen in love? Of course not! Fallen in love? It was out of the question. How could the heir to the Mastery ride out to view his future bride, and fall in love with the wrong woman?

15

The secret of the Mastery

Bowman rode back with his master to the High Domain, eager for the first opportunity to return to his family. Ortiz had required him to remain in the city-palace overnight, allocating for his use a room more suited to a friend than a servant; but he had still not told Bowman what his particular duties were to be. He treated him with courtesy, and sought his assistance as if he were asking a favour rather than giving an order. Therefore Bowman hoped he would grant his urgent request.

However, once back in his quarters, Ortiz dismissed all the others, and asked Bowman to stay. He beckoned him to join him on his private terrace. Here, where a fine view of the city was laid out before him, Ortiz was accustomed to come when he wanted to reflect.

Bowman was just preparing to make his request when Ortiz said abruptly,

'What did you think of my bride?'

'Your bride?'

'Her beauty? The sweetness of her voice? Her temper, her manner, her understanding?'

'But – she was veiled. She never spoke.'

'Exactly.'

'Sir –'

'What is marriage?' Ortiz was talking as much to himself as to Bowman, driven by confused currents within himself. 'An arrangement, nothing more. Not love. Not even happiness. Only a fool expects to love his wife.'

Bowman hardly knew how to respond to this, so he kept silent.

'So you see, love has nothing whatsoever to do with this marriage. The wedding proceeds as planned. Business as usual. I can tell the Master that I am perfectly satisfied. Is that clear?'

'Yes, sir.' Bowman had been so full of thoughts of his sister that he had not been paying close attention to Ortiz. He now realised he had no idea what was going on inside his young master.

'I suppose you wonder what I'm talking about.'

'Yes, sir.'

'I'm talking about nonsense, about moonshine, about dreams and shadows. Look!' He gestured over the glowing domes of the city. 'Has there ever been so beautiful a city? Have men ever lived so well? This is real, this is lasting. Not some fleeting glimpse of how it might be to – to – what? To be interested in another person? To catch their eye? To hope for an answering smile?'

He turned an eager face to Bowman's, and Bowman caught the excitement of his feelings. Like all lovers, Ortiz was overwhelmed by an impulse to share his emotion with someone else.

'I can talk to you, can't I? You understand me, at least a little, don't you?'

'Yes,' said Bowman; beginning, belatedly, to investigate.

'One look! Isn't it absurd? How can so little lead on to so much? I feel as if I've peeped through a tiny hole in a door, a pinhole, and seen on the other side – myself, leading a different life.'

Bowman was thinking fast. This burst of passion could not have been prompted by the veiled Johdila Sirharasi.

'One look from a pair of dark eyes!' said Ortiz with a sigh.

Now Bowman was there.

'The Johdila's servant?'

'Ah! You saw her too?'

'Yes. I saw her.'

'I tell you, if I wasn't about to be married, I would hope – I would ask – I would wish – to know her better.'

Bowman's mind explored this new development. Somehow, he was sure, he should be able to turn it to the advantage of his enslaved people.

'You don't have to go through with the marriage,' he suggested.

'It's the Master's wish.'

'You don't have to do everything the Master wants.'

Ortiz turned to stare at Bowman.

'I don't have to –? Of course, I'm forgetting. You're new here. You don't yet understand. This –' a sweep of one hand over the view, 'this perfect world is the Master's creation. It exists and prospers because we do his will.'

'A perfect world for you,' said Bowman. 'Not for the slaves.'

Ortiz looked at him again, in an odd sort of way.

'Are you sure about that?' he said. 'Don't the slaves of the Mastery live well? In comfort and safety? Don't they do good work here, their best work, and grow fat and rich and well-respected? What more can any man want?'

'To be free.'

'Why?'

'Why?' Bowman was taken aback. 'Everyone wants to be free.'

'Everyone wants? Like everyone wants chocolates? It's not always good to be given what we want, is it?'

'No, but – but freedom is –'

Bowman began to feel confused.

'Freedom is what?' said Ortiz. 'I'll tell you. Freedom is vanity. Freedom is greed. It sets man against man. It makes savages of us all. The Master has shown us the terrible cruelty of freedom.'

It was madness, but Ortiz seemed to believe it, and with conviction. Bowman forgot for the moment that he was a slave, and that this was a man who had power over him.

'I've seen cruelty,' he said, letting the anger into his voice. 'I've seen innocent people burned alive.'

'Of course! Every one of us here has seen that! But that's not cruelty. That's terror. A single act of terror forces obedience. Without obedience, there's chaos. With obedience comes peace and order. First we obey in terror. Later we obey in love. The Master has taught us so. And this rich and beautiful world is our reward.'

Once again Bowman said,

'For you. Not for the slaves.'

Ortiz then reached out his right arm before Bowman, and in silence, drew back the rich fabric of his sleeve. There on his wrist was a branded number.

'We're all slaves here,' he said. 'That's the secret of the Mastery.'

Bowman stared.

'All?'

'All but one. The Master bears the burden of freedom for us all.'

Bowman looked from Ortiz to the view of the city, and the lake, and the well-tended fields beyond. He saw farm workers following the plough. A team of wagons plodding down the road. A troop of chasseurs trotting briskly over the causeway. He recalled the young lords in Ortiz's party, and the dance teacher; the manacs, and the choirs singing in the dusk. All slaves?

'Are you telling me that we're slaves of slaves?'

'Yes.'

The view from the terrace seemed to lurch and spin round him.

'Then why don't the slaves rise up? Why don't they rebel?'

'First we obey in terror. Then we obey in love.'

'I don't understand.'

'It takes time. You're new. But little by little, you'll come to see all that you've gained from your loss of freedom. This country will become your country. You'll help to build it. You'll become proud of it. You'll see how we all serve each other, because there's only one Master. And so your fear will turn to love.'

'I will never love the Master.'

'You will! You think you won't now, but you will!' A sudden idea came to him. 'I'll take you to meet him. I have to report on my viewing of the bride. You shall come too.'

'Not now. Tomorrow. Let me go back to my family tonight. They'll be worrying about me.'

'No, now, now! At once!'

'You want the Master to know about your new interest?'

'My new –? No, not at all! Is it so obvious?'

'It is.'

This calmed Ortiz down.

'Maybe you're right. Maybe a night's sleep will settle

me a little. I do feel strange, and – and unlike myself. Yes, very well. Go back to your family. I'll send for you in the morning.'

Mist the cat was waiting for Bowman on the causeway.

'Have you been here all night?' asked Bowman.

'Here and there,' said the cat, not liking the note of pity in the boy's voice.

'You should go home,' said Bowman. 'There's going to be trouble here.'

'There's trouble everywhere. Also, I don't have a home.' He ran beside Bowman, who was walking fast. 'When are you going to teach me to fly?'

'I told you. I don't know how to fly.'

'If Dogface can fly, you can fly,' said Mist. 'You're just not trying.'

'I'm sorry. I have more important things to do.'

'More important?' Mist came to a stop. 'I can always teach myself, you know.'

Bowman hurried on, and this time the cat did not follow him. He was angry at what he saw as the boy's selfishness, and lack of ambition. His pride was offended that the boy thought so little of him. But then it struck him that perhaps he really could teach himself to fly. He'd watched the boy practising with the stick. It had been largely a matter of concentration. Why shouldn't flying be the same?

He looked round for a suitable spot to start practising: somewhere to jump off, but not too high, so that he wouldn't hurt himself while he was learning. His eyes followed Bowman up the road, and came to rest on the tall wheeled cages called monkey wagons.

* * *

Bowman found his parents sitting alone in their barracks room, deep in quiet conversation. His father had a sheaf of paper in his hand.

'Bo!' cried his mother as soon as he entered. 'Shut the door. Your father needs to talk to you. Oh, we are unhappy people indeed.'

'No, no,' said Hanno. 'It'll all turn out well in the end. There's nothing to say it won't.'

'First I have news for you,' said Bowman. He sat down on the bed and took his mother's hands in his and squeezed them. 'I've seen Kestrel.'

'Oh, my dear.' Tears welled up in Ira Hath's eyes. 'My darling child! Is she all right?'

'Alive and well.'

'Where is she?' asked Hanno.

'She's with the wedding party that's just arrived. A princess has come to marry the Master's son, the one called Ortiz.'

'The one who sent for you?'

'Yes.'

'Did you speak to her?' asked Ira. 'What does she say? How does she come to be with these people?'

'We couldn't speak much. She doesn't want to be found out. She's a servant of the bride.'

'Servant of the bride?' Ira Hath was bewildered. 'I want to go to her. I want to see her.'

Hanno Hath had already taken in the possible advantages of the situation.

'Leave her alone, my dear. She doesn't want to be given away. I'm sure she has something in mind. Did she tell you, Bo?'

'No. Not yet.'

'You must try to meet her alone. Are they far from here?'

'Not so far. And pa –' Bowman was eager to tell all he had discovered that day, 'the people in this country, the lords and the ladies even, they're all slaves! It's a country of slaves!'

'All slaves!' said his mother. 'That's ridiculous. How can you have slaves of slaves?'

'That's how it works. They're all slaves except the Master. They all do what he says.'

'Do they now?' Hanno Hath didn't seem as surprised as Bowman had expected. 'The Master must be a remarkable man.'

'I'm to meet him tomorrow.'

'You're to meet the Master?'

'With Ortiz.'

'The Master puzzles me very much,' said Hanno thoughtfully. 'He collects old Manth manuscripts. He's said to know something about our prophet Ira Manth. It's good that you're to meet him. Tell me what you find.'

'What should I look for?'

'I don't know.' He shook his head, annoyed with himself that he couldn't find the hidden connection. 'When is this wedding?'

'Very soon. Just a few days, I think.'

'We have so little time.'

He gave Bowman some of the sheets of paper he was holding. They were covered in his handwriting, scribbled at great speed.

'There are things you too must know.'

'Oh, my darling boy!' Ira Hath put her arms round Bowman, as if he would soon be taken from her. Bowman let his eyes run over the writing, as he listened to his father's quiet steady voice.

'I've found the Lost Testament of Ira Manth. It tells us many things, and when we have time we'll talk over all of them. But there's one part that affects us all now, and you and Kestrel and Pinto most of all.'

Bowman looked up and saw that his father was smiling at him. That smile told Bowman there was a great sadness coming. His mother stroked his hands.

'We spoke before about the Singer people. I understand now their full purpose, and the price they pay to achieve it.'

'They protect us from the Morah.'

'More than that. They, and they alone, have the power to destroy the Morah. But in doing so, they die.'

'They die? And the Morah dies?'

'And returns again. As the Singer people return. Read.'

Bowman read aloud the first lines of his father's handwritten transcript.

A child of my children will always be with you at the time of the consummation. In this way I live again, and I die again.

'I never asked for this, my darling,' said Ira, kissing him. 'All I ever wanted was for us to be an ordinary family, leading an ordinary life.'

'You mustn't mind, ma,' said Bowman gently. 'Not for me. I think I've always known.'

'Known what, my Bo?'

'That there's something I'm to do. Something waiting for me. Something that makes sense of being the way I am.'

'You may well be right,' said his father quietly.

Hanno then explained as best as he could what he had learned from the newly-discovered manuscript. It seemed that the old Manth people had a name for the vital force in all living creatures, and this name was *mor*. They understood that the *mor* was a good and necessary energising power, that drove people to do their best, to work hard, to aspire to make their dreams come true. To the old Manth people, the *mor* was the source of courage, and honour, and worthy pride. However, this same noble power, when allowed to grow too strong in a man or in a people, turned courage into violence, and pride into anger. As the *mor* swelled, it empowered the people, but it also led them into conflict with each other. They made war, and learned to fear and hate, and the more they feared and hated, the more they called on the power they believed would protect them. In this way, the time came when the *mor* filled every person to the brim, and bursting the skin that separates one from another, it merged into a single force, that fed on itself and all its member people, and could never thereafter be destroyed. This great, terrible, united power was called the Morah.

Bowman knew it all, even as his father told him of things he had never known. Had he not been touched by the Morah?

One of many, part of all. No more fear now. Let others fear.

'Ira Manth speaks of three generations,' said Hanno. 'A time of kindness. A time of action. And a time of cruelty. At the end of the third generation, the power of the Morah is at its height. Terror follows terror, as men forget how to love, and are driven to rule or be ruled, to kill or be killed. At such a time, the Singer people return.'

'And die.'

Hanno nodded his head. Bowman understood.

'We're living in such a time now, aren't we?'

'I believe so,' said Hanno.

'I know so,' said Ira, shuddering. 'The wind is rising. We must reach the homeland. The wind will blow everything away.'

Bowman did not speak. How could he explain to his parents that more than anything else he felt deep within him a sweet relief? He felt as if at last everything that was strange in him, everything that made him solitary and apart, was now part of his true purpose. He had to be as he was, to do as he must do. Even his failure all those years ago in the halls of the Morah, when he had surrendered to that sweet deadly power; even that, for which he had so long blamed himself, now became part of his destiny. In his fear, he had let the Morah touch him and possess him. Now he was grown older, and the time was approaching when he would redeem himself.

He read once more the first line of the transcript.

A child of my children will always be with you at the time of the consummation.

Hanno looked at him searchingly.

'I'll be with them, pa.'

'No!' cried Ira. 'My own boy!'

'Don't cry, mama. I'm happy. It's what I've been waiting for.'

'What will they do to you, my darling? What is this wind on fire?'

'I don't know. I need to have a little time on my own. Let me read. Let me think.'

'Yes, darling.'

She let him go. As he slipped out of the room, she looked after him with awe, as if he were her child no longer.

'What will happen, Hanno? What are we to do?'

'Our task, my dear,' he said, 'is to prepare our people. Somehow they must be persuaded that this powerful, rich and beautiful country can never be their home.'

'They don't listen to me any more.'

'Even so, we must prepare them. The time of cruelty is coming. They'll listen to us then.'

Let them live in the stillness, and know the flame. They will lose all and give all.

Bowman read all that his father had been able to copy from the Lost Testament, and then he read it again, until the last light faded from the sky. Then he took the papers back to his father.

'I'm going to find Kess,' he said.

'Be very careful,' said his father. 'If anyone sees you –'

The slaves were under orders to stay in their quarters at night. Everyone knew the punishment for disobedience.

'No one will see me.'

He spoke with such confidence that Hanno said no more. Bowman was changing fast. The discovery of what he believed to be his destiny had unlocked something within him, and suddenly he felt there was nothing he couldn't do. Hadn't the man with one eye, the Singer, told him he had the power? His great task, he knew, was yet to come: the time when he would lose all and give all. Between now and then, what could hurt him?

He waited until all the lights in the High Domain were extinguished, and the land lay silent in the night. Then he set off on foot, following the road back up the hillside and into the trees, towards the encampment on the borders of the Mastery. He walked fast, treading lightly, making almost no sounds. His mind reached ahead towards Kestrel. He thought of how it would be when she came out to meet him, how they would hug each other –

'Stop right there!'

Bowman froze. A tall Johjan Guard strode forward, his sword raised. Bowman cursed himself. Why had he not guessed there would be sentries?

The guard glared at him.

'Come with me!' he barked, reaching out his left hand to take hold of Bowman.

Bowman took a step back, raised his eyes to the guard, concentrated all his energies on the man's forehead, and – struck. His own body remained perfectly still, but the blow landed with such force that the guard was sent sprawling backwards, onto the ground. There he lay, unmoving, stunned. Bowman felt a little giddy. He hadn't lifted a finger. He hadn't thought about what he was doing, or how he was to do it. In the urgency of the moment, he had struck in the only way he could. What was it the one-eyed man had said? *It's just a matter of wanting it enough.*

He felt a rush of exultation sing through his body. His power was growing! This was more than lifting pencils: he had stunned a man twice his size. If he wanted, he could do more, and worse: he felt it in him now, like a young wolf that has tasted its first blood. He could send great pain. He could kill.

What am I thinking?

He forced himself back to the reality of the moment. Ahead lay the great encampment, where soldiers and courtiers slept in lines of tents and carriages. Kestrel was there. He must find her.

Moving softly, alert now for other sentries, he crept past the tents, careful not to trip on the guy-ropes. He could feel his sister, he could hear the quiet rhythm of her breathing as she slept.

Now he was come to the cluster of royal carriages. In the darkness of night there was no way to tell one from another, but he could have found his way with his eyes shut. He came to a stop before the Johdila's carriage, and very gently reached out with his mind to wake his sister.

Kess . . .

He felt her stir, and climb sleepily out of her dreams.

Is that you, Bo?

Then she was wide awake. He couldn't see her, but he was tracking every single move she made. She was sitting up now. She was looking across at the sleeping Johdila.

I'm outside.

Now she was pulling on a robe over her nightclothes, and feeling under her cot for her slippers. Now, treading lightly, she was passing down the carriage to the door. Now the door was opening.

She flew down the carriage steps and into his arms. He held her tight and close, feeling her heart beat by his, and pressed his cheek to her cheek, first on one side, then on the other. Then he pressed his brow to her brow. In silence of voice and mind, they remained like this, arms wrapped tight round each other, for many long minutes. They had been cut in half, and now were becoming whole again.

Then they parted, and held hands, and looked deep into each other's eyes.

You've changed, my brother.

In answer, he let her feel the new power that was growing in him: letting his mind press against hers. She reeled back.

'How do you do that?'

'Hush! Speak softly. I don't know.'

He drew her away into the trees, where they could talk without fear of waking anybody. Even so, they dared not stay together long. There were other sentries, who might pass close enough to see them. If Bowman were sent back to the Mastery under guard, accused of spying, the fires would be lit again beneath the monkey wagons.

Kestrel heard of the Mastery's ways of enforcing obedience with anger.

'They're monsters! I'm going to kill them all!'

'We will, Kess. We're going to destroy them.'

Kestrel marvelled that her gentle brother could say such things. What had changed him? There was so much to ask, so much to tell, and so little time.

'I know how we can do it,' she said. Speaking rapidly, she told Bowman about Zohon and his ambitions. 'He doesn't want this marriage. He'll use his army to stop it. He wants the Johdila for himself.'

'Everyone fears the Mastery. Are you sure this Zohon will make a fight of it?'

'I know how to make him sure.'

'We have to get all our people away together. If any are left behind, they'll be killed.'

'When the fighting starts, that's our chance. But our people must be ready.'

'They will be.'

Bowman took her hands and squeezed them. He was sure now. Together, they could do anything.

'Kess, there's more you need to know –'

But just then they heard a soft voice calling from the camp.

'Kestrel! Where are you, Kess?'

'The Johdila! You must go! Don't let her see you!'

Bowman gave her one last quick hug, and slipped away through the trees. The Johdila appeared from the other direction just in time to catch a glimpse of his shadowy departing form.

'It's him, isn't it?'

'Hush!' said Kestrel. 'You should be asleep.'

'Call him back, Kess. I want to meet him.'

'Not now. Nobody must know. It's our secret.'

'Why did he come? What did he want? Did he want to see me? Did he ask about me?'

Kestrel led the Johdila back to her carriage, doing what she could to calm her excited spirits.

'He came to see me. We've missed each other very much.'

'Yes, I do see that, darling. But he's seen you before hundreds of times, and he's never seen me at all. I really do think it's my turn, you know.'

'Maybe soon. But now we must both go back to sleep. Who knows what tomorrow may bring?'

16

Master! Father!

Bowman reported to his master, Marius Semeon Ortiz, early the next morning. The streets of the High Domain were awash with water, as they were hosed down and swept clean for the coming day. Ortiz himself was bright and eager, full of nervous tension.

'The Master has sent for me! We'll set out right away. This is a great, great day for me. You'll say nothing about my little fancy of yesterday, will you?'

'No, sir.'

'All nonsense, of course. A whim of the moment. I've hardly given her a single thought since I woke this morning. The first rule is, obey the Master. Then everything else works itself out. You'll see.'

He led Bowman out onto the gleaming street.

'By the way,' he said, 'if you don't agree with anything I say, you're to speak up. The Master teaches us that those in power quickly lose touch with how matters really are. No one will tell them the truth, you see. Everyone tells them what they think they want to hear.'

He stopped and turned his handsome face to Bowman with a smile.

'I never did tell you your particular duties, did I?

You're to be my truth-teller. I picked you out on the march. It seems to me you go your own way. Was I right?'

Bowman was very surprised, and a little impressed. This eager young warlord became more complicated all the time.

'For example,' said Ortiz, 'when I say I've not given a moment's thought since I woke up to a certain pair of dark eyes, you as my truth-teller might reply, then why do you speak of her now? Do you see? I offer that merely as an example.'

'What if the truth I tell is painful, or dangerous?'

'Dangerous how?'

'Suppose I were to tell you I was going to kill you.'

'Going to kill me?' Ortiz was a little taken aback. But true to his word, he listened, and thought about it. 'I don't think that's truth-telling,' he said after a few moments. 'That's future-telling. I'm not asking you to tell the future, because no one knows the future, not even you. Now if you were to say, I want to kill you – that would be truth-telling. You'd be speaking about your own desire, which would remain true whether or not you actually carried out the deed. Do you see the difference?'

'Yes, sir,' said Bowman, amused in spite of himself.

'So go on. Tell me a truth.'

Bowman thought. It didn't take long.

'You'll never be a Master to others so long as your greatest ambition is to please your own Master.'

'Great stars above! Do you think so?'

They had now reached the staircase that led to the upper levels.

'That's good! I'll have to give that one some

thought. But here we are now. Don't mind if the Master ignores you. He has a great deal on his mind at present.'

They ascended the stairs and entered the wide bright upper levels. The Master was striding up and down with a pair of binoculars clamped to his eyes, gazing out over the streets of the High Domain, and making strange signals with his free hand. His servant Spalian stood beside him, holding his violin.

'There! No, he still can't see me. There!'

'He sees you now, Master.'

Meeron Graff was stationed a little way away, also with binoculars to his eyes. The Master waved his left hand above his head. Across several streets, a tiny figure on a high roof terrace waved back.

'Got him! Mark it!'

Ortiz and Bowman waited and watched. The Master seemed to be establishing a number of lines of sight, to people posted in windows, and terraces, and on rooftops, all down the main avenue of the High Domain. The upper levels reached along part of this avenue, but by no means all. Some of the more distant lookouts were equipped with telescopes, so that they could track the Master's signals. Bowman's immediate thought was that a great trap was being prepared, for the members of the wedding party and their armed escort.

He fixed his mind on the Master, and probed as far as he could. He felt the power of the man radiating out from him like heat from a fire; and beneath the surface heat, he felt the Master's deep inner coldness. What came as a surprise was the jangle of energy, the restlessness, the brittle rage so quickly lost in brittle laughter –

in all, the unexpectedly high level of anxiety. This huge man, with his crimson cloak flapping about him, and his gold-belted belly, and his streaming white hair, was fighting some secret fear.

'There, Graff! Those are their positions. Make sure they know them.'

'Yes, Master.'

'The timing is crucial. There's to be no delay. On my signal, they begin.'

'Yes, Master.'

The Master now lowered his binoculars and turned to take in the waiting Ortiz. He paid no attention to Bowman, who stood quietly behind him.

'Ah! You've come.'

Ortiz at once prostrated himself on the floor.

'Did you see her?'

'Yes, Master.'

'Up! Up! What's she like? Will she do?'

'I'm content to marry the Johdila, Master, if that's your wish.'

'I asked you what's she like, not what you wanted.'

'She was veiled, Master.'

'Veiled!' The Master burst into booming laughter. 'Excellent! So you've no idea! That's fine, I must say. A surprise package. This calls for a wager. I say she's a beauty – well, passably pretty, at least. I'll stake – what? The Sovereignty of Gang! How about that?'

'Master?'

'If she's pretty, you get the pleasure of a handsome wife. If she's a shocker, you get an empire of your own. How's that for a bet?'

'You're more than generous, Master.'

'I'm going to give you the wedding of all time, Marius!

These primitives from Obagang will never have seen anything so glorious in all their miserable lives! It will be a living work of art! Food!'

This last word came out as a sudden bellow. A slave appeared, seemingly from nowhere, holding out a tray on which lay several small pastries. The Master took one of the pastries, put it whole into his mouth, and after two or three vigorous chews, swallowed it.

'Delicious!' he exclaimed. 'There's a new pastry cook, a kind of genius. Try one.'

Ortiz accepted a pastry, and ate it rather more slowly. The Master took a second, and demolished it as ferociously as the first. Bowman watched him in growing surprise. The man clearly had enormous appetites, which he made no effort at all to control.

'It's your wish, then, Master, that I marry the Johdila?'

'Yes, boy. Why not? Someone must.'

'And that I . . .' Ortiz cautiously left his sentence unfinished.

'And that you? And that you?'

Ortiz bowed his head humbly.

'Be named your son, Master.'

'Well now, that's quite a jump, isn't it? For a man to acquire a son at my age. Let's take a look at you.'

Ortiz knew what that meant. Trembling, he raised his eyes to meet the Master's. He felt the Master reach into him, deeper and deeper. His heart beat fast, but he did not turn away.

Suddenly the Master growled with menace.

'What's this, Marius? What secret are you keeping from me?'

'Secret, Master? I have no secrets from you.'

'Liar!'

The Master's eyes flashed with anger. His bearded chin jerked, and Ortiz crumpled to the floor with a cry of pain. There he writhed and contorted, while the Master tossed him as if with an invisible pitchfork. Bowman watched in horror, knowing exactly what the Master was doing. He was holding Ortiz in a mind-wrench, tormenting him with crushing pain. It was the same power the hermit had taught him, though in the Master it was far stronger. Bowman knew he must find out just how strong, because the time would come when he would face the Master's power himself. Carefully, not wanting to attract the Master's attention, he extended his senses into the crackling energy that gripped Ortiz.

'What's this dirty little secret of yours?' thundered the Master, as Ortiz thrashed and screamed at his feet. 'You belong to me, do you hear! All your thoughts and all your passions belong to me!'

'Yes, Master!' sobbed the stricken man.

'Tell me!'

'Only a pretty face, Master! Only a servant girl who caught my eye – aaah! –'

'A girl, eh?'

As abruptly as he had gripped Ortiz, he let him go. Ortiz let out a long breath, the pain still shuddering through his aching body.

'No harm in that,' said the Master. 'You're young. It's to be expected. Look at me again.'

Fearful but obedient, Ortiz looked up from where he lay. This time the Master smiled on him, and as he smiled he healed him of all the pain he had inflicted, and filled him with sweet sensations of joy. Ortiz felt his body relax. He bathed in the warmth of the Master's love, and tears sprang to his eyes, tears of joy, and rolled streaming down his cheeks.

'I love you, Master. All that I do, I do for you. I love you now and forever.'

'Well, well,' said the Master, his voice now soft with kindness. 'You shall marry, and you shall be named as my son. Does that suit you?'

Ortiz crawled onto his knees, and from there, prostrated himself before the Master, flat out on the floor at his feet.

'Master!' he cried. 'Father!'

Bowman was taking care to veil his feelings, and to keep his eyes down, not wanting to attract attention. However, when Ortiz rose up again, his wet eyes still shining with joy, he was so brimming with love for the Master that he couldn't resist turning to Bowman and saying,

'Now you see why all his people love him!'

'Yes, sir,' murmured Bowman.

'Master,' cried Ortiz, 'I have taken this young man as my truth-teller.'

'Truth-teller, eh?' The Master looked at Bowman for the first time. 'Young for a truth-teller.'

'He's one of the Manth people, Master.'

'Is he, now?' His eyes were still on Bowman, but Bowman himself looked resolutely down at the floor. 'Ever heard of a prophet called Ira Manth?'

'Yes, sir,' said Bowman.

'Yes, Master!' thundered the Master.

'Yes, Master.'

'Look at me, boy. Let me see your eyes.'

Bowman raised his head and looked. He emptied his mind, making it as blank as he could, while the Master explored him. After a few moments, the Master looked away with a shrug.

'I'd say he was more of a simpleton than a truth-teller, Marius. I shouldn't pay too much attention to him if I were you.'

I will destroy you.

'What was that?' The Master jerked round, eyes blazing. 'What did you say?'

'Nothing, Master.' Bowman drained his mind once more. He was angry with himself for letting his true feelings out, even for so brief a moment.

'He said nothing, Master,' said Ortiz.

The Master ignored him. He came up close to Bowman. His eyes flashed as he gripped him with his mind. Bowman forced himself not to resist. He let the Master shake him, wincing at the pain.

'Be careful,' said the Master. 'Be very careful.'

He let him go.

'Graff!'

The Keeper of the Master's Household hurried forward.

'Tell Marius everything he's to do. Marius, you'll play your part precisely as you're instructed. This wedding will be a symphony! It will be one great seamless work of art! I am the artist, my people are my medium! I make beauty out of life itself! Fiddle!'

Spalian stepped forward and gave the Master his violin. Bowman saw with relief that he had been forgotten. As Graff now led Ortiz away, and Bowman trotted meekly behind, the Master raised his violin to his shoulder and began to play.

When they were out in the street once more, Ortiz turned eagerly to Bowman.

'He's astonishing, isn't he? Such power! Such love! But perhaps he frightened you.'

'Yes,' said Bowman truthfully. 'He did.'

The Master had great power, and Bowman had felt it. But even as the Master had shaken him, Bowman had sensed the limits of his strength. When the time comes, he thought to himself, it may be me who frightens him.

Now that the wedding was only days away, there were consultations between Meeron Graff, the Keeper of the Master's Household, and Barzan, the Grand Vizier of Gang. The Grand Vizier then summoned the members of the court to explain how the ceremony was to proceed.

'You must go too,' said Kestrel to Sisi, wanting to be at the meeting for her own reasons.

'Barzan is the most boring man in the empire,' said Sisi. 'You go, darling, and then tell me whatever I need to know.'

Sisi was much more interested in the final fittings for her wedding dress. She didn't at all want to be married, but she did want to wear the dress.

So Kestrel attended the meeting, keeping herself discreetly at the back, and listened with close attention as the Grand Vizier explained the order of the main events.

There was to be a processional entrance into the High Domain, in which the Johdila would ride in an open carriage, in her wedding dress, watched by thousands. She would enter the great domed hall on foot. Here there was to be a display of the famous manaxa. Immediately after this, the bride and groom would dance the tantaraza. They would then take the five steps towards each other and exchange vows, and as man and wife would sit down to a huge banquet, that would last the rest of the day.

'A huge banquet, eh?' said the Johanna. 'Quite right, too. What's a wedding without a banquet?'

'I understand there's to be music,' said Barzan. 'The Master is very fond of music.'

'Music's all well and good,' said the Johanna. 'But the banquet's the thing.'

When the meeting was over, Barzan noticed with satisfaction that Zohon was once again in conversation with the Johdila's servant. All this talk of weddings, he trusted, had put the Commander in a romantic mood.

Barzan was right.

'I think of her day and night,' Zohon was saying to Kestrel. 'Let her only command me, and I will take her away from all this. But I must know she loves me.'

'Only the free can love,' said Kestrel.

This struck Zohon with great force.

'The Johdila is not free?'

'Neither she nor her country. Often I hear her sighing and murmuring, "Oh for the man who will make my country strong again, and set my people free!"'

'That's me! Who else?'

'Perhaps the Mastery will be too powerful even for you.'

'We shall see about that!' Zohon smacked his silver hammer into the palm of his left hand. Then his eyes turned with sudden suspicion on Kestrel.

'How do I know any of this is true? How do I know you're not lying to me?' This doubt took root rapidly in his mind. 'The Johdila has told me nothing herself. All I know comes from you. Who are you? What do you want? How do I know you're not tricking me?'

Kestrel thought fast.

'You know, because the Johdila has given you the secret sign.'

'When? I haven't seen it.'

He stared at her with hard suspicious eyes.

'She's very discreet. You must watch all the time.'

'I've watched, but I've seen no sign. I must see this sign for myself.'

Kestrel looked round, as if to assure herself that they weren't overheard, and then said in a whisper,

'This evening, after supper, I'll walk with the Johdila between the trees. Place yourself out of sight by the carriages, and watch. I'll tell the Johdila you're watching. Then you'll see.'

'I hope so,' said Zohon grimly. 'For your sake.'

Kestrel had no difficulty in getting the Johdila to take a stroll with her alone. Sisi had matters of her own to talk over in private with her friend. Kestrel half-listened, waiting for the moment when she could give Sisi their secret friend sign. Sisi would then do the same for her, and Zohon, watching from the shadows, would be satisfied.

'When will I see your brother again, Kess? I must see him before the wedding. It's tremendously important.'

'Sisi, you must forget about my brother.'

She was making sure they walked in such a way that Sisi was facing the carriages.

'Why? I like him. I think maybe I love him.'

'No, you don't. That's all nonsense. You don't know anything about him.'

'That doesn't matter.' Sisi was surprisingly persistent

on the subject. 'Mama says that no one ever knows anything about the person they marry. They learn to like them afterwards.'

'Well, I don't think he'd like you.'

Sisi stopped walking and stared at Kestrel, shocked. Kestrel had been hardly thinking what she was saying, and at once regretted her words. She rather wondered why she had said them.

'I don't mean that,' she said.

'Yes, you do,' said Sisi, blinking back tears. 'You think I'm silly, and vain, and useless.'

'No, I don't –'

'And you're right. Only what you have to understand is, until I met you, that's what everyone wanted me to be.'

'Please, Sisi –'

'So you see, I've been trying my best to please everyone, only I've chosen the wrong everyone to please. Now I've decided to change, and I will change, because although I am silly and vain and useless, I can tell there's another way I can be, which is more like you. And that's what I've decided to be.'

'You're a better person than I am,' said Kestrel sadly. She knew that Zohon was watching from his hiding place. Now that the moment had come, she found it was much harder than she thought. It felt too much like betrayal.

'Please go on being my friend, Kess,' said Sisi. 'You don't know how important you are to me.'

'Of course I will.'

Then, without Kestrel prompting her, she put the palms of her hands together, and interclasped her fingers, in the sign that Kestrel had told her meant secret friendship. Zohon, hiding between the carriages, saw her make the sign that Kestrel had told him meant eternal love. It was all he had been waiting for. Convinced now that Kestrel had told him the truth, he slipped away to prepare his men.

Kestrel heard him go, even as she pressed her hands together in the return sign. Tears sprang into her eyes. Forgive me, Sisi, she said silently. I wasn't going to betray you. But it's happened now.

That evening, word spread through the slaves quarters of the Manth people that Ira Hath the prophetess had had another vision of the future, and wished to pass it on to her people. There were still a few who believed that Ira Hath had the true gift, but most of the large crowd who gathered to hear her were merely curious.

They arrived through the evening shadows in little groups of threes and fours, not wanting to arouse the suspicions of their masters. Ira had seated herself on the ground in front of a large open fire, and the Manth people gathered in an ever-widening ring around its warmth. Dr Greeth came, as the Haths had known he would, and placed himself near the front, where if necessary he could speak against the prophecy. The others regarded Ira Manth's utterances as entertainment. Jessel Greeth believed her to be dangerous.

When they were all settled, Ira Hath stood before them.

'Thank you for coming to hear me,' she began.

'Can't hear!' shouted voices from the back. And, 'Say, O unhappy people!' shouted those at the front.

'O unhappy people!' said Ira Hath.

'O unhappy people!' chanted back the jokers in the crowd, delighted.

The effect of this mockery on the prophetess was predictable. She became angry. Wanting to wipe the smiles off their foolish faces, she called down on their heads the full catastrophe to come.

'This city will burn!'

'Burn!' they wailed back at her. 'We'll all burn!'

The more she doomed them, the more they laughed.

'The wind is rising! The wind will carry all before it!'

'Wooo-wooo!' they cried, flapping their arms.

'We must seek the homeland! The time of cruelty is coming! Be afraid!'

'Oooh!' they shivered, giggling. 'Oooh-aaah!'

'Laugh now! Soon you'll be weeping!'

'Boo-hoo! Waa-waa!' they cried.

Hanno Hath stood up beside his wife. It was hopeless. He knew it, and she knew it. But it was his duty to try to warn them.

'My friends,' he said in his most reasonable voice. 'Tonight my wife's prophecies make you laugh. But when you see the city burning, remember her words. Return here, to this hillside. Bring food, warm clothes, anything you can carry. And together we will seek the homeland.'

This was different. Nobody laughed. Instead, they fell to talking nervously among themselves. Jessel Greeth had been content while everyone was mocking the Haths. But now he felt he had better take control of the situation.

'This woman,' he said, pointing at Ira Hath, 'tells you the city will burn. But we know who will burn if we pay any more attention to her wild ravings. Our loved ones will burn, as they burned before.'

There were nods and murmurs of agreement to this all over the crowd.

'Why do we listen to her?' cried Jessel Greeth. 'Why do we go on letting this mad family put the rest of us in such danger? Let's leave them to prophesy to themselves.'

People began to leave. Pinto tugged at her father's sleeve.

'Lift me up on your shoulders, pa!'

Hanno swung her thin body up onto his shoulders, and there where they could all see her in the flickering fire-light, Pinto spoke to the crowd.

'Babies!' she cried. 'You're not Manth, you're just slaves and babies! We'll go without you. We'll find the homeland without you. We don't need you. So pooa-pooa pocksicker to you all!'

The crowd responded with a big cheer. No one quite knew why they cheered. Perhaps it was because they thought it was brave of a seven-year-old child to be so defiant. Perhaps they just cheered because it was good to hear the old oaths again.

Third Interval:

The tomb

The sea is rough today. High waves suck and roll, gathering themselves ever higher until they break at last, and crash in fury onto the shore. Gulls are hurled in the wind overhead, screaming their long thin screams. The coarse sand seethes with foam.

Dogface the hermit stands looking out across the grey water to the island. His robe flaps about his legs. He's cold, and tired, and hungry. Further along the shore other solitary figures stand as he stands. They're waiting, as he waits, for a lull in the wind.

As the day ends, the sea at last begins to grow calm. The water's surface still rises and falls in heaving swells, but the direction of the wind is changing, and the hermit knows he can make the crossing now. He prepares his mind, and begins his song, aware that along the coast the others are doing the same.

He rises in the air and glides out over the breaking foam. The others do likewise. Soon there are many figures to be seen skimming low over the water, rising and falling with the sea's swell, flying to Sirene.

As Dogface reaches the island he hears the chant coming from the hilltop, and knows he is still in time.

They have begun the song of opening, a song that will last through the night. He comes to land on the island's stony shore, and begins at once to hurry up the long winding path. Behind him he hears others following; ahead, the ever-louder surge of song that he has sung before in training, but never in earnest. His heart beats with excitement, and he too joins in, singing aloud. The song is like a succession of drumrolls, it powers onward, its rhythm intensifying with each cycle, until the Singers feel their bodies move in a slow rocking stamp, forward and stamp, backward and stamp, in time with the driving wordless chords.

Singing, striding to the beat of the song, Dogface reaches the top of the hill. Here before him, lit by the silver-grey light of a sun setting in cloud, rise the towering roofless walls. Within the hall stands a great crowd of Singer people, more than a hundred, all singing, rocking, and stamping together. As Dogface takes his place among them he looks round and sees faces he remembers from his time of training; but there are no answering looks of recognition. They are deep in the song.

By the time those who followed the hermit reach the hall, Dogface too sees no one and hears nothing but the song. This is the beginning of the destiny he chose, many years ago. This is what he trained for, and has waited for so patiently. The time of consummation has almost come.

All through the night the Singer people sing their song. As they sing they feel beneath their stamping feet the slow shudder of the earth. They feel its spasms, and they know that slowly, unseen as yet, it is opening. They sing on, the rhythm never abating, urging the ground to swell, and stretch, and tear.

At first light, the opening begins. Those standing where the thin crack appears jump aside, but never pause in their pulsing song. They sing now with all their power, forcing the sound out and up with a shout, a stamp and a shout, a clap and a stamp and a shout. Still more Singer people are arriving, as they have been doing all through the night. They come singing, and the song grows ever louder.

Now there comes a jarring juddering cracking sound, followed by a long rumbling groan: the sound they have long expected, but have never heard. They are the lucky ones. They are the generation who will know the wind on fire.

All down the long roofless hall, the ground is shivering and cracking, tearing itself apart like a wound that has healed and now opens again. Fragments of rock sheer off the sides and rattle down through the great space to clatter on the floor below. The Singer people sing on, rocking and stamping, feeling the earth part beneath their feet. As dawn breaks, the soft light reaches down to reveal the walls of the ever-widening rift, and the dusty vastness of the great cave below.

The ground stops moving at last, and the song ends: or rather, it changes, and becomes a quieter chant. Immediately, those close to the edge step out into space, and float slowly down. The others, singing all the while, wait their turn to follow after, in a steady stream.

Now it's Dogface the hermit who steps off the crumbling edge, and lets himself float down into shadows. The torn rock walls widen as he falls, slanting away to meet the smooth stone floor of the great cave. To one side, in a deeper chasm cut by the fast-flowing water, there runs an underground river, an undersea river, which disappears into vaults of rock. High above him now, the lightening sky. All around him, his brothers and sisters. And before him, raised on a platform carved from the rock floor, the stone tomb.

Four columns support a shallow-pitched roof. Within, on a stone bier, there lies the grey and wizened body of a long-dead man. Here, in the stillness of the underground cave, he has lain undisturbed since the day he died, hundreds of years ago. His flesh has shrivelled away to the bone. His face has become a skull shrouded in fragments of yellow skin. His hands rest clasped on his chest, bones on bones.

When he lived, his name was Ira Manth. They call him the prophet. He has died, but his powers remain. They live on in his followers, the Singer people. And they live on in his children.

Now the song is ending in the great river cave of Sirene. The singers fall quiet. They know that they must wait, for an unknown length of time. They are accustomed to waiting. During this time, more and more of their people will come, until they are all gathered together. Then the child of the prophet will come. Then it will be time.

In this way, the prophet promised, *I live again and I die again.*

17

A city in song

Creoth sat on his stool in the cowshed, his hands drawing hot milk from the udder of the patient cow, and watched the dawn over the misty land. The milk hissed into the wooden pail in rhythmic spurts, the notes growing deeper as the pail filled. The cow tugged hay from the bulging net hung up before her. Others in the small herd lowed softly, impatient to be milked in their turn.

Now the sun rose above the rim of the far hills, and the burning red disc spilled sudden colour over the chilled fields. The grey forest sparkled and turned pink: and for a few moments, before the sun climbed into cloud, the world glowed as if newborn.

'Quite a show, eh, Cherub?' said Creoth. He dipped a ladle into the pail and drank warm milk for his breakfast, moving his arm slowly, taking slow sips. Then he rose and emptied the pail into the big churn on the wagon behind him, and moved his milking-stool to the next cow. He sighed as he settled down, wriggling his fingers to keep them supple.

'Yes, yes, yes,' he murmured to the restless cow. 'I know you had to wait, but I'm here now.'

The cow swung round her mournful head to gaze at him.

'And good day to you too, my Star,' said Creoth, and set to work. Star reached for the hay-bundle, and the disappearing sun turned the underside of the clouds gold.

So it went each morning, and Creoth was content. He was not a young man any more; and his former life, already slipping into oblivion, had been solitary, quiet, and regular. Cows suited him. They made no sudden movements. They did the same things at the same time every day. Most of all, he liked their smell. The milk, of course, with its rich froth of bubbles in the pail; but also the smell of their damp hide, and of the fields they grazed, and of their manure, which was the smell of cows and grass and earth all mixed up together.

As he finished the morning's milking, he heard the rattle and tap of wagons moving down the distant high road. Looking up he saw framed in the cowshed doorway a long procession of horse riders and carriages. Some of the carriages were very grand indeed, decorated in gold pinnacles, drawn by double teams of horses. They were making their way towards the lakeside, and the causeway to the High Domain.

'That'll be the bride,' said Creoth to the cows. 'There's to be a grand wedding today.'

He told his cows everything. They looked solemnly back at him, meditating on what he said, never replying.

'May she be happy, eh, Star? May she be happy.'

When the guards came to the slave quarters that morning to make their usual selection for the monkey cages, Pinto whispered to her father, 'I'll take my turn today.'

Hanno shook his head.

'No, darling. Today's the most dangerous day of all.'

'I know,' said Pinto. 'You and ma have work to do. But I have nothing.'

'Well, let's hope they don't pick me or your mother.'

But the guards picked Ira Hath. At the same time a message arrived for Hanno Hath, requiring his presence, wedding or no wedding, in the academy library. This left no one to prepare for their escape.

'You see,' said Pinto. 'It has to be me.'

'Darling,' said her mother to her, 'you can't go in the cage today. This is the day. I feel it. We can't be sure the people in the cages will get out in time.'

'Ma, look at me.' Ira met her younger daughter's earnest eyes. 'I'm only little. I can't do anything. But I can do this. Don't you see? At last I can be of some use.'

'You don't know what you're saying.'

'Don't I?' She leaned forward and kissed her mother's cheek, and whispered in her ear. 'I'm saying maybe I'll die in the cage, so that you can get our people away.'

It was that quick kiss that moved Ira Hath most.

'Oh, my dearest. Have you grown up too? Must you leave me too?'

'You know I'm right. You must gather our people. I can't do that. Today's the day.'

Her mother turned to Hanno, unable to make the decision. Hanno looked at Pinto, and saw the pride in her eyes.

'The child's right,' he said. 'Go then, my darling. We won't let you come to harm.'

Pinto ran to the guards and told them that she was taking her mother's place. The guards were indifferent. So long as they had one member from each kin group, their job was done.

Hanno Hath went with her to the crossroads, and watched as she was locked into one of the monkey wagons. Pinto smiled as she stood there, holding the bars, and waved at him to show he mustn't be afraid for her.

'I'll be back for you,' he said. And went on his way with a heavy heart.

Sisi sat veiled in her carriage, looking out of the window, trembling with nervous excitement. There were labourers out in the fields already, and all of them were standing still, staring at the endless procession of carriages.

'Lunki!' said Sisi in amazement. 'They don't cover their eyes!'

'The poor heathens!' said Lunki. 'They don't know any better, my pet.'

'Do they know they'll all have their eyes put out?'

'I should hope not,' said Lunki. 'My good baby is wearing her veil.'

'Oh, so I am. I'm never quite sure if it's there or not.'

'Baby drink a little milky?'

'No, Lunki. Take it away. This is my wedding day. I can't possibly eat.'

'Drinking's not the same as eating. My baby hardly needs to make her mouth move at all.'

Sisi shook her head, and turned to Kestrel.

'What are you looking at, Kess?'

Kestrel was sitting gazing out of the other carriage window at the Johjan Guards. The mounted soldiers rode two by two in front of their carriage as far as she could see, and behind, all the way to the bend in the road. Kestrel felt as if she was leading her own army into the heart of the enemy stronghold.

'I'm looking at where we're going.'

In the distance now she could see the lake and the causeway, and the walls of the High Domain. Ten times the size of Aramanth at its greatest, the amber city with its tumble of jewelled domes awed her gaze. This extraordinary city-palace had been built by the people who had burned her home and enslaved her family. And yet, glorious as it was, beautiful even, Kestrel had laid plans for its destruction. This skinny fifteen-year-old with no title and no position had judged the Mastery and passed sentence of death. Her weapon was her own passionate and merciless will. Today was the day of the wedding, and the day of the execution.

I am the avenger.

'You said something would happen to stop the wedding,' said Sisi. 'But nothing's happened.'

'You're not married yet,' said Kestrel. 'They can't make you be married if you don't want to.'

'They can,' said Sisi. 'If everyone expects you to do something, and they're all looking at you, then you do it.'

'You'll know what to do when the time comes.'

What Kestrel couldn't tell her was that if all went as she planned, Sisi would have no decision to make.

'There, you see, my pet,' said Lunki. 'You're not to worry, like the friend says.'

Lunki didn't approve of Kestrel. She knew nothing of Kestrel's concealed plans, and had no opinion about her opinions. Her objection was that the Johdila Sirharasi of Gang should not have a friend. It demeaned her high status. Ordinary people had friends. Royalty had subjects. Lunki could not imagine venturing any criticism of her mistress, certainly not aloud, so she limited herself to calling Kestrel 'the friend', as one might say 'the hairdresser', 'the dance instructor'. In this way she turned Kestrel into a functionary like herself, and was satisfied.

Two carriages ahead, the Johanna gazed out of his window at the High Domain, and he in his turn was awed. It was smaller than Obagang, his own capital city, heart of the Sovereignty of Gang: but by comparison with this jewel of a city, Obagang suddenly seemed shabby. The great buildings of his capital were made of stone, but they were squat heavy structures, quite unlike these exquisite domes. And the bulk of his city was nothing but timber hovels, crowding one upon another like so much refuse. He had never felt this before. As ruler of the greatest empire of the civilised world, he had been accustomed to a comfortable all-pervading sense of superiority. It came as an unpleasant shock to find himself entering a palace grander than any he possessed. The Grand Vizier, he reflected, had been quite right in arranging this marriage. The man who had formed this country out of nothing at all, the man they called the Master, would make a powerful enemy. How had he done so much, so quickly? This lake, for example: there had been no lake here before. This had been a desolate region, inhabited if at all by passing nomadic shepherds. No one had wanted it. No one had minded when a group of strangers had camped here, fifty years ago. He recalled his late father saying, 'Let them be. We need a caravan stop out there.' A caravan stop! If his father could see it now! The lake alone must be several miles long, and all dug out of the rocky ground at the command of this one man.

'Sit up straight, Foofy,' said his wife. 'Remember you're the Johanna of Gang, and all these people we're about to meet are dirt under your feet.'

'Dirt under my feet. Yes, dear.'

'You're not to simper or pick your cuticles or eat with your mouth open. When anyone speaks to you, remember to glower.'

'Yes, dear.'

'Show me your glower.'

He glowered.

'There, now. You look just like your father.'

Zohon, Commander of the Johjan Guards, magnificent in his dress uniform, rode at the head of his men. All three thousand guards were either riding behind him, or marching in double lines on either side of the procession of royal carriages. He had not asked if this mighty escort would be welcome in the host city. Nothing had been said on the matter. The Johanna had made no objection, for all Barzan's efforts in that direction. So Zohon proposed to lead all three thousand men into the heart of the High Domain.

Secretly, as he sat tall in the saddle, and the lakeside came nearer, he expected to be stopped. Should that happen, his plan was to attack at once. A heavy iron battering-ram lay concealed under one of the carriages, for smashing down the gates. But no one stopped him. No armed force of any kind was to be seen, other than his own men. And across the long causeway ahead, the great gates were open.

The procession came to a stop at the land end of the causeway. The ceremonial open carriage, as yet unoccupied, was now drawn forward into the lead, and a picked squad of mounted Johjan Guards, all exactly the same height and colouring, took up their places on either side. The Johanna and the Johdi put on their crowns, which were impressive, but also heavy and uncomfortable. And as Kestrel watched, the Johdila was dressed at last in her wedding gown.

It was a remarkable creation. The dressmaker insisted that the Johdila wear no underclothing of any kind beneath it, which Sisi found thrilling. Not that the dress revealed any part of her slender young body: the perfectly-cut white silk sheath covered her from throat to ankles, lying so tight and close to her body that it was almost a second skin. Over her head was drawn a close-fitting white silk cap, cut to follow the curve of her neck down to her shoulders. Over her face hung a simple square of white gossamer, which fluttered in and out as she breathed. But all this was no more than the inner part of the creation. Over and around it, over her white-clad head and body, sustained by fine wire supports fixed to her head and shoulders, there floated an entire body veil made of the lightest silk, so fine that it was almost invisible: more a swirl of mist than a garment. Within this all-enveloping aura her slender silk-skinned body moved like a mystery of seduction, offering to the entranced eye of the onlooker everything and nothing, charged with the intoxicating promise of beauty.

'Oh, Sisi!' cried Kestrel, as she gazed on the finished result. 'I've never seen anyone look so beautiful in all my life!'

'There, pet,' murmured Lunki. 'My baby's happy now.'

The dressmaker fretted about her, adjusting the fall of the body veil.

'Must she ride in a carriage?' he kept saying. 'The material is cut to hang. If she sits, it will crumple.'

Sisi herself was torn. On the one hand, she didn't want her dress to crumple. On the other hand, she didn't want to walk over the very long causeway. So she allowed herself to be handed into the open carriage, where she sat facing her father and mother.

The procession now set off once more, the horses' hooves booming on the boards of the causeway. Zohon rode immediately behind the royal carriage, making his horse perform a high-prancing trot to hold it at the procession's slow pace without himself seeming to amble. The long line of carriages, escorted by close ranks of Johjan Guards, rolled along behind, covering so great a distance that by the time the front of the procession reached the great gates, the tail was yet to set foot on the causeway.

As the open carriage carrying the bride passed through the gates, an orchestra struck up, and a choir began to sing. The Johdila looked round in wonder at the beautiful buildings she was passing. In every window, on every terrace, musicians were playing their instruments, and groups of singers were singing. At the same time small children, squeezed between the performers, were throwing flower petals in an unending cascade. The petals came skittering and floating down around Sisi, settling here and there on her body veil, filling the air with colour and mingling with the streams of song, so that it seemed as if it were the falling flowers themselves that flooded the street with such sweet sounds.

Zohon, prancing proudly behind her, his handsome face looking round, concealing his intense excitement, saw no signs of any armed men. All he saw, in astonishing numbers, were musicians. He almost laughed aloud. Not much danger from a bunch of fiddlers and warblers!

Kestrel leaned out of the window of the Johdila's carriage to gaze at the city of her enemy, and she too was amazed. This nation of murderers and slavers was beautiful, its streets charming, and its citizens – musical. And how musical! She realised as they rolled slowly up the street that the great anthem was modulating from one group of performers to the next, so that the melody was always taken by the musicians closest to the royal carriage, while the harmonies continued to swell from behind them, and from further up the street. She began to notice that the eyes of the performers were raised, all looking in the same direction. Following their gaze, she caught a glimpse of a curving glazed roof terrace, where an indistinct figure was moving back and forth, beating the air with outstretched arms.

The Master pounded the upper levels, conducting his multiple orchestras and choirs, singing the great anthem himself as it rolled out over his city below. Lost in music, white hair flying, with the sweep of his arm he caused a hundred singers to burst into song five streets away, even as the violins below him poured out their eager melody. He stabbed a finger, and trumpets sounded from the flower market; turned his hand, and two hundred drummers stationed in the plaza began their insistent toccata. Now the bass fiddles started up their thrumming, all over the city, making the air vibrate with a sound deeper than sound. The Master tugged the air, and a thousand sopranos hit the first thrilling high note of the final movement, the sound bursting skywards like a field of larks. Here came the strings, the sweet yearning of the violas, the loving murmur of the cellos, weaving into the call of the pipes – he strode over the glowing spaces to the far end to punch one finger towards his massed male choir, and with a shiver that was felt all over the High

Domain fifteen hundred bass voices began to sing, and the Master, lost in the glory of his own creation, was singing with them.

A city in song, a city become a symphony, to welcome the lovely young bride. Let them see, thought the Master, passionate in his moment of command, let them see the true meaning of mastery! This is the world I have made, this is my gift to my people, this is my promise of a new world!

Hanno Hath heard the music that signalled the coming of the bridal party, and knew that Kestrel was somewhere in the procession. With Professor Fortz's permission, he went to the high window of the academy library to watch the bride go by.

'Weddings!' said Fortz in disgust. 'Sugar now. Pill later.'

'You're not married yourself, Professor?'

'Marriage is a leisure activity. Don't have the time.'

'It's given me the greatest happiness of my life,' said Hanno.

'Has it?' Fortz was very surprised. 'I dare say you like hot meals.' He stood on a chair to look out of the window himself. 'Great stars! Who are these people? All that gilding. So provincial!'

The choir in the building facing the library, taking their cue from the Master above, now burst into song, making Fortz jump. The waves of co-ordinated sound, however, seriously impressed him.

'The man's a genius, you have to admit. Listen to that! The sound of a people united in song!'

'United in slavery, too,' murmured Hanno.

'What of that? Ask yourself what makes a nation prosperous. Good order, and hard work. What sort of people do as they're told, and work hard? Slaves. Strip away all that sentimental old nonsense about rights and freedoms, and what do you get? The most prosperous country in the world!'

From the street outside came a series of trumpet fanfares, climbing, heaping, towering over the song of the massed choirs.

'The bride must have reached the great hall,' said Fortz.

Hanno had not seen Kestrel.

'I wonder,' he said, 'if I might go out to watch.'

'Well, why not? No one can concentrate in all this din.'

Hanno left the library at about the same time that the Johdila was stepping down from her open carriage, before the entrance to the great hall. However, he did not try to push his way through the crowd to watch the ceremony. He turned the other way, and headed through the gates and across the now deserted causeway.

It was time to prepare for their departure.

18

Mumpo fights the manaxa

K estrel was shivering. From the moment the huge bridal procession had entered the High Domain, she had been expecting Zohon to strike. Column after column of his Johjan Guards came marching up the street, and nowhere could she see any force of men with which the Mastery could resist them. But the Commander rode smilingly onwards, and the ceremony proceeded as planned.

She climbed out of the carriage with Lunki, and followed the bride up the steps leading to the great domed hall where the wedding was to be celebrated. The music swirled all round her. From within the hall came the sound of a choir singing a joyful song. The Johdila, already out of her open carriage, flanked by the Johanna and the Johdi, was being met at the high arched entrance by the Keeper of the Master's Household, bowing low and sweeping out his arms. Now they were all processing into the hall. Kestrel followed.

The hall amazed her. The immense intricately-carved stone pillars sustaining the floating domes; the arena erected for the wedding, formed out of a lattice of slender oak supports, bearing cushioned seats, surmounted by a crimson gold-fringed canopy; the great glowing light-filled space above, shining like a private sky; and filling all of this vast space, soaring up to the sunset-coloured glass itself, the triumphant song of the four hundred singers of the Master's personal choir. They stood on two specially-constructed stands of their own, on either side of the entrance doors, all wearing long-sleeved robes of crimson and gold.

'The bridal chorale,' the Keeper whispered to the Johanna. 'Composed by the Master for the entry of the bride.'

'Composed by the Master!'

'All the music for the wedding is composed and conducted by the Master himself.'

The ranks of tall Johjan Guards came pouring in on all sides, still marching in perfect time, and filled the spaces behind the timber arena. Kestrel realised that if there was to be a battle, it must begin here, in this awe-inspiring but ever more crowded hall. She looked round to discover the various routes of escape. There were entrances on three sides: one to the main street, through which they were passing now, and two side entrances, both of which were closed and jammed with spectators. There was an internal passage on the far side, leading to further rooms within the great hall. And across the hall there was a narrow flight of stairs rising to a gallery, which ran all round the hall just below the level of the lowest dome. But before she could examine this further, she must follow the royal party into the arena itself.

There was sand on the arena floor, which seemed out of place on such a grand occasion. Also, she realised as she stepped upwards, the floor was raised, like a wide stage. The Johdila was now being led to a special bridal throne, in the centre of the left hand bank of benches. Kestrel took her place behind the royal party.

'Quite a place, isn't it?' the Johanna said to his wife. 'Why can't we get our fellows at home to build us something like this? Look at those pillars! Carved all the way to the top. You'd swear they were real leaves growing there.'

'Too fussy for me,' said the Johdi. Her gold cloak made her hot, and her crown hurt her head.

'So what's going to happen here, Barzan?' The Johanna gestured at the sand-strewn platform before them.

'They call it the manaxa, mightiness. It's a kind of fighting. They think very highly of it here.'

'Does it go on long?'

'I don't believe so, sire. After it there will be the tanta-raza. The bridal dance.'

'Does that go on long?'

'Altogether perhaps an hour, gloriousness. The wedding banquet is to be eaten at noon.'

The Johanna signed. Already breakfast seemed a long way away.

With a roll of drums and a shout from the male voices in the choir, a second procession now entered, bringing the bridegroom. In the lead came twelve young lords of the Mastery, chosen by Ortiz to be his attendants for the ceremony. They wore their finest garments, the long-trained robes over the richly-embroidered tunics, in the style that was currently the height of fashion. The light falling from the high domes above stippled them in orange and gold, until they passed under the canopy, and all the air turned rosy pink. The colour scheme seemed arbitrary as the various elements in the composition moved about the hall, but once they were all in their places a design emerged, in which the dominant tones of the canopy, the sand, and the outer blue light, were picked up and heightened by the subtler costumes of the guests, all leading the eye to the centre of the composition, the pure white simplicity of the bride. The only discordant elements were the ones out of the Mastery's control: the purple of the Johjan Guards, and the turquoise markings on the body of Ozoh the Wise.

Now Kestrel, watching every moment, saw the entrance of the bridegroom himself. Marius Semeon Ortiz wore white; though the straps, buckles and belts of his garments were all silver. His tanned face and his tawny hair looked particularly handsome set off by the surrounding white. Walking tall and proud, he advanced to his own crimson throne facing the Johdila's across the arena, bowed low to the royal court of Gang, and sat down. The young lords sat down round him. His personal servants lined up at the back. Kestrel found Bowman among them, and for a short secret moment their eyes met.

The massed choirs now delivered their final stirring chord, and the storm of music which had swept the High Domain for almost an hour was finally stilled.

The Keeper of the Master's Household stepped forward.

'To celebrate the coming union of your people and ours,' he proclaimed, 'the Master is pleased to present his finest fighters, who will meet in the noble art of manaxa.'

Kestrel's eyes sought out Zohon. He stood with his arms folded, watching the ceremony. His men entirely surrounded the arena, standing six deep. There was nothing to stop him. What was he waiting for?

Ba-ba-ba-bam! Ba-ba-ba-bam! The drums beat for the entrance of four manacs, who now appeared through a tunnel beneath the stands, and filed into the ring. Oiled bodies gleaming, limbguards and blades polished to a high shine, they jumped up one by one onto the platform and bowed in deep respect, first to the Johanna and his family, then to Ortiz. Lars Janus Hackel the trainer watched from his position by the tunnel entrance, and led the courteous applause for each contender.

First came strong-muscled many-scarred Dimon, veteran manac and master of the art. He held his bladed helmet under one arm as he paid his respects. The Johdila accepted his bow with a delicate inclination of her lovely veiled head. Then she let her eyes, concealed as ever, reach past the manac, past the throne where her future husband sat, to Bowman, standing behind. It seemed to her that her friend's brother was watching her with his thoughtful eyes. The Johdila sat very still and straight, too proud to show her nervousness, but deep inside she was shivering. Oh, Bowman, she was thinking. What am I doing here? Why can't you and I just creep away somewhere all on our own and talk, and get to know each other?

Bowman was looking at Kestrel.

Don't, Bo. It's dangerous.

He couldn't help just reaching out, and stroking the edges of her mind. She was very tense, which was to be expected, but also very excited.

When will it begin?

I don't know, she replied. *Be ready.*

She turned again to watch Zohon.

Ba-ba-ba-bam! Ba-ba-ba-bam! Up onto the sandy boards jumped lean Cadiz, the manac with the longest reach of them all. Slim and hard as corded wire, he bowed his courtesies, and acknowledged the applause.

Zohon was gazing down the tiered seats to the Johdila. The curve of her slender neck beneath the close-fitting cap was so seductive that he longed to caress it with his strong hand. He thought he saw her tremble as he watched her, and avert her gaze from her bridegroom. Never fear, beloved! he called to her in his heart. I will save you! And he turned his gaze on his enemy, the arrogant young man who presumed to marry his own Sisi, and stared at him with steady hatred. To his great satisfaction, he saw Ortiz blush, and drop his eyes.

Ba-ba-ba-bam! Ba-ba-ba-bam! Now it was great Arno, huge Arno, the most feared manac of them all, who straddled the stage, vast arms akimbo, and lowered his bull's head for the royal visitors.

Ortiz acknowledged Arno's bow, his cheeks still burning. He had blushed because he had been looking across the arena at Kestrel, and she had met his look, and her eyes had flashed with sudden fire. Why is she angry with me, he asked himself? There could be only one answer. She saw in his eyes that he loved her. This thought filled Ortiz with a sudden wild delight. That bright eager face, that now seemed to him to be more beautiful than all others, that vivid spirit, had been touched by his emotion. Perhaps she even returned his love! Madness to think it, madness and chaos and impossibility!

Ba-ba-ba-bam! Ba-ba-ba-bam! The fourth manac ran onto the platform to bow before the dignitaries, and it was Mumpo. Kestrel recognised him with shock, and only just prevented herself from crying out. He looked so different. His bare oiled body gleamed, his way of moving was supple and assured. Now in control of her responses, she watched and marvelled. She didn't yet know the nature of the manaxa, and so felt no immediate fear for him. Bowman, watching from the far side, knew all too well, and he shuddered.

The drums now fell silent. In the silence, the sound of the many spectators shuffling to get comfortable slowly faded into a nervous stillness. Into this stillness came three low raps, the sound of a violin bow tapping on a railing: rap, rap, rap. All eyes turned upwards. There in the shadowy gallery above the arena, the figure of a man could be made out. A huge crimson-robed form, on his head a golden helmet with a mane of golden chain, in his hand a violin. One word rustled down the benches.

'The Master! The Master!'

The Johanna was disconcerted.

'Shouldn't he be down here?' he whispered to Barzan. The Grand Vizier whispered to the Keeper of the Master's Household. The Keeper whispered back. And so the whisper returned to the Johanna.

'The Master is conducting the music. He will have the honour of meeting you after the exchange of vows.'

'I see. Oh, well. All right, then.'

Fresh sand was strewn over the platform. The drums rolled once more to signal the start of the manaxa. And the first pair sprang into the arena. Dimon faced Cadiz, the wily master against the young giant. A single rap came from the gallery above, and the fight began.

The manacs circled each other, mirroring each other's steps without making contact, the short blades on their knees and fists glinting in the rose-coloured light. Gangling Cadiz sprang first, spinning as he leapt, but Dimon was gone when he landed, and already counter-striking. *Clang*! The sound of blade on arm guard was followed by a bewilderingly fast exchange of blows, as knees danced and fists flew, *calla-calla-calla-clang*! and both manacs spun gracefully away, unharmed.

Sisi was electrified. With that first strike she realised the game was serious. The fighters meant to hurt, to wound, perhaps even to kill. Each move mattered, each flash of steel could end a life. Suddenly the fighting seemed to her the most beautiful thing she had ever seen in her life. The feints, the strikes, the blocks and parries, executed with such economy, such precision, such daring! All that exposed skin, just waiting to be cut, sliced, torn, gouged! The almost blood of it! Her heart beat fast and her eyes shone bright as she followed the steps of the deadly dance.

Wily Dimon swung round and beneath his opponent's long arm, his left knee rising even as Cadiz sprang back. Out drove Dimon's right arm, Cadiz blocked with his left, and sprang back again as Dimon's right knee pranced.

'Ha!' cried Dimon.

With this one move, Dimon had gained control of the rhythm of the manaxa, as the other watching fighters and their trainer knew. Helpless now, Cadiz blocked and retreated, until he was at the very edge of the platform, from which, with a graceful high-arcing leap, he conceded the fight.

The applause was generous. A classic bout, conducted with skill by fighters at the top of their form: but no blood. Ortiz, watching, guessed that the trainer had so ordered it. Visitors who had not been raised on the manaxa were sometimes shocked by its more brutal aspects.

Kestrel turned to look at Zohon. His eyes were glittering: he was fascinated. He'll make no move so long as the manaxa lasts, she told herself. Then all thoughts of Zohon and the coming battle were driven from her mind. Mumpo was entering the arena.

The drums rolled, and Arno clambered up onto the platform, to face the novice Mumpo. A strange pairing, Arno so vast and fleshy, Mumpo so slim and lithe. Curiously, Mumpo seemed if anything to be moving more slowly than his huge opponent, almost as if he was in a trance. Ortiz, seeing this, at once recognised the pre-fight concentration of the true manac, the fighter who makes his moves without conscious thought. He's a natural, he said to himself with approval. This will be a fight to remember. His eyes turned to Kestrel, and he noted how she too seemed to be fascinated by the young manac. 'She understands. She feels the power of the manaxa. I knew she would!'

The signal was given, the fight began, but neither manac seemed to be in a hurry. They moved with an exaggerated slowness, almost within reach of each other, responding to one another's turns and sweeps exactly as if they were dancing. In reality, they were intently engaged in finding each other's rhythm, that subtle beat that lay at the heart of the manaxa. Dreamily, eerily, they swayed and curved, turning all the time, seeking control.

Then Mumpo curled in close, and Arno struck. An obvious lure, an easy parry: but now the tempo of the fight increased. Mumpo seemed to have his eyes shut, to be sensing rather than seeing the big man's movements.

He was astonishingly graceful, each turn beginning and ending with an unhurried ease that made it seem he knew in advance all that was to come. Arno too, now that the action was accelerating, had a breathtaking command of his body. As nimble as Mumpo, as fast to strike, he possessed twice the power. One lethal blow from that great spiked fist, and Mumpo would not recover. But the blows did not land, on either side. The formal sequences of strike, parry, riposte, and counter-strike were unfolding in textbook formation, a true masterclass in the high art.

Lars Janus Hackel, seated by the arena tunnel, watched with satisfaction. The boy will come to no harm, he thought to himself. He's too good. He saw the profound level of concentration with which Mumpo was fighting, and knew that the big champion would never break those defences. Now the moves were flowing at dazzling speed, quick tight moves that were over before you could track them, each blow delivered before the mind of the fighter could calculate its effect, following patterns of combat in which both fighters had been drilled. *Dikka-dikka-dikka-dik*! went the blades, just touching each other or the limb guards, wasting no power on fruitless thrusts. Faster and faster now, turning, leaping, the manacs were locked in a ceaseless and accelerating dance that made the spectators hold their breath. Surely any moment now one of them would miss a beat, would fail to anticipate the next strike, would see the flying blade burst through the unprotected skin? But on they went, each yielding nothing, holding perfect concentration, and the tension grew.

Sisi could hardly bear it. She gripped her hands tight and leaned forward in her seat and willed the fighters to

– to what? With a flush of shame she realised she wanted the climax towards which this dance of blades was speeding, the moment of blood and pain. She couldn't help it. Everything about the manaxa called for its culmination. Captured by beauty, the spectator cried out for the release of blood.

Kestrel felt it too, but for her the excitement was darkened by dread. She could hardly bear to watch, and yet couldn't remove her eyes. With all her being, she was willing Mumpo, calling silently to him.

Jump, Mumpo! Run away! Don't be killed!

On whirled the manacs, now so close and so fast that they seemed to be embracing. They had reached the point in the manaxa where the first fighter to break the rhythm takes control of the other, and in an attempt to do this both were varying their moves at every turn. Arno tried a succession of left sweeps, hoping by sheer repetition to catch Mumpo unprepared: but after the fifth sweep Mumpo was blocking with his knee, which forced Arno to defend himself against the dangerous two-fist strike, and they were back into more familiar patterns. Suddenly Mumpo launched a forward spring that brought all four body blades into play at once, a move that usually forces the other fighter back. Arno, too experienced to retreat, responded with a full-arm forward thrust, that should have driven deep into Mumpo's belly, but that he leaped and twisted in midair, and caught the blade with one armoured shin. And down, round, and back, fists flashing: a beautifully-executed attack and defence that was greeted with awed applause.

The fighters were tiring now. How could they not, after such a punishing pace? In wordless agreement, they allowed the space between them to widen, and the speed of attack and counter-attack to lessen. This was always a danger point in a fight. One or both would let his concentration slacken, and the other would seize the advantage. But the invisible cord that held the two manacs to each other remained taut even as they parted. Circling carefully, the fight entered a new phase. The trainer looked at the champion and knew precisely what he would do next. Mumpo was too new a fighter to predict his opponent's move. There simply hadn't been time to teach him everything.

And here it came: the famous wild man charge. Arno rose onto the tips of his bare toes and hurled himself forward, thrashing the air before him in crazy stabbing movements that followed no pattern at all. Flailing and kicking, he bore down on Mumpo, hoping to draw him into an answering wildness: at which point, as Hackel had seen so many times before, Arno would switch in an eye-blink to a deadly precision, and it would all be over. But Mumpo stayed solid as a rock. He made no attempt at all to block the wilder outer strikes, keeping his full attention on Arno's own exposed torso. This forced Arno onto the defensive, and the attack ended as quickly as it had begun. Then, skilfully using his failure, Arno made a sudden turn, briefly offered his back to his opponent, and Mumpo took the lure. He reached out in attack, and Arno's left fist blade span round, slicing Mumpo's upper right arm. The bright blood poured out of the cut, and down into the armoured lower arm. The crowd all gasped at once. Hackel shook his head: the boy shouldn't have fallen for that. Kestrel, horrified, cried out loud.

'No! Don't hurt him!'

Mumpo's head jerked round. He had recognised her

voice. Now he saw her, for the first time. Astounded, he could only throw her one look before the big champion was attacking once more. Now Mumpo was in confusion. He backed away, buying himself time, all his concentration gone. Hackel saw it with dismay, Ortiz saw it with surprise: the boy had fallen apart. Arno drove down on him with relentless power, knowing that the fight was now his for the winning. His objective was to force Mumpo to the edge of the platform, and there, with a slight glancing blow, to topple him to defeat.

Mumpo backed and parried, the blood dripping from his right hand to the sand. His defences were still good, but he had lost the initiative. Big Arno was now dictating the rhythm, and inexperienced though he was, Mumpo knew that meant he would lose. The fundamental rule of the manaxa was that the attacker wins. Arno was increasing the speed of their engagement with every strike, denying him the chance to turn his ceaseless reactive defence into an attack. Moreover, out there on the benches watching him was Kestrel. He kept throwing glances towards her, and every glance took him out of the fight.

Now Hackel was gravely concerned. The boy was making mistakes. He'd better jump, and soon. Even now, as he watched, Arno broke through once more, and one knee blade caught Mumpo on the thigh, drawing more blood. The crowd gasped again. Mumpo, not even feeling the wound, looked up and caught the anguished look on Kestrel's face. All at once, his confusion cleared. Kess doesn't want me to lose, he found himself thinking. So I won't lose. A burst of happiness exploded in his heart, and he sprang back as Arno attacked again. He saw now exactly how he would do it. Bracing himself, instead of preparing himself to defend against the next strike, he spread his arms wide.

Ortiz saw and half-understood, rising from his seat in excitement. 'He can't!'

Hackel saw, and went white. 'He can't!'

Arno saw, and drove forward into the expected sequence of thrust, parry, riposte, counter-thrust. But Mumpo didn't parry. Arno's strike flew between both arms, and the fist blade drove into Mumpo's chest. Kestrel screamed, 'No!' Everyone on the benches sprang to their feet. But Arno did not strike again. He was standing, motionless, and Mumpo's right arm was reached out towards him. Only then did the crowd realise that Mumpo had accepted the blow in order to strike himself. He had executed the notorious double-kill manoeuvre: and his fist blade had plunged deep into the big champion's heart.

Slowly, in utter silence, Arno fell, pulling his own blade out of the side of Mumpo's chest as he dropped. The huge body thudded onto the sanded boards, and did not move again. Mumpo stood motionless, bleeding steadily from arm and thigh and chest. And the applause began. First they stamped their feet, then they beat their fists on the benches, then they screamed: a howling hammering explosion of emotions that could not be contained. The beauty had ended in a kill. The dance had turned to death. Sisi howled and hammered with the rest, swept by surges of passionate feeling that left her drained and exhilarated. Only Kestrel did not scream. She sat still, shaking all over, and kept her eyes on Mumpo.

Slowly he raised his arms to acknowledge the applause. He seemed dazed. Hackel gave a signal, and arena slaves climbed onto the platform to remove the corpse of Arno. It took six of them to lift him. Hackel himself led the victorious manac out of the arena, to have his wounds cleaned and dressed. Mumpo turned as he went, and threw one last glance towards Kestrel.

19

Kestrel dances the tantaraza

As soon as the manaxa ended, the Johdila rose, and accompanied only by her young servant, left the arena. Zohon, still elated by the fight, was caught by surprise.

'Where is the Johdila going?' he demanded.

Hasty enquiries revealed that the Johdila had retired to a side room to prepare her clothing for her dance.

In the side room, Sisi was tearing off her wedding dress as fast as she could, as she and Kestrel exchanged clothing. The emotions roused in Sisi by the manaxa, added to nervousness over the coming deception, made her hands shake as she hooked Kestrel into the tight dress.

'Oh, Kess! What if they find out?'

'They won't.'

'You're trembling too. I can feel you.'

'That's because of the fight.' She shuddered.

'Did you hate it, darling? I hated it so much it made me go hot and shake all over.'

'I didn't hate it,' said Kestrel in a low voice. 'I should have done, but I didn't.'

'Didn't you? Oh, Kess, do friends tell each other what they really feel?'

'They do if they want.'

Sisi whispered. 'I felt excited.'

'So did I.'

'Did you? Oh, thank you, Kess darling! Sometimes I think I'm so bad I shouldn't be allowed to go on living. There – now the cap.'

Kestrel drew the cap over her head, and lowered the veil in silence. She was gripped by a new fear. What if Zohon made his move now, while she was dancing the tantaraza?

She looked up at Sisi and saw tears in her eyes.

'What will happen, Kess? Something strange and terrible is coming. Don't you feel it?'

'Yes,' said Kestrel. 'We must be brave.'

While the ladies were preparing for the dance, Ortiz found himself suffering an almost unbearable restlessness. The manaxa had stirred his blood to such a degree that he was ready for anything, however unthinkable the consequences. He knew that after the dance came the exchange of vows, and then it would be too late. Somehow, he must speak to the unknown lady now.

He beckoned to Bowman. Speaking low, so that only he could hear, he pointed towards the private room to which the Johdila had retired.

'You see where they went? Her servant went with her.'

'Yes.'

'Go and find her. Tell her I must speak to her.'

'How? Where?'

'There's a passage over there. It leads to a garden. I'll go there directly after the dance. Have her wait for me there.'

Bowman did as he was told, glad enough to have this unlooked-for chance to talk to Kestrel alone. He made his way unobtrusively round the back of the raised arena, towards the private room. As he did so, Kestrel, wearing the wedding dress and the face veil, but not the outer body veil, came out of the room and entered the arena from the front. She never saw Bowman, nor did he see her. She didn't notice that Bowman was gone, because she was shivering with nervous anticipation. For all the danger of what she was doing, Kestrel felt a sudden surge of excitement. She had learned to love the tantaraza.

She looked up at Zohon as she entered. He stood at the back, where he had stood from the start, staring proudly down on the arena stage. Quietly, she pressed her hands together, and interclasped the fingers. He stiffened, and gave a very slight nod. He had seen. She then made a second gesture with her hands, stroking the air before her with downward strokes, to indicate, slowly, slowly, not yet. She hoped he understood.

The dancing master, Lazarim, who had watched the manaxa with an admiration that had turned to awe, now realised that the great tantaraza was to be danced on the blood-soaked sand of the arena. He had forgotten that he was party to a high-risk deception, and that it would not be the Johdila in the arms of the bridegroom. Only now, as he saw the slender white-clad figure return to the arena, did he realise that this must be the Johdila's young servant. As he turned to watch the bridegroom, an icy sweat of fear broke out on his brow.

Marius Semeon Ortiz did not spot the deception. His mind was elsewhere: in the room where Bowman was even now, he supposed, speaking to the lady with the dark eyes. But here and now, in the arena, his bride was before him, and he must bow, and offer her his hand. Together they stepped up onto the platform, and presented themselves first to the Johanna, then to the Master in the gallery above. Ortiz caught the eyes of his dance teacher, Madame Saez, who was staring at him sternly, warning him to concentrate on the coming dance. She was right: the tantaraza was not easy. He wondered whether the Johdila would be any good at it. He supposed not.

Their respects to others paid, he now held out his right hand, and aligned his body. His partner took his hand with a firm grasp, pivoting on the balls of her feet to adopt the correct opening position. Ortiz was agreeably surprised. She moved well. Perhaps the dance would be a pleasure after all.

Up in the gallery, the Master raised his violin to his shoulder, and started to play. The musicians below joined in: not a mere pipe and drum, but sixteen instruments, all in the hands of experts. Lazarim, standing at the back among the servants, forgot his terrors, as with all his will he reached out to his young pupil, saying in silence, fly like a bird! Fly away, child! Fly away!

The musical introduction ended, and the dance itself began. Ortiz moved to the left: step, step, step. She was with him. To the right: step, step, step. And the salute. Perfect! No attempt at grand gestures, just the correct move, pure and unadorned. And now, with the sudden sweep of the music, round into the spins, round! Round! Round! And stop! She was there! What an arrest! Madame Saez saw it, Lazarim saw it, Ortiz felt it thrill through his body. She could dance! Hands out, heels and toes clicking, they came in for the re-join, and as he took her in his arms he sensed her joy in the dance, and all other thoughts, all other hopes and fears left him. This was the tantaraza, the dance of love, and he was in love, and he would dance as he had never danced before. Round and round they swirled, lost in the rhythms of the music, their flying feet barely touching the blood-soaked sand.

Now that all eyes were on the dancers, Bowman approached the door to the side room, and quietly opened it. There was a young woman sitting at the far end with her back to him. She wore the clothes Kestrel had been wearing, and she was looking out of a window at a small garden beyond. Her head was bowed, her face was in her hands, and she was crying. But he knew at once that she was not his sister.

He was about to turn and leave, when the young woman turned her tear-stained face, and seeing Bowman, uttered a low cry of joy.

'Bowman!'

Bowman was too astonished to move. The weeping lady dabbed at her eyes and looked at him in a strange intent way.

'You are Bowman, aren't you? Kess has told me all about you.'

'Who are you?' How could she look at him as if they were intimate, when he had never seen her in his life before?

Sisi realised that he hadn't worked out the exchange she had made with Kestrel. He had no idea she was the Johdila Sirharasi of Gang. After all, she was wearing the dress of a servant.

'I'm called Sisi,' she said. 'I'm one of the Johdila's servants. Like Kestrel.'

'Where is Kestrel?'

'She went out earlier. The Johdila likes to have her by her side all the time. They're friends, you see.'

Sisi found saying all this quite delightful. But Bowman was already turning to leave.

'I have to find her.'

'Not yet!' cried Sisi. 'She doesn't want anyone to know about you. You're her secret.'

'But she told you.'

'That's because we're such close friends. Come, sit down. Wait till the dance is over.'

Reluctantly, Bowman sat down. There seemed to be nothing else he could do. He was still bewildered. How had Kestrel left without him seeing her?

'I know all about you,' said Sisi, watching him intently. 'Kess was going to arrange for us to meet, and now we have.'

She smiled radiantly.

'Do you think I'm beautiful?'

Bowman blushed.

'I don't know,' he said, hardly aware of what he was saying. 'I've never met you before.'

'What difference does that make? You have only to look.'

'No, it does make a difference.'

'Does it?' She looked disconcerted. 'How long do you need? You can look as much as you like. I won't let them put your eyes out.'

'Who?'

'Oh, anybody.' Sisi covered her mistake as best as she could. 'Go on looking. Are you getting to like me?'

'What an odd person you are.'

'Odd, but beautiful. Go on, admit it.'

'Yes. You are beautiful.'

'Hurrah!' Sisi clapped her hands with joy. 'That means you love me!'

'No, it doesn't.'

'Of course it does. Everyone knows that. Men always love beautiful women. Are you a tiny bit stupid?'

Bowman looked at her, and for the first time made the effort of reaching inside her mind. He found a confusion of childish fears, and a simple longing for affection.

'Why were you crying?' he asked more gently.

'I don't want to be –' She was about to say 'married', but stopped herself just in time. 'I don't want to be alone.'

'May I give you some advice?'

'Yes. Please.'

'Leave. There's going to be trouble here.'

'Oh, yes. I know.'

'Tell your mistress. Ortiz won't marry her. It would be better for you all to go home.'

'He won't?' She stared at Bowman, greatly astonished. 'Are you sure?'

'He's in love with someone else.'

'You mean I won't have to – with who? Who's he fallen in love with?'

'With Kestrel. With my sister.'

Sisi stared and stared. How was it possible that a man who had the chance of marrying her could prefer a funny-looking person like Kestrel? She felt no jealousy, only bewilderment. Then –

'Of course! The veil! He's never seen – her. Or me. I expect if he saw me, he'd fall in love with me. Don't you think so?'

'Yes. I expect so.' Bowman smiled. Sisi was lovely, but she was absurd. 'Now I'm going to go.'

'All right. Go if you must. But you'll find out you do love me in the end, you just wait and see.'

'If I do, I'll let you know.'

'Promise?'

'Promise.'

Bowman slipped out, and returned unnoticed to his place at the back of the arena: unnoticed because every eye, every heart, was captured by the dance. Ortiz and Kestrel, like birds on the wind, were carried by the pulsing sweeping melody, round and back, falling into each other's arms and allowing themselves to be tossed away again, like the very soul of yearning fickle love itself. Bowman watched, and knew at once that it was his sister out there on the sand. Lazarim was following every move with miniature echoing moves of his own small body, and without realising it, his mouth was uttering low cooing sounds of ecstasy. The Johanna was so absorbed that he forgot the discomfort of his crown, and tipped his head this way and that as the dancers flashed before him. Madame Saez watched in complete rigidity, her body straining, her mouth open, frozen in anticipation of each unfolding beat. And as for the dancers themselves, they were possessed. Ortiz no longer thought of the sequences of steps, or of guiding and leading his partner. Neither of them led. They flew together, in the only way possible, the way the music commanded and their bodies desired – away, away, and round, reaching, not yet touching, and away! And back! Spinning into each other's arms – ah, so lightly, barely brushing as they met, before passing and leaping, down on one foot, the spin! The return! The clasp!

Kestrel danced as if after this dance her life would

end: as if nothing and no one existed but this man, this music, this small spinning stage. He was her enemy, the man she must destroy, and he was her partner, her lover, herself: for as long as the dance lasted, they were two bodies become one.

She felt his strong arms around her as she fell back, confident that he would not let her fall; and felt his beating heart as she rose again, her breast pressed to his chest. She spread her arms wide and he lifted her, and as she dropped to the ground, feeling almost weightless, the broken drumbeat began again, that sound of startled birds crackling up out of bracken, *clacka-clacka-killacka-clack*, and together, within the same heartbeat, they exploded into free flight. One mind, one song, two bodies in motion: precise poise and total abandon, melting together in a dance that was one long unfolding embrace. In this state of grace, Kestrel knew there were no rules, no limits, her body could do anything, because everything it did was beautiful and necessary and right. She danced like one who falls from an unthinkably great height: to fall truly she need do nothing, except not resist. And so, smiling, glowing, lovely, she fell towards the climax.

The pipes and the fiddles came surging back, to tell the raptured dancers that the final phase had begun. Without conscious thought, both slipped into the arise, parting, hands raised, meeting for the merest fingertip touch, parting again, in an accelerating rhythm. With each retouch they came closer together, though by no more than an inch, and held their touching hands higher; with each parting they spun farther away from each other. So that as the music began to hammer towards its climax, they were hurtling away and throwing themselves back, into an almost-embrace, closer, closer, arms higher, higher, and on the long high call of the pipes, arms up high above their heads, face to face, breast to breast, they turned slowly, still not touching, the spectators hardly daring to breathe, famished for the promised embrace, until the music released them at last, and they fell into each other's arms.

Silence. The Master lowered his violin. Then a great sigh arose from all over the arena. Then the applause. Not the crazed screams that followed the manaxa, but the deep steady satisfaction that greets a true ending. Only Zohon stood, still as a statue, and silent.

'That,' murmured Lazarim, weeping, 'that is the tantaraza!'

Ortiz held Kestrel close, and felt her shiver as she panted to regain her breath, and saw that her face veil was fluttering away from her lips with each breath. He leaned his head close over her shoulder and whispered,

'May I dance with you till the day I die.'

It was no more than the conventional compliment of the bridegroom to the bride at the end of the tantaraza, but he meant every word. He was also watching her veil. She did not give the customary response, but her breath moved the light silk, and for a moment he glimpsed her mouth and chin. It was enough. He had been studying that face all morning. Somehow, impossibly, his partner in the dance was not the princess he was to marry, it was the unknown lady he loved. Bursting with joy at the discovery, thinking nothing of the consequences, made bold by her presence in his arms disguised as his bride, he moved to kiss her.

Zohon's eyes flashed towards his waiting captains, and

his hand began to rise in the signal for attack. But before he could complete the movement, Kestrel turned away, slipped out of Ortiz's embrace, and ran off the platform.

A ripple of surprise rose up from the arena. Ortiz bowed to the Johanna, and to the Master, and returned to his place. Here he beckoned Bowman to his side.

'It was her!' he whispered. 'Did you see the dance?'

'I saw,' said Bowman.

'She's the true princess! Only a princess could dance like that!'

Kestrel re-entered the side room, her feelings in a turmoil.

'Kess!' cried Sisi, jumping up. 'I met him! I talked to him!'

Kestrel hardly heard. Her fingers shaking violently, she began unhooking the bridal dress as fast as she could. She was burning with shame inside. How could she have danced with her enemy? No, far worse, how could she have allowed herself to love the dance?

'Bowman! Your brother!'

'What?'

'He was here. We talked. Oh, Kess, he's so sweet. So grave and kind. He thinks I'm one of my servants. He says I'm beautiful. He's going to love me.'

Kestrel stopped thinking about the dance, suddenly aware that the critical moment was now upon them. She pulled off the tight white dress and helped the Johdila to put it on.

'But Sisi, you're about to be married.'

'No, I'm not. I'll never marry him. Never ever ever.'

'What will your father say?'

'I don't care.'

She pressed her pretty lips together and made her most stubborn face. Kestrel finished dressing herself, and then took the Johdila's hands in hers and spoke to her gravely.

'Listen to me, Sisi. I'm your friend. You must realise what you're doing.'

'Oh, I do, darling. I'm going to my own wedding and not getting married.'

'There'll be trouble.'

'Of course there will. Everyone will be frightfully cross.'

'Trouble, and fighting, and danger.'

'Yes, I expect so.' A flicker of anxiety clouded her amber eyes. 'What should I do?'

'Stay close to your father and mother. The guards will protect you.'

'And you, Kess. You're my friend.'

'No. I must go with my brother.'

'I want to go with him too.'

'It's impossible, Sisi. You know it as well as I do.'

'I don't know it! How do you know what I know? You're not me.'

'I know you're a princess, who's always been looked after by servants. You won't like it where we're going. It'll be too hard for you.'

'No, it won't! Why are you being horrid to me?'

'You'd have to walk all day, with the wind and rain on your face, and sleep on the hard ground. You wouldn't be beautiful any more.'

'Oh.' That gave Sisi pause for thought. She frowned as she struggled to understand her own feelings.

'I wouldn't like not to be beautiful. But I wouldn't like to lose you and Bowman, either.'

'Who knows what will happen to us all?'

She gave Sisi a quick hug, and a kiss on her cheek.

'Just in case we don't meet again. I've liked being your friend.'

She lowered the veil over the Johdila's sweet and troubled face, and let the gossamer cloud of the body veil drop around her, and opened the door.

20

The wedding goes wrong

The Master looked down on all he had created, and was pleased. This great domed hall was his own design; as was the palace-city of which it was a part, and the lake from which it rose, and the nation all round it. He had given his life to the making of this nearly perfect world, in all its details. Year after year he had drawn the best from his people, and caused them to work together without conflict. Year after year he had weeded out the shoots of rivalry and discord, he had given discipline to the idle and purpose to the lost. By his will alone he had forged out of the mess and muddle of humanity this work of art: and now, with this wedding, which effectively made him the ruler of the civilised world, he was weaving all the threads of his creation together into a single great performance. His people were his instrument. From them he was drawing his sweetest melody, his most stirring music. He was playing the world.

The climax of this long-planned masterwork was to be the exchange of vows. All the musical motifs, from the moment the bride had entered the High Domain, had been designed to culminate in the mighty chords that were about to rise up from every player and every singer in the Mastery. United in sound, all would rejoice as one.

As the Master waited for the bride to return, he let his gaze travel over the packed hall below. At first it had irritated him to see the great mass of Johjan Guards occupying the space he had set aside for his own people. But then he had reflected that these soldiers too were now in effect his people. Let them see, and hear, and marvel. Their ruler and his fat wife looked up as if the whole proceedings overawed them, which was as it should be. Young Marius had danced to perfection, which made the Master smile down upon him. And there behind him –

A young man was looking up at him. Their eyes met. The young man at once dropped his eyes. The Master frowned. It was Ortiz's truth-teller. There was something about him that wasn't right. The Master felt irritated. This was not the time for petty distractions. What was wrong with the boy? Ah, yes, that was it. The boy wasn't afraid of him.

Curious, that. But there would be time enough to investigate later. The last movement of his great symphony was about to begin, as soon as the bride returned.

Zohon too waited with mounting impatience for the Johdila. His men were all in place, his plan was now heading towards its trigger moment. Ever since he had seen the Johdila sign to him through the trees, he had been sure of her love. Knowing she loved him, he was sure she would not give herself in marriage to the heir to the Mastery. And now, here in this very hall, he had seen her repeat her pledge to him, and sign to him to wait before ordering his men to strike. There was only one possible explanation for this. She meant to declare her true will to all the world. She herself would call on him, and he would be ready for the call, with his invincible army at his side. That way when battle commenced, there could be no doubt as to his intentions. He would be acting in defence of the Johdila. Even the Johanna would see that. The result of the battle would be the defeat of the Mastery. The Johdila would be free to marry the man she loved. The Johanna would pass on his crown to his new son-in-law. The Sovereignty of Gang would be supreme again. And he, Zohon, would at last look on the face of his beloved Sisi.

When would she call on him? And how would she show her rejection of the bridegroom? She had only the one word to utter, to consent to the marriage. Zohon, believing her to be a gentle and timid creature, thought it most likely she would choose to remain silent. When she did not speak, he would allow a pause for all the onlookers to hear her silence, and then he would strike.

Mumpo lay on a bench in the manacs' robing room, while Lars Janus Hackel himself massaged his tired muscles.

'Boy! Boy!' said Hackel, sighing. 'You're myself reborn! You have the gift, as I had it once.'

Mumpo said nothing. His bandaged wounds throbbed with pain, but he paid the pain no attention. He was elated and appalled, both at the same time, and the two feelings seemed to be mixed up with each other. Kestrel had returned. And he had killed a man. Where had Kestrel come from? Did she need his help? Why had he killed his opponent? For what? The big man had not been his enemy.

At the time, within the ritualised world of the manaxa, it had seemed necessary, even inevitable. But now as he lay on the bench and felt the blood singing through his veins, he was aware that another man lay on another bench nearby, and that he would never rise again. Kestrel had returned, and he had ended a life. Why?

'How did you know?' marvelled Hackel. 'There was only the one move would beat the big man, and you chose it. I never taught you that.'

'I didn't mean to hurt him so badly.'

'Badly enough. He's fought his last fight.'

'I'm sorry.'

'He entered the arena ready to die, just as you did. That's the manaxa for you.'

Mumpo lifted himself up into a sitting position.

'I have to go back.'

'Want to see the wedding, eh? So you shall.'

A group of slaves were scrubbing down the dead man's body, preparing it for the funeral rites. A woman, presumably his wife, was kneeling by his head, stroking his dead face.

'I won't fight again,' said Mumpo.

'Every manac says that after his first kill,' responded the trainer, unperturbed. 'But they all come back. Once you've felt it, you can't do without it.'

Mumpo reached for a training robe and pulled it on, grimacing at the pain as he moved.

'I have to go back,' he said again.

Something was wrong, he knew it. Kestrel would need him.

The Johdila re-entered the arena at last, followed by her servant, and was led to her position on the bride's side of the sandy stage. Marius Semeon Ortiz stood in his position, on the other side, and waited as he had been instructed for the music to begin. He noticed that the Johdila was trembling. Let her tremble, he thought. She's not my responsibility. His eyes were on Kestrel.

Now that the exchange of vows was imminent, the Johdi began to cry. She snuffled noisily behind her veil, and Lunki, hearing her, also began to weep. 'Oh my pet,' she crooned to herself. 'Oh my poor baby.'

Mumpo entered quietly, and took up a position by the tunnel entrance, where he could see Kestrel. Kestrel, braced for the critical moment, was watching Sisi. Sisi was looking across the arena towards Bowman. Bowman was looking up, at the Master.

The Master raised his violin to his shoulder, settled himself down, and drew the bow softly over the strings. The first low sweet note sounded over the arena. The other players responded, and the movement was begun. On the eighth bar, all perfectly together, the choir began to sing. From now on, the tempo of the music dictated every move in the ceremony.

Ortiz took one pace forward, and was still. The Johdila, quietly guided by Meeron Graff, took a pace forward in her turn, and was still. The Master's violin led the next phrase, and the other musicians followed. Outside the domed hall, linked by chains of assistant conductors who signalled to each other, every choir and every ensemble in the High Domain was playing the same theme, at the same time.

Ortiz followed the steps he had rehearsed as if he were in a dream from which he would shortly awake. His slow paces would carry him towards the Johdila, five steps in all: but his eyes were on Kestrel. He heard the

Master's violin, and he took the second step, and even within his dream-like state he knew that he faced an unbearable choice. It was his beloved Master's wish that he marry this princess. How could he not obey? But as he looked on the young woman with the dark eyes, the one who had danced the tantaraza with him, the one who had become for him all that was life itself, he thought, how can I love anyone but her?

He took the third step.

The Johdila felt the gentle tug of Graff's hand, and she took her third step, coming ever closer to her husband-to-be. She looked up now, as her mother had taught her. She saw her white-clothed groom before her, and beyond him she saw Bowman, looking pale and grave. He told me there would be trouble, she thought. He thinks I'm weak and foolish, and have to be protected. But I'm the one who's going to cause the trouble. He'll see, and then he'll know. I'm not as useless as they all think.

Then the solo violin was playing once more, and the Keeper of the Master's Household was pulling on her body veil, and so she took her fourth step.

Zohon watched in fascination, as bride and groom glided over the blood-stained sand, in slow motion, towards each other. With each arrested step, the music grew a little louder, a little more urgent, as it drove the betrothed pair towards their vows. The players outside the hall could be clearly heard now, so that those in the arena were doubly cocooned in music. Zohon checked his captains, to be sure that all were alert for his signal. It would come soon now.

Up in the gallery above, intoxicated by his own music, the Master drew from his violin the opening notes of the fifth passage, and saw Ortiz below take the fifth and final step. Then, as the other players followed him, here in the hall and all over the city, he caught a sudden note of danger. Turning sharply, focusing all his powers of attention, he tracked its source. It was Ortiz. The boy was going to disobey him! Without ceasing playing, he came close to the gallery's railing, and stared down at the bridegroom.

Ortiz felt the Master seize his mind from above. He looked up, and was at once flooded with the Master's own pure will. He felt himself go icy cold. At the same time, his skin prickled and burned, as if he was on fire. Then the coldness and the burning left him, and he found he was filled with calm: more than calm, a limpid and invulnerable tranquillity, the calm of unclimbable mountains, of unreachable stars. Now all was simple again. He had only to love his Master, and obey.

Bowman, standing not far behind, felt the jolt of the Master's power, and understood exactly what had been done. In that same moment, he understood that it was this supreme will alone that sustained the entire Mastery. If the Mastery was to be destroyed, the Master's will must first be broken.

The music surged on towards its climax. The Johdila took her fifth step. Ortiz now stood before his bride, close enough to reach out and touch her, with no thoughts and no desires left. Remotely, as if recalled from some far-off place in space and time, he felt a sense of loss: but it had no face, no name. His Master made the music that directed his steps. He had only to love and to obey.

Suddenly the music paused, in mid-phrase, almost in mid-chord. This was the Master's desire, that the few but necessary words be spoken in a space formed by the music itself, a space dynamic with tension, straining for release into the grand climax.

Ortiz knew his part. Now he was to speak.

'With these five steps, I stand before you as your husband. Do you receive me as my wife?'

The Johdila was silent. The silence, the not-music, stretched out in long agonised seconds. Zohon braced himself for action.

'Say the word, radiance,' murmured Graff.

No one could see the Johdila's face through the two veils, but tears were welling up in her eyes, and now were spilling over to trickle down her perfect cheeks.

Ortiz realised that his bride was not going to speak. Kestrel met Bowman's gaze across the arena.

Any moment now –

The silence became unbearable. The Master, waiting in mounting rage, suddenly realised that this was not a matter of nerves or shyness, but an act of defiance. At once he focused his powers on the bride, to hammer her spirit into line with his will, and so sweep on to the glorious climactic chords of his masterwork –

'No!'

The Johdila cried out the one electric word. There was a moment of stunned silence.

'Go!' cried Kestrel. 'Run, Sisi, run!'

The Johdila turned and ran from the stage.

Consternation filled the hall.

Zohon's hand struck the air. All his men drew their swords.

'In the name of the Sovereignty of Gang,' he cried, 'surrender or die!'

Barzan saw the Johjan Guards moving in to control the exits, and shouted in despair,

'Idiots! What do you think you're doing?'

The Master lowered his violin, and closing his eyes, poured out his will all over the High Domain. The message was wordless, but all heard it, and all obeyed. Every able-bodied man in the hall, from the trumpet players in the orchestra to the young lords in Ortiz's entourage, was transformed into a fighter. The question that had so puzzled Zohon – where is the army of the Mastery? – was now answered. The Master's people were his army. From beneath robes and tunics came weapons. Within minutes, the great domed hall was a scene of bloody battle.

Zohon saw this with shock. But his guards were surely better trained than any citizen rabble. It was only a matter of holding his nerve.

'Cut them down! Kang! Kang! Kang! The Hammer of Gang!' he cried, fighting his way through to the terrified Johanna and his wife.

'You fool!' wept Barzan, stamping his feet. 'You great stuffed booby!'

'Where's the Johdila?' demanded Zohon.

Bowman and Kestrel had both moved towards the doors at the same time. All they wanted now was to escape the battle-filled hall and find their parents. Mumpo leaped up and followed them, careless of the danger. Finding one of the Johjan Guards barring his way brandishing a sword, Mumpo struck out with his bare fist, broke the guard's neck, and ran on.

Ortiz, filled with his Master's will, took charge of the mass of fighting men.

'Close ranks! Strike hard! For the Master! Fight and die!'

Bowman and Kestrel pushed their way through the

open doors to the street. Outside, to their astonishment, they saw columns of armed people advancing, summoned by the will of the Master. They came from all directions, in seemingly limitless numbers. The Johjan Guards would never be able to resist such an onslaught. Bowman gazed on the swarm of people, saw the single-minded gaze in every eye, and understood what it was he must do.

'I have to go back.'

'No!' cried Kestrel. 'This is our only chance!'

'Get out of the city! I'll join you as soon as I can.'

'No! I'm coming with you!'

'Please, Kess!' He turned on her fiercely, knowing he had very little time. 'You'll weaken me. Get out of the city. All this is about to be destroyed!'

Kestrel stared at her brother, shocked. Never before had he chosen to face a danger without her.

'How will I weaken you?'

Mumpo came running up to join them.

'Kess!'

'Mumpo! You're all right! Bo –'

But he was gone.

'Don't be afraid, Kess. I'm a good fighter. I won't let anyone hurt you.'

'I know, Mumpo. I saw.'

She turned and looked down the street at the advancing streams of armed men, and decided she must do as her brother wanted.

'Let's go and find ma and pa.'

Bowman went back into the domed hall, where the fighting was now intense and chaotic. A Johjan Guard, striking wildly at anyone and anything, made a swing at him. At once, in instinctive self-defence, Bowman turned his burning eyes on him, and without raising his hand, struck him a single concentrated blow. The guard fell like a stone.

Bowman looked up to the high gallery, where the Master still stood, eyes closed, pouring out his limitless will. Bowman saw how the Master's people fought, sustained by this power, without regard to their own safety. They would never be defeated until this one man's power was broken.

This is what I've been sent to do.

He focused his attention on the figure of the Master, and sent a shock-beam from his mind towards him. At this distance it lacked power, but it still struck the Master with such force that he jumped, and let go of his violin. The violin fell from the high gallery, and smashed on the stone floor below. In fury, the Master sought out his attacker, and found Bowman. At once he sent out a wave of power, but Bowman was waiting for it, and well-defended. To the Master's astonishment, he stood his ground, blocking the assault, redirecting the stream of energy to drain harmlessly into the ground.

As suddenly as he had attacked, the Master pulled back. It was now Bowman's turn to be caught by surprise. Surely it couldn't be over so easily? But the Master had turned, and with a flurry of his crimson robes, he was striding away.

Bowman searched for the way to reach the high gallery, and quickly saw the narrow open staircase climbing the wall on the far side. He crossed the stone floor towards it in a straight line, using his growing power to hurl the fighting men out of his way as he went. Some Johjan Guards were already on the staircase. Bowman plucked them off as if they were insects, and dropped them to the floor below. He ran up the stone stairs to the gallery. It was empty. A long passage led away, to a further flight of stairs. At the bottom of the stairs he found the Master's violin bow, lying discarded on the floor. He climbed the stairs three at a time to a small landing at the top. Here lay the Master's golden helmet, and his crimson cloak. Before him was a small door with an iron handle.

As Bowman put his hand to the iron handle, he knew that he would find the Master inside. He could feel him. The door would not be locked. He would enter. And the real battle would begin.

21

The mind duel

The space beyond the door was dazzlingly bright. Bowman realised that he must be in the topmost part of the highest dome. Above him, through a great enclosing cup of clear glass, clouds were marching across a grey sky. Before him stretched a plain timber floor, on which stood a narrow iron bed, a table, and a chair. The bald simplicity of the furniture gave the room, if room it could be called when it seemed to have neither walls nor roof, the look of a prison cell. On the single chair sat a stooped old man, with his back to him. He wore a robe of coarse undyed wool. His feet were bare.

Bowman stood and stared in confusion. The door swung shut of its own accord behind him. As the latch clicked, the old man turned his head.

The same mane of white hair, the same strong mouth and ruddy cheeks: but the eyes were different, withdrawn, no longer powerful. The Master looked at Bowman with a curious kind of detachment, as if interested to see what he would do, but not personally involved.

'You're a Singer?'

'Of course,' said the Master. His voice was low, almost

300

a whisper. 'Or I was once.'

'Then why –?'

'Why rule? Somebody must, boy. We can't all sing songs.'

Bowman had come to fight, if need be, to kill: but here before him was no resistance, no power. He no longer knew what to do.

'They don't understand this in Sirene.' The Master gestured with one hand at the city beyond the glass. 'Sirene has sent you, of course.'

'Yes.'

'I knew it would come one day.' He studied Bowman carefully. 'Are you strong enough?'

'I don't know.'

'If necessary,' said the Master, 'you can call for help. One of many, part of all.'

Bowman felt a shiver of fear. This was what the one-eyed hermit had said to him. How could the Master know so much?

The Master was smiling at him.

'What exactly did they say you were to do?'

'To destroy and to rule.'

'Ah, yes. First you destroy. Then you rule. How little changes! So you're just like me after all.'

Bowman struggled to hold on to his sense of what was right and true.

'No,' he said. 'I'll set the people free.'

'Free?' The Master chuckled at the thought. 'What makes you think they want to be free? You think I compel their obedience?'

'You're the Master. They obey you.'

'I am what they have made me.'

The smile faded. Like a curtain being drawn aside, the

old man allowed Bowman to reach deeper into him. There he felt again the power of a being with no fears and no desires.

'Do you see it now?' said the Master quietly. 'You've come not to free them, but to free me.'

Bowman said nothing. He could feel the Master gathering his strength. He wanted to be ready when the blow fell.

'Then, after I am gone, you will become me.'

'Never!'

'Poor Marius. He thought it would be him. But he's not like me.'

'I'm not like you. I don't want what you want.'

Why pretend? Do you think I don't know?

The thought cut into Bowman's mind like a knife. Just in time, he braced himself. The Master's eyes were on him, his mind rearing up over him –

Destroy me if you can! If you can't, I will destroy you.

Bowman staggered under the impact of the Master's will. Out of that great body streamed a jet of power that scrambled his mind and sucked away his thoughts.

Let's see how strong you are.

Desperately, Bowman struggled to retain control of his own will, and realised with mounting panic that he could not. He felt as if he was growing heavier, and his muscles were growing weaker. He felt his knees buckle.

Come, let's have more of a fight than this.

Bowman sank to his knees. His lips started to form words, words of submission and obedience. In his heart he felt a desire to serve, to please, to be loved. But even as he bowed his head, he knew what it was he must do. He must not resist. There was nothing that could resist so overwhelming a will. Not resist: let go. He must meet this great emptiness with his own emptiness. He must fight nothing with nothing.

With a last desperate throw, he flung open the doors of his mind; emptied it in the way he did when listening for his sister. At once, as his own confusion dropped away, he felt the Master's will lose its grip. He had become slippery.

He raised his head and met the Master's eyes.

Better, said the Master. *Now we shall see.*

He held the Master's eyes, and let himself enter his mind, with no intent to harm or to control, only to know. He found there silence; and behind silence, power; and behind power, anger; and behind anger, hurt. The longer he remained in possession, the further he reached, the weaker the Master became.

Forget me, said the Master, *but don't forget what I have made.*

He saw the old man shiver.

'You're cold.'

'Of course. I grow colder as you grow warmer.'

Bowman felt a twinge of pity. At once the Master struck, rocking his mind with an explosion of naked power. Bowman reeled, closing his eyes, clutching at his temples.

Not so easy after all, boy. Take care, or I shall crush you.

Once again, drawing a deep breath, Bowman cleared his mind, and raising his eyes, returned to the silent duel. Back beyond silence and power, beyond anger and hurt, to a long-buried dream of glory –

Do you feel it, boy? It's your future. First you destroy, then you rule. But you can't do it alone.

* * *

Out in the city, the fighting between the people of the Mastery and the Johjan Guards was reaching its climax. Zohon now realised his mistake in bringing all his force inside the great hall. As more and more armed men arrived outside, he found he and his guards were surrounded, and facing greatly superior numbers. He had no choice but to form his men into a defensive square, and fight for survival itself.

Ortiz saw that the battle was all but won. The Master was no longer at his position in the gallery above. He must have withdrawn to his private quarters. As he looked over the scene of struggle, he saw a slight figure slip into the hall, and weave her way round fighting men to the far side. It was the young woman with the dark eyes. At once, all his love for her came bursting back. But where was she going?

Kestrel had reached the very gates of the High Domain when she had felt Bowman's pain. At once she had turned back, saying to Mumpo, 'You go on, find the others. I can't leave him.' She had raced back up the street, filled with a terrible foreboding. Bowman was in trouble, and she must find him.

Now, following that sense that was neither sound nor smell, but through which she felt her twin, and careless of the danger around her, she ran up the stone stairs, knowing he was not far now, and he was suffering.

Not many strides behind her, also running, came Ortiz.

Bowman stood in the Master's cell, his eyes closed, locked deep in the mind duel. His face felt cold, very cold. His body was going numb. He had lost all sense of time. Had he been here for seconds, or for centuries? He no longer knew. The Master faced him, still and expressionless, in silent struggle with his younger opponent. Each had entered the other's mind, and slowly, with ever-increasing force, sought to stifle it. To Bowman it was as if he had reached out an invisible hand, and now held it clamped over the old man's face, crushing and suffocating him: while at the same time the Master's hand was on his own face, and it was hard for him to breathe. So hard, so slow –

There came a distant rattle of sound, somewhere far away. A figure entered the room, seeming to float, it moved so slowly. With it came a familiar feeling, warm and strong, tugging him out of his duel.

Kess!

At once, seizing the break of concentration, the Master's will surged into Bowman like a river in spate. Bowman fell slowly, so slowly to the ground, choking, drowning. All around him the air was full of a thick buzzing, like a cloud of sleepy flies.

Bo! Use me!

Kestrel was sending him all her fierce young will, to fight the dark flood. Bowman stirred and revived a little, and began doggedly to claw his way back, assisted now by Kestrel's will.

Ah! murmured the Master, feeling the change. *Two become one.*

With a sudden push, Bowman was back in the Master's mind, and the duel resumed. Calling on all his strength, he drove deeper, further than he had gone before, but however deep he went there was more.

Two is better than one, mocked the Master, *but you'll need more. Call for help and help will come.*

Never!

Don't say that, boy. Even you may need help.

He gave a twist of his mind-grip that made Bowman gasp with pain. But Bowman did not let go. They had reached so far into each other now that they were sharing a heartbeat, and Bowman found with shock that he could look out of the Master's eyes. The duel moved at lightning speed, but outside the two of them everything else was moving so slowly it barely moved at all.

It was with this slowed double vision that Bowman saw Ortiz enter the room: first though his own eyes, then through the eyes of the Master. He saw Ortiz turning, his arms reaching out to seize and hold Kestrel. He heard the low buzzing sound that was Ortiz's voice.

'Mmmmaaasssterrr . . .'

Ortiz was asking for orders. Before his request could be completed in the form of spoken words, the Master was replying.

'Kill her! Kill her! Kill her! Kill her! . . .'

He spoke the words only once: the echo came from within Bowman, as he heard through the Master's ears, and through his own, round and round in an eternal loop of sound.

No!

Through the Master's eyes he saw Ortiz's face contort with pain. Through his own senses he felt Ortiz's agony, as obedience clashed with love. Of course! He remembered now, faintly, from so long ago. *He loves my sister. He won't kill her.*

But already Ortiz's right hand was tracking down through space to find the pommel of his sword, and the left arm was crushing her tight against his chest.

'I obey, I obey, I obey, I obey . . .'

The fuzzy words echoed in Bowman's ears as he felt the Master's power hold him too in its grip, so still and unfathomable and merciless. Dimly, far-off, he heard Ortiz sobbing, and saw the tears crawl slowly down his face, and knew that he wept for Kestrel, who he loved and must kill. Out slid the bright sword, longer and longer in the slanting light from the sky, until it flashed free. Bowman saw that slow dazzle from one side, from the other, saw the sharp blade turn and start to float, to drift, ah, so slowly, towards his sister's breast.

Furiously, wildly, hopelessly, Bowman beat with his own will against the Master's implacable power. The old man sat still, his eyes open, the faint smile still lingering; but behind that filmy gaze lay the force he could not overcome. Not alone. Not with Kestrel. Not without help.

Kill her, kill her, kill her, kill her . . .

On sailed the bright blade, driven by the obedient tormented hand of Marius Semeon Ortiz, slave of his Master's will. Kestrel's eyes looked round, reached out, uncomplaining, filled with pity, not for herself but for the brother she loved more than herself –

Love you, Bo –

So close now, and he knew he could not break the Master's grip, not alone, not without help. What choice did he have? *Quick, now, quick*! Had he not surrendered before? What innocence had he to protect? *Now, now*! Would he not die for her, his dear one, his half-self, his sister? Then why not call for help from the only source greater than this old man, this well of desirelessness, this Master? *Must she die for my purity*?

'Help me!' he cried aloud, his voice sounding thin and strange. 'I can't do it alone!'

He saw the Master's face twist into a smile of victory, even as he felt the power come pulsing into him.

One of many, part of all!

He drew deep strong breaths. He grew. He swelled. He burned. The sword was still in motion towards its deadly goal, but now Bowman was overtaking it in its flight, overtaking time itself, as the bright pure spirit of the Morah rose within him.

We are legion! We are all!

Kestrel saw in his eyes the many eyes, the hundreds of eyes possessing him, and knew what he had done for her. But she could not stop him now.

No more fear now! Let others fear!

As the power grew and grew, he turned it on the Master, bearing down on him, suffocating him, crushing him. He heard the old song in his head, and marching now to its tune, though his body never moved, he felt the savage joy blossom within him.

Kill, kill, kill, kill! Kill, kill, kill!

The old man's power dwindled before him, unable to resist the legion that was the Morah. *Kill!* said Bowman, pressing, squeezing. *Kill!* he cried, forcing the life out of his enemy without moving a finger. *Kill!* as he felt the old man fading, and he laughed and rejoiced, and would not let him go.

Ortiz sensed the Master's power leave him, and the sword stopped in its path, an inch from Kestrel's breast. Still holding her tight, wracked by anguish, he bent his tawny head over her shoulder and sobbed.

This is how Mumpo found him as he burst into the room. This is how Mumpo saw him, from the back, his sword still seemingly poised to strike. Springing forward without a second thought, his fist struck Ortiz at the base of his skull with all the power at his command. Ortiz died in that instant, with Kestrel in his arms, and the tears fresh on his cheeks. Mumpo seized him in his fury, and tore him away from Kestrel, and hurled him aside.

'Has he hurt you?'

'No,' said Kestrel, shivering and shivering. 'I'm not hurt.'

She looked down at where Ortiz lay, and he looked unhurt, and beautiful in death. She had her vengeance. But nothing was the way she had supposed. There was no rejoicing in her heart.

The Master's eyes had never left Bowman's. The light of life was fading fast now. He fought no more. The great will that had built and sustained a nation was broken.

'Free at last,' he murmured; and the light went out.

Kestrel felt the shudder of separation go through her brother. She felt him come slowly from a dark deep place, back into the light. When at last he turned to look at her there was such anguish in his eyes that she cried out loud and ran to him, to take him in her arms. He let her embrace his burning body, and kiss his fiery cheeks. Slowly he raised his arms to hold her. Slowly, recognition returned to his eyes.

Couldn't let you die, Kess. Couldn't live without you.

Kestrel thanked him with her eyes as she kissed him. But she knew they had very little time.

'Help me, Mumpo. We must get him away.'

22

The anger of slaves

The defeat of the Master changed everything. The armed men fighting in and around the hall, pressing in on Zohon's embattled Johjan Guards, let their sword arms fall and stood bewildered, uncertain what they were doing or why. They looked at each other, and didn't recognise each other, and it seemed to them that the men who had been fighting at their side were strangers. The Johjan Guards understood none of this: only that the tide of battle was turning. Zohon urged his men to renewed efforts, crying,

'Kang! Kang! Kang! The Hammer of Gang!'

To his astonishment, his encircled men broke through at last. The enemy were giving ground. The enemy were – inexplicably, but all too obviously – giving up.

Kestrel, Bowman and Mumpo made their way back down the stone stairs into a scene of grisly revenge. The Johjan Guards were now advancing on all sides, and killing without mercy. Mumpo protected Bowman and Kestrel, sweeping armed men aside with brutal skill, as they crossed the great domed hall.

A stout man with a raised sword, who had been fighting his way forward in obedience to his Master's will, suddenly turned right in front of them and swung his sword against the carved stone of a pillar. Thock! went the blade as it bit into the delicate stonework. He yelled out loud. Thock! Thock! He yelled ever louder as he hacked, sliced and mutilated the pillar. From outside in the street there came a loud crash. A group of people had overturned a flower stall, and were stamping and trampling on the flowers. Cries and jeers rose up on all sides. Crash! A window was broken. Suddenly, as if released by the sound, everyone was breaking windows, swinging at them with swords, pelting them with stones, even kicking them in with their boots. Crash! Crash! Crash! on every side. A crowd surged into a wine shop and reappeared with their arms full of bottles. Crash! Crash! Crash! as they hurled the bottles against walls, screaming as they did so, howling with laughter.

In the hall, a tall man stood over the fountain, swinging an axe in both hands. With his first blow he smashed the marble birds. With his second and third blows, he broke the bars of the marble cage. The water gushed on as before, but now there was no cage to contain it, and no birds to fly the rising wave. Fragments of delicate marble littered the floor, along with shards of broken glass and blood.

First you destroy –

Destruction indeed! The slaves were free at last, and they were using their freedom to smash and tear, hurt and kill, with no purpose or advantage other than to taste the power so long denied them. Musicians were trampling on their instruments, dairymen danced in butter, horses stampeded, and children urinated in the streets. Trees were stripped of their branches in the squares. The gilded carriages of the bridal party were smashed to matchwood. Crazed men even broke into the academy library, and set about hurling books out of the windows. Down in the maddened street the books could be seen descending, their pages fluttering apart like the wings of wounded birds. Everyone was screaming, either in the wild joy of destruction or in pain from random injuries. And now fires were being started.

The guards round the monkey wagons had spent the morning watching the antics of a wild grey cat. It had been scrabbling up onto the top of one of the cages, and hurling itself off again, in the most comical manner. They had tried to pet it, and had offered it food, but it had paid them no attention. Now it was back on top of the cage, preparing yet again to spring into the air.

Then the shouts and crashes began in the High Domain. The guards turned to see what was going on. The cat too looked across the lake. The prisoners in the cage became frightened, and reached out to hold each other's hands. As the sounds of destruction grew, the guards became agitated. They looked from the slaves locked in the cages to the city on the lake and back again, as if aware that they must do something, but not sure what. Pinto Hath watched them from inside her cage, keeping alert but quiet, holding tight to her neighbour's hand to give her courage.

All at once her father was there. He had come racing down the hillside to plead with the guards.

'Listen! Can't you hear? It's all over! Everything's changed now! You can let them go!'

The guard stared back at him with frightened eyes. He was a Loomus, and his mind moved slowly.

'Let them go?' he said.

'Take out the key,' urged Hanno, speaking clearly and forcefully. 'Unlock the cage. Let them go.'

'Let them go?' said the guard again.

A stream of acrid smoke from the city was carried over the lake by the wind. One of the slaves in Pinto's cage saw the smoke and cried out,

'Look! It's burning!'

'No!' cried Hanno. 'Don't say it!'

But he was too late. Already the Loomus guard was turning to his companions and saying,

'Burning! Burning!'

Their wide nostrils snuffed the smell of the smoke, and hearing the distant screams they started to utter small screams of their own. The general confusion seemed to have unhinged them.

'Burning!' they shouted, jumping up and down like children at play. 'Burning!' They started to laugh. One of them went to the fire and drew out a glowing stick. He held it out for the others to see. 'Burning!'

'Burning!' they agreed, nodding eagerly.

Hanno threw himself at the guard as he headed for the monkey wagon. The guard never even paused. He just swiped at Hanno with his free hand, and Hanno fell gasping, winded, to the ground. The guard thrust the burning stick into the dry kindling beneath Pinto's cage. Pinto and the others tried to push their fingers through the grid to dislodge it, but the mesh was too small. Already the dry kindling was catching fire. The grey cat felt it, and leaped from the cage-top to the ground.

The Loomus guards watched with excited delight. Dancing from foot to foot, they mimed how it would be to be burned alive in the cage, and found it uproariously funny. The people in the cage crept away to the point furthest from the flames. Pinto settled herself down here, and fixed her eyes on her father, and made not a sound.

The causeway was jammed with people fleeing the burning city. It took Mumpo some time to force a way for himself and his companions. The crush was made far worse by the looting. People were dragging with them bundles of silverware, fine dresses, rolls of bedding, even an iron bed itself. Where the way forward was blocked, the people pushing from behind clambered over those who had stopped, and the unfortunates beneath were trampled to death. Many were running along the causeway's low wooden balustrades, but the timber rails weren't built to take such weight, and collapsed in several places at once. The people on them tumbled into the cold waters of the lake, where those who couldn't swim thrashed and screamed and were ignored, until the screaming stopped.

On the hillside above the monkey wagons, Creoth was driving his herd of cows, riding in a horse-drawn wagon that carried the day's supply of milk. Hanno Hath had called him, and now he was coming to join him on his promised escape, bringing with him his cows, his wagon, and the four big churns of milk. The first he knew of the battle was the agitated lowing of his cows. Then he saw fires burning in the High Domain. Then he heard Hanno calling to him.

'Creoth! The milk!'

Creoth didn't understand what Hanno meant. Then he saw the people in one of the monkey wagons all crowded to the far end of the cage, and the fire crackling away at the near end, and the Loomus guards dancing and laughing.

'On the fire!' Hanno was shouting. 'Throw the milk on the fire!'

'Beard of my ancestors!' muttered Creoth to himself. He pulled the wagon to a halt, jumped down, and ran round to the milk churns on the back. The churns were heavy, but he was a big man, and with both arms clasped tight round the churn's middle, he could carry one. Staggering under the weight, watched by the laughing guards, he heaved it to the cage, and tipped it over. The rich creamy milk gushed out of the churn to one side, and spread in a white puddle over the road. The guards doubled over and smacked their legs and howled with laughter. The people in the cage, crying now, felt the fire crawl towards their feet.

Creoth slapped himself on the face.

'I'm a disgrace to my ancestors!' he wept. 'Why am I so useless?'

'Help me here.'

Hanno was already back by the wagon, struggling with a second churn, but it was too heavy for him to lift. Creoth hurried to his side, and wrapped his strong arms round the churn. Hanno went with him to guide it as it tipped. This time the milk poured onto the burning wood, and with a hissing and a bubbling, doused part of the flames. The rich smoky smell of burned milk filled the air.

The guards stopped laughing and goggled in surprise. Then with a bellow of anger, one pulled out his sword and turned on Creoth, while the other took up a bundle of dry wood to re-kindle the fire. Up went the blade, as Creoth cowered by the overturned churn, and down it came, slashing the air. Creoth had rolled under the cage. Frustrated, the guard ran round, swiping and poking with

315

his sword, while Creoth kept out of his reach between the wheels.

Mist saw the second guard carrying the firewood towards the cage, and understood what it meant. The guard was some way away, but the cat was angry. All morning these two fools had laughed at him because he couldn't fly. Now they laughed at people being burned to death. Goaded beyond endurance, Mist coiled his body, and sprang. Claws outstretched, he hurtled through the air, further than he had ever sprung before, faster, higher, to land full on the guard's face. Tearing at his cheeks and neck with his claws, he forced the guard to stumble and release his firewood.

'Yow!' shrieked the guard, pulling the cat from his face. Mist dropped to the ground, and looked back in surprise. How had he jumped that far? Had he jumped?

Did I fly? Was that flying?

A scream came from the guard with the sword. He had been so absorbed in catching Creoth that he never heard the arrival of the others.

Mumpo struck the first guard a single deadly blow before he even knew he was under attack. The second guard, hearing the dying scream of his companion, looked round in time to see Mumpo's flying fist: and it was all over.

Hanno was already tearing the key from the dead man's belt. Bowman was by the cage, reaching through the bars to Pinto. Ira Hath had found Kestrel, and folded her in her arms.

The cage door swung open, and the terrified prisoners came tumbling out. Pinto waited until all the others were out before leaving herself, and letting herself be gathered up into her father's arms. Then for a few short precious moments she and Hanno and Ira and Kestrel and Bowman and Mumpo all pressed close against each other, and none of them spoke.

Then Hanno said,

'Time to go.'

Zohon was now in undisputed control of the High Domain; if it could be called control, to rule a city that was given over to smashing, looting and burning. But Zohon was not concerned to save the beauties of the Mastery. It gave him grim satisfaction to see the elegant domed structures burn and fall. Let the High Domain and all its glory die. Let it return to the barren dirt from which it had been raised. Let its people slaughter each other. He, Zohon, the master of the Mastery, the conqueror of the world, had a greater goal in view. At the head of his victorious Johjan Guards he would march in triumph back to Obagang, and there declare himself the new supreme ruler: the Zohonna of Gang. He needed only to find his beloved, his true bride, the one who would legitimise his seizure of power and bring joy to his proud heart: the Radiance of the East, the Pearl of Perfection, and the Delight of a Million Eyes.

But she was nowhere to be found. His men had searched the state rooms. They had found the body of Ortiz, but not the Johdila.

'Someone has taken her!' Zohon raged in his fury. 'Someone is hiding her from me!'

He had the miserable Grand Vizier dragged before him, along with the royal augur. Ozoh the Wise was incoherent with terror.

'Where is she?' yelled Zohon. 'I will be told!'

'I don't know,' wailed Barzan.

Zohon took out his hammer, and reversing it to present the sharp steel blade, he slashed the front of Barzan's tunic. Barzan screamed. The blade had cut through fabric and skin to leave a streak of welling blood.

'Must I cut deeper?'

'I swear, I swear I don't know,' blubbered Barzan in pain and fear.

Zohon looked on him with disgust.

'Have you no manliness? Stand up straight.'

Barzan tried to stiffen his cringing back.

'To think a worm like you believed he could oppose me! Can't you recognise true greatness when you see it?'

'I didn't know,' stammered the Grand Vizier.

'You know now. Kneel!'

The hammer's sharp blade hovered close. Barzan hastened to kneel.

'I am the Zohonna, Lord of a Million Souls!'

'Yes, yes.'

'Yes, what?'

'Yes, mightiness.'

Zohon turned to the augur.

'Ozoh the Wise,' he said, sneering. 'If you're so wise, you'll tell me where the Johdila is.'

'My wisdom is fled, mightiness,' wept Ozoh. 'I have lost my egg. I know nothing.'

'Take down your trousers!'

Ozoh hurriedly pulled down his baggy pantaloons, letting them drop to his ankles. His bottom and his upper thighs were revealed: naked, pale, unadorned.

'Paint!' said Zohon. 'Just paint, after all! I knew it! Boil him.'

Poor Ozoh was dragged away, weeping with fear. Zohon turned to his attendant officers.

'Here is my command to the people of the Mastery,' he announced. 'They are to bring me the Johdila Sirharasi by dawn tomorrow, or they will die. Every last one of them! Every man, woman, and child! Not one living creature will be left alive, if the Johdila is not restored to my strong and loving arms!'

23

Sisi turns her cheek

Twilight was gathering as Hanno Hath led his followers up the hillside and out of the Mastery. The terrible events of the day had proved Ira Hath to be a prophetess with the true gift, and this had brought some more to join their group. But most stayed behind, to loot, to take over the abandoned farms, to work the already-cultivated land. For as they said, where were the wanderers going? No one knew. How would they be protected? What would they eat? How would they keep warm when winter came?

'Is it far?' they asked the prophetess. 'This homeland of yours?'

'Far enough,' she said. 'But not too far.'

How else could she answer? She had only seen it in a dream. Where it was or how far away she had no idea.

So in the column that now trudged up the stone road as the day drew to a close there were just thirty of the Manth people, five cows, one horse-drawn wagon, and a grey cat.

Some of the Manth people who were staying behind gathered to wish them well on their way. But it was a subdued leave-taking. The ones who were staying were exhausted, afraid, and full of doubts of their own. The ones who were leaving knew they were only carrying enough provisions for the first few days, and after that they must find food on the road or starve. They would also have to forage for firewood, and the means to shelter themselves at night, for winter was approaching fast. So altogether it was a band sustained by faith and hope, more than any sensible expectation of survival, that waved good-bye and wound its way up the hillside into the trees.

Hanno Hath led the way, with his wife at his side. They proceeded on foot, as they had done on the slave march. Behind them came their children, Bowman, Kestrel, and Pinto. Mumpo took upon himself the role of guardian, and together with the two eldest Mimilith boys roamed back and forth along the straggling column watching out for danger. Scooch had joined them, along with the Mimilith family, and fat Mrs Chirish; and Creoth, driving his cows, who were lowing pitifully, because it was past their time to be milked.

They made their way through the trees, past the stone pillars that marked the borders of the Mastery, and out onto the bleak uplands. Here, Ira Hath stood still a moment, until she felt on one cheek the far-off warmth that only she could feel. Guided by this faint but sure sense of direction, they turned north. Hanno's intention was to put as much distance as possible between them and the Mastery before they stopped for the night. But darkness was falling, and his companions were weary after the terrors of the long day, and so, sooner than he thought wise, he was obliged to call a halt.

They lit a fire with some of their small store of wood, and all gathered round it. Creoth milked his cows at last, apologising to each one as he emptied the straining

udder. 'Better you carry it than me.' Then there was
fresh milk for all, and bread taken from the stores. No
one would go hungry that first night. The days to come
were another matter.

Pinto curled up close in her father's arms and whispered to him,

'What happens when we've no more food?'

'It falls from the sky.'

'No, really.'

'I only mean to say,' he explained, kissing her bony
cheek, 'that if we're going the right way, somehow we'll
get there.'

'I do love you, pa.'

'And at least we're together again.'

Bowman hardly spoke at all. He had been virtually
silent since the end of the mind duel. He seemed greatly
weakened, and almost ashamed. For company, he chose
only the grey cat that went with him everywhere. He sat
apart from the rest, with the cat curled up on his lap,
and together they stared in silence at nothing.

His mother partly understood, and knew there was
nothing she could say to undo what had been done.
Instead of trying to console or reassure him, she
reminded him that his help was still needed.

'There are hard days ahead,' she said. 'We need your
power. Whatever it costs you.'

This was just what Bowman wanted: to be allowed to
pay the price for what he had done.

'I'm not afraid,' he said. 'I'll face any danger. I don't
care what the risk. I'll do anything.'

'You'll do what you're called upon to do,' said his
mother gently.

This at last comforted Bowman, this hope that his

battle was not yet over, and so he had not yet lost. He allowed his mother to draw him in to the wish-huddle before they slept. There, their arms tight around each other, their heads touching, Pinto the youngest wished first.

'I wish for us family always to be together.'

Then Kestrel wished the same.

'I wish for us family always to be together.'

Bowman felt the familiar warmth of the others pressing against him, and even though he didn't believe it would be possible, he wished the same.

'I wish for us family always to be together.'

Ira Hath said softly,

'I wish for strength.'

Hanno Hath said,

'I wish for all my dear ones to be safe and well for ever.'

Mumpo kept watch while the others slept. It was a dark night, with low cloud overhead blotting out the stars. As the flames of the fire flickered and died into glowing embers, he found he could see almost nothing; so he closed his eyes and did his guard duty by sound alone. Sitting still, feeling the ache of his wounds throb softly in his flank and in his leg, he allowed his thoughts to turn to Kestrel. She looked at him differently now, he was sure of it: with gratitude, and better still, with respect. There had been no time to talk to her; nor would it have been right. There would be time later, when their journey was done. For now, his job was simple: he must protect her, and keep her from harm. He must protect all these good people he loved. The Mastery had taught him that he was strong, that if he chose he could fight and he could kill. He still found this surprising, and regarded his ability as something accidental, unearned, even a little frightening. But he was proud to know he too had a part to play, and that Kestrel needed him.

So he sat quietly and listened to the noises of the night. Somewhere nearby a stream trickled over a stony bed, its soft murmur blending with the fading hiss of the fire. From time to time a night bird passed overhead, its wings barely moving, a quiet sigh in the air. Some small unseen creature scratched at the earth by his feet: scree-scree-screek, scree-scree-screek. And all the time, beneath the other sounds, there was the steady drumbeat, slow and muffled, of his own heart.

Wind gusted across his face. He opened his eyes, and found the clouds were moving overhead, rolling away to the west. Stars began to appear, and a thumbnail moon. He looked for the familiar constellations, the Axe, with its long handle, the Crown, with its three points.

'Are you awake, Mumpo?'

He started. It was Pinto.

'Pinto! Why aren't you asleep?'

'I can't sleep.'

'You have to sleep. We'll be walking all day tomorrow.'

'So will you. And you're wounded.'

'I'm all right. I'm strong.'

'Well, so am I.'

He looked at her fondly, and saw how she was shivering.

'I'll make up the fire.'

He stirred the embers together, drawing in the unburned ends of logs, and the fire flickered back to life. In its gently-spreading glow, the others returned to his view, lying asleep in tangled heaps, pressed together for warmth. Mumpo's eyes sought out Kestrel, and found her curled up between her brother and her mother, one hand folded in Bowman's sleeping hand.

'Do you still love her, Mumpo?'

'Yes,' he said simply.

'What if she were to die?'

He looked at Pinto, shocked. 'Don't say that.'

'No, but what if?'

'I don't want to think about it.'

'You'd forget her and start loving someone else. That's what people do.'

'Well, nobody's going to die.'

'Don't be silly, Mumpo. Everyone's going to die.'

'Not for a long time.'

'Kess'll die before me, because she's older than me. Then there'll just be me. You can love me when you're old.'

'All right,' said Mumpo, touched by her fierce loyalty. 'I'll love you when I'm old.'

For a few moments they sat in silence and watched the caverns forming in the fire. Then Mumpo's sharp ears caught a different sound, more regular than the pop and crackle of the burning wood. It was approaching footsteps.

He leaped to his feet, and drew his sword.

'Stay here!' he commanded Pinto.

As she shrank back against her sleeping parents, Mumpo loped away silently into the darkness. Pinto too could now hear the footsteps, but a sudden gush of bright flame from the fire made the night around impenetrable. She heard the footsteps stop. Then came the indistinct sound of voices: women's voices. Then Mumpo was returning to the ring of orange light, and with him came two women, one fat and one thin. They were shaking with cold, and looked badly frightened. Mumpo led them up to the warmth of the fire. The fat one said,

'There, my pet. Now my baby will be warm again.'

The thin one said nothing at all. She just huddled up close to the fire and bowed her head.

Mumpo whispered to Pinto.

'See if you can find them something to eat.'

Pinto nodded, and felt her way to a nearby wagon. She brought back two chunks of their precious store of bread. The fat woman took the bread without a word and gave a small piece to the thin woman. The thin woman held it for a moment, and then let it fall to the ground.

'Don't do that!' said Pinto, dismayed. 'We don't have enough food to feed ourselves.'

The thin woman frowned, and turned to look at Pinto. Then she looked down at the fragment of bread she had dropped. Slowly, she picked it up and reached it out to Pinto.

'Sorry,' she said, her voice low and sad.

'Oh, my precious.' The fat lady gave a shuddery sob. 'My precious must eat or she'll die, and what will her Lunki do then?'

'Hush,' said Mumpo. But it was too late. Lunki's sob had woken Bowman. As he sat up, his movement woke Kestrel. Bowman stared in confusion at the firelit vision of the Johdila Sirharasi, still in her wedding dress but unveiled, gazing back at him with such sweet sadness on her lovely face. Thinking he was in a dream, and that all this would melt away as he woke, he reached out one hand and said,

'Don't go!'

Then Kestrel was up, and alert.

'Sisi!'

'Oh, Kess!' Sisi burst at last into the tears that had been waiting within her, and fell into her friend's arms.

'There, my pet,' said Lunki, weeping herself with relief. 'There, the friend will make everything all right.'

'Who is she?' said Pinto to Mumpo in an undertone.

'She's the princess who came to be married.'

Kestrel calmed Sisi down and got her to tell all that had happened.

'Zohon has arrested mama and papa, and he's killing everyone, and he says he's going to marry me, but I hate him, so I'm going to come with you instead, because you're my –' she broke once more into sobs, 'you're my – you're my – friend.'

'But Sisi,' said Kestrel gently. 'We're not your people. You'd find it strange with us. We don't have princesses, or veils. We're just ordinary people.'

'That's what I want to be. Look, I'm not wearing my veil. I let him see me.'

She turned to point at Mumpo.

'No other man has ever seen me. Oh yes, your brother has.' She turned to find Bowman gazing at her. 'He thinks I'm my servant. Well, I might as well be now. Lunki, you can't be my servant any more. We're going to be ordinary people from now on. You'll have to be my friend.'

Lunki was dismayed.

'I don't know how to be a friend. I only know how to be a servant.'

Sisi was still looking at Bowman.

'Do you mind if we come with you?'

Bowman said nothing.

'Why won't he speak to me?'

'It's not you, Sisi,' said Kestrel. 'He's hardly spoken since – since we left the palace.'

'It is me. He thinks I'm odd. But he said, don't go.' She set her lips in a stubborn expression, as if he might deny it. 'You did say so, so I won't.'

'Let's talk about it in the morning,' said Kestrel.

But Sisi had recovered her determination.

'There's nothing more to talk about. I shall come with you, and I won't be a princess, and anybody can look at me whenever they want to, until their eyes pop out.' She turned on Pinto, who had indeed been gaping at her. 'Even little girls.'

Pinto wasn't afraid of her.

'I'll look at whoever I want.'

'I'm glad I'm so interesting.'

'You're not interesting,' said Pinto. 'You're just beautiful.'

'Oh! Oh!' exclaimed Sisi. 'Lunki, beat her! Put her eyes out! The little wildcat! Don't you dare speak to me like that, I'm – I'm – No, I'm not, am I? Oh! I don't know who I am any more.'

'Come along,' said Kestrel kindly. 'You can lie down next to me, with Lunki on your other side. Is that all right, Lunki? We're quite near the fire here. We'll not get cold.'

After some grumbling, everyone settled back down to sleep, except Mumpo, who insisted on standing guard once more, and Bowman, who claimed he had slept enough.

Mumpo was a little in awe of Bowman now. He had become so quiet and grave. He was almost exactly Mumpo's age, but lately he seemed to have grown much older. It was as if he had been away on a long journey, and had learned things that none of the rest of them knew. Mumpo would never have presumed to ask his friend about those experiences; but deep into the night, greatly to his surprise, Bowman began to talk.

'Do you remember the Morah, Mumpo?'

'Of course.' It was long ago, but he had forgotten nothing.

'The Morah didn't die. The Morah never dies.' For a moment he was silent. Then, 'But you know that, don't you? You've felt it too.'

'I think so.'

'The Morah's back in me, Mumpo. I did it to save Kess.'

'To save Kess? But I thought I –' He broke off. He could see it all so clearly. Ortiz with his sword descending. His own fist powering through the air. 'I thought he was going to kill her.'

'He was.'

'Then what – how –?'

'I was wrong. I did nothing.'

Bowman fell silent, leaving Mumpo uneasy and confused. But then after a few moments Bowman spoke again.

'If I have to go, will you look after Kess for me?'

'Of course. Always.'

'She thinks she's the one who looks after me. But it'll be hard for her.'

'I'll look after her as long as I live.'

'I know you love her.'

'I do.' Mumpo was filled with a simple happiness just to be able to say it. 'Do you think that one day, not now, but when all our troubles are over, she might love me back?'

'She loves you now.'

'I mean more than as a friend.'

Bowman said nothing for a moment. Then, quietly,

'I don't think so. She doesn't want to marry anybody.'

Mumpo hung his head. He didn't dispute Bowman's answer. He had heard Kestrel say it too many times, in the old days of Aramanth.

'What is it she does want, Bo?'

'I don't think she knows yet.'

'I know what I want. I know it so clearly I can almost see it.'

'What do you want, Mumpo?' He stroked the cat, curled up as always on his lap.

'I want to be married. I want to have a house with a porch. And I want to have a son. I shall keep my little boy so clean, and dress him in such neat clothes, that everyone will love him. He'll play with his little friends, and never feel lonely, and laugh all day long.'

Bowman smiled in the firelight.

'What will you call him?'

'I thought at first I'd call him after my father. But then I thought, no, I'll call him after myself. He'll be Mumpo the Second. That way I'll be able to sit on the porch of my house in the summertime and hear the children calling, "Mumpo, come out to play! Mumpo, we're waiting for you! We can't start without you, Mumpo!"'

'May we all live to see that day, my friend.'

In the silence that followed, Mist spoke to Bowman, knowing Mumpo couldn't hear him.

'Boy,' he said.

'Yes, cat?'

'Did you see me in the fighting? I fought too.'

'Yes, I saw.'

'And boy?'

'Yes, cat?'

'I think I flew. I think it was flying. I'll teach you to fly, if you'd like that.'

'Yes, cat. I'd like that.'

Mist was content.

Little by little now, the light was returning to the sky. The clouds had all dispersed. High above, sharp stars still shone in the night, even as the first pale watery-green tints of day seeped over the eastern horizon. The cows were rousing each other, and heaving themselves up onto their legs to tug at the sparse grass. In distant trees, waking birds began to call.

Then Mist pricked up his ears.

Faint and far away, there came the sound of a bugle: ta-tara! ta-tara! Mumpo leaped to his feet. Another distant sound followed on the breeze: the thunder of horses' hooves. The cat jumped off Bowman's lap as he stood up.

'Quick! Wake everyone!'

Hanno Hath was already rising.

'What is it?'

'Horsemen,' said Bowman.

Mumpo was motionless, listening attentively to the sounds. The horses were advancing in formation, keeping time with each other.

'Soldiers!' he said.

Now all the travellers were awake and rising. Ira Hath turned over to find Sisi curled up close to her.

'Who are you? Mercy, what a pretty child!'

Sisi heard the horsemen and started to tremble.

'They're coming for me! Don't let them take me! Please!'

'Quickly, quickly!' called Hanno. 'Load the wagon!'

'We have to hide her,' said Kestrel to her mother.

'Into the wagon,' said Ira, understanding there was no time for explanations.

Sisi and Lunki were lifted into the wagon and covered up with blankets alongside the supplies of food. The horsemen now came thundering into view, over the crest of the hill: a full regiment of Johjan Guards, led by Zohon himself.

The Manth people made no attempt to flee. They stood quietly, shivering in the pre-dawn cold, as the horse-soldiers formed a circle all round their camp. Zohon rode up to the leaders by the fire, and pointed his silver hammer at them.

'Where is she?' he demanded. 'Hand her over!'

'Who?' said Hanno, as politely as he could.

'You know who! The Johdila!'

'What is a Johdila, please?'

'The princess! Give her to me!' Zohon had passed a sleepless night on his search, and was now in such a state of exhausted fury that the slightest resistance drove him wild.

'We have no princesses here.'

'You defy me?' Zohon screamed. 'Kill them all! Every one of them!'

The tall Johjan Guards dismounted from their horses and drew their swords.

'Why kill us?' reasoned Hanno. 'It won't get you what you want.'

'How do you know what I want?' screeched Zohon. 'Start with him! Kill him!'

He pointed his silver hammer at Hanno. A guard came striding towards him. Mumpo gripped his sword tight and braced himself to spring. The Manth people looked on, frozen with horror. The Johjan Guard raised his sword –

'Stop!'

Out rang a clear high commanding voice. Everyone turned to look. Out from behind the wagon stepped Sisi, head held high, magnificent in her sleek white dress, and veiled.

Zohon's entire appearance changed. He softened. He smiled. All the bitterness and anger left him. He gestured to his men to sheathe their swords. With a light look now brightening his weary but handsome face, he swung down from the saddle.

'My lady,' he said, and he made her a bow.

Sisi stood absolutely still, and said nothing. Zohon had half-expected her to throw herself into his arms with a cry of gratitude. But it struck him now that she was a princess, and not aware of recent developments.

'My lady,' he said, 'you see before you the Zohonna of Gang, Lord of a Million Souls.'

Still Sisi said nothing. Zohon began to find her silence awkward. Perhaps she was concerned about her father and mother. That would be natural enough.

'Your esteemed father,' he explained, 'has relinquished the throne to me. He and your mother are safe, and under my protection.'

Still Sisi did not speak. Zohon began to twitch the silver hammer in his right hand, not aware that he was doing so. There remained only one more thing to say. No doubt in her modesty it was this she was waiting to hear, before lifting her veil and taking him in her arms.

'I ask, my lady, for your hand in marriage.'

Slowly, at last, Sisi raised one hand, and drew the veil

from her face. Zohon gazed at her in wonder. She was so beautiful! More beautiful than even he had ever dreamed!

'My lady! May I dare hope –?'

He went down on one knee.

'Stand up!' commanded Sisi. 'Never address me in this way again!'

Zohon turned a deep red, and rose to his feet.

'My lady, I understood –' he turned to glower at Kestrel, 'that you shared my hopes.'

'Kess! Did you tell this person that I had any interest in him of any kind?'

Kestrel marvelled at Sisi. She was so grand, so imperious.

'I told him you would love the one who set you free,' she said. 'The one who made your country great again.'

'There, my lady!' Zohon recovered some of his composure. 'Who but I can make our country great?'

'Are you the heir to the throne?' said Sisi with withering scorn. 'I shall make our country great myself.'

Zohon gaped. He still couldn't quite take in what was happening.

'You reject my proposal?'

The Johdila inclined her queenly head.

'Am I to be given a reason?'

'You are a nothing,' said Sisi. 'I have no need of you. I have no interest in you. You may go now.'

The scene began to swim before Zohon's eyes. His hands started to sweat, and he heard a galloping pounding noise in his ears. He struggled to speak, but hardly knew what to say. Then he heard a muffled choking sound, followed by another like it. All at once he realised that everyone was laughing at him.

The red mist cleared from his brain. His mighty vanity came flooding back. He stood tall once more.

'Draw your swords!' he commanded his guards. 'If anyone moves, kill them!'

He then gestured brusquely to two of his men.

'Seize this woman! Hold her!'

Two officers stepped forward and grasped Sisi by either arm. Angrily, she shook her arms to release herself, but the guards did not let go. Zohon drew a long breath. He felt calm and strong once more.

'My lady,' he said, 'I will put my proposal to you in a different way.' He spun his silver hammer round, so that the sharp steel blade was towards her. 'You will marry me, or you will die.'

'Baby, no!' cried Lunki, vibrating with horror.

No one else made a sound. They're not laughing at me now, thought Zohon grimly. The Johdila stared back at him, her eyes ice-cool with defiance. She looked more beautiful than ever. What a couple we'll make, thought Zohon. How handsome our children will be!

'Kill me, then!' said Sisi.

Zohon blinked. For a second, his new-found confidence wavered. Then he understood.

'You don't believe me.'

'Oh, I believe you. This is just the kind of battle you like best. An unarmed woman held helpless before you. What a fearful foe! How brave you must be to stand up to her!'

'Be quiet!'

'Let everyone see the Hammer of Gang strike his most glorious blow!'

'Enough, I say!' He lowered his blade. As he did so, he caught in her eyes a flash of contemptuous triumph.

With that one look, all his stored love turned to hatred. As intensely as he had wanted to kiss her and caress her before, he now wanted to hurt her. She had wounded him in his deepest heart, which is to say, in his pride, and now he wanted to humiliate her in return, to take from her everything she had, to break her high spirit, to make her crawl and beg for forgiveness. He no longer wanted her to die. He wanted far more, and far worse. He wanted her to live, and suffer, and regret. He wanted her to curse the day she lost his love, and with it all her chance of happiness.

As the hatred rose within him, he looked on her and marvelled at her beauty. It seemed to him that she taunted him with this beauty that he could not possess. Then the rising wave broke within him, and hatred flooded his mind. With one quick movement, he swept his blade down her left cheek. A line of scarlet beads followed the blade, and swelled, and flowed into each other, and rolled down her face. The watching people went still with shock, not moving, barely breathing.

'I kill your beauty,' said Zohon.

Sisi never so much as blinked. Instead, slowly, proudly, she turned her unmarked cheek towards him. Still defiant! With a second savage slash of his blade, Zohon cut that cheek too.

'May the scars never heal!'

With these bitter words, he gestured to his men to release her, and strode back to his horse. Once in the saddle, he called in his commanding voice,

'Ride on! There's nothing worth having here!'

The Johjan Guards formed up, and rode away over the brow of the hill. Sisi stood where she had been left, the blood now streaming down both cheeks, and over her neck, to stain her white wedding dress. Lunki hurried to her on one side, and Kestrel on the other, and they staunched the flow of blood with the sleeves and hems of their garments, and called for water, and washed her face and neck. All this time, while Lunki sobbed and Kestrel issued commands, Sisi stood still, her eyes dry.

'Get her something to drink! She's trembling.'

'Oh, my pet, oh, my sweetie, oh, my baby! All gone, all gone!'

'The cuts are shallow, said Kestrel. 'Look, the bleeding's stopping already.'

'But her sweet lovely face – oh, oh, oh!'

Ira Hath brought Sisi a cup of milk, and held it up to her lips. Sisi sipped a little.

'You're a very brave young woman,' she said.

Sisi shivered. The wind was growing colder as dawn broke. All round the camp, people were rolling up their blankets and preparing to leave. Beyond the wagon, Creoth was milking his cows. The driver was harnessing the horses.

'Bring her a blanket,' said Kestrel. They wrapped a blanket round Sisi's thin trembling body. Lunki went on dabbing at the cuts on her cheeks until Sisi pushed her away.

'Get me a mirror, Lunki. I want to see.'

'No, baby, no. You don't want to see.'

'I do. Get me a mirror.' It hurt her to talk. Lunki saw her wince, and wrung her fat hands with grief.

There were no mirrors. Kestrel poured water into a bowl, and when the water was still, Sisi bent over the bowl and looked at her reflection. She looked carefully, seeing how the two cuts ran in converging diagonal lines from cheekbones to jaw, changing her appearance utterly. All the softness was gone, all the delicacy. She looked older, harder, wilder. The blood was congealing in two irregular lines, dark red against her cold white skin.

'I'm so sorry,' said Kestrel.

'Don't be sorry,' said Sisi quietly. 'I can be me now.'

Kestrel bit her lip. Sisi's quiet acceptance touched her more deeply than all Lunki's wails and sobs. She saw her brother watching them, and knew he felt it too.

'Can I still come with you?'

'Of course. You can ride in the wagon.'

'No, I'll walk, like everyone else. Is it a very long way, where we're going?'

'Yes. A very long way.'

'I'm glad.' She looked round, and saw Bowman. She made a slight fleeting gesture towards her disfigured cheeks. 'You don't have to love me any more. You don't even have to talk to me. But I would like sometimes to talk to you.'

'I'd like that,' said Bowman.

Sisi tried to smile for him, but the smile hurt her wounded cheeks, and she had to stop.

'I can't even smile any more.' She spoke without self-pity, as if her new state was an inconvenience that had very little to do with her. 'How different everything is going to be.'

24

Departure

The travellers were now ready, the wagon hitched, the firewood for the coming night gathered and stowed. A white sun was appearing over the hills to the east, and there were flurries of snow in the air. Hanno Hath called them all together, and asked his wife to speak to them before they set out on their journey.

'What can I say to you that I've not already said?'

She looked over the crowd of familiar faces, and saw there their hope, their fear.

'We have very little time. The journey will be hard. But the homeland waits for us. We will be safe there.'

She stopped, because she had remembered her dream. She herself would not enter the homeland: these good people, her people, would go on without her. She did not tell them how her strength was slowly but surely draining away. *My gift is my disease. I shall die of prophecy.*

'This is all that matters,' she said, reaching out her arms as if to embrace them all. 'That we hold together, and love each other. We are the Manth people. Let us make our own Manth vow.'

Hanno Hath, understanding what she meant to do, took her left hand, and held out a hand to Bowman.

Kestrel took her mother's other hand. Pinto held Bowman's hand, and called to Mumpo to join her. Kestrel reached out for Sisi's hand, and so Sisi joined the ever-growing chain. Sisi brought Lunki with her, and beside Lunki stood Creoth. Beside Mumpo was Mrs Chirish, and next to her, little Scooch, and the Mimilith family, and Principal Pillish. And so they all joined hands, all thirty-two of them, and Ira Hath led them in the old familiar vow. Sisi, who had never heard the words before, felt tears fill her eyes. She wasn't crying for the wounds on her soft skin, or for the loss of her beauty. She was crying because the words seemed to come out of her own longing, and to tell of a love she had never had.

'Today begins my walk with you.' They spoke together, their voices sounding softly in the cold air. 'Where you go, I go. Where you stay, I stay. When you sleep, I will sleep. When you rise, I will rise. I will pass my days within the sound of your voice, and my nights within the reach of your hand. And none shall come between us.'

So bound together, they pulled their coats close around them, and began their journey. They marched north, by the light of the rising sun. Snow was falling, lightly but steadily, small hard flakes that stung the face and blew in swirling eddies over the stony ground. It was the first snowfall of the coming winter.

FIRESONG

Volume III of
THE WIND ON FIRE

They must seek shelter, they must reach the safety of the homeland, before the storm breaks; or the coming wind will carry them away.

In the time of cruelty, the Manth people march back to their homeland. They grow weak with starvation. Ira Hath is the only one who knows the way, but she is dying. Bowman eagerly awaits his calling to join the Singer people, but when his sister Kestrel is taken by bandits, he must use his powers to find her. Together they fight . . . until their destinies lead them apart. And all the while they wait for the wind to rise . . . Only one will sing the firesong.

WILLIAM NICHOLSON
Smarties Gold Award Winner

William Nicholson is one of the greatest and most imaginative writers of today and has won countless awards for his work in television, plays and films. *The Wind Singer*, the first title in the Wind on Fire trilogy, won the Smarties Prize Gold Award and the Blue Peter Book Award. His latest novel, *Rich and Mad* – his first for teenage readers – received much praise, and he has written several successful adult novels. He is an acclaimed Hollywood screenwriter; his work includes *Elizabeth: The Golden Age*, the Bafta award-winning *Shadowlands*, and *Gladiator*, for which he received his second Oscar nomination. William Nicholson lives in Sussex with his wife, Virginia, and their three children.